Meant To Be

Also by Fiona McCallum

Paycheque
Nowhere Else
Wattle Creek
Leap of Faith

The Button Jar Series:
Saving Grace
Time Will Tell

Fiona McCallum

Meant To Be

H HARLEQUIN® MIRA®

First Published 2014
Second Australian Paperback Edition 2015

ISBN 978 174369333 9

MEANT TO BE
© 2014 by Fiona McCallum
Australian Copyright 2014
New Zealand Copyright 2014

Published by
Harlequin Mira
An imprint of Harlequin Enterprises (Australia) Pty Ltd.
Level 13, 201 Elizabeth Street
SYDNEY NSW 2000
AUSTRALIA

® and TM are trademarks of Harlequin Enterprises Limited or its corporate affiliates. Trademarks indicated with ® are registered in Australia, New Zealand and in other countries.

Printed and bound in Australia by McPhersons Printing Group

Fiona McCallum lives in Adelaide, South Australia, and is a full-time novelist. She is the author of five Australian bestsellers: *Paycheque*, *Nowhere Else*, *Wattle Creek*, *Saving Grace*, and *Time Will Tell*. *Meant To Be* is her sixth novel and the third (and most likely final) in *The Button Jar* series.

More information about Fiona and her books can be found on her website, www.fionamccallum.com. Fiona can also be followed on Facebook at www.facebook.com/Fiona McCallum-author.

*In loving memory of my nanna, Nancy Price
– much treasured, long gone, but never forgotten.*

Acknowledgements

Many thanks to Sue, Cristina, Michelle, and everyone at Harlequin Australia for turning my manuscripts into beautiful books, for all the wonderful support, and for continuing to make my dreams come true. Thanks also to editor Lachlan for his hard work and patience to make my writing the best it can be.

Thank you to Jane and the team at Morey Media for putting the word out, and to the media outlets, bloggers, reviewers, librarians, booksellers, and readers for all the amazing support. It really does mean so much to me to hear of people enjoying my stories.

Finally, huge thanks to friends Carole and Ken Wetherby, Mel Sabeeney, Arlene Somerville, NEL, and WTC for continuing to provide so much love and encouragement, and for being the best friends a person could ever hope to have. I am truly blessed.

'True friends are like diamonds, precious and rare. False friends are like autumn leaves, found everywhere.' (Origin unknown.)

Chapter One

Emily lay in bed with Jake spooning against her. As the first rays of daylight slowly lit the room, she was wide awake. But he slept on, his strong arms around her and his deep breathing stroking her back in long warm whispers. She felt like leaping up and greeting the day, but couldn't bear to break the spell. Instead she lay there with a warm glow in her belly, thinking that she could quite possibly be the luckiest girl in the world.

She had a kind, gentle man who loved her and whom she loved in return, and she was so grateful to Simone for bringing about their reunion. The trip to Melbourne had changed everything. She was so glad she'd been there for Jake when he'd needed her. If only the circumstances had been different.

Death had been such a theme in her life recently – her gran's passing, John's fatal accident, and now the incident on Jake's work site – hopefully that was all behind her. She'd been through so much and survived, and she now knew she could get through anything else that came her way, especially with Jake by her side.

After all the financial stress, she no longer had to search for a job – at least for a while. Thanks to her inheritance from John and the annual lease payments from Barbara and David on the land, and the income from the sheep, she was fine for the time being – and for life if she was careful.

Emily still felt a little guilty about how it had all come about, but at least she had the blessing of John's parents. She just hoped the Wattle Creek locals would be as understanding. A townie, a woman, inheriting a decent slice of prime land and everything with it was one thing, but how would they feel when they heard she'd moved a new man in just days after John's funeral?

Speaking of which. She felt him stirring behind her.

'Good morning sleepyhead,' Jake said, kissing the back of her neck. She rolled over to face him, kissed him deeply in reply, and wrapped her arms around him.

'Hmm,' she groaned as he pulled her towards him.

Later they lay entwined, just like they had last night before going to sleep. Emily could feel her breathing matching Jake's, their chests rising and falling together.

'God, you smell good,' he said breathily.

'I was just thinking the same thing,' she said, smiling at him. 'How are you feeling? Did you sleep okay?'

After the flights from Melbourne, the long drive from Whyalla, and then David and Barbara staying on for dinner, they had both been exhausted. They had spent the next two days taking it easy, going on gentle strolls, and making a huge fuss of Grace, who Emily had missed terribly whilst she'd been away. The little border collie was such an important part of her life – they'd been through so much together in such a short amount of time.

'I slept okay. But I'm still pretty tired. I can't seem to shake it.'

Emily knew how debilitating grief could be.

'I've got to go into town to run some errands. Do you want to come along?' Emily asked.

After lingering over a big breakfast, they were standing side by side doing the dishes – her hands in pink rubber gloves beneath a thick layer of suds, his tea-towel-covered hand stuffed into a mug.

'If you don't mind, I'd rather stay here. If that's okay?'

Once upon a time she'd have been hurt. 'Of course it's okay, Jake. We've both lived alone long enough to not need another person to entertain us all the time. Although don't get me wrong, I do enjoy your company,' Emily added, starting to get a bit flustered. Isn't that what love was? Wanting to be with someone all the time?

Jake let out a sigh. 'It's not that I don't want to spend time with you. I do. But I'm just not used to having someone else around all the time.'

Emily nodded.

'You've probably only just got used to living alone. And I wouldn't mind betting you've quite enjoyed being independent,' he said, looking at her sympathetically. 'So, can we make a pact? Can we agree that it's okay to spend time apart without getting all paranoid about why? That it's not a sign there's something wrong between us?'

'I guess,' Emily said, not quite convinced. *Where is this coming from? Maybe he's had a clingy girlfriend before.*

'I don't mean to sound pushy, but I once had a girlfriend who came to stay and insisted on spending every second of every day together. It drove me nuts.'

Bingo!

'Sorry. The only peace I got was in the loo,' he said with a gentle smile.

'It's fine, Jake, we all need our space,' she said.

'So it's a pact?'

'As long as we also agree that if one of us has a problem – big or small – we discuss it,' Emily said. 'I don't want to end up where we were last time.'

'Okay,' Jake said.

'And while we're on ground rules...' Emily continued.

'Uh-oh, here we go,' Jake said, smiling at her.

Emily flicked a handful of suds at his chest.

'I'm being serious,' she said. 'I want you to feel at home; come and go as you please. But it would be helpful to know what meals you will and won't be here for.'

'Now you're making me sound like a boarder.' He went behind her, wrapped his arms around her waist, and nuzzled at her neck. 'I mean it when I say I love you. I'm serious about us, about this working out, even though it's so new. I only meant I want to be free to head off for a walk on my own if I want to. I might not even want to.'

'I love you too. And I mean it when I say I want you to feel at home – what's mine is yours. Honestly, you should feel free to use the car, internet, phone; whatever you need.'

They finished the last few dishes and then sat at the table to write up a shopping list. Jake gave her some money towards expenses, which she very reluctantly accepted, and she handed him the spare key to the sliding glass door.

'Right, last chance to change your mind,' Emily said, collecting her handbag and keys from the bench. 'Sure you don't want to visit the thriving metropolis?'

'I'll pass, thanks,' Jake said, getting up and going over to her. 'I *am* looking forward to getting to know the area, but

I don't think I'm ready to become the talk of the town just yet. I know what small towns can be like. I might just go for a stroll. Maybe take a few shots. I'm planning on being here for a while, so there's no rush – for anything.' He gave her a peck on the lips. 'Have fun.'

'You too. Gracie, you look after Jake for me while I'm gone,' she said, bending down to ruffle the border collie's ears.

Jake was standing at the glass door when she backed out of the shed and drove off. She returned his wave and the kisses he blew her.

Before driving to town, Emily drove a short way up the road to run a quick errand. David had put the sheep on the stubble in the paddock over from the cottage ruins, where she and Jake could keep an eye on them. She'd promised to check the trough each day. Under their lease agreement, David was taking care of them in exchange for a profit share, but there was no point in him driving down just to check that a trough had water in it.

After satisfying herself that all looked well with the trough and the sheep, she did a U-turn and headed off to Wattle Creek.

Emily collected her mail and paid a couple of bills at the post office, and visited the newsagent to get *The Advertiser* for Jake. Being Thursday, Wattle Creek was swarming with people – well, as busy as a district of two thousand people could get. Tuesdays and Thursdays were the main shopping days, thanks to the delivery of fresh fruit and veg. Emily had to go around the block twice to find a park halfway between the bank and the supermarket where she could just pull in – she was no good at reverse parallel parking.

As she walked the aisles, every second person stopped her to enquire if it was true that Donald and Trevor's cousin, Tara Wickham, had turfed her out of the house she had an arrangement with them to buy. 'And is it true that you've moved back to the farm?'

'Yes,' Emily said. There was no point in being evasive. When asked how John's parents, Thora and Gerald, were doing, she replied, 'As well as can be expected,' whilst kicking herself for her forgetfulness. She'd been in touch with Gerald by phone about John's estate, but hadn't seen them since the funeral. And they'd been so good to her the day she'd gone out and told them the truth about her and John. She vowed to keep in touch.

At least without Jake beside her she didn't have to deal with, 'Ah, so who is this? And where are you from? And how long will you be visiting with us?' Locals – particularly the elderly – could be very nosy around newcomers. And then there would be the raised eyebrows, along with, 'So you're staying at the farm with Emily, are you?'

She could see how Jake moving in mere days after John had been laid to rest could be seen as inappropriate. It was hardly surprising that tongues were wagging. It had been fine while Jake could be seen as just a friend of her cousin Liz…

But love doesn't work to a timetable.

If only Jake had happened about a year into the future, she thought, as she stowed the three green eco bags of groceries in the boot. Then it would all be aboveboard. She let out a deep sigh as she shut the lid. But he hadn't, Barbara would say; he was meant to be there now. The universe had all this stuff sorted out and everything happened when and how it was supposed to.

Maybe so, but it still didn't make it any easier to deal with the gossip.

Emily had sometimes fantasised about leaving Wattle Creek. But where would she go? The truth was, she couldn't see herself living anywhere else. And having already moved house twice in a matter of weeks, she was keen to stay put.

Perhaps Jake would want to spend time in Melbourne down the track and gradually she'd be able to tear herself away. Could she consider living there, if that's what he wanted?

God, who was she kidding? Other than seeing him and meeting his sister Simone, she hadn't enjoyed her trip to the big city at all. Dealing with all that traffic and so many people in such close proximity, practically running everywhere, was overwhelming. No, thank you very much. And the low cost of living was a major redeeming feature of life in the country.

Just before Emily left town she remembered to pop into the bank. She wanted to consult the spinning displays for term deposit and other investment brochures, but was also hoping to see Nathan Lucas, a friend who had recently moved to Wattle Creek from Adelaide to become the Assistant Manager.

A few weeks ago – a lifetime ago it seemed – Nathan had wanted Emily to rent him a room in the house she'd bought from the Bakers; correction, *nearly bought*. While she'd desperately needed the extra money, she'd turned him down. She'd needed more time on her own. Then she'd been evicted. Thankfully they had remained friends.

Thinking of Nathan made her realise with a bit of a shock that she didn't have many people she considered friends. She knew plenty of people to wave to in the street, say g'day to and chat about the weather. But there were very few she trusted enough to confide in – only really her dad, David and Barbara, and now Jake. But surely it hadn't always been like this. What happened?

Prior to getting married, when she'd worked in the insurance office, Emily had had lots of friends, and had always felt a part of a community. But she'd become withdrawn whilst being with John. They'd had a few dinner parties in the first few months together, but then stopped – they hadn't been much fun; she'd done all the work in the kitchen and John had just got drunk and belligerent. And their friends had never reciprocated. Or perhaps John had never passed on the invitations.

Emily paused by the wall of the bank and pretended to study her shopping list. But what she was really doing was wondering how she'd come to have so few close friends. She was easy to get along with. Wasn't she?

She'd had plenty of girlfriends in high school and during her twenties. But one by one they had moved away to the city in search of work and men. She'd just moved to the next small town over. And then she'd married John and he'd become her world.

Stepping inside the bank, she spotted Nathan in his glass-walled office, tapping away at his computer keyboard. When he looked up and saw her, he grinned and waved her over.

'Come in,' he said, pecking her on the cheek. 'Sit down, take a load off,' he added and slumped back into his chair.

'How are you settling in?' Emily asked. 'Have you found somewhere to live yet?'

'Yep. One of the girls from the other bank, Sarah Poole, has a spare room. *They* provide housing for the Assistant Manager. I'm clearly with the wrong bank.'

'Isn't it a conflict of interest, or something?'

'You mean sleeping with the enemy?' He winked. 'No idea. I'll just have to spend more time with my non-bank friends – like you. So, how're things?'

'Great. Speaking of housemates, remember I told you about my friend Jake, in Melbourne, who came for Christmas? Well, he's staying again. Hopefully for a few months.' *Hopefully forever.*

'Ooh, do I detect romance?'

'You do, indeed,' Emily said, blushing slightly.

'Well, I hope you checked his horoscope before letting him move in.'

'And I hope you've checked your compatibility with Sarah,' she said with a laugh.

'I have, actually. And you might scoff. But take it from me, you can save yourself a lot of heartache if you ask the question up front. As a Capricorn, you need a Taurus or a Virgo. But your love-life is your business. I've said my piece. Just being a friend and looking out for you.'

'Thanks Nathan. I appreciate it,' she said, wondering about Jake's birthday. He knew that hers was New Year's Eve, because he'd sent the lovely plans for the Bakers' house to Barbara and David's that night. But when was his?

'So, did you just drop in to say hi, or was there something of a banking nature I can help you with?'

'Well, I did want to say hi. But I've been thinking I should look at some investment options.'

'How are you going with settling the estate?'

'Okay, I think. It seems to be just a matter of putting information together and applying for probate – I've mainly let the lawyers deal with it. John's dad was kind enough to send them a list of assets, which saved me a lot of palaver. Hopefully in two months it'll all be rubber stamped.'

'That's good. I've heard these things can be a nightmare.'

'Well, it helped that John was recently bought out of the family company and had plenty of cash on hand for me to pay the outstanding bills.'

'Phew for that.'

'Yes. There was also an insurance policy. The payout from that should come soonish. And then there will be the proceeds from the estate to think about. I want to be sensible, do the right thing for my long-term future.'

'Right, then, let's see what we've got to offer.'

Nathan ran through some of the bank's choices – the interest rates, potential returns and costs involved, but said if she was talking about investing large amounts she should probably think about seeing one of their visiting financial planners at some point. By the time he finished, Emily's head was swimming.

'Hey, do you and Jake want to go and do some wineries or have lunch sometime? Sarah's quite new in town too, and we need to make some friends.'

'I'd love to.' *I should give Jake a proper welcome, too.* Maybe over the weekend they could all splurge on lunch with Barbara and David.

Emily hadn't visited any of the cellar doors that had popped up on the far side of the district in the past few years. Her deceased husband hadn't been one for romantic Sunday drives. Farming, football, beer, and sex were the extent of John's interests. But she was really looking forward to playing tourist with Jake.

'God, this is just like high school all over again, isn't it?' Nathan said.

'Ha ha. I'll see what suits Jake and let you know.'

And then Emily was on her way back out of town, thinking again about what a whirlwind the past few months had been.

When she'd driven away from the farmhouse that day with Grace curled up on the passenger's side floor of the car she'd thought – hoped – it would be the last time she would ever drive this particular dirt road. And now look where she was. Life certainly was full of surprises.

Lost in her thoughts, Emily was suddenly jolted by two hard clunks as first the front tyre and then the rear one hit a large pothole – one she usually managed to avoid.

She slowed. The car seemed to be okay, so she continued on. But one thing was for sure; when the insurance payment came through for John's written-off ute, she would definitely replace it. Now that she owned a farm, she really needed something all-terrain. But what sort? And should she keep the car as well, or was running two vehicles too extravagant?

She was glad she had Jake to discuss these sorts of things with. Proud as she was of her newfound independence, there certainly were benefits to having a man around.

Chapter Two

'Hi honey, I'm home!' Emily called, smiling to herself. *What a cliché! I sound like a character from a soap opera.* She dumped the four heavy bags of groceries onto the lino floor of the kitchen, then rolled the stiffness out of her neck and shook the circulation back into her fingers.

'Jake?' She shut the sliding glass door she'd shouldered open moments before. *He mustn't be far away to have left the door unlocked*, she thought.

Emily quickly unpacked the groceries, all the while listening for movement. If Jake was inside he would almost certainly have come to help carry everything in; he was that sort of guy. And Grace would normally have bounded up to greet her. She wandered through the house, but found no trace of either.

By the time she finished she was starting to get concerned. She checked her watch; almost two p.m. She went to the bedroom to change into her farm clothes, thinking she'd look for them outside. Maybe Jake and Grace were exploring and hadn't heard her return.

Entering the room, she said hello to Granny Rose via the big jar of buttons on the tallboy. The old Bushells coffee jar had been her gran's last gift to her, and together with its precious contents, it meant more to her than anything. Emily wrapped her hands around the cold glass and put her chin on the rough, slightly rusty, faded red lid.

Again she found herself wondering if Gran had remembered the rough diamonds in there amongst the buttons. The frustrating thing was that she'd never know. But she would have treasured it anyway, even if it weren't for the diamonds.

Being a sentimental romantic, Emily loved the button jar for the symbolism it held. Trust Gran to hide her wedding gift from the Indian prince in there. Was it before or after that – because of the precious stones – that she'd decided never to take any buttons out?

Over the years Emily had seen many added – usually when Gran was cutting up worn-out clothes for rags – and had never understood why Gran would drag her off to the shop to buy new buttons whenever she needed one. One of her favourite things to do as a child – well, actually, even now – was to rotate the tightly closed jar and listen to the hiss, whoosh and rattle the different buttons and other objects made against themselves and the glass.

She couldn't believe that in all that time she'd never spotted one of the seven diamonds lurking about in there. Or perhaps she had and had dismissed them as one of the other strange things Gran had added over the years: old coins, buckles, hair clips, the odd seashell. It wasn't like diamonds in the rough were anything that would catch your attention.

But what a beautiful, sentimental gift. Emily thought about the prince's letter – the evidence that the family story had been no myth.

When Jake had first discovered the diamonds, she had immediately wanted to phone her mother up and gloat, 'See, Gran was telling the truth.' But that would have opened one big old jack-in-the-box – and there was no way Jack could be stuffed back in again. She had since decided to keep them a secret. If they found out, Enid and Aunt Peggy would no doubt argue they belonged to them as heirs, and then they'd cash them in for sure.

Emily was grateful every day for whatever had caused Gran to thrust the button jar into her arms on that last visit, rather than see it end up amongst all the things they'd had to sort through after her death. Back then she wouldn't have had the courage to defend her choice of keeping such an obviously sentimental – and apparently worthless – item. She was now much more able to stand up for herself. 'Oh Gran,' she whispered. 'I wish you were here to meet Jake. You'd love him.'

As she absently glanced out of her bedroom window, she looked past the ugly steel skeleton of the half-built hayshed to the pile of rubble behind it. Once it had been her beloved cottage – before John had taken a front-end loader to it.

Something caught her eye – Jake's red shirt. It stood out like a beacon against the pile of pale limestone around him. He was sitting amidst the ruins of the cottage, leaning against the base of what had once been the stone chimney to the original outdoor kitchen. Grace was lying at his feet.

Emily hugged the button jar again, put it back down on the tallboy, and got changed.

As she made her way over to the pile of rubble, she wondered if she would feel less sad about it if she had it removed. Would she eventually forget what had been there and who had been responsible for its demise?

'Hey there you two,' Emily called as she approached. Jake looked like he might be snoozing, and she didn't want to startle him. He and Grace were mostly in the shade, but their legs were stretched out in the sun. Grace raised her head and slapped her tail a couple of times before lying back down and becoming still again.

'Hello,' Jake said, smiling up at her. 'How was the thriving metropolis and cesspit of gossip?'

'Thriving,' Emily said, smiling back. 'You look like you've found a good spot.'

'Sure have. Care to sit?' He patted the smooth patch of earth beside him.

'Don't mind if I do,' she said, sitting down. Grace immediately got up, stepped over Jake's outstretched legs, and flopped down with her head in her mistress's lap.

'Hello girl,' Emily said, giving Grace's ears a rub as the dog stared up at her adoringly. 'I thought you'd traded me in for Jake.'

'Not a chance. She was just being polite to the new guy, weren't you, girl?' Jake said, reaching over and patting the dog's belly. As he leant back again he paused to kiss Emily. Her heart surged.

'So, what did you guys get up to while I was out?'

Jake checked his watch. 'I've actually been sitting here the whole time you've been gone,' he said, frowning.

'Really?' She looked at him closely. 'Are you okay?'

'I'm fine.'

'Are you sure? If you've been sitting here all this time without realising…'

'Really, I'm fine. Just feeling a bit washed out.'

'You'd tell me if there was something wrong, wouldn't you?' She watched as he plucked at the dried grass. 'Jake,

I'm worried about you. Is it about Shane?' Emily's heart began to race a little.

Jake shook his head, but kept his gaze down.

'There's a psychologist in town, Jacqueline Havelock, if you think she might be able to help. Or there's Doctor Squire. Though, it can take a while to get in – one of the pitfalls of country life...' She shut her mouth abruptly, aware she was babbling. She was scared. What was going on with him?

Jake looked up and fixed his gaze on her. He looked worse than a bit washed out. There were beads of sweat on his forehead. As he brought his hands into his lap, she saw that they were shaking.

'It's not a big deal. I didn't want to worry you. I *don't* want to worry you.'

'Now you are worrying me.' She tried to sound light-hearted, but failed.

He grasped her hands and took a deep breath.

'Last week, before you came to Melbourne, I saw my GP.'

'Okay. That's good. And?'

Emily didn't like prying, but poor communication had been a problem for her in the past. It had almost lost her Jake and her two best friends, Barbara and David, and she was determined not to repeat her mistakes. She bit her lip in an effort to wait out his excruciating silence.

'I'm fine. Well, I *will* be fine, in time. I need to take it easy for a bit. Lots of rest. My GP thinks I have adrenal fatigue, but we'll know more when she gets my test results back.'

'Is it like chronic fatigue syndrome?'

'Quite different, as far as I can tell. With chronic fatigue, you're always exhausted and just want to sleep. With me, I'm often fuzzy and weary, but not in the way I want to actually sleep. I'm quite tired in the mornings, but I seem to often get a second wind in the afternoons and evenings.'

I've noticed that – in Melbourne and the other night with Barbara and David.

'A lot of the time I feel jittery. It's like a fight-or-flight response – surging adrenaline – but for no reason. And you can't stop it.'

'You poor thing, it sounds awful. Did something happen – other than Shane's death – or is it because you're too stressed? Until I saw you in Melbourne, you always seemed so okay with everything.'

'I'm always busy with work, and I've usually got a lot on my mind. I guess I just accepted that. But Shane's death seems to have triggered something, tipped me over the edge.'

Emily felt terrible that their tiff might have contributed to his stress as well. 'So, did something happen, something specific, that saw you go and see your GP?'

'On Thursday morning – I think it was Thursday, anyway, last week is all a bit of a blur – I was watching the news on TV. Suddenly the noise seemed miles away and I couldn't make out the specific voices. It was like everything was distorted, out of focus. And then I couldn't get up. I felt glued to the couch. My heart started racing. I was sweating. And when I thought about what I was meant to be doing, I couldn't remember. I couldn't think. It was terrifying. I didn't know what was happening to me – if I was having some sort of seizure or stroke. Eventually things became clear again, like coming out of a fog. I'd probably only been like that for minutes – maybe half an hour – but it felt like I'd lost a whole day. I didn't know what else to do, so I phoned the clinic. I was really freaked out. Thankfully they could fit me in that morning.'

'God, you poor thing.'

Fiona McCallum

'I guess it's being based in a city and dealing with so many stressed people, but my GP picked it straight away. She thinks the test results are just a formality. It'll be good to know for sure, but it won't really change anything. Regardless, she wants me to take three to six months off.'

'Can you afford to take that much time off?'

'I don't see I have a choice. If it happens again, there's a chance I could find myself totally catatonic, like a complete shutdown, and not be able to move. Imagine if it happened when I was driving.'

'That's a scary thought.'

'So, I'm looking at Shane's death as a big wake-up call. If there's one thing good that can come out of that, I'll take it. What's the point of working so hard if it's just going to kill you? I've got some good people working for me. And Sim's got someone in mind as project manager. I'm not too concerned about the business. And I'm fine for money, thanks to a good insurance policy. I have to focus on getting better, at this stage just take each day as it comes. It's all about playing it by ear and listening to my body, really.'

'So, Simone knows everything?'

'Yes.'

Sometimes Emily wished she had a sibling to confide in. 'And there really isn't any specific treatment?'

'Just lots of vitamins and long walks in the country. Watching my stress levels and concentrating on getting myself healthy through diet and exercise. I've cut way down on caffeine too. I was drinking coffee right through the day. I had no idea how many cups I was having – I always had one on the go in the office.'

'Actually, I had noticed you weren't drinking so much coffee. And I did wonder about all the vitamins you've been taking.'

'Yes, I practically rattle in the mornings now.'

'You know you can always talk to me about things. If this is going to work, I don't want there to be secrets between us.'

'Thanks for understanding,' Jake said, pulling her to him and kissing her.

'Of course. I love you,' she said, snuggling into him. 'I'll take good care of you.'

'I love you too.' After a short cuddle, they sat back and spent a few moments looking about in silent contemplation. Jake was the first to speak. 'It's such a shame about the cottage, because there really is something quite magical about this place. It's got good energy, or something.'

'I felt that the first time I came over here,' Emily replied, picking up a small stone from beside her. 'I thought it was the building, but perhaps it's the trees and nearby creek.'

'Well, I can certainly see why they chose here for their home,' Jake said.

In front of them, the dry creek bed twisted its way through the paddock. 'The stream would have run most of the year before they dammed it way back up in the hills in the nineteen fifties. Why does progress have to be so brutal on the environment?' Emily said wistfully, running a hand through Grace's soft fur.

'It doesn't have to be. The old and new can coexist. I've made a business out of blending them. It just takes some thought and sometimes a bit more effort.'

'I bet it isn't easy convincing people to keep the old when the new is so often cheaper.'

'The people who approach me tend to know and like my work, and be serious about having me involved. There's not a lot of convincing to be done. I guess I've been lucky that there are enough people out there who still have a conscience and also appreciate traditional aesthetics. Speaking of aesthetics, what are you going to do with that?' Jake said, nodding towards the half-built hayshed a little way off.

'David said he could use the extra storage, so I wouldn't mind it moved down to the end of the other sheds. I don't know why John didn't put it there to start with,' she said, shaking her head.

'I had a quick look on my way past,' Jake continued. 'It's just bolted together like a giant meccano project. Shouldn't be hard to deconstruct.'

'Yeah, that's what I thought,' Emily said, rolling her eyes. 'But I've learnt my lesson about trying to do it on my own.' She was still embarrassed about not knowing how to start the tractor and then getting stuck up the ladder, but was starting to see the funny side of the incident. 'Thank goodness Barbara and David came along when they did. I might have been stuck up there forever.'

'I think between the two of us we might be able to manage it,' Jake said, patting her knee. 'But perhaps it would be more sensible to get David involved. He'd know more about this sort of thing than me. I'll ask him.'

'I would so love not to have to look at it from the bedroom window each morning. And all this rubble,' she added. 'What do you think I should do about it? John said he was going to just push it into the creek.'

'I've been sitting here wondering the same thing myself.'

'And?'

'I reckon we sort out that monstrosity and then tackle this. One thing at a time. What do you say?'

'Fair enough. Now, would you like something to eat? I know it's late, but I got some fresh rolls and ham from the bakery.'

'Sounds perfect,' he said, getting up and then holding out a hand to help her up.

They walked back to the house with their arms around each other and Grace bounding ahead of them.

'Hey Jake?'

'Yeah?'

'When's your birthday? Since you know mine, it's only fair.'

'April twenty-third. I'm coming up to thirty-six.'

'Okay. Great.'

'I'm a Taurus, which I understand is highly compatible with Capricorn – you,' he added with a cheeky grin.

Yes, yes, YES! 'Oh, really? Cool,' Emily said, impressed at how nonchalant she'd managed to sound. 'I don't know much about astrology,' she added with a shrug, and put a little skip into her step.

Chapter Three

An hour later, Jake had just announced he was making a bolognaise sauce for dinner when the phone started to ring.

'Would you like me to get that?' he asked, reaching for the handset.

'If you don't mind.'

'Hello,' Jake said into the phone. 'Yes, this is Jake. Oh, hi, Enid,' he said, looking at Emily with raised eyebrows and a smile. She felt herself become tense. She hadn't yet told her mother about him moving in.

'A couple of days ago. We came back from Melbourne together.'

'Oh, right. Well it all happened rather suddenly,' he said.

'Yes, I did. It was a bit of a shock, but thankfully not a close friend. I'll leave it to Em to tell you all about it,' Jake said, his eyes fixed on her. 'Let me hand you... How long am I staying? I'm not sure yet. Look, Enid, it's been lovely talking to you, but Emily is here now and I have to um... I have, er, something I must attend to.' He handed the phone over with a look of huge relief, and headed off into the pantry.

'Hi Mum, what can I do for you?' Emily said, watching Jake returning with onions and mince.

'You didn't tell me you were bringing Jake back from Melbourne.'

'Well, as Jake said, it all happened rather quickly. Chopping board is under the sink,' she said in response to Jake's chopping charade, holding her hand over the mouthpiece.

'And are you going to tell me why you had to run off in such a hurry? Your father said it was for a funeral.'

'Yes. Someone Jake knew. I went to support him.'

'So why is Jake staying with you?'

'He just needed a break away, Mum. Tomato paste and herbs are in the pantry – sorry, only dried,' she whispered to Jake who nodded in return. He was getting everything out before starting to chop. She smiled; it was the same way she cooked.

'Well, it must be serious between you if you drop everything and race off to Melbourne. You've just ended your marriage, for goodness sake!'

Emily sighed. 'Mum, was there a particular reason for your call?' She probably sounded a little rude, but it was better than 'Mind your own bloody business,' which was dangerously close to the tip of her tongue.

'We haven't spoken for a couple of days,' Enid said, sounding indignant. 'I just wanted to make sure you had settled back in okay.'

'Yes. All is well. I'm fine, thank you.' *Can I go now?* She knew she should ask Enid about her own last few days, but couldn't muster the energy to listen to the ensuing twenty minutes of waffle. 'Look, Mum, it's a bit rude of me chatting on the phone when I have a guest. If there was nothing else?'

'Well there is, actually. Your father and I are heading out. We'll be there in around thirty minutes – put the kettle on.'

'Um, now?' It was Emily's turn to shoot Jake a stricken look. 'That really isn't convenient,' she said. She mouthed and made hand gestures that she hoped he'd understand. She was too rabbit-in-the-headlights stunned to actually speak the words out loud.

His response was a series of hand movements which she translated into 'You and me are going for a drive.'

'Are you still there, Emily?'

'Yes. But, Mum, we're actually heading out in a few minutes.'

'Where are you going?'

Oh shit! 'Um, I'm going to show Jake around.'

'Oh, I love a nice drive. We can all go together. You can just wait for half an hour.'

'No, Mum. We have somewhere to be and are already running late. We'll have to catch up another time,' she said.

'But I thought you were just going for a drive,' Enid said.

'Thanks for the call, Mum, gotta go. Bye,' she said, and hung up. Emily suddenly felt very heavy. She sat down on the nearest chair.

'Not good at taking hints, is she?' Jake said.

'That's the understatement of the century.'

'You couldn't have made it more obvious.'

'I wouldn't be surprised if she turns up in half an hour or so.'

'Well, we won't be here,' Jake said, gathering up the ingredients and taking them back to the fridge and pantry.

'But don't you want to cook that for a few hours?'

'I'll do it tomorrow instead,' he said over his shoulder. 'Your mother needs to learn that no means no. Anyway, I need to take you on a proper date. Come on, you've got ten minutes to get back into your jeans,' he said, grasping her by the hand and leading her out of the kitchen.

'We could *pretend* we're not here,' Emily said, pulling him close as they entered the bedroom.

'Somehow I don't think Enid would believe you weren't here if the car was still in the shed. And I don't think we should be stooping to hiding it, or ourselves. You're allowed some privacy, Em. She'll just have to learn that.'

'Thanks, Jake. I probably would've just given in to her.' *Like I usually do.*

'Happy to help.'

'I feel a bit mean.'

'There is absolutely nothing wrong with saying no, Emily. You're an adult. You're allowed your own life. Come on, we'd better get out of here. You stay here, okay Gracie?' Grace looked up from her cushion on the floor and flapped her tail.

In less than fifteen minutes they were locking the glass sliding door. Emily had hesitated at the bathroom mirror, thinking that she ought to put on some make-up. But Jake had wrapped his arms around her from behind, kissed her on the cheek and said to her reflection in the mirror, 'No need for that. You look perfect just the way you are.'

Emily smiled and grabbed his hand. She had never been much into clothes and make-up. Throughout her twenties she'd religiously slathered stuff on her face, and carefully added colour to her eyes, lips, and cheeks. But she'd never enjoyed doing it, and didn't like leaving the house feeling not quite herself. What was wrong with looking natural anyway? And why the hell should she put on all the ridiculous war paint for a man? Look where that had got her.

She hoped Jake wasn't just being nice, because she was done with all the try-hard crap – she'd leave that to younger women. Not that she was unkempt. Emily was always clean, tidy, and presentable, and did wear make-up for evenings out and special occasions. She just couldn't be bothered trying to look like she was ready for a magazine shoot every time she left the house.

'I like that you don't wear make-up every day,' Jake said over the crunch of the rubble as they walked over to the car.

'Thanks Jake,' she said, smiling at him.

'I honestly don't know how you women do it.'

'No, whenever I wear it I tend to spend the whole time feeling like I need a damn good scrub.'

'Well, it's lucky I love you just the way you are then, isn't it?' Jake said, and pulled her to him more firmly. 'Now, shall I drive since it's our first proper date?'

'That would be lovely,' Emily said, beaming. She gave him a peck on the cheek before making her way around to the passenger's side.

But Jake darted ahead of her and opened the door with his left hand while giving a flourish with his right. 'My lady.'

'Why thank you, kind sir,' Emily said, and got into the car.

Jake went back around to his side and then climbed in. But instead of starting it up, he turned to her. 'You know we won't be able to hide from Enid forever, don't you?'

Emily frowned. 'I'm learning to say no to her. I am. And I really do appreciate your support. Far too often it's just easier to give in.'

'Short-term gain, long-term pain,' he muttered. 'Anyway, you did stand up to her. You said no. She just didn't listen.'

'Hmm. You know, leaving John was probably the first time I've ever really stood up to her. And that was mostly because of my love for Grace, and need to protect her, not...' She fiddled with the strap of her handbag in her lap.

'Yes, but it overrode your habit of just falling into line. I know she seems to be very – how shall I put it? – self-righteous? But surely she just wants to see you happy. I would've thought that was the most basic mothering instinct of all – to protect your child from pain.'

'I honestly don't think my mother cares about my happiness,' Emily said sadly. She hadn't really meant to say the words aloud. 'Or if she does, it comes a distant second to I-will-not-have-my-daughter-embarrass-me-by-daring-to-divorce. And, yes, before you say it,' she said, holding up a hand, 'I am fully aware this is not the nineteen fifties.'

'Oh well, as frustrating as she can be, I think what you have to do is limit the impact of her behaviour. Each of us is responsible for our own wellbeing. And, playing devil's advocate for a moment, she is your mother. As much as she drives you mad, at least you still have her in your life to drive you nuts.'

'I know. And I'm sorry you and Simone lost your parents when you were so young.'

'Thanks. But I didn't say it for sympathy. I've had plenty of years to come to terms with it. Hopefully you'll come to terms with Enid one day, and accept that she just is the way she is. I mean, if we ever have kids, I'd like them to have their grandparents in their life.'

Crikey! Kids? Where did that come from? Emily nearly poked her finger right through the leather of her handbag.

Emily couldn't picture Enid as a doting grandparent letting kids run around her immaculate home, but had to concede that people did continue to have the capacity to surprise.

She blinked back the initial shock, and looked up and across at him. 'You want kids then?' she asked.

'One day. Of course. Do you?'

'One day.'

There was a moment of silence, as if Jake was going to say something. Instead, he turned the ignition. Emily put her handbag at her feet, took a deep breath, and settled back into her seat.

'Well, let's get out of here before we get caught. I must say, I do like your dad,' Jake said, as he carefully backed the car out of the shed.

'Me too.' Emily felt a familiar stab of guilt. She'd sold Des Oliphant short for so many years, assuming he was gutless when all the time he was most likely biding his time and choosing his battles wisely. She wished her father had been more influential in her upbringing than her mother. Maybe then she'd have chosen her life partner better and not have had the mess of the past few months to deal with.

'So, which way?' Jake asked, idling at the end of the short driveway beside the house.

'Left if you don't want to risk bumping into Mum and Dad. They'll be coming from that way if they come,' she said, indicating with her head. 'It's a forty-minute drive to the nearest winery, but we don't have to go all that way if you don't want to. We can just drive around.'

'I don't mind if you don't. Let's do a bit of exploring and then have an early bite to eat if we see somewhere we like the look of. Sound like a plan?'

'Perfect. Left here and then the next right and then left – we'll take the back roads; the scenic route.'

Emily took them along a road where a number of partial ruins, abandoned stone cottages and larger homesteads were scattered about the undulating landscape. Most were constructed from pale cream, almost white, limestone – the same as her cottage ruins – but a few were of the darker brown ironstone.

Jake stopped wherever a building was close enough to take a photo without trespassing. A number of times Emily tried to assure him that the owners really wouldn't mind them entering the property for a closer look, but he said he'd rather get their permission first. She liked how respectful he was – about everything.

Eventually they turned onto the bitumen highway, drove a few more kilometres, and then turned in at a glossy painted sign swinging in the slight breeze that read:

Ocean View Winery
OPEN

'Vineyards have only been in the area a few years, hence how bare everything looks,' Emily explained. 'And cellar doors with cafés and restaurants have only really started popping up in the past twelve months.' What she didn't say was that she hadn't been to one before.

Jake let the car roll on slowly across a large rubble car park where a few young, spindly gum trees had been planted. They would make good shade one day and return some of the character to the area, Emily thought. She cast her eyes down the undulating landscape with its neat rows of bright green vines on their timber and wire trellising. The scene was very striking against the wider patchwork of pale yellow, grey and brown stubbles remaining from the recently harvested winter crops. They were on a small rise, and in the far distance she could just make out the blue of the Spencer Gulf.

'Isn't it a shame they left those lovely stone buildings back there to rot? They could have reused one of them instead of putting up something completely new,' Jake said, bringing the car to a halt. Emily was having the same thought at the same moment. 'Don't get me wrong. I'm a huge fan of corrugated iron,' he continued. 'I just think it's sad to see all that old charm and quality workmanship going to waste.'

'Hmm,' Emily agreed, looking at the structure in front of them. Its high-pitched roof and row of skylights gave it a certain charm. But still it looked somehow temporary. Perhaps when the trees and shrubs grew it would look more in keeping with the surrounding landscape.

They parked, got out, and walked across to the building. She followed Jake through the bank of café doors and looked about at the interior – concrete, corrugated iron, and visible steel beams. At first glance, the place was just a shed with nicer doors and windows. Though, looking more closely, she realised that only the main beams were visible. The building was lined in corrugated iron, no doubt with insulation between the inner and outer sheets. There was a solid timber bar running almost its whole length. Emily was turning around and slowly taking it all in when she heard a familiar voice.

'Well, look what the cat dragged in.'

Her face lit up as her gaze settled upon a couple at a table in the corner.

'Barbara! David! What are you guys doing here?!' She rushed over and hugged them both.

'The riff raff they let in,' Jake said, grinning at them. 'Hello you two.' He hugged Barbara and shook David's hand.

'Sit, sit,' Barbara urged, patting the wooden bench beside her.

'What can I get you to drink, Em?' Jake asked, wrapping an arm around her waist.

'Their rosé recently won a prize,' Barbara said.

'Would you like one, Barbara? David?' Jake said.

'No thanks, we're having an alcohol-free day,' David replied.

'At a winery?' Emily laughed.

'We came for coffee and hot chocolate.' He suddenly seemed a little uncomfortable. And Barbara was looking down at her hands in her lap.

'Another bottle of water then?' Jake asked, picking up the empty one.

'That'd be good, thanks,' Barbara said.

'Yes, water, thanks,' David said.

Emily noticed her friends visibly relax. So what if they didn't want to drink? She wasn't about to make them feel awkward by quizzing them on it. In her opinion, most people drank far too much anyway.

'Em?' Jake asked.

'I think I'll just have water too, thanks,' she said, smiling at him.

'Righteo,' Jake said cheerily. 'Water all round it is then.' He tucked the empty bottle under his arm, collected David and Barbara's used mugs, and walked the few metres across to the bar. Emily sat down next to Barbara, who leaned in towards her.

'Jake's looking a little brighter,' Barbara said.

'Yes, he is, isn't he?' Emily watched him. They didn't know about Jake's adrenal fatigue, but this wasn't the time to share. 'He'll be fine. It'll just take some time,' she replied.

'And plenty of fresh country air and TLC from you,' David said.

Jake returned with a bottle of water and four glasses. He sat next to David, across the table from Emily.

'To good friends,' Barbara toasted when they each had a glass in hand.

'Good friends,' David, Emily, and Jake replied, and they all clinked glasses to complete the ceremony.

'We would have invited you to join us, but we thought we'd give you your space,' Barbara said, after they'd all taken a sip. 'Wasn't expecting to run into you lovebirds quite so soon,' she added with a knowing expression, which caused both Jake and Emily to blush slightly.

'Actually, we're hiding from Mum,' Emily said with a laugh.

'Oh?'

'She phoned and then wouldn't take no for an answer about dropping by for coffee,' Jake said. 'So we decided to give her a little wake-up call.'

'Oh, bravo!' Barbara said.

'I told her it wasn't convenient; that we were heading out,' Emily said.

'And she said she was coming over anyway, right?' Barbara said.

'How did you guess?' Jake laughed. 'If I hadn't got all insistent, she'd probably be interrogating poor Em as we speak,' he added, stroking Emily's hand that was wrapped around her glass on the table. 'So, here we are.'

'Good! I've been telling her for ages she needs to redraw the boundaries,' Barbara said.

'She was doing okay, just needed some reinforcement,' Jake said. 'But I'm here now.'

Hello people, I'm sitting right here.

'So, other than hiding from the lovely Enid, we're actually here on our official first date. And what are you guys doing so far from home?' Jake asked.

'First date, eh? About bloody time,' David said jovially.

'Yes,' Barbara agreed.

'Here's to many more.' David raised his glass and they again went through the ritual.

'And here we are making you celebrate with water,' Barbara added with a tight laugh.

'You're not *making* us do anything,' Emily said.

'Well, anyway, it's just lovely,' Barbara said.

'So…?' Jake asked, looking from David beside him to Barbara across the table with raised eyebrows.

'So, what?' David said nonchalantly, though Emily didn't buy it for a second.

Jake continued to look at them expectantly.

'Oh. *Us*? Oh, well, we're um, er,' David stammered, looking at Barbara.

'We're actually here celebrating the anniversary of the day we met,' Barbara cut in.

'Yes,' David said, taking a slug of water.

'Silly, really,' Barbara added, looking down at the table.

'Not at all,' Jake said.

'I don't think we do nearly enough celebrating,' Emily said emphatically, trying to cover up the slight unease that seemed to be hanging over them all. Something just wasn't quite right. Not actually between David and Barbara; they were as close as ever. Just as she had the thought, they exchanged another doe-eyed look.

'Right, who's for one of these wood-fired pizzas?' David said, picking up the stiff, laminated menu cards from the end of the table. He handed them each a copy.

Emily reluctantly dragged her mind back from her misgivings, accepted the card with a thank you, and tried to focus on the long list of pizzas on offer.

It took them ten minutes to decide they would share one large pizza – half gourmet meat for the guys and half barbeque chicken and roast capsicum for the girls.

After they ordered, Jake raised the topic of moving Emily's unfinished hayshed.

'Good idea,' David agreed, 'but I'm busy rolling stubble for the next few days – if the forecast of hot weather turns out to be accurate. I'm happy to look into it after that.'

'What's rolling stubble?' Jake asked.

'After harvest, we roll the stubble flat so it breaks down quicker for the next season – just like putting down a layer of mulch in a garden, really. We used to heap it up and burn it, but it's all about putting it back into the soil now. But you need the weather to be hot enough for the stalks to snap and stay lying on the ground. Otherwise they just spring back up and you've just wasted your time and fuel.'

'Can I go with you and watch?' Jake asked.

'Sure. Though it's not very exciting; it's just going round and round on a tractor.'

'Well, since I've never done that, it might be quite interesting to a city boy like me.'

'In that case, you're on. I'm working at Emily's tomorrow, so I'll drop in and pick you up on the way past. Depending on how quickly it heats up, it probably won't be until around lunchtime. You'll want to pack a sandwich and a water bottle – in case you don't get bored after the first two laps,' David added with a laugh. 'I won't stop until evening when it comes in cooler.'

'Cool, I'm going to play farmer for a day,' Jake said.

'Mate, I wouldn't get too excited,' David said. 'Tractor driving can be as boring as bat shit.'

While David and Jake discussed the various tractor-driving jobs involved in life on the land, Emily and Barbara quietly swapped the latest gossip they'd heard in town. It turned out they'd both been in that day without the other knowing.

Barbara seemed a little quieter than usual, and looking harder at her friend, Emily thought she also looked a little pale. Hopefully she wasn't coming down with something. Though, didn't they say people often got sick when they slowed down after a busy time? David and Barbara had just had David's father's death and funeral, and a houseful of guests to deal with.

With Jake off with David, tomorrow would be a perfect opportunity for the two of them to spend some quiet time together. If it was going to be hot, they wouldn't want to be out and about. It was better to hibernate in that sort of weather.

'Hey, Barb,' Emily said, suddenly. 'Do you fancy hanging out tomorrow and watching a DVD or two while the boys are off?'

'Sounds very indulgent. Probably just what we both need after the last few months. I've got a couple of recent chick flicks.'

'Perfect.' The only DVDs she had were action movies of John's.

'Well, how do you like that? We menfolk will be hard at work and you'll be inside with your feet up,' David teased.

'We'll be sure to pine for you. Will that help ease your burden?' Barbara replied, batting her eyelashes.

'It certainly will.'

Finally their pizza arrived with an apology for the delay. They oohed and aahed over it, and set about devouring the meal with little conversation.

Afterwards, the men went up to the counter to settle the bill and then the four of them made their way outside.

They spent a few moments admiring the bright orange and pink sunset before hugging and getting into their separate cars.

'Well, that was nice. Thank you,' Emily said as they drove out of the car park.

'You're welcome. But I guess it means we still haven't officially had our first date. I don't think a double date counts,' Jake added with a laugh.

'I don't mind. It wasn't like you knew they'd be here.'

'No, but I still owe you one.'

'You saved me from my mother, remember? I think we can call it square.' She smiled at him.

'I saved *myself* from your mother,' Jake said.

'Hey, did you notice how cagey they got when you asked why they were there?' Emily asked, deliberately changing the subject.

'I did. Something's up that they clearly don't want to share.'

'I hope they're okay,' Emily said.

'Well, they seemed happy with each other – more affectionate than usual, I reckon. If we're meant to know, we'll find out,' Jake added, patting Emily's thigh. 'Just leave it be.'

'Yeah, you're right. It's just that after all they've done for me, I'd like to return the favour if I can.'

'You'll get your chance, if and when you're meant to.'

'I hope so.' Emily leaned back into the seat and tried to put the nag of concern out of her mind.

'I'm excited about going out with David tomorrow,' Jake said, after a few minutes of silence.

Emily smiled at his boyish enthusiasm; he sounded like a kid about to enter a candy shop.

'That's great, you'll have fun,' she said, beaming at him. 'But make sure you don't overdo it. You're here to recuperate, remember?'

They entered the house to find the red light on the answering machine blinking in the dark kitchen. Emily turned on the overhead fluoro light, dumped her handbag beside Grace, who was snoozing in her bed, and pressed the button to play new messages.

'Oh! Des, it's the damned answering machine,' Enid's voice rang out. 'Emily, it's your mother here. We're outside. Where are you? I told you we would be stopping in. We've been sitting here in the car for ten minutes. Call me back when you get this.'

'Unbelievable,' Jake muttered.

Emily shook her head slowly and sighed. Just hearing her mother's voice made her feel very tired. Thankfully, it was almost too late to phone back – well that would be her excuse. Enid didn't take calls after nine p.m. *Actually, no, I'll get it over with now*, she thought, grabbing the phone and plastering a smile on her face, as she'd once been taught in an office skills course. 'A smile makes for a friendly sounding voice,' she'd learnt during training.

Enid picked up straight away. 'Enid Oliphant speaking.'

'Hi Mum. We've just got home and got your message.'

'Where were you?'

'I told you we were going out. It's not my fault you chose not to listen.'

'Oh, Emily, don't get all high and mighty with me.'

'Was there something you wanted?'

'Yes, actually. We'd like to meet this young man you have staying.'

'It's Jake, Mum, and you've already met him. At dinner with Liz.'

'Well, as it now seems he's your *boyfriend*, we'd like to meet him properly. I need to have you both for dinner, but all my evenings are booked for the next two weeks.'

'That's all right, we've got a lot on too.'

'What could you possibly have on? You're a lady of leisure, and Jake's on holidays, isn't he?'

'Sort of. Mum, you don't need to go to the bother of dinner. We'll just drop in for a cuppa soon. Okay?'

'Well, then, please give some warning so I'm definitely here.'

Emily smiled wryly and shook her head slowly. *As if you won't be there.* She was starting to see the funny side of Enid.

As she hung up and deleted the message, she wondered why her mother hadn't just called her mobile in the first place. Why bother leaving an answering-machine message Emily might not get for hours? Maybe Enid thought she and Jake had been hiding inside.

Chapter Four

At eleven the next morning, David's ute pulled up outside. They went out, Jake swinging John's blue lunchbox-sized esky and a small matching water bottle filled with ice cubes that rattled when he walked. Emily stopped short of the gate at the end of the concrete path and wrapped her arms around him.

'Are you sure you're up to heading out?'

'I'm tired, but I'm fine. I promise I'll call you to come and get me if I'm not up to it.'

'Okay. I don't mean to nag, I'm just concerned. And you don't seem to be taking it easy at all.'

'I am. Just changing environments is a huge help, I think. And not having to make business decisions. I'll check in tomorrow. But I'm sure all is well in Melbourne.'

'Well, okay, if you're sure. Take care,' she said, stretching up and nuzzling his neck.

'See ya,' Jake said, giving her a final firm kiss. He walked around to the passenger's side of the ute, where Barbara was stepping out.

Emily returned his wave as the ute drove away and Barbara leaned into her embrace.

'I come bearing chick flicks, microwave popcorn, and soft drink,' Barbara said, holding up a green eco shopping bag.

Her friend didn't look nearly as bright and cheery as she sounded. But Emily shook her doubts aside. Jake was right; if something was up, Barbara would tell her if and when she wanted to.

'It's going to be a hot one, so let's get inside and batten down the hatches,' she said, leading the way back up the path. Thanks to the thick stone walls and their layer of concrete render, the house usually managed to stay cool through three days of full-on South Australian heat if kept closed up. Two more days and it would start to get stuffy.

Emily idly wondered what it would cost to put in ducted air conditioning. She'd probably be able to afford it. But was it a luxury that should wait, or be done at all? In her three and a half years with John she could only remember a handful of nights when they had been unable to sleep due to the heat. Winter wasn't too bad either. They'd tended to shut off most of the house and just live in the kitchen, bedroom, and lounge – all of which were clustered at one end of the house and could be heated with small electric heaters. The lounge had an open fire, which she would have liked to use more, except her husband had refused to cut wood himself or get any delivered.

'Coffee?' Emily asked as Barbara sat heavily onto a chair in the darkened kitchen.

'Actually, I'd prefer a tea. I seem to have suddenly gone off coffee,' Barbara said.

'Are you okay? You look a little pale.'

'Just a bit queasy. Must have picked up a virus or something. If I could just throw up, I'm sure I'd feel better.'

'God, you poor thing. You should've cancelled.'

'It comes and goes.'

'Well, I'm sure a nice cup of tea will help.'

'Thanks. Yes,' Barbara said. But suddenly she was leaping up with a hand to her mouth and disappearing from the room.

Emily had just consulted her watch and decided to give Barbara one more minute, when she returned looking even paler.

'False alarm,' Barbara said. It was clear she was trying to sound bright.

'Have you seen a doctor?' Emily asked. She frowned as Barbara sat down, nodding.

'I've booked. But of course I couldn't get in until next week,' she said, rolling her eyes.

'Well, you could always go to emergency at the hospital.'

'I'm not that bad. And I am feeling a bit better.'

'If you need me to do anything, you only have to ask.'

'Thanks. I know.'

Emily was stirring sugar into Barbara's tea when it finally dawned on her. 'Um, tell me to back off, but would you by any chance be pregnant?'

Barbara looked up sharply. She was on the verge of tears.

'What is it?' Emily asked.

'Yes. I'm pregnant,' she said.

Gosh! Emily wasn't sure how she felt, other than stunned and, if she was completely honest, a little nervous at the prospect of losing her best friend to a baby.

God, could I possibly be a worse friend? After everything Barbara's done for me...

There had been so much upheaval in recent months, she really just wanted things to be settled for a while, not change. But she put her concerns aside with the stern reminder: *It's not about me.*

'So what's wrong? Isn't this a good thing? You guys want kids, don't you?' She placed the two mugs on the table and sat down on the end around the corner from Barbara.

Barbara nodded. 'I'm just so scared,' she said, and began sobbing. 'I'm a mess.'

'Is it the hormones?'

'No. I wish.'

'Is there a problem with the baby?'

Barbara fiddled with the handle on the mug and then without looking up said, 'I've had two miscarriages in the year since we've been married. I'm so scared of going through it again. But not enough to stop trying,' she added with a wan smile.

'Oh Barbara, I'm so sorry.' Emily put her arm around her friend's shoulder again, this time loosely. 'Why didn't you tell me?'

'Because I wanted to be positive, put it all behind me – us.'

'Well, let's hope it will be third time lucky,' Emily said softly, giving her a gentle squeeze.

'Hmm.'

'So how far along are you? When does morning sickness set in?'

'I'm only a couple of weeks. It should be too early for morning sickness. I think my problem is the stress and anxiety.' She took a tentative sip of her tea and then sat with her hands wrapped around it for a few moments.

Emily waited her out.

Barbara finally looked up. Her forehead was creased with concern. 'I'm sorry I didn't tell you, but we didn't want anyone to know until three months was up and we were in the safe period. Although that's a bit of a misnomer;

I lost Isabella at four months. She was the second one. They were both before I knew you.'

'I'm so sorry,' she said, hugging Barbara again.

'The doctors haven't been able to find anything wrong,' Barbara said with a shrug, answering the question on the tip of Emily's tongue. 'Just bad luck, not meant to be, and all that,' she said with a resigned shrug of her shoulders.

'God, I feel so helpless,' Emily said. 'I can't even begin to imagine how you must be feeling.' She wondered why Isabella had a name but not the first baby. But she wasn't about to ask.

'We're just trying to be as normal as possible and try not to jinx things. We know you guys didn't buy our non-drinking story last night,' she said, smiling weakly. 'We discussed it on the way home. David's going to tell Jake today too.'

'Well, you tell us if there's anything we can do for you – both of you – no matter what it is, or what time of the day or night. Promise me you'll call if there's anything at all – big or small,' Emily said.

'I promise. Thanks, Em, that means a lot.'

'God, Barbara, after all you guys have done for me...'

They hugged briefly.

'Now, should we start our totally indulgent and lazy day while the men folk are out toiling the fields?' Barbara asked.

'Yes! And let's pop the corn! It can be lunch,' Emily declared.

'I was hoping you'd say that,' Barbara said, grinning. 'I seem to be craving popcorn at the moment.'

Halfway through the movie – the new Julia Roberts – Emily's phone began to ring. Barbara paused the DVD as Emily picked it up from the coffee table.

'Sorry, I'd better get this,' she said, looking at the screen. 'It's Simone, Jake's sister,' she added, and answered. 'Hi Simone.'

'Hi Em, how is everything?'

'I'm good, but what you really mean is, how's Jake, right?'

Simone laughed. 'Yes, I guess I do.'

'He's doing well, a lot more relaxed than he was in Melbourne. And he told me about his suspected adrenal fatigue. Right now he's out with my friend David on the tractor. I'm a little concerned he's overdoing it, but he's assured me he will take care. Perhaps the fresh air and change of scenery is the answer,' Emily added.

'I hope you're right,' Simone said. 'Oh, well, he's a big boy, he's seen a doctor, so we can only really be here for him.'

'And how are things with you?' Emily asked.

'Great. Your lovely comments about my paintings have got me all inspired. I'm painting like a demon every chance I get.'

'That's great. I can't wait to see more of your work.'

'So, are you making any more jam?' Simone asked. 'It's just that Billy emailed me and...'

'To be honest, Simone, I haven't had much chance to think about it. And it's really a bad time for fruit at the moment – everything has finished. I should have access to figs in a few months and then oranges over winter for marmalade. I was going to see if the blackberries are still running rampant at the back of the farm, but I haven't had a chance to get up there. I'm really sorry.'

'Don't be, you can't help when fruit is ripe,' Simone said with a laugh. 'And, anyway, you've probably got your hands full looking after Jake. It's not a problem; Billy just wanted to know for certain where it all stood. Look, I'd better go. I just wanted to know Jake was okay. I'll give him a call.'

'It was lovely to speak to you, Simone. Thanks for calling.' Emily hung up. 'Simone was checking up on her brother. Isn't that nice?'

'Hmm,' Barbara agreed. 'So, shall we continue?' she asked, nodding at the television.

'Yes, sorry about that.'

They resumed watching the movie, but Emily was unable to totally immerse herself back into the story again. She was distracted by thoughts of Simone and her art, and a nagging within her that she couldn't quite grasp.

Emily didn't know much about painting, but she liked Simone's bold style of having a single brightly coloured bloom take up most of the space on her huge canvases. If not for the slightly raised, thick paint, some of them might have been mistaken for photographs. The gorgeous texture made you want to reach out and touch them. And she wasn't the only one who appreciated her talent; Jake had a couple of her paintings hanging in his apartment as well. Emily had particularly loved the one of red and green chillies on a bush in his kitchen. If only she knew someone who could get her art out to a wider audience.

She wished she could somehow return the help Simone had given her with selling her jam when she was so desper-ate financially. Not that Simone had known just how desperate her situation was. All she'd known was that Jake had brought back the apricot jam to Melbourne because he liked it and thought it might sell well at the markets. And it had, thanks to the gorgeous labels Simone had designed, and the scones she'd taken the trouble to make and serve with it. All without even having met her.

If Emily hadn't suddenly inherited everything from John, jam making could well have become her lifeline. She felt the overwhelming need to do something in return. Frustration grew inside of her, so much so that she became physically restless. Grace eventually got up from the couch with a harrumph and went to lie down on the floor.

'Are you okay?' Barbara asked.

'Yeah, sorry.' She tried to tell herself that the chance to help would arise when and in whatever way it was meant to. She just had to be patient. Jake was bound to have an idea, or at least a sensible pep talk. Meanwhile she was missing the movie.

Just as they finished the second DVD, they heard two toots of a car horn; the signal that David was back. After gathering Barbara's things together, they headed out. Sure enough, David's ute was outside and Jake was walking towards the path. When Emily opened the door, a blast of hot air hit her with the intensity and dryness of an oven.

'Bloody hell,' she said. She checked her watch and was surprised to find it was almost six o'clock. 'Quick, get into the cool ute,' Emily urged, giving her friend a quick goodbye hug. 'See you or speak to you soon.'

'Thanks, it's been a fun day,' Barbara called, hurrying down the path. 'Sorry, too hot to stop,' she said to Jake, pecking him on the cheek on the way past.

'God, it's hot,' Jake said, leading Emily back into the house.

'You look shattered. Jake, you're meant to be taking it easy.'

'I was in an air-conditioned cab. The hum of the tractor is actually quite soothing when you're not in charge of anything. I had a few power naps along the way. But, yes,

I am feeling quite done in. Oh, and I got my test results. It took some effort to convince them to give them to me over the phone...'

'And...?'

'Positive. It's official, I have adrenal fatigue. But at least I don't need to look any further into what's wrong with me. And I know I'll get better. The results weren't as bad as my GP had feared. She told me to just carry on with what I'm doing and in time I'll be my old energetic, chipper self again.'

'If you take it easy and don't overdo it,' Emily warned.

'I love that you're worrying about me, but I'm fine, honey, honestly,' he said, kissing her.

'Did, um, David tell you their news?'

A huge smile burst across Jake's face. 'He did. Isn't it exciting?'

'Hmm. Barbara seems more scared than excited. I'm a bit worried about her.'

'David seems genuinely thrilled, though he's quite concerned about Barbara too. I can only imagine what they must be feeling. I guess all we can do is hope everything will be okay and be there for them if not.'

'I guess.' Cross that bridge if and when we get to it, as her gran would have said.

Emily was in the kitchen when Jake came in after his shower with a towel around his waist. She smiled at his wet, mussed boyish hair sticking out in all angles. As he moved towards her she noticed the water droplets glistening on his smooth chest. He leaned down, nuzzled her ear and then started nibbling at her earlobe. Her stomach turned molten and her knees went weak.

'Fancy taking advantage of my evening burst of energy?' he whispered.

Emily stood on quivering legs, accepted Jake's outstretched hand, and allowed herself to be led to the bedroom.

Chapter Five

Each day flowed into the next and soon more than two weeks had passed since Jake's arrival. Emily loved him being there, but was constantly concerned he was doing too much. But she had to trust that he knew his body and was listening to its needs. She didn't want to become a nag. She was damned lucky to have him in her life, and didn't want to put that in jeopardy.

They had settled into an easy existence where they spent plenty of time together, but also plenty of time apart as Jake went off with David playing farmer and she did the housework. He was happy. She was happy. Most importantly, they were happy.

When they were both home, they often made love in the late afternoon or early evening. Afterwards Emily would stay with Jake for part of his hour or so of resting. She felt so blessed to have this time together; it was so decadent. But she always left him alone after a while, and always when he disappeared into the lounge to lie quietly on the couch – accompanied by Grace. A few times she had caught herself watching him sleep, looking for signs he was doing better. Really, other than a slightly drawn, pale look about him, most people wouldn't have known there was anything wrong.

But Emily was beside him when the night sweats soaked the sheets. She saw the shake in his hands and the confusion and vagueness in his eyes, and knew it wasn't the real Jake. He was making an effort, but he was certainly not the vibrant, cheery fellow who had visited her those first two times. When they were with other people he was more exuberant than when he was at home with her. She could see it took a lot of effort for him to be sociable.

They went out to lunch with Sarah and Nathan and David and Barbara one Sunday and had a wonderful time. On the way home they'd agreed that Nathan and Sarah had looked a lot closer than mere flatmates. A few days later at the bank when Emily had signed up for an at call investment account, Nathan had admitted they were officially an item. She was glad to see her friend happy. He had promised to invite them to a dinner party at his and Sarah's house. But a week or so on, nothing had eventuated.

Emily wasn't surprised. Sarah and Nathan worked full-time, so they only had the evenings and weekends together. Besides, they were in the flush of young love, just like she and Jake were. They'd get around to it eventually.

Meanwhile, she was so grateful for this time with Jake. The heat of the South Australian summer kept them close to home, and more than once they had spent the whole day in bed. It was a charmed, wonderful existence. But she was starting to yearn for something more constructive to do with her time when Jake wasn't around. She'd imagined he would need more taking care of, but he seemed to be doing fine. It was just a long, slow process of getting the body better.

He was spending a lot of time with David learning how a working farm operated, and also taking plenty of gentle strolls with his camera – often over to the old cottage ruins.

The idea that she really wanted to somehow help Simone bubbled away in the far depths of Emily's brain, but a tangible solution still hadn't presented itself. She was also more and more feeling the need to do something with her life. It was nice to have the means to while away her days – and she was very grateful – but it just wasn't in her nature to be idle for long.

One morning, Emily was staring out the bedroom window, wondering what to do. Jake was out with David again, and she was at a loose end. She was standing next to the tallboy beside Gran's button jar, where she often stood and contemplated life. She knew it was ridiculous, but she always felt better when the object was nearby. And answers quite often came to her while she was standing there. She liked to think Gran was still with her while she was close to her treasured object.

Emily frowned. She really wished she could move the damned hayshed herself. It was such a blight on the landscape. David and Jake had discussed it, but David was still busy rolling stubble. Grace nudged her leg and she bent down to pat her briefly before returning her attention to the jar in front of her and her musings.

'What I need is some purpose – a project,' Emily said aloud, and then looked up at the ceiling. Suddenly she laughed at herself. What the hell was she expecting? A bolt of lightning and Gran's booming voice telling her to take up knitting or something?

Nothing happened, except that she felt a sharp, enduring stab of shame deep within her. Granny and Grandpa had been through so much, so many tough times over the years, and here she was complaining because she had plenty of money and too much time on her hands.

'Come on Gracie,' Emily called, and left the room. The guilt stayed with her as she made her way through the house to what had been John's office and was now also home to Jake's suitcase and laptop.

Gran had filled any spare time she had with working for the community. Barbara had asked Emily to join CWA and, as much as she'd have enjoyed more time with her, she'd resisted. She couldn't knit, crochet, or arrange flowers. Therefore, she argued, she was absolutely not CWA material. Though, she'd always be happy to lend a hand with baking for fundraisers.

Perhaps driving for Meals on Wheels might be the way to go. As a child during school holidays she'd loved walking up to the door with the tray of food while Gran sat in the idling car nearby. But Gran had lived in town. Emily was a little too far out. She'd have to think about it.

Or was it time to have a child? As the thought crossed her mind she was disappointed at how practical – how rational – it sounded. Where was the ticking biological clock, that desperate need she'd heard other women talk about? She shook her head. The time wasn't right. It was definitely too soon for her and Jake, and, really, she needed more distance from all that had gone on in her life recently.

While it often felt like years had passed since she'd left John and he'd had a car accident and died, the reality was that it was all very recent.

Emily found herself wondering if Gran had felt time passing quickly or excruciatingly slowly while she lived with Alzheimer's and was up in the hostel on the hill. The poor old dear had really just been marking time for a number of years. *Which is exactly what you are doing right now.* The words in her head sounded uncannily like Gran's.

Emily sat down at what had been John's desk in the spare room. Jake's laptop sat closed beside the monitor connected to her tower-style PC. The rest of the large desk was covered in paperwork. There were carefully arranged piles of bills and receipts to be filed, sheets of correspondence from the lawyers regarding the estate, bank statements, and a stack of assorted miscellaneous items she wasn't sure how to file. She considered getting it all into the empty filing cabinets and out of sight, but she couldn't muster any enthusiasm. She was feeling restless to do something, but admin was the last thing she felt like doing.

She walked through to the adjoining room. It was empty except for a plain double ensemble bed covered in an old-fashioned powder blue candlewick bedspread. With its rose-patterned wall-to-wall carpet that was around nineteen forties or fifties vintage, it was a more feminine room than the office, which had carpet in an autumn leaf design – oranges, browns, and dark pinks on a plain pale grey background.

Grace trotted in and began snuffling her way around the room.

John never used to come in here because it was the room his grandfather had passed away in. Emily didn't have a problem with it; if his grandfather was haunting the place, she figured he wouldn't confine himself solely to this room, and would have surely shown signs of his presence before now. Not that she knew anything about ghosts and how they operated.

Occasionally relatives of John's had stayed here over the years, apparently without complaint. Now, as Emily sat staring around her looking for inspiration, she wondered if her life with John might have been better if she'd had a room of her own to indulge in some hobbies. Why hadn't she pushed harder to get her own computer? Well, that one was obvious: John would have said it was hardly worth the expense when she'd probably only need it for the odd hour here and there. And how could she have argued with that sort of logic?

Emily closed her eyes and tried to conjure up her perfect office space, not that she really needed an office. Though, now there was no one to tell her so, she liked the idea more and more. And anyway, she was running a business now, wasn't she? The farm was hers – well, it would be when the probate came through and the estate was officially finalised.

God, the thought of all it entailed made her head fuzzy. She and David had signed the agreement for the sheep, and he'd promised to take her over the farm and give her a bit of a rundown on it all when he got the chance. Meanwhile, Emily was a little embarrassed to admit that she quite liked remaining blissfully ignorant.

Staring at the beige walls around her, she suddenly burned with inspiration and the desire to act NOW. If she could choose any colour she liked, what would it be? She looked down. The carpet was a multitude of pinks, purples and a few greens depicting foliage on a beige background. There was a great choice of colours right there in front of her, and not so many as to be overwhelming. She felt herself drawn to the pinker tones. But if she chose one, how was she then to get it translated into a paint colour? She couldn't exactly cut out a chunk of carpet and have it matched. *Ah, but I could go and get a heap of sample pots.* That would be fun. She stared at the floor for a few moments, trying to commit the colour to memory.

Emily didn't think she'd take the carpet up even if she wasn't in such a hurry to put her own stamp on the room. It was really quite lovely. She would give it a decent vacuum and the walls and woodwork a decent wipe-down before painting, and perhaps even get the visiting carpet-cleaning guy in next time he was in town. But for now she was off to the hardware shop to get some paint. She practically skipped out of the room in her excitement.

A few days ago, Jake had said he wouldn't mind checking out the shops selling antiques and bric-a-brac scattered about the district. It would be nice to go looking for something in particular, rather than just browsing aimlessly. Maybe Barbara and David could come along too. It would be great to have Barbara's opinion and then Jake and David could chat together while she and Barbara shopped guilt-free.

She almost pulled the car over to get out her mobile phone. No, she'd discuss it with Jake first. For all she knew he was planning to visit Whyalla and check on the project he was involved with up there. He had mentioned the need to get back up there in the next few weeks.

Emily had been a little concerned that he was getting into work again too soon, but he'd reassured her that he was okay and taking careful note of any signs his progress might be slipping. And how could she say otherwise when his face lit up a little at the mere mention of a project or a client.

He was so kidding himself if he thought he could take three to six months off work. A slight sadness descended on her, but she pushed it aside. He had made no mention of going back to Melbourne.

Chapter Six

Emily was standing in the doorway surveying her work when she heard the glass sliding door open and close.

'Em? Sweetie, are you here?'

'Up here in the spare room,' she called whilst continuing to stare at the fresh paint job.

It's very pink, she thought. *Should I have perhaps just done a feature wall?*

It was what Doris at the hardware store had assumed she was doing. Emily was now wondering if her comment had in fact been a hint that doing a whole room in that colour would be too much. Perhaps if she did the skirtings and door and window frames in white it would look better. But she couldn't help feeling that it would be sacrilegious to cover up the lovely grain of the timber. Weren't people falling over themselves to strip back the woodwork of old houses these days?

'Wow! Haven't you been busy,' Jake said, appearing behind her and wrapping his arms around her waist and laying his head on her shoulder. 'Great colour.'

'Do you think so? Honestly? I'm beginning to wonder if it's too much.'

'No way. I love it. I think when you get some more furniture in here it'll make all the difference. You just need time to get used to it. And if you don't, we can paint over it again. So, what is it to be – spare room, or what?'

'Office-slash-whatever else I decide it is.'

'I hope this isn't a sign I'm outstaying my welcome,' Jake said, suddenly serious.

'Why would you say that?'

'Well, you already have a perfectly adequate office next door.'

'No, this is about me putting my stamp on the house. I love having all this time on my hands, but I think it's sending me a little nuts. I just got a sudden urge. If I wanted that room, I would've asked you to move in here.' She put her arms around him. 'Honestly, I love having you here.' *And I don't want you to ever leave*, she added silently. 'So you really don't think it's too much?' Emily asked when they parted.

'Not at all, but you will need to be careful about what window covering you end up using – to make sure the room isn't too busy. What great carpet,' he added, peeling the drop cloth back a bit and staring at the floor.

'I was thinking of leaving the bed and just adding a desk and chair and maybe an arm or wing chair and lamp. But it'll all depend on what's out there and how much everything is. I don't want to spend a fortune.'

'Well, I reckon Simone would match the covering on the chair to the curtains and put a matching cushion on the bed to tie it in,' Jake said thoughtfully.

'Hmm,' Emily agreed absently while still taking in the new colour. The longer she looked at it, the more she liked it. And she was also starting to see where pieces of furniture could go. It was actually quite exciting.

Looking back down at the carpet, she noticed that there was quite a bit of black in the design. By bringing out the deep pink of the roses, she seemed to have also inadvertently highlighted their subtle black edging. It was interesting how colour worked.

Perhaps black and white check would work for the curtains and upholstery. Emily brought a finger to her lips and tapped while she thought. Suddenly a bubble of inspiration burst in her head. She opened her mouth to share, but Jake, who had been silently taking in their surroundings, spoke at exactly the same moment.

'I think a mossy green check might work well for the upholstery and curtains – and you could do a matching roman blind for extra insulation, if it's needed.' Jake was now squatting on the carpet and tapping a finger on it. 'See, there's quite a bit of green in here.'

Emily laughed. 'I just had the same thought. Why try to be clever when someone else has already done the colour matching for me?' she said.

'Exactly. And it really is lovely carpet. I bet it cost a fortune in its day,' Jake added.

'It's pretty feminine,' Emily said.

'Nothing wrong with that. I happen to like feminine,' he said, standing upright and drawing her into another hug, and nuzzling her neck.

'I need a shower. Care to save some water with me?'

'Well, I've probably got some paint splotches I need help removing.' She grinned.

Later they lay stretched out naked in bed. They had made love and snuggled, and finally become too warm.

'So how was your day playing farmer again?' Emily asked, rolling onto her side to look at Jake.

His face lit up. 'Great. Today I got to see a boom sprayer in action! I wish they didn't have to use chemicals, but it seems there's no getting around it. I thought it was lovely and green, considering it's the middle of summer. But David tells me the summer weeds are a big problem. It's hard to follow sometimes. I thought farmers always wanted rain. But apparently the last lot they had has now caused problems. Beats me.'

Emily fleetingly thought about how lax John had been with chemical safety – he'd never even worn gloves for measuring out chemicals. 'I hope you wore safety gear.'

'Yeah, David's a stickler in that department. You hear about farmers taking risks and not being careful, but we were covered from head to toe.'

'So, are you off with him again tomorrow?'

'Yep, if that's okay with you – just a couple more hours rolling up at his place. So, I'll need the car, unless you need to go anywhere?'

'No, that's fine. But as long as you're not overdoing it.' Emily hated being a nag, but she was concerned about him.

'I'm feeling good. Even better now...' he said, grinning cheekily at her. He reached an arm across and traced a finger the length of Emily's bare belly, causing her to shudder with pleasure again.

★

Emily woke the next day feeling very excited. She and Barbara were heading to Port Lincoln for a girls' day out – an all-day shopping trip. Since meeting, they'd idly discussed it a number of times, but Emily had never fully committed. It wasn't that she hadn't wanted to go, but she had always figured that being unable to actually spend money on anything but the barest of bare essentials would make for a depressing day. And window-shopping wasn't her idea of fun.

What could be worse than seeing all those beautifully displayed windows, shop floors, and advertisements when one couldn't afford to indulge? What if she lost her will-power for a moment and whipped out her credit card as if it wasn't real money leaving her account? So, Emily had decided it was best to avoid the temptation altogether.

Today would be an entirely different story, though she would still have to keep herself in firm check. Having been so tightly restrained for so long – whilst married to John and then so cash-strapped for the past few months – a stray purchase was bound to signal something in her brain akin to opening the floodgates. Luckily Barbara wasn't a frivolous shopper, so she would help keep her on the straight and narrow.

For a fleeting moment Emily wondered if Barbara would want to spend the day trawling baby shops. It was still very early days, but it might be nice to pick up a little present for the baby. Would that make her clucky? Oh well, she'd just have to wait and see.

Jake was still asleep, so she carefully got out of bed, stepped around Grace in her position on the floor, dragged her bathrobe from the hook on the back of the door, and made her way through to the bathroom to shower.

A few minutes later, Jake wandered in while she was rinsing her hair and humming to herself.

'Someone's chirpy this morning,' he said, opening the sliding shower screen to give her a quick peck. 'Nothing like the lure of the big smoke full of bright, shiny objects, huh?'

'Yep. Can't wait.'

'I can tell. So do we need a big breakfast? You know what they say about not shopping on an empty stomach.'

'No, thanks. And I think that only applies to food shopping. We're going to start with cake and coffee when we get there. Not ideal nutrition, but hey!' Emily said, turning off the shower and then stepping out into the towel Jake held out for her. 'So what are you up to today, more playing farmer with David?'

'Something like that.'

Emily caught an odd sort of look cross his face ever so briefly, almost like caginess. Perhaps it was slight embarrassment at her gentle ribbing. But it wasn't like he'd complained before.

'I'll have you know,' Jake continued, full of mock seriousness, 'the fact that I can now competently operate a tractor and boom sprayer means I've risen above the ranks of mere "playing".'

'Does that mean you're looking at a career change, dear?' she asked.

'Becoming a farmer? Hell, no! God, far too many things can go wrong that you have no control over! Though, I have to admit, I am quite enjoying being David's lackey – all care and no responsibility. It's kind of nice for a change. But all good things must come to an end.'

'Surely you're not thinking of heading back to your business already. I didn't think you'd last six months, but it's only been a couple of weeks! Are you sure it's wise? You seem fine, but what if...?'

Jake placed his hands on each side of her face and looked deeply into her eyes. 'Don't worry, petal, I'm not getting fully back into work mode, and I'm not thinking of leaving you to head back to Melbourne.'

Emily coloured slightly. 'Oh, I'm not worried about me, I…'

'It's okay. I only meant I need to get back in touch with things a bit. Starting with going up to Whyalla to check on the Civic Centre project. Actually, I've been considering setting up an agency over here. There doesn't seem to be anyone else doing old buildings – especially in stone.'

And with that he walked out, leaving Emily with a head full of questions. An agency? Here in Wattle Creek? Was he just winding her up? She stood there dripping onto the bathmat for a few moments until her brain kicked back into gear and she remembered she didn't have long to get herself ready.

As she started the hairdryer, she told herself not to worry; Jake wasn't one to drop a bombshell like that and walk away unless he was just joking.

One thing was true, though. As far as she knew, there wasn't anyone on the whole of the Eyre Peninsula who specialised in building with stone. That was no doubt why the new cellar doors popping up about the place were constructed out of corrugated iron and why old homesteads were being torn down and replaced with kit homes and transportable buildings. One of the huge problems with living so far away from the big cities was that freight made everything more expensive. The lack of competition didn't help either.

As Emily put some sunscreen on her face and added pale pink lipstick, she thought Jake might have just struck upon a good idea. Knowing him, he wouldn't have mentioned it without at least looking part way into it. She wouldn't be surprised to learn that he'd started looking into possibilities after that first trip with Elizabeth, or even that that was why he'd visited the area in the first place.

She let out a sigh as she told herself to leave the subject alone. She was desperately trying not to be like her mother – who asked questions non-stop and pried and prodded unnecessarily. No, she would be mature and non-controlling and not say a word until Jake brought it up again. And she would certainly not be all needy and demanding to know if he was planning to stay.

Just let it be, she told herself. It was a phrase that ran through her head often when spending time with her parents.

'You look nice,' Jake said, looking up as Emily wandered into the kitchen all ready to go.

'Thanks.'

'Time for a coffee?' he asked, getting up.

Emily checked her watch. 'Yes, please, but I've only got ten minutes.'

As Jake made her coffee, Emily sat down with her list. 'Are you sure there isn't anything you want me to get you?' she asked.

'Actually, I wouldn't mind a new book to read – some crime, say from James Patterson, Lee Child, one of the Kellermans – if you go into a bookshop,' he said, putting a mug of steaming milky coffee in front of her. 'I really want to get back into reading now I've got the time.'

'Okey-dokey,' she said, adding the authors' names to her list. She picked up her cup. 'Mmm, thank you.'

'I'll get you some money,' he said.

'No, don't worry about it. We can sort it out later. Or, I can take it in kind,' she said, leaning towards him and planting her lips on his.

'Aren't you becoming quite the little minx?' he said. 'I don't want you to go now.'

'Hmm.' Emily enjoyed the effect her kisses had on him.

'Okay,' he said, running a hand through his hair and drawing a line in the conversational sand. 'That's some list you've got there,' he said, leaning over.

'Uh-huh,' Emily said, trying to banish thoughts of Jake's naked body from her mind. 'It's mostly stuff I want to check out – you know, furniture and decorating ideas for the study.'

She had initially wanted to add curtains, quilt cover, sheets and towels, but had stopped herself. While it would be nice to start afresh, she couldn't go blowing money just for the sake of it. It would be far too easy to leave behind her lifetime of frugality and go crazy.

'I'd like to visit a few antiques and bric-a-brac shops. You know, to find some one-off pieces with character. But it won't hurt to check what's available new.'

Suddenly there was the sound of a friendly *toot toot* of a car horn.

'Well, that's me,' Emily said. She leaned over for what was meant to be a quick peck, but Jake grabbed her around the waist and pulled her onto his lap and the kiss became more passionate.

'God you're sexy,' she growled, shaking her head with frustration as she eased herself out of his clutches.

'Jesus, you can't say something like that and then just walk out the door.'

'Sorry,' she said. 'Hold that thought until tonight.'

'Do you want to drive me crazy?' He groaned and put his head in his hands on the table.

The truth was, if Barbara wasn't outside waiting for her, she could imagine them tearing each other's clothes off right there in the kitchen. Emily was a little shocked at the strength of her feelings. She took a deep breath and shook her head.

'Bye Gracie.' She gave the dog a brief pat before retrieving her handbag from the nearby chair.

'See you later. Have fun,' Jake said.

'I will, you too,' Emily called, already halfway out the sliding door. She gleefully skipped down the path before leaping into Barbara's car.

'Ready for a fun day of shopping?' Barbara said after they'd exchanged quick kisses and hugs.

'Yes, onwards James!' Emily said, clapping her hands together.

As they drove onto the main dirt road, Emily noticed a ute coming towards them. They returned David's wave as he drove past.

'What are those two up to, anyway? Jake was weirdly vague.'

'Dunno. You know men,' Barbara said with a shrug. 'Probably just pottering around on the farm; secret men's business and all that.'

Emily glanced at her friend. Was Barbara trying to avoid saying something? 'Well, we've got our own secret women's business going on,' she said, and slapped her hands on her knees a little more forcefully than she'd intended.

★

Emily spent the whole day unable to wipe a slightly ridiculous grin off her face. She couldn't help it; it was just so wonderful to be out with her best friend, shopping, and with not a care in the world.

After an hour-and-a-half drive, they arrived at the shopping street that ran along the picturesque foreshore of the seaside city. They found a park right outside their chosen café and headed in. Without consultation, they both ordered lattes and carrot cake, laughing at their synchronicity.

'How totally decadent,' Emily declared as she pushed her fork into her cake with its luscious cream cheese icing.

'Yes, should be more of it,' Barbara agreed.

After coffee and cake, they shopped, ate a lovely café lunch, and shopped some more, scouring the two main shopping strips for everything on their lists. A number of times they laughed about how exhausting shopping was – usually just as they pushed the door open into another store.

Despite wandering the shops all day, Emily only purchased some necessities and two books for Jake. She saw plenty of things she liked, especially in the large furniture store, but with big, expensive items like chairs, desks and curtains, she wanted to take her time and make a careful, informed decision. She did, however, manage to surreptitiously take lots of photos with her mobile phone while Barbara distracted the sales staff.

They visited a shop chock full of baby gear, and Emily oohed and aahed over the tiny items of clothing Barbara held up, imagining the little person who might one day wear them. But as they roamed the racks, cooing over booties and singlets and onesies, Emily was a little disappointed to find no stirrings of a maternal nature in herself. It was a pity. How good would it be for two best friends to have their kids grow up together? Even better if they had a boy and a girl between them. She shook the thoughts aside as she realised Barbara was leaving the store, and hurried to catch up.

'You didn't buy anything?' she said. 'I thought you were going to get that cute little jumpsuit.'

'I was, but I got scared. I don't want to jinx things.'

'It's okay to be scared,' Emily replied, and linked her arm through Barbara's to reassure her. 'But you can't have the poor little thing arriving into the world with no clothes to wear,' she added, smiling warmly.

'I've got plenty of time,' she said, clearly trying to sound more exuberant than she felt.

'I guess that means we'll have to come back for another shopping trip!'

They reluctantly declared the day's shopping over at five o'clock, leaving just enough time to have a fortifying hot chocolate before embarking on the long trip home.

Weary and all talked out, they both sat silently staring into their mugs for a few moments.

Emily found herself again thinking about her life with John.

She remembered how he'd encouraged her to give up her job when they got married. At the time she'd seen it as his way of showing he loved her and his desire to take care of her; fulfilling his duty as husband. Now she could see how naïve she'd been. It wasn't anything to do with love. It was all about control.

God, she wished she could stop thoughts of John popping up, and of her mother for that matter. Enid was Enid. She wouldn't ever change. As Jake said, she'd have to learn to live with her and stop bitching about it. Well, he hadn't been quite so forceful… She laid her teaspoon on the saucer and picked up her mug and sipped, concentrating on the hot earthiness and soaking up its comfort.

'How much fun is this?' Barbara said. Emily was jolted from her reverie.

'Yep, brilliant,' Emily replied.

'So what's up?' Barbara asked, putting her cup down and looking at Emily.

'Nothing. Why do you ask?'

'Well, you've been all smiles all day and suddenly you look like…'

'Just tired, I guess,' Emily said, and took another sip of hot chocolate.

Barbara continued to stare pointedly at her friend with raised, questioning eyebrows, but said nothing.

'All right, you win,' Emily said with a tight laugh. She fiddled with her teaspoon. 'I was just thinking how long it's been since I was able to shop without worrying about every cent. And then about John's reaction when I got home.'

'Which should have you feeling ecstatic, not glum!' Barbara declared with bewilderment.

'I made such a mistake marrying him, and giving up my job,' Emily continued wistfully.

'Yes, we all know that. But you fixed it. You left the brute. And now he's gone. So, come on, you have to let it go. We all make mistakes; it's what you do with what you've learnt that's the important thing.'

Hmm, something Gran might have said, though probably not quite so gently. Granny Mayfair could never abide self-pity, and wasn't afraid to point it out if she saw it.

'And don't you dare mention that crap about being a failure! That's Enid's bag, not yours. Might I remind you again, my dear friend, that this is the twenty-first century and that you don't need a man in order to be fulfilled. If you *want* one, fine! And you've got a bloody nice one waiting at home, who I know for a fact would do anything to make you happy! So stop feeling sorry for yourself, finish your drink, and let's head on home to our gorgeous menfolk!'

'Okay then.' As Emily drained her cup, she smiled to herself. Barbara sounded so like Gran sometimes. It was nice, but it also made her feel the teeniest bit sad. 'Are you okay to drive, or would you like me to?' she asked, more out of politeness than the desire to drive. She was probably a little too weary, though she could feel the sugar from the hot chocolate starting to kick in.

'Thanks, but I'm fine.'

Emily was pleased to be once again seated in the car, and was now realising how painful her feet were. She'd worn what she thought were comfortable shoes, though the amount of walking and standing around browsing they'd done would have rendered anything dressier than sneakers uncomfortable, she thought wryly. She was seriously out of practice with this shopping caper! Thankfully she had Jake and his beautiful hands to make her feel all better later...

Just as Barbara was fishing the keys out of her handbag her mobile phone rang.

'It's David,' she said as she answered. 'Hello darling, how did your day go?'

Emily couldn't hear the other side of the conversation, but the way Barbara was looking at her – seemingly trying not to – told her something was being said she wasn't meant to hear. And the slight flush to her friend's face confirmed it.

'Oh, right. Okay. See you later then.'

That's one of the shortest conversations I've ever heard between those two, she thought as Barbara ended the call and tossed the phone back into her handbag. Her friend looked decidedly cagey.

'That was David,' Barbara declared.

'So you said. Is everything okay?'

'Yep.'

Barbara put the key in the ignition, which Emily took as a sign their discussion of the phone call was over. She itched to ask more, but reluctantly accepted that if Barbara wanted to tell her something she would.

They backed out of their parking space and joined the slow-moving traffic on the shopping strip. After a few minutes they were out on the open highway where the traffic was light.

The molten orange sun behind them cast deep shadows into the car. Emily leaned back into her seat. The radio played music quietly in the background. She cast her gaze between the windscreen and the side window while Barbara kept two hands on the wheel and peered past it to the road ahead. Emily tried to keep her eyes open, but with the late-afternoon sun coming in over her shoulder and the steady, gentle movement of the car it was more and more difficult.

She must have nodded off, because suddenly she woke to find Barbara indicating and taking the right-hand turn into the seaside town of Tumby Bay. Golly, she must have been asleep for nearly half an hour! Emily sat up straighter and blinked a couple of times. She felt quite refreshed and not groggy at all. But she frowned slightly.

'Why are we stopping in at Tumby Bay?' Barbara had made no mention of it earlier, and all the shops would be shut.

'I thought we might have an early dinner,' Barbara replied. 'I hear the hotel on the foreshore has a new chef.'

'Oh. Okay, great.' *I guess.* Emily felt like she'd been eating all day. And she was keen to get home to Jake. 'I should ring Jake and let him know I won't be home for tea,' she said, starting to fish about in the handbag at her feet for her phone.

'No need, that's what David was phoning about. They're probably at the pub as we speak,' Barbara added quickly. A little too quickly, Emily thought.

So why didn't you say that before?

For about the third time that day, she had the feeling there was something going on between her friends she didn't know about. But again, in the interests of being less Enid-like, she refrained from questioning it.

'Oh, okay then. I won't disturb him,' Emily said, letting go of her bag and sitting back. But the feeling that something a little odd was going on refused to fully leave her.

'So what *were* they up to today, anyway? Jake was vague when I asked him,' Emily ventured.

'Oh, I don't know, this and that,' Barbara said, taking her right hand off the wheel and waving it about a bit before returning it to its position. 'Farmer stuff.'

Emily gnawed at the inside of her cheek as she pondered Barbara's response – Barbara who was David's right hand, Barbara who had her finger totally on the pulse. *Farmer stuff, my arse!* They were up to something. *God, I hope they're not planning some sort of surprise. I hate surprises.*

Oh God, she thought, her blood feeling like it had stopped in her veins. Jake wouldn't. No, he wouldn't. He had said himself that they weren't going to rush things – and by God, mere weeks sure would be rushing things! No way would he be planning to propose so soon.

But if not that, what the hell were they up to?

Chapter Seven

It was well after dark when Barbara dropped her off. As they drove towards Emily's house, the lights shining through the windows from behind curtains and blinds in the distance made her smile. It was so nice to be coming home to a friendly presence – well, now *two* friendly presences. But, gosh, she was exhausted. At that moment she yawned, followed immediately by Barbara.

'You'd better stop in for a break before the last stretch,' Emily said.

'I'll be okay. Yawning is contagious, you know.'

'Why is that?'

'No idea, but that is too deep a question after the day we've had.'

As usual, whenever she was turning into her driveway, Emily glanced at the site of the old cottage across the way. It was a habit she was trying to break.

Tonight, as the headlights panned around the corner, something seemed a little different. She was probably imagining things, or was too tired and not seeing things correctly.

Or perhaps it was just her position in the passenger's seat rather than the driver's that had made things seem different.

Barbara stopped at the gate by the house. Jake came out, followed by Grace. He was dressed casually in shorts and a light navy-and-white-striped polo top. His hair was damp and mussed. Whatever he'd got up to that day with David, he must have only been home long enough to shower.

Barbara got out to help Emily sort through the bags of shopping in the boot.

'Hello there. Have we had fun?' Jake asked, coming down the concrete path to help carry.

'I did, but I missed you,' Emily said, wrapping her arms around him.

'That's lovely. I missed you too,' he said and kissed her deeply.

She bent down to give Grace a hug. 'Did you miss me too?' The dog wagged her tail so hard the whole length of her wiggled.

'Looks like you two were busy,' Jake said, looking down at the mass of shopping.

'We were, indeed!' Barbara and Emily said in unison, and then chuckled.

'Right, I think that's it,' Barbara said, and shut the boot lid with a thud. The women hugged.

'Thanks so much for a wonderful day,' Emily said.

'Thank *you*,' Barbara said. 'It was a great day. See you soon.'

She got back into the car, waved and called, 'See you Jake,' as she pulled away.

Jake and Emily stood with an arm around each other and watched as Barbara drove off. Grace was sitting patiently beside them.

As the car became a hum in the distance, the silence was filled with a multitude of creatures settling into their night-time symphony. It was a gorgeous warm summer evening with a slight cool breeze.

Jake gave Emily another quick kiss, and then bent and gathered up the handles of most of the shopping bags. She picked up the rest.

'Anything exciting in here?' he asked as they made their way inside.

'Not really, although I did find you some books.' Looking at all the bags they carried between them it seemed like Emily had bought heaps. But in actual fact, she'd only bought a couple of cheap t-shirts and light track pants, some novels for Jake, a couple of beach towels on sale to use as bedding for Grace, and two bags of groceries. She and Barbara had picked up favourite items that the local supermarket in Wattle Creek didn't stock. But her most treasured purchases were the latest editions of four interior decorating and house-and-garden magazines. Emily loved flicking through the glossy pages, but had rarely ever bought them new – they were such a luxury.

'So, what did you get up to today?' she asked as she scurried back and forth putting the groceries away in the pantry.

'Oh, nothing too exciting, just hanging out with David.'

'Have you eaten? I can make you something.'

'Thanks, but I'm fine,' he said, reaching over and dragging one of her magazines towards him. 'Mind if I have a look at this?'

'Not at all, go for it.' Emily wasn't sure why, but again she had the feeling that something wasn't quite right. When she flipped up the lid on the rubbish bin she noticed a soup tin and bread bag.

'Have you only had toast and soup for dinner?'

'Yeah, just now. We got caught up.'

But Barbara said you were going to the pub hours ago. What's going on? She kept the words to herself.

'I can fix you something more substantial if you like. It won't take long to thaw out some steak.'

'No, thanks, I'm fine. But I won't say no to a big breakfast in the morning,' he said with a cheeky grin. 'I know it's early,' he said, now up from the table and wrapping his arms around her waist from behind, 'but I'm sure you're exhausted. How about a massage?'

'Ooh, that would be lovely. But after a quick shower, I feel all grimy.'

'Okay, only if I can join you.'

'Haven't you just had one,' Emily said, reaching up a hand and ruffling his hair that was still damp.

'Well, one can never be too clean.'

★

The next morning, Emily stirred, rolled over sleepily and kissed Jake. But instead of wrapping his arms around her and seeing what happened next, Jake leapt out of bed and flung the curtains open. Emily was momentarily disappointed. She'd been hoping for a little entanglement in the sheets.

It was Australia Day, but they had decided against going to any of the special breakfasts being held around the district. Emily had thought Jake would definitely be up for a bit of lovemaking. If not, he'd be sleeping in. Instead, he was standing at the window in his tight black trunk undies, looking out.

'It's a lovely morning,' he said.

'Yeah, not meant to be too hot today,' Emily said, lying on her back and linking her hands behind her head.

'It's really quite a spectacular view.'

'I'm sure it is.' *What's going on? He's seen morning from that window plenty of times now. They're all pretty much the same this time of year – bright, clear and beautiful, but predictable. Seen one, seen them all.*

'Aren't you getting up?' Jake said over his shoulder.

'Aren't you coming back to bed?' Emily tried for seductive, but her voice came out more like a whine.

'No, come and have a look at this.'

'Why?'

'Because it's beautiful.'

'Beautiful? A pile of rocks and building debris and a giant meccano set? I'd rather just look at the view from here,' she said, staring at Jake's smooth bare back and taut upper thighs.

'Oh ha ha,' he said, still facing the window. He was beginning to shift on his feet, as if getting impatient, or needing to pee, or something. With a sigh he finally turned away and got back into bed beside her. They snuggled into each other, became entwined, and started to kiss. But something didn't feel quite right. Jake seemed distracted. She pulled away.

'What? What's wrong?' he asked, frowning.

'That's what I was about to ask you.'

'Nothing's wrong, why?'

Emily just looked at him with arched eyebrows.

He shrugged and stayed silent.

'What's up with you this morning? You leap out of bed like you're on fire – which has never happened in all the mornings you've been here – and then you stand at the window going on about the view, which you've seen plenty of times, and one we both know isn't worth commenting on thanks to my late husband's intervention. Has a spaceship landed out there overnight, or are you having some kind of *episode*?'

'No and no,' Jake said, sighing deeply.

'Well, what's going on?'

'Emily, just go and look out the damn window,' he said with a groan. 'Go on, do it for me. Please.' He was lying on his back and shaking his head slowly.

'Why?' She eyed him suspiciously.

'God, you make some things hard,' he said with a laugh. 'Okay, don't,' he said with another, and got out of bed.

As he started to gather clothes and get dressed, Emily's heart gripped. *Shit, we're not having a fight are we? Surely not about me not looking out the window! God, that's almost as silly as me last time.*

'Okay. All right. If it means that much to you, I'll look out the damned window.' She got out of bed and padded over to the nearest of the two bedroom windows – the other one to where Jake had stood. She glanced out. Yes, it was indeed a bright, sunny, glorious summer morning – cobalt blue sky, a couple of wispy clouds. *So bloody what?*

'Hmm, yep, I agree, it's lovely,' she said brightly, despite still feeling very perplexed. She turned back to Jake, who was putting on socks.

'Just thought it was a morning worthy of appreciating, that's all,' he said with a shrug.

'Well, let's get out in it and go for a walk then, shall we?' Emily said, opening the first drawer in her tallboy to gather clothes.

They laced up their shoes and left the house. Grace bounded ahead but stopped just outside the gate on the rubble driveway area. Emily had trained her that they now went straight ahead, down past the sheds, rather than left out onto the public road that ran through the middle of the farm, which was near where the old cottage had been.

Emily's shoes didn't feel quite right, so she stopped at the end of the concrete path and bent down to retie them.

'So, which way would you like to go – left or straight ahead?' Jake asked.

It struck Emily as an odd question since they had only ever gone straight ahead since Jake had been there. Perhaps he was just being polite, making conversation, or perhaps he wanted a change. Too bad. She didn't want to see what was over that way.

'Straight ahead. Definitely straight ahead,' she said, standing up and leading the way. As soon as she saw which way they were headed, Grace raced off ahead. *She's growing so fast*, Emily thought, as she watched the border collie's flickering tail.

She smiled and looked up at Jake as he grasped her hand and linked their fingers together. It was as perfect a morning as it had looked from inside the house. Cool, not a breath of wind, and with the sun shining brightly. The forecast was for it to be warm, and Emily had already decided to spend it inside going through the photos from yesterday and trawling through her glossy magazines searching for decorating inspiration. She was eager to complete her office.

After their shower the night before, they'd both sat up in bed flicking through her new magazines. They'd had fun nudging each other and pointing out things they liked. Eventually Jake had put down his magazine, shuffled in closer and they'd gone through the one publication together. Much better. That they so clearly had a shared interest made Emily's heart glow. And they seemed to like a lot of the same things. It certainly boded well for the future.

So far, so good, her gran would have said. Emily felt sure Gran would have loved Jake and it made her a little sad that she wasn't around to see how happy she was with him.

As they walked, she kicked a stone and watched it bounce and bobble along the ground in front of her. Their steady footsteps, and her occasional kicks, were the only sounds other than the usual morning calls of birds.

'You're very quiet,' Jake suddenly said. So deep in thought was Emily that she started slightly.

'Oh. Sorry. Just thinking about Gran. Wishing she was here to see me so happy. She would have loved you.'

'And I'm sure I would have loved her too. I get the impression she was quite the character.'

Emily smiled up at him. As she began to look back down at the stone she'd been kicking, her attention was caught by something behind Jake. She stopped in her tracks as she saw a new steel structure standing beside what had been the last shed. She looked from it to Jake with her mouth open.

He smirked back at her. 'Surprise,' he said, opening his arms wide. He now grinned broadly.

'Wow. WOW! You moved it! Oh, thank you, thank you, THANK YOU!' she said, throwing her arms around him.

'David's the one you need to thank, but I'll always take a hug,' he said, wrapping his arms tightly around her and kissing her neck.

After a moment, Emily pulled away and got her mobile out of her pocket. It was only seven-thirty, but hopefully it wasn't too early for David and Barbara. She found their number and pushed the green key to make the call. As she waited for it to be answered, she stared at the steel structure, the excitement building inside her. She was all but jumping up and down on the spot when Barbara picked up.

'Oh my God, oh my God, OH. MY. GOD!' she cried into the phone.

Barbara laughed and said, 'I take it you're talking about the shed.'

'Yes I'm talking about the shed! Thank you, thank you!'

'I'll put David on.' A split second later, David was on the line.

'Hey Em, I take it you like your surprise then,' he said.

'Do I ever! I'm just so blown away. Thank you so much.'

'You knew it was going to happen sometime soon.'

'Yes, but it's actually done! Again, thank you!' The words seemed inadequate, but what else could she say?

'It's my pleasure. We'll be over tomorrow to do the iron. The footings need a day to cure; perfect timing being a public holiday and all.'

'Who's "we"?'

'Jake and me, Bob Stanley, Steve Olsen, and Grant Anderson. And don't worry, I made sure Jake didn't overdo it – I had him in the tractor operating the loader bucket.'

'Thanks so much. I really appreciate it. I'm happy to pay everyone for their time, just let me know...' At that she looked up to find Jake shaking his head.

'I can't speak for Jake, but there's no need to pay me or the other guys. Grant and Steve are on annual leave, and Bob owed me a favour. They're all happy to help you out. They thought you got a rough deal with John and wanted to go some way to evening the score. Steve and Grant feel bad about snubbing you that day just after you'd split up from him too. You've got a lot of friends around here, Em. Just you remember that.'

Emily felt her throat suddenly tightening and tears gathering behind her eyes.

'Thanks David,' she managed with a croak. 'Can you put Barb back on?'

'Yeah, she wants to speak to you again too. Here she is.'

'I hope to hell you're not crying!' Barbara said, causing Emily to laugh.

'Maybe just a little,' she said.

'Well, I'll leave you to it. See you soon.'

'Okay. See ya. Thanks so much, again, both of you.'

'It's our pleasure. See ya.'

Grace stood beside them with her head cocked to one side, showing obvious concern for her mistress. Emily pulled a crumpled tissue from her sleeve, blew her nose hard, wiped away the couple of tears that had escaped, and took a deep breath.

'Shall we continue?' she said, giving Jake a weak smile.

'Yes, let's,' he said, offering a bent elbow for her to slip her hand through.

Grace, sensing all was well again, bounded off ahead of them.

Just as they started to pick up speed again, Jake said, 'Or would you rather go the other way now?'

'No, the rubble is still there – unless you guys moved that too,' she added, sounding hopeful.

'No, but I've been thinking about that.'

'Yes? And?'

'Why don't we rebuild it?'

'How much would it cost? I remember you saying it would be a pretty big job.'

'Well, it won't be cheap, but the stone is there, and I'll happily throw in my labour.'

'You can't do that.'

'Of course I can.'

'You're meant to be taking a break. Resting.'

'I'm fine. And maybe a bit of manual labour is just what I need. As I said, I've been thinking about it anyway. It could be a win for both of us. I could use it as a sample of my work – like an advertisement – and you could have your B&B.'

'I think I've gone off the B&B idea,' she said, a little apologetically.

'Well you could have your cottage, for whatever you want to do with it. You could rent it out for extra income, set up a shop, or a café. The options are pretty endless.'

She thought about it. 'So you were serious the other day when you talked about setting up an agency for your business here?' Emily said.

'Yeah. It's certainly worth crunching a few numbers. It's a pretty low-risk proposition for me because my main business is so well established. I'm not talking about taking over the world or anything, just the odd project here and there to keep my hand in. The cellar door market might appreciate stone buildings if there was someone local to keep costs down. If I'm going to stick around I'd like to keep doing something I love – but without the pressure of dealing with big corporations and government depart-ments. So what do you say?'

'Are you trying to make me cry again?'

'It's nothing to cry about,' he said. Jake stopped walking. He turned to face Emily and grasped her by the shoulders. 'I love you. I want to be here for the long haul if that's what you want too. I know I said we wouldn't rush things, but I want you to know that I'm serious about us, serious about staying.'

'But what about Melbourne?'

'Hmm, big city, lots of cars, squealing trams, a strange road rule called a hook turn,' he said, grinning at her. 'What about Melbourne?'

'Er, you have a thriving business there.'

'There are plenty of good project managers around. It's a well-run business, but I'm not arrogant enough to think I'm indispensable. And it's not as if I'm totally walking away. I'll keep an eye on things, but from a distance, and not so often.'

'Won't you miss the hustle and bustle of city life?'

'I don't know. Maybe. But then a trip back now and then would probably be enough.'

'But what about your gorgeous apartment?'

'Rent it out, sell it if I need the money. It's only a building, Em,' he said with a shrug.

Only a building.

'Different things mean different things to different people,' he said, as if sensing her thought. He took her face in his hands. 'I know how much the cottage means to you – and how much your husband hurt you when he pulled it down. I can make that better for you. And I want to. Please let me. You'll never know how much it meant that you dropped everything to come to Melbourne for me when it was so out of your comfort zone. I'd like to repay the favour. And you'd be doing me another favour by letting me use it as a display, remember?'

'But what about your adrenal fatigue? You're meant to be taking time off...'

'I think this will be okay, it'll be a scaled back version of work. Besides, I'll be bored in a few months if I don't do something. This will all take time to get up and running; I've only just started to think about it...'

'I'm just concerned you're taking on too much too quickly.'

'Unless, you don't want all this, us,' he said suddenly, looking at her. 'It's just that you're finding a lot of reasons for me *not* to do this.'

Emily rushed to reassure him. 'It all sounds perfect to me,' she said wistfully. 'As long as you're sure.' She felt all warm and cosy inside.

'There's still a lot of research to do, planning, decisions to make, figures to go through...'

'Well, if you're in, I'm in,' she said decisively, with a nod of her head. How good would it be to have her cottage back, an even better version? And what could be more romantic than building a house with the man you loved? Emily felt excited to be embarking on a major project together.

There would probably be a considerable financial cost, of course, but this certainly was true love. She was just thinking she couldn't walk – she was so deliriously happy – when Jake grasped her hand and gently pulled her forward.

'Come on,' he said. 'Let's earn ourselves a big breakfast and a day inside making plans.'

'Hmm, actually, I've got another form of exercise in mind,' Emily replied, leading him back towards the house.

Chapter Eight

After a big bacon-and-eggs breakfast, they walked over to the mound of rubble that had once been Emily's dream. Her stomach flip-flopped. Could they really do it?

Again she found herself wondering about the family that might have lived there over a hundred years ago. It didn't matter that she was no relation. The feeling that she wanted – no, *needed* – to do this for them engulfed her. Her heart rate rose. Maybe simply putting up a little weatherboard place would make more sense financially. But it just wouldn't be right. This was absolutely the place for a limestone cottage.

Not to mention Emily's desire to right John's wrong. She felt as strongly about that as she did about anything else.

As hard as this will be, it will be worth it. If it wasn't meant to be, the universe would have sent a sign.

She couldn't wait to get started. She knew it was all a little silly, melodramatic, overly romantic – whatever you wanted to call it – but she just could not shake the feeling.

And she had Jake to thank. She looked up at him and smiled warmly, and forced her romantic notions aside to focus on what he was saying.

'I think building just in front would be a good idea. That way we won't have to move everything twice.'

Emily stared at the rubble pile. In the months since John had knocked it down, the mishmash of bricks, timber, corrugated iron, stone and other unidentifiable building debris had become overgrown with weeds. As the scale of it struck her, she started to feel a dose of reality seeping in.

'Jesus, where do we start?'

'First we'll have to go through it all to sort the rubbish from what is reusable.' Jake was getting more animated. He went to the edge of the pile and picked out a few rocks.

'See,' he said, holding up two for Emily to examine. 'We'd need to chip off the old mortar and get the stone clean. It's not hard, just time-consuming. You could do it – I can teach you, if you're interested. We could do it together.'

Emily closed her eyes and breathed in deeply. *Ah, bliss.* She could imagine them spending whole days working side by side; taking rocks from one pile, chipping away to clean them up, adding them to a new pile, stopping to eat and sip on water, taking the occasional rest together. At the end of each day they'd walk back to the house, exhausted but happy and fulfilled. Hopefully not too worn out to make love…

The next morning they'd return – hand in hand – and start all over again. Maybe it was a bit pathetic, but it was totally romantic too. Not unlike men in her grandparents' era building their future brides a house as a wedding gift.

Oh, Jake, could you be more perfect?

Standing there in the partial shade of the large gum trees with the sun gently drumming on her back, Emily literally felt warm and fuzzy right through to her bones. Her negative voice tried to tell her he wasn't actually building her a house – she was paying for it – but her positive voice wasn't having a bar of it. *This is going to be great.*

'It won't be easy, but it can be done,' Jake added, as he put the rocks back down onto the pile. Emily suddenly had the feeling Jake was losing enthusiasm. Perhaps because she was just standing there looking all weird and vacant.

'If you think it can be done, it can be,' she said enthusiastically. 'And I'm willing to get my hands dirty,' she added, linking her arm through his. Wasn't this what she'd dreamt of with John? Back then she'd hoped they would run the farm shoulder to shoulder, but what did the project matter? What mattered was a mutual goal to work towards.

Suddenly Emily could see how Gran could have given up her posh home life with all its trappings to become the wife of a mere farmer – no disrespect to Grandpa. She had loved her man, and had known they could do anything as long as they were together. Their goal had been the farm and raising a family. Emily's was a little different, but she felt sure the feelings were the same. At that moment she felt on top of the world; like she could achieve whatever she put her mind to.

'Come on, I want to start making some notes and calculations,' Jake said, leading her back towards the main house.

Part of her wanted to stay and start sorting through the rocks, but there was no point going at it like a bull at a gate, as Gran would say. As a professional, Jake would want to formulate a sound, workable plan. Slow and steady wins the race. If it was meant to be, it would be.

Back inside, Jake strode up the long enclosed verandah to the room he was using as his office before returning to the kitchen. He dumped his laptop and a few pads of paper, loose sheets, pens, pencils, and erasers on the table. Emily stood by, feeling a little dazed and a lot useless.

'It might help to have your photos of the cottage,' Jake suggested.

Emily went to the bedroom and got her folder out from under the bed; the scrapbook of ideas she'd put together for the original cottage, which contained notes, photos, fabric samples and paint charts, and old magazine clippings of furniture, interiors, exteriors, and landscaping ideas. On the way out, she also grabbed her selection of glossy new house magazines, despite knowing it was way too early in the process for interior decorating. She added her contribution to the now cluttered kitchen table.

'You look over all this while I make your coffee,' Jake said.

Looking at the rough sketches he had laid out for her, Emily was impressed at how much work Jake had already put into the project. Clearly he'd been thinking about it for a while. No wonder he'd been spending more and more time up in the office.

'It's more cost-effective to go bigger to start with than having to add on later,' Jake explained, as he put down their mugs. 'I've done what I think will give the most options,' he added.

'Hmm, looks great,' Emily said, nodding in agreement. Not knowing what all the little symbols and abbreviations meant, she struggled to follow the plans beyond where the doors, window, fireplaces and other features were. She turned to a list of projected figures.

'Without knowing exactly how you want to fit out the interior of the cottage, they're pretty rubbery,' Jake explained. 'And they're just my suggestions; it's your project.'

'It's *our* project.'

The figures were mainly rounded to the nearest five thousand, and when she looked at the total at the bottom she was neither shocked nor disappointed. When John's estate was settled she would have plenty of money to play with. Not that she wanted to be silly about it; that just wasn't in her nature. Emily Oliphant was conservative through and through, and proud of it.

The lease on the farm would pay for most of her living expenses for the year, considering there was no rent or mortgage. David had assured her that the troughs, fences, and sheds looked pretty good and that she shouldn't be up for any major maintenance bills for the next few years. Though there was always the chance of the unforeseen cropping up, he'd hastened to add. Emily had experienced plenty of unforeseen events in recent times, but she chose to trust that all would be okay.

Anyway, if she was smart about the cottage she could make money from it. She'd have to do something with it or else in twelve months – or however long it would all take; they hadn't got to that bit yet – she'd have an empty cottage instead of a pile of debris and still be wondering what to do with her life.

She was sure she didn't want to run a B&B. After spending ages thinking about it, she'd concluded that she didn't want to cook and clean for other people and have to deal with potential complaints, mucked-up bookings, and non-payers and no-shows.

Emily loved to cook. It was a release and a great form of relaxation, but she suspected that that would all change when she *had* to do it, and under pressure. She'd always coped okay with the pressure of feeding the masses during shearing, but that was only for a week or so each year. If the business was successful – which, obviously, she hoped it would be – she'd be under that sort of pressure every weekend.

Maybe she could open a shop? Selling jam was a totally different proposition to running a B&B, because she could cook at her leisure. But she wasn't convinced a viable business could be made, despite all Barbara's protestations and encouragement that she could be the next Maggie Beer. It was sweet that her friend believed in her, but there was no getting around the fact that there was no fruit in season during certain times of the year. And even if she planted an orchard, it would be years before the new trees fruited.

No, what she needed was something simple where she could make some money without actually making the product herself. Of course she'd sell jam when she had it; it would be a nice country touch for city visitors travelling through.

Emily was startled when Jake spoke. 'Where were you just now?'

'Sorry?'

'You were lost in thought,' Jake said.

'I'm just wondering what to do with the cottage when it's done. What does the district need? We've got enough cafés and small restaurants with the new wineries, and I think there are plenty of shops selling furniture and home-wares,' she said, thinking aloud.

'I'm sure you'll come up with something. You've got plenty of time to think about it. Maybe Simone might have an idea?' he offered, as he went back to scrutinising his plan and making notes.

'Yes, she's bound to have some great ideas,' she mused.

And then it came to her. Of course! She'd been thinking about Simone from totally the wrong angle.

'I've got it!'

Jake looked up at her in surprise. 'Sorry, what's that?'

Emily shook her head and opened her mouth to speak. *I know what I want the cottage to be!* But no words came out. She closed her mouth and then opened it again. *Stop it, Emily, you look like a bloody goldfish!*

'Are you okay? Do you need water or something?' Jake said, starting to get up.

'No, I'm fine,' she finally said with a laugh, her voice suddenly working again. 'I've just realised what I want the cottage to be. Of course it's just an idea. I'll have to make sure it can be viable and…'

'Well? Come on. I thought you were having some sort of seizure. Just tell me! What is the cottage going to be?'

'A gallery! To exhibit Simone's paintings, and your photos, and sell my jam, and whatever else I like. It'll be called The Button Jar, because what's inside will be an eclectic mix. Obviously I wouldn't sell buttons; that would be silly.' She chuckled. 'And, anyway, there are plenty of places to buy buttons. No one would want to by buttons from me. But no one's selling good-quality art around here, are they? Ooh, I can see it so clearly…'

Emily was suddenly aware that she was becoming a little out of breath. And Jake hadn't said a word. Well, she hadn't exactly given the poor bloke a chance.

'So, what do you think?' She said almost inaudibly, afraid that saying it all out loud might mean it sounded ridiculous.

'Well, I do feel very flattered, but I'm not sure I'm good enough to exhibit,' Jake said, blushing slightly. 'Simone certainly is, though.' Emily was surprised at how shy Jake had become. Staring down at his almost empty plate, he was like a little boy.

Not good enough to exhibit! Are you mad? The shots she'd seen – especially the photos of specific architectural features taken from unusual angles – were incredible. She'd put money on people lining up to buy them. Well, she would be, literally, if she went ahead. She almost giggled, but managed to turn it into a gasp.

'And I love the name,' he said, deflecting the conversation away from him. 'The Button Jar. It's perfect. That would give you leeway to stock whatever you wanted to. Aren't you clever?' he said, leaning over and kissing her.

'And it'll be a tribute to Gran,' Emily declared, the idea dawning on her. 'It's thanks to her wisdom that I'm here, like this, now. I know some of her clichéd quotes seem quite silly – even irrelevant – but some are actually quite profound.'

'I think it's a lovely idea,' Jake said, kissing her again. 'And I know she would be very proud of you.'

While Gran had never directly said, 'you should do this' or 'do that', Emily was seeing more and more that the old lady had gradually been setting her up to deal with the hard knocks in life. If only she'd had the courage to leave John when Gran was still alive. Then she'd have known her granddaughter would be okay. But it was the way it was meant to be. Perhaps Gran had known she'd be okay because she'd been carefully and surreptitiously steering her right.

Unlike her own mother. Shouldn't that have been Enid's job? Emily almost snorted aloud. From the age of around ten, Emily had realised that no matter what she did she would never gain her mother's acceptance or approval. But despite knowing this, she'd continued to try.

She'd married the richest, apparently best catch in the district, despite reservations – yes, she could admit that now. She'd stayed at home and played wife, thrown the occasional elaborate lunch, afternoon tea, and dinner party. But every time Enid would find fault. And Enid was always invited, because if she wasn't she would sulk and subject Emily to the silent treatment and whatever other emotional blackmail tactic she could use. It was easier just to invite her and for Emily to accept she wouldn't be nearly as free to enjoy herself as if she were just amongst friends.

There would be that slight edge to her mother's compliment, 'Yes, Emily, it was a very nice meal,' that really meant, '*but not as nice as one of mine.*' And that was a spoken example. There had been plenty of down-the-nose looks over the years too.

Thank goodness her father was completely different. Whilst he didn't gush the words, Emily knew he adored her, no matter what mistakes she made in life. The bottom line was he just wanted her to be happy.

'Are you okay? You're suddenly very quiet?' Jake asked.

'I'm fine. Just thinking about stuff.'

Chapter Nine

During lunch, Emily's phone rang and Barbara's name was on the screen.

'Hey, what's up?'

'I totally forgot to tell you. About tomorrow. Are you okay to feed the guys? Sorry about the short notice.'

'God, did you do all the catering in time to pick me up at eight yesterday? Jesus, how did you manage to do a whole day shopping, including all the driving, and not collapse? Are you Wonder Woman or something? You should have asked me to help.'

'What, and ruin the surprise? Not bloody likely!'

'Well, thank you so much. I owe you big time.'

'I'll remember that,' Barbara said with a laugh. 'We couldn't have your reputation for fine food tarnished. You know Steve and Grant only agreed to do the work because they've heard shearers rave about your catering.'

'Oh ha ha, Barbara. You're hilarious, but I'll take a compliment any way I can get it.'

'Hey, I'm not lying. You ask David next time you see him. They don't say a way to a man's heart is through his stomach for nothing, you know.'

'So, now I have to live up to *your* even higher standards tomorrow? Please don't tell me you served them homemade Kitchener buns or anything too elaborate,' Emily said with a groan.

'Damn, wish I'd thought of that,' Barbara said, and laughed. 'No, I just did chicken and salad sandwiches and apple teacake for morning tea, and meatloaf and salad and stewed nectarines with cream for lunch. Actually, you'd better check your ice-cream supply. David mentioned they had that as well.'

'Okay, thanks. Sounds like I'll be doing a big shop this afternoon now anyway. What did you give them for afternoon tea? I don't want to serve anything the same and blemish this reputation I supposedly have,' Emily said.

'Carrot cake, and ham, cheese and mustard sandwiches for the non-sweet tooths. You know, every time I do this sort of catering, like for shearing, I can't get over how much food they put away. All David brought home was empty dishes.'

'Well, Grace probably demanded her share as well.'

'Probably. So I hereby hand catering duties over to you,' Barbara said. 'I look forward to wonderful reports tomorrow night from David.'

'No pressure! Let's hope there's still some fresh fruit and veg left in town. And seriously, thanks again. For everything.'

'My pleasure. I actually really enjoyed it. It took my mind off…you know.'

'You're going to be fine, you know. Hey, why don't come down and cook with me this afternoon and/or tomorrow if you want,' Emily said. She loved it when the two of them cooked together.

'Not a chance! I'm on strike. I've even got David cooking tea tonight.'

Emily laughed. 'Fair enough. I'll let you go. Someone has a menu to go off and plan!'

'Good luck.'

'Thanks. See ya.'

'See ya.'

'Looks like my afternoon is spoken for,' Emily said to Jake as she put the phone back on the table. 'I'm going to be cooking for you guys tomorrow.'

'Do you want some help?'

'Thanks, but I'll be fine. It's not hard, just takes time. But first I've got to go and do a big supermarket shop. Thank goodness they're opening to take advantage of everyone being in town for the big Australia Day breakfast and award ceremony.'

'Oh, how come we're not going?'

'Um. Sorry. I didn't want to go, but I should have mentioned it. I used to go with John, but he always drank so much, and...'

'It's okay. It doesn't matter, Em,' he said, touching her arm. 'The different shopping hours are something I still have to get my head around,' he continued, changing the subject. 'Most things in Melbourne tend to be open all day every day – including public holidays. So, do I get to come with you to the zoo, I mean, Wattle Creek?' he said with a cheeky grin.

'If you're very, very good,' Emily said, laughing. Although he'd been staying with her for more than three weeks, they still hadn't been into town together. 'I'm sure you'll be spending a lot of time there over the next few months if we go ahead.'

'Yes, I'll need to know all the movers and shakers.'

'Well, start with Doris at Mitre 10 – she knows everyone who's anyone in the building trade. Her cousin, Will, owns the place. You'll like him.'

'Duly noted,' he said, tapping his head. 'So, do you want to head off now?'

'No rush. I need to plan a menu first, and write a list. And I wouldn't mind going over this a bit more, unless you've had enough for today,' Emily said.

'Never! It'll be great to nail down some details and get the plans drafted,' he said, clearly excited.

Emily found planning her menu easy – she had a few tried-and-tested favourites, which thankfully, Barbara hadn't served. While she wrote a comprehensive shopping list, Jake tinkered with the rough floor plan of the cottage – not that anything Jake did was rough – and looked over the figures. Emily couldn't believe how straight he could draw freehand.

'Years of practice,' he said when she commented.

'Right,' she said. 'Tell me if you think this menu is okay, and if there's anything you want to add.' She handed him her pieces of paper.

'Yum. Yum. Yum. Yum. And yum,' he said, making his way down the page and putting a tick next to each item. 'Looks wonderful.'

'And the shopping list?'

'Actually, I know it's naughty, but I'd love some barbeque chips.'

'Craving salty foods.' She lifted an eyebrow. 'Isn't that one of the symptoms of adrenal fatigue?' After he'd told her about his condition, she'd got on Google one day while he'd been out with David. Thank goodness he hadn't shown any signs of another symptom – loss of sexual appetite.

'It could just be that I like them and haven't had them for ages. Can I have some, please, can I? Pleeeease!' He pretended to whine like a child.

'Oh, ha ha,' Emily said, slapping playfully at his arm. 'Of course you can, my love,' she cooed, and leaned over to kiss him.

'Don't start that or else we'll never get to town,' Jake groaned, and pulled away reluctantly. 'And I want to show you what I've come up with.'

They agreed the design should be as versatile as possible so that the building could cope with multiple uses. The original cottage had consisted of just two main rooms divided by a central hallway that opened onto a lean-to style extension housing a simple kitchen with a small bathroom off it. They were keeping the basic design, but modernising and enlarging it.

Instead of just a bullnose verandah on the front like the original cottage, they were planning to go right around, incorporating an outdoor living area beyond the kitchen. But, of course, it all depended on how the budget looked down the track.

Their finalised plan showed four large square rooms with a central hall. At the back there was a sizeable open-plan kitchen and living area, a laundry, two bathrooms, and a powder room. One of the bathrooms opened into one of the main rooms, which could be used as a master bedroom with ensuite if the building ever became a B&B or permanent residence. Emily was pleased to note that Jake had factored in wheelchair access.

If she went ahead with the art gallery idea, the separate powder room would accommodate visitors and the full-sized kitchen would be ideal for any functions they might have. The four rooms at the front would have high ceilings with large walls for hanging art, and plenty of floor space for displaying sculptural pieces or whatever else she chose to sell.

'I'm not sure about polished concrete floors – I had floorboards in mind.'

'Trust me, they'll look amazing – not at all drab like those in the winery we were in the other week. Ours will sparkle. And be warm. You'd be surprised how efficient underfloor heating is.'

'Oh, I thought we'd have a wood heater or two.' Emily's heart sank. She wanted the place to be classy, but also to have a country hominess about it – even if it was a business.

'Trust me, the novelty of real flames will wear off pretty quickly – it's very labour intensive. And you'd be surprised how much more dust you'll end up with – not something you want around paintings. Gas log fires in each room will give a nice ambience and extra heating when it's really cold, and be labour-free. Also, gas is much cheaper than electricity.'

'Are you sure, when you'll have big gas bottles to deal with?'

'Sorry?'

'Gas doesn't come by pipe or cable out here like water or electricity – you have to cart large bottles back and forth. Or have it delivered. I'm not sure how much it costs.'

'Oh. I hadn't thought of that. I don't think it'll be a problem. And I'm sure it'll still be cheaper. We definitely want gas for the kitchen.'

'I'll have to take your word on that too – I've only ever had electricity. Though, I have heard that gas is what serious cooks prefer.'

'It's still a much better option than dealing with wood and ash for heating. I think electric hot water, especially if we're going to have to do gas in bottles. Trust me, Em, I know what I'm doing,' he added, clearly noticing her concern.

'Okay. I know. I'm sorry. I'll try not to question you so much. It's just that it's all so new to me. I only want to be sure.'

'It's okay. And it's okay to question. You're spending a lot of money – you need to be sure, and happy. But, remember, it's a joint project. I'm going to be using this to advertise my business – anything less than great will not be good enough.'

Emily relaxed. She would let herself trust him. He had years of experience and she had zero. And, God, he was sexy when he was in business mode and all commanding!

Jake explained that with careful thought to positioning and with thick walls, plenty of insulation in the ceiling, and well-fitted doors and windows, the cottage wouldn't need air-conditioning at all. It could always be added later if needed.

'What about double glazing?' Emily asked.

'Easy enough to get a basic costing. Or we could go double laminate glass instead of the standard. I'll look into it,' he said, making a note. 'Now, lights. I'm thinking down lights.'

'As in, those little disks set into the ceiling?'

'Yes. What do you think?'

'They're very modern looking.'

'And perfect for an art gallery. You want nice clean lines and unobtrusive views for art. If you go with pendants, they'll have to be really plain so they don't distract from the art, anyway. And with down lights you can change the direction to highlight pieces better and avoid shadows.'

'Hmm, fair enough, I guess.'

'Honestly, it's what all the galleries do.'

'Well, if I'm not allowed to have a central light in each room, I'm going to have a dirty great crystal chandelier inside the front door,' she said with a harrumph, and folded her arms in mock defiance.

Jake laughed. 'That was actually going to be my next suggestion,' he said. Emily felt a new burst of warmth flood through her at the thought that they weren't too far out of synch with their ideas. And if they ever were, he'd steer her right. She just had to have more faith.

They chose a classic look, with a neutral colour scheme for the bathrooms, powder room, and kitchen. They both agreed that it was best to limit the use of bold colour to accents and objects that could be changed easily and relatively inexpensively.

It had all yet to be costed, so they ran two lists: Must Have and Wish List items. For instance, Emily wanted floor-to-ceiling tiles right throughout the bathrooms and toilet, but not if it meant she had to have an ordinary vanity and basin.

She was very impressed at how much Jake knew about pricing and what was out there. She said she thought architects just did the design and plans, but he explained that he was a lot more hands-on than most architects. He also had some great contacts that would help to keep costs down and give good advice.

'But we'll try to source as much as we can locally,' he said. 'I don't want to go upsetting the local businesses.'

'Good idea. But we'll have to allow plenty in the budget for freight.'

It wasn't that she thought Jake would forget anything, but she wanted to make sure they had as many costs factored in as possible, so as to avoid getting bitten down the track. Country people were at a considerable disadvantage compared to those living in the city with freight adding significantly to the cost of almost everything.

They had now finalised the hand-drawn plan and were ready to get the big, proper plans drawn up. They also had enough of an idea about the quality of the fit-out and a comprehensive list of what they would need in order to get a quantity surveyor involved. Emily had never heard of such a person, but Jake assured her it was the best way to go. Apparently the woman he worked with would be able to come up with a pretty accurate costing, even at this early stage. Emily didn't see how someone in Melbourne could cost something for Wattle Creek, given the extra freight involved and not knowing what was stocked locally, but, again, she had to trust Jake. She knew diddly-squat about any of this stuff.

Once the plans were done, Emily could put in a building application with council. They didn't anticipate any problems. Being out on a farm there were no neighbours to be concerned about overshadowing. Development approvals on farms tended to be just exercises in rubber-stamping, if there was an application put in at all.

'God, in Melbourne, planning and building approval can take years, depending on which council you're dealing with,' Jake said.

With such a huge area, geographically, to police, there was no way the council would have the resources to check that all the sheds and outbuildings that popped up on farms had building approval. And no farmer would ever dob in another farmer. It just wasn't done; the whole place worked on a what-goes-around-comes-around philosophy.

Emily had asked David about council regulations when they had first discussed moving the hayshed and had been told they should just let sleeping dogs lie. He was pretty sure John wouldn't have bothered with the mere formality of gaining approval in the first place. Oh well, if it came back to haunt her, she'd worry about it then.

Chapter Ten

After an hour or so of discussion, they sat back in their chairs, satisfied with their progress. They'd now go and do the shopping and then Emily would cook while Jake hunkered down in the office to start the ball rolling on the next phase. Emily was feeling very excited and positive about it all. What a great day!

Suddenly they were startled by a brief knock followed by the hiss of the glass door sliding open. Emily and Jake exchanged quizzical expressions.

'I'll get it,' Jake said, getting up.

Emily hoped it might be Barbara, despite her friend making no mention of a visit. In all her excitement, she'd forgotten to tell her about the cottage – she'd got side-tracked by the food. She looked forward to getting her friend's input. But she was going to have to stop referring to it as a cottage – the place was really quite big.

Emily's smile faded when she heard her mother's voice. Part of her started emotionally searching for somewhere to hide. Fight-or-flight response. The feeling Jake had been living with almost constantly, thanks to his adrenal fatigue.

'Hello Enid. Hello there Des,' Jake said.

Enid entered the kitchen, followed by a sheepish-looking Des. Both were dressed smartly in crisp, neatly ironed shirts – Des: navy and white check; Enid: plain white – and navy slacks. Des's wiry grey hair was standing up a little, as if he had been running his hands through it, but not a hair was out of place in Enid's grey bob. Jake came in after them. *Must remember to keep the door locked*, Emily thought grimly.

'Oh, there you are,' Enid said. 'Happy Australia Day.'

'Hi Mum, hi Dad, come in,' she said, getting up from the table. Her sarcasm was clearly lost on Enid, but not Des, who mouthed, 'Sorry.'

Emily performed the air-kiss ritual with Enid and then wrapped her arms around her father.

'So what brings you by, Mum?'

'We're on our way home from the ceremony. We went to Wattle Creek this year at the invitation of the Greens. We thought you might have been there.'

'I didn't feel like it this year.'

'Well, Jake might have enjoyed getting out and meeting some people. Not everything is about you, Emily.'

'We did discuss it, Enid, but I didn't actually feel up to it,' Jake said. Emily's heart surged with gratitude. She really hadn't known what to say.

'Oh. Are you unwell? What brings you so far from home, anyway, Jake? Surely not just to visit our Emily.'

Why wouldn't *he come especially to visit me? Thanks a bloody lot, Mum!*

'Oh. Just a bit of a break in the fresh country air,' he said, starting to look a little flustered.

'So, you haven't said what brings *you* by,' Emily said.

'You haven't been to visit, so we thought we'd come to you,' Enid replied haughtily. 'Do I have to make an appointment now to see my daughter, my only child?'

That would be preferable, yes.

'So, are you going to offer your parents a seat and a cuppa, or just have us stand here like statues?'

Emily shrugged and waved a hand as an invitation to sit down.

'You sit, Em. I'll get the coffees.'

'Thanks, Jake. I'll have tea, please.' As Emily sat down, she realised that her mother was peering at the plans they had been working on. *Shit!* She wished she'd thought to gather up the papers and stuff them in a drawer. Not that she'd had time.

'Tea for me too – white with one, thanks Jake,' Des said, taking a chair.

'Coffee for me, thank you. Milk, no sugar,' Enid said.

'Coming right up.'

Emily watched as Enid dragged the plans towards her and began scrutinising them.

'Do I smell fresh paint?' Des asked. It was silent in the room except for Jake's rattling around at the nearby bench.

'You do, indeed, Dad. I'm doing myself an office,' Emily said proudly.

'Looks like you're doing more than that,' Enid said in an accusatory tone as she jabbed a fingernail into the plan.

Uh-oh, here we go again.

'Oh, that's something of mine,' Jake said.

'It's okay, Jake,' Emily said in practically a whisper. 'It's actually a joint project,' she now said boldly, looking directly at her mother. 'We're going to rebuild the cottage across the way. Though it'll be considerably bigger than the original cottage.'

'Whatever for?!'

'Because I want to. Because *we* want to,' Emily said, fully aware her chin was now jutting out stubbornly.

'And how much is that going to cost?' Enid continued.

'That's really none of your business, Mum,' Emily said, forcing the words to come out slowly and calmly. She noticed her father's eyebrows rose up a notch, felt a little guilty for him having to be part of this, but pushed it back.

'Well, it sounds like a silly idea to me. I thought you'd have learnt your lesson after that other dreadful house.'

The blood rushed to Emily's cheeks. She tried to remain calm. 'Mum, it really makes no difference what you think. It's my idea, my money, and my life.'

'But, Emily...'

'But nothing, Mum.'

'Enid, I'm sure Jake and Em know what they're doing,' Des said.

Emily was relieved when at that moment Jake delivered the mugs and sat down. Murmurs of thanks made their way around the table.

'So, who won the Citizen and Young Citizen of the Year for Wattle Creek?' she ventured.

'If you had any interest in your community, Emily, you would know,' Enid said, making an exaggerated show of picking up her mug and taking a sip.

'I really can't take a trick, today, can I?' Emily said, putting on a laugh in an attempt to calm the situation.

'Emily, you can't possibly think this is a good idea,' Enid said, jabbing at the papers again. 'You already have a perfectly suitable house.'

'Can we please just change the subject?' Emily said, desperately searching her mind for something benign to discuss.

'But, Emily, you're not being sensible. You need to think it through.'

'I have. *We* have, Mum.'

'Enid, I wouldn't be supporting Emily in this if it wasn't a viable proposition. I'm a not-too-shabby businessman, actually.'

'Well, you can't be a very good businessman if you think this is a good idea. And you barely know each other.'

'Enid,' Des warned.

'Clearly *someone* needs to be the voice of reason here.'

'Mum, please…'

'It's okay, Emily, your mother is entitled to her opinion,' Jake said, laying a hand on hers. 'Can we please just enjoy our cuppa and our time together? I've been looking forward to catching up.'

How can he be so calm? I want to knock her bloody head off!

'I've lost my appetite,' Enid said, putting her mug down and pushing it away with a sneer. She got up. 'Come on Des,' she said, gathering her handbag from the floor beside her. 'We've clearly caught Emily at a bad time. We'll visit again when she's in a better frame of mind.'

Emily fumed but kept her mouth shut.

Des Oliphant remained seated. Enid stood over him and tugged at his elbow.

'Des, now, we're leaving.'

The wall clock counted the passing seconds loudly in the silence. Finally, Des looked up at his wife. 'Actually, no, Enid. You can go, but I am not. I'm interested to hear about Emily and Jake's plans. You can wait in the car or come back later and pick me up. Or not. I can easily find my own way home.' At this he shot Emily a slightly stricken look, which she answered with a nod.

'But. But…'

'Enid, go. Just go.'

For a moment it looked like she was about to sit back down. *Please don't*, Emily pleaded silently. She so badly wanted this time with her father. And to give him a big hug and say thank you, thank you, *thank you* for standing up for her.

Jake got up and followed Enid as she stomped out to the glass door.

Although they were on the other side of a thick stone wall, their voices could be clearly heard. Emily wasn't surprised by what her mother said next, but she still cringed at Enid's nerve, even in obvious defeat.

'Jake, clearly Emily is suffering some sort of midlife crisis.' Emily imagined Enid holding his arm and feigning sincerity. 'Though surely she's a little young for that. Anyway, whatever is causing her to be so wilful needs looking into. I suggest you book her in to see the new psychologist, Jacqueline Havelock.'

'Emily is fine, Enid,' Jake replied in a pleasant, even tone.

There was an audible harrumph and then the sound of the glass door *whoosh*ing and shutting with a bang, followed by the faint thud of court-shoe heels on concrete. Jake returned and sat back down heavily at the table.

'I'm sorry about all this, Des,' Jake said.

'Why are you apologising? Please, Jake, honestly, it's quite refreshing to hear Emily stand up to her mother. I'm afraid I've let her down on that score far too many times.'

Well, you've certainly made up for it today, Emily thought, looking sympathetically at her father.

Des looked gutted. Her heart lurched. It must be awful to be caught between the two women he loved, trying to be loyal to both at once. He was between a rock and a hard place, as Gran would have said. Emily wished it wasn't like this, but she certainly hadn't set out to provoke her mother. All she'd done wrong was not hide the evidence of the cottage project. Why couldn't Enid be supportive? She didn't have to agree, or even understand, just nod politely and say, 'It's your life, dear, whatever makes you happy.' How hard was that?

'I'm afraid Enid can be a bit insecure about her place in the world,' Des continued. 'And any happiness or success Emily finds just seems to magnify it. I wish there were something I could do, but I'm afraid she's not going to change now. Maybe she's just too set in her ways.' He sighed deeply.

Emily stared at him, wondering if he was actually thinking of leaving her mother after all these years. 'I'm sorry I upset her, Dad. I didn't mean to.'

Des nodded and patted his daughter's hand in response.

They cocked their heads slightly at hearing a car door slam, engine roar to life, and the spray of gravel. There was a collective breath of relief now they knew Enid wasn't outside waiting.

'Looks like I might need to trouble you guys for a ride home,' Des said, shaking his head.

'Do you think she'll be back?' Jake asked.

Des winced. 'I doubt it.' He was obviously upset but trying not to show it.

'I have to go and shop for groceries anyway,' Emily said. 'I'll just get them in Hope Springs instead of Wattle Creek. They're open on the public holiday, aren't they?'

'Yes. So,' Des said, clearly making an effort to be more up-beat, 'how about we start again. Tell me all about this exciting plan you have.' He looked from Emily to Jake and back again.

'You tell the story, Em, and I'll fill in the gaps,' Jake said.

As Emily showed her father the plans for the gallery, telling him all they had been discussing that day, she was pleased to hear his genuine enthusiasm. She wished her mother had shown the same excitement. Had Enid *ever* been excited for her? About anything? A wave of sadness swept through her before she could push it back.

'It sounds like a great idea,' Des said. 'I don't know much about art or any of that sort of thing, but I think something else for tourists to look at can only be good for everyone. There seem to be a lot more people traipsing over this way nowadays thanks to the wineries and such. And I'll happily sit and chip some mortar off rocks if you can do with the help,' he added.

'Careful what you offer, Dad,' Emily warned.

'It'll be nice to get some fresh air and sunshine,' he said with a wave of his hand, 'though you might find I'm a bit of a fair weather labourer. Honestly, if there's anything at all I can do to help, you only have to ask,' he added, patting Emily's hand.

'Thanks, Dad. We'll let you know. Though, as you can see, it's very early days yet.'

An image of them working together on the old house she'd rented from the Bakers crept into her mind. It had been a great bonding time, but it seemed so long ago.

After half an hour they offered to drive Des back to Hope Springs, since they hadn't heard from Enid and Emily really had to get to the shop before it closed. As they walked over to the shed where the car was garaged, she remembered the hayshed. So much had been running through her mind since seeing it, she'd forgotten to mention the wonderful surprise from that morning.

'Dad, there's something you have to see before you go,' she said, changing the direction towards the newly erected frame, which was only fifty metres away but hidden by the large shed next to it.

'David and Jake organised for the hayshed to be moved,' she continued, practically skipping. 'The iron is going on tomorrow after the footings have cured. It's so exciting. I only found out this morning. It was a total surprise.' She stopped in front of the large steel structure and waited for her father and Jake to catch up.

'It'll be nice not to see it out of your bedroom window anymore,' Des said, gazing at the steel shining in the sun. 'Sounds like you're really settling in and making your mark on the place, Em. I'm so pleased for you,' he said, draping an arm around her shoulders. 'And I really appreciate all you're doing, Jake,' he added.

'I'm enjoying being here,' Jake said, beaming at Emily. He grasped her hand and gave it a squeeze.

'Hey, Dad, you're welcome to come and hang out tomorrow while the guys are putting the iron on – if you've got nothing else to do,' Emily said. 'I'm making scones for morning tea,' she added in an enticing tone.

'Oh, well, there's no way I can resist the call of your scones, Em. Count me in. But as long as I'm not going to be in the way,' he added, looking at Jake.

'You'll be no more in the way than this city boy,' Jake said, smiling back.

'Great, thanks. I'll come on by. Right about smoko time, I reckon,' Des said, grinning cheekily.

'Thanks very much for the ride. Time to see what sort of mood awaits,' Des said wearily, as he got out of the car idling at the kerb of Emily's parents' home.

Emily wondered for a split second if she should go in and speak to her mother. Ordinarily she would have.

As they drove away, she thought about how much time and breath she'd wasted over the years being the adult to her mother's childish tantrums. Even more annoying was the realisation of how Enid always managed to manipulate her into feeling that she was the one in the wrong. Not anymore.

They parked in front of the small supermarket, but just as Emily was about to get out of the car, Jake placed his hand on her thigh.

'I wanted to say this earlier, but I didn't want to embarrass your father. I'm so proud of the way you handled your mother today.'

'Thanks, Jake. I don't think it'll make much difference, but I sure feel better for standing up for myself. If only she could see that not everything is about her,' Emily mused.

'You did the right thing. You're a lot stronger than you give yourself credit for. Look at all you've had to deal with over the past few months.'

'I'd rather not, if you don't mind,' she said, with a laugh. 'But thanks.' She leant over and kissed him before opening the car door and getting out.

Chapter Eleven

The following morning Emily kissed Jake goodbye when the first vehicle drove in, a friendly honk signalling its arrival. There wasn't time to go out and meet and greet – the first smoko would be around before she knew it and she was already busy in the kitchen. She had planned a veritable feast stretching out over the day: scones with jam and cream or cheese and tomato, and an assortment of sandwiches for morning tea; roast chicken, sliced ham and salad for lunch; homemade pasties, another different assortment of sandwiches, and buttered date loaf for afternoon tea.

Back in the first year of their marriage, John had told her how important it was to serve good food during shearing. According to him, the best, most plentiful meals ensured their shed would receive priority the following year. If you served up average food you were apparently relegated down the list and the shearing team manager would send the slower, less experienced people.

Emily had sometimes wondered if this was just something John had concocted to shift the blame if things didn't go his way. Perhaps people might put his shed last on the list simply because they objected to having abuse shouted at them. But what did she know? She'd been on the farm about five minutes in the scheme of things and, as he had regularly reminded her, she was a born-and-bred 'townie' anyway.

The discussion of food for shearing – or rather his insistence she provide exceptional meals; he'd made it quite clear he wasn't interested in discussing it in any finer detail than that – was the closest John ever got to sharing farming facts with her. She still didn't have a clue how many fleeces made up a bale, or how many bales they might get from their flock. They were all things she should probably get up to speed with now.

Apparently speed was everything when it came to shearing. It was a major job that few farmers enjoyed (and many absolutely hated) and stretching it out just added to the annoyance. One of the things that would send John into a rage was if everyone had to come back for a half-day to finish off. It had happened only once in her time, and as far as Emily could see it wasn't really anyone's fault. She was actually just as inconvenienced as John was, through having to do more cooking, not to mention the additional cost of providing the extra few meals. It didn't sound like much, but as Emily had soon learnt, feeding six or seven men three times a day really added up.

If all went well today, the men would be finished cladding the shed by early evening. She had called David when they'd been in the supermarket the day before and offered dinner as well, but he'd phoned back a few minutes later to say that Steve and Grant had meetings that evening and wouldn't be able to stay. Since she wasn't paying them, she was even more determined than ever to feed the men well.

She wondered how their wives felt about them working for her on their holidays. She'd have to put on a barbeque sometime later to thank everyone. It would be nice to get to know them better, and potentially useful if she was going to be running a business down the track.

As Emily measured out the ingredients for the date loaf, she thought about how much fun she and Barbara had had cooking together. The company would have been nice, but she could totally understand Barbara's declaration of being 'on strike' after all the work she'd done for the day before, especially whilst being pregnant. She hoped Barbara would have a nice quiet day and rest up. *Meanwhile, I'd better stop daydreaming and get cracking!*

Even though she was under pressure to get the meals out at certain times, the prospect of a day in the kitchen filled Emily with a sense of calm and serenity. She'd never understood why her mother claimed to hate cooking.

As she sifted flour, Emily shook her head, remembering how Enid had briefly taken up jam making after Jake had raved about her own apricot jam. Barbara had suggested that Enid was just feeling threatened because Emily was good at something, and trying to compete as a result. Emily had been a little annoyed; lately Enid seemed to copy everything she did. Like getting her hair cut into the same chin-length bob. Oh, well, perhaps she'd tire of that like she had the jam. According to Des, two attempts tasting like burnt toffee had put an end to the jam hobby.

At nine-thirty, Emily filled a large box with scones – fresh from the oven – plus pots of jam and cream and a variety of other sweet and savoury condiments. She added a Tupperware container of sandwiches, thermoses of tea and coffee, and all the requisite paraphernalia.

'Come on, Gracie, let's go feed the hungry workers,' she said, and left the house to carry it all down to the far end of the large rubble area flanked by corrugated-iron sheds. The men seemed to be making great headway. In just a couple of hours they had already done half the roof. Below, the steel uprights remained naked.

'Smoko time!' she called uselessly above the two idling tractors. She was relieved to see Jake driving one rather than involved in heavy labour. There was no sign of Des. He must have decided not to come after all.

Clutching the box that was growing heavier by the second, she looked around for a place to lay everything out. Grace stood beside her, her tail wagging gently.

Suddenly the tractors were turned off and silence reigned.

'Here, I'll take that,' David said, taking the box as Jake stepped down from his tractor and rolled a forty-four gallon drum towards them. Emily would have loved a show of affection from her man, but he was clearly in work-site mode. He looked happy and in his element, though a little tired and drawn.

'Thanks so much for doing this, you guys,' she said to Steve, Grant and Bob, as they brought three smaller drums over.

'You're very welcome,' said Bob, the older, slightly shorter and more thickset of the three, with a wave. Emily nodded back. She'd seen it plenty of times; when men had been working and their hands were dirty, instead of offering a hand to shake, they lifted one in greeting.

'No worries,' Grant added, scraping at the dirt with the toe of his boot. 'Good to see a few things going your way. Steve and I are really sorry about snubbing you after, you know...'

'All water under the bridge,' Emily said to the pair of tall, lean agronomists. Steve and Grant might have been difficult to tell apart except for Grant's mop of light-brown hair and Steve's short black spiky haircut. 'I just can't believe you'd do this for me during your time off. It's amazing. Thank you.'

'It's just a couple of days. And we do far too much sitting behind a desk or driving around these days. So it makes a good change, eh, Grant?' Steve said.

'Yup, sure does.'

'Well, it means the world to me. So, again, thank you,' Emily said, feeling a sudden rush of emotion grip her.

'So, is it going to be for hay?' Grant asked.

'Up to David – he's running the place. I'm not sure if he's planning to cut hay down here this year. He might use it for storing equipment. But, don't worry, it'll be put to good use one way or another.'

'Well, at least it's in a much better spot now. I don't know what John was thinking,' Bob said.

The men passed around a small bottle of hand sanitiser, and David laid the first of two small checked tablecloths on one of the tall drums. 'Who's for tea and coffee?' he asked.

'There's Milo too,' Emily said.

'Or Milo,' David added.

'Tea, thanks,' Steve and Grant said together.

'Coffee for me, thanks,' Bob said.

'Milo, thanks,' Jake said as he brought another couple of smaller drums over and put them in the centre of the semicircle.

'This all looks great. Are you staying, Em?' David asked, raising a mug and wiggling it at her.

Emily had packed extra food and a mug, but until that moment, she hadn't been sure whether to join them or not.

She actually didn't feel as out of place as she thought she might.

'Sure, why not? Tea, thanks. White with one.' She sat down on a drum.

'I'll let you do the doctoring,' David said, leaning over and putting the jars of milk, sugar and teaspoons onto the cloth Jake had just draped across two of the smaller drums. He passed out plates and serviettes then put the basket of scones and condiments and knives on one drum and the box of egg sandwiches on the other. Emily accepted the hot mug and took a scone. She liked having the men waiting on her.

Just then they all turned at the sound of an approaching vehicle. Des Oliphant got out and made his way over.

'Ah good, not too late I see,' he said, grinning and rubbing his hands together.

He gave Emily a quick hug and shook hands with each of the men, greeting them by name.

'Don't worry fellas, I'm not here to check up on your work. I'm quality control for the catering,' he added jovially, and took a seat on the last remaining empty drum.

Cheeky bugger, Emily thought with a smirk as she sipped her tea. It was good to see him looking cheerful. Hopefully that meant Enid hadn't given him too much of a tongue-lashing.

There was a collective chuckle and hum of voices as the small group settled down to the food, murmuring with relish about how good it was.

As Emily walked back to the house with Grace trotting along beside her, she wondered what Steve, Grant and Bob must think about her being shacked up with another bloke so soon after the death of her husband. But she shook the thought aside; like Barbara had said often enough, she couldn't control what people thought, or what they said behind her back. Anyway, she had done nothing, and wasn't doing anything, wrong.

Jake had been staying with her for just over three weeks and still hadn't been with her to collect the mail or groceries in Wattle Creek. She wasn't consciously hiding him, but she was pleased she'd been spared a little while from becoming the focus of gossip all over again. Though, Enid was bound to have told someone by now – if only to utter her disapproval. Anyway, Emily was sure someone from Wattle Creek would have seen them together in Hope Springs the day before. So word was definitely already making its way around the district. And now that Steve, Grant and Bob had been here... Oh, well, maybe the sooner the tongues started wagging, the sooner they would stop.

Chapter Twelve

Emily was just finishing re-packing the box after afternoon tea – unsure if it would be needed again or not – when her mobile began to ring. She dragged it off the bench and stared at the screen: Cousin Liz. She sighed and sat down.

She wasn't sure why, but for some reason she didn't feel like talking to Liz. Emily had always got on well with her cousin. At Gran's funeral they'd had a great heart to heart and Liz had encouraged her to leave John, even offering a haven in Melbourne, if necessary. But she hadn't liked the way Liz had behaved towards Jake when they had visited. And she really didn't fancy being quizzed about their relationship, and why he was back there again. Jake had assured her there had been nothing between him and Liz, but they both knew she had feelings for him.

It was naïve to think that Liz hadn't been in touch with her mother and that Peggy hadn't been in touch with Enid, and that they didn't all know the latest details of Emily's life. Oh, Liz would know everything all right. How would she feel about her plain, unsophisticated country cousin ending up with the man she'd wanted? Liz was competitive through and through; it was no doubt how she had done so well in her career as a business analyst – whatever that entailed.

Emily toyed with not taking the call, but just as she'd decided she'd let it go to voicemail she found her finger scooting across the screen and answering.

'Hi Liz,' she said, more brightly than she felt. 'How's things?'

'What's this I hear about Jake being over there?'

Emily was taken aback at her cousin's abrupt manner. *Uh-oh.* 'Yes, he's here. He's having a country break.'

'Are you two an item now?'

'Yes, we are, actually.'

'Oh. Right. And what's this I hear about you being in Melbourne and not even calling me?'

'I wanted to, but Jake said you were overseas at a conference or something.'

'It was *then* you were here?' Elizabeth said, a little subdued.

'It was a spur-of-the-moment thing.'

'It's not like you to be so spontaneous.' Emily could picture the sneer on her cousin's face. And, God, she sounded like Enid.

'Oh, well, maybe I'm changing.'

'So why the rushed trip?'

'Jake was going to a funeral. I went along for moral support.'

'I could have done that, saved you the bother.'

'It wasn't any bother, Liz. And you were away, remember?'

Liz didn't seem to have a response to that. 'So, who died?'

'A business acquaintance. Nobody you know, I should imagine.' Emily hoped she was saying all the right things.

Really, this was a conversation Liz should be having with Jake. 'How was the conference?' she asked.

'Bit boring, but not the worst I've been to. At least the hotel was five-star. So, I hear you've moved back to the farm. Mum told me about John's accident. And I hear you're rich. Quite the turnaround.'

'Not exactly *rich*, but if I'm careful I should be okay.'

'I know plenty of money men and women if you want some financial advice. I can do some introductions if you like,' Liz said.

'Thanks, but I'm fine,' Emily said.

'And what would you know about investing wisely?'

'Jeez, don't hold back, Liz,' Emily said.

'Sorry. I'm just trying to look out for you.'

'I'm fine. The bank here is helping me. And I have Jake for advice if I need it.'

'That does sound serious,' Liz said with a tight laugh.

We are, Emily thought, but didn't say it.

'Remember, he's an architect and builder, Emily, not an expert in money matters,' Liz said.

'Was there something particular you wanted, or did you just call to give me a hard time?'

'I heard about the cottage,' Liz said, hesitating.

Uh-huh. So she's been instructed to talk me out of it.

'Why don't you just put up a cute little wooden hut if you want extra accommodation? It'd be a lot cheaper.'

'And what business is it of yours?'

'Well, it's not really. I just don't want you blowing your money on something silly.' The words could have come straight out of Enid's mouth. And the tone was pretty spot on as well.

Emily fumed. 'What, you'd rather I blew it on some get-rich-quick scheme instead?'

'You at least need to get your money working for you. And you don't want to over-capitalise. You'll never get your money back if you sell.'

'I'm not going to sell,' Emily said.

'What, you're going to stay out there in the sticks and play at being a farmer?'

'Is that what my mother told Peggy to tell you to say? Surely you've got enough going on in your own life without wasting time being messenger for our mothers. You need to grow up, Liz, and stop playing this silly game of theirs.'

'Gosh, we are a little touchy, aren't we?'

'What are you talking about?'

'Things not working out so well with Jake?'

'Everything is working out perfectly well between Jake and myself, actually,' Emily said. 'In fact, he's thinking of staying permanently, perhaps even setting up an agency here. Not that it's any of your business.'

Damn. She knew she'd said too much. It wasn't her story to tell. Liz would now go back to Aunt Peggy with her news, and Peggy would spread it back to Enid. God only knew what information would get changed along the way. Chinese whispers, indeed!

'Clearly I've caught you at a bad time,' Liz said cautiously.

'No, not at all. But I don't see why you're wasting your money and both of our time by phoning to quiz me about my life, only to then put it down.'

'I'm not.'

'Oh, really? Not once have you said, "Em, I'm sorry the other house didn't work out" or "Em, I'm really pleased your financial situation has eased" or "Em, I'm happy that you've hit it off with Jake" or "Em, isn't it great that life is finally starting to treat you better". Not once have you ever called just to say hi or be supportive. You only ever call when you want something – whether it's to stay so you can try and impress Jake, or whether it's to appease your mother or mine, or to somehow make yourself feel better by hearing all about my poor, sad life.' She was ranting, but she couldn't stop.

'Well I've had enough, Liz. You use people. You can deny your feelings for Jake all you like – hint that he's gay and all the other crap you pulled when you stayed – but the truth is, you're jealous. You're jealous because he's chosen me over you, and you're jealous of the fact that I have a more meaningful life than you because I'm not obsessed with money and impressing people who don't really matter.' She was becoming a little breathless, but she blundered on.

'Well, Liz, you can't compete with me or lord it over me, or whatever you're trying to do, because that game takes two to play and I'm not interested in playing it. I don't care about flash cars, posh restaurants, five-star hotels, designer clothes, or being seen in the hippest Melbourne café sipping on a latte. If that makes me the poor country hick cousin, then fine, that's what I am. But that's my choice and it's none of your business, or your mother's, or even *my* mother's, for that matter!' Suddenly Emily stopped. She was struggling for air.

There was silence on the other end of the line.

'I've got to go,' Emily said after a moment. 'I don't need this. I've grinned and put up with all this crap for long enough!' And with that she hung up. Her face was flaming. She felt exhilarated, a little light-headed, and a wee bit guilty. It was the closest she'd ever got to hanging up on someone.

She ran her hands through her hair.

'God, what's happened? Are you okay?' Jake asked, full of concern.

Shit. He must have come in mid-rant because she hadn't heard the sliding door. 'No, I'm bloody wild!'

'What's happened?' He sat down.

'Bloody Liz! I wish I didn't let her get to me, but she pushes my buttons every time! I guess this time I cracked,' she said, smiling weakly.

'Well, she can be pretty full-on,' Jake said, choosing his words carefully.

Emily held her hands up. 'I know she's a good friend of yours, but she's a back-stabbing, smarmy, manipulative bitch who only thinks about herself.'

'Yep, she's all of that, and more,' Jake said thoughtfully. He shuffled his chair closer and put his arm around her. 'What did she say to upset you?'

'I don't know,' Emily said, exasperated. 'She was going on about how the cottage is over-capitalising, or something.'

'Like she'd know,' Jake said.

'Can't she just be pleased that I'm doing something that makes me happy?'

'She's jealous of us too, right?' Jake asked.

'I think so.'

'Emily, she's jealous of *you*. You're naturally beautiful…'

'Yeah, right.'

'Let me finish,' he said, holding up a hand to her. 'You're naturally beautiful; you don't go in for all the make-up, fancy clothes…'

'Because I can't afford to,' she started, but was halted by Jake's steely, warning gaze.

'You know who you are and you're content. You don't feel the need to impress people. You're like, "Right, here I am, if you don't like it then bugger off."'

Actually, that's pretty recent. He was right that she no longer felt the need to impress people, but she had spent years desperately seeking her mother's approval and had always wanted to make John happy.

'You're you, Em. You're real. What you see is what you get. That's what I love most about you. I think deep down Liz envies you. She tries to distract everyone with flash window dressing, but I think underneath it all is a pretty insecure, unhappy person.'

'So why are you friends with her? Not that it really matters.'

'I suppose I feel a bit sorry for her. For a long time I didn't see her for what she really is. Actually, it's spending time with you that's done it. In fact, the very first time I met you I saw how comfortable you were in your own skin – despite everything you were going through.'

'Come on, I was a complete bloody basket case!' Emily said with a laugh. But it was lovely to have someone saying such nice things about her.

'No you weren't. You were the perfect host: warm, friendly, welcoming. To a complete stranger at that.'

'Well, you were a friend of Liz's.'

'And even though she was a complete cow most of the time, pretending to flirt with me or making me out to be gay, you kept your cool. Don't think I didn't notice what was going on.'

Emily's eyes were wide. 'And you just smiled and put up with it. I've done that a lot in my life.'

'And it's part of your charm. But you don't need to pretend with me. Now you're getting your life sorted out, you need to concentrate on standing up for yourself.'

'God, I was a bit rude,' Emily said, a little sheepishly.

'And she probably deserved it.'

'Why can't they just say, "You know what, whatever makes you happy. If you're happy, we're happy"?' Emily was annoyed to find her eyes filling with tears. She swiped roughly at them with the back of her hand. Of course what she really meant was: Why can't *Mum* say these things?

Poor Liz. She probably wasn't as bad as Emily was making out. They'd had good times over the years. Her timing was just bad. Or was it good? Barbara would say that the universe was in charge; she wouldn't have said these things to her cousin if she wasn't meant to.

'Well this is why they say you can choose your friends but not your family,' Jake said kindly, and passed her a clean but crumpled tissue from his pocket. 'It's just lucky you've got me, and Barbara and David, and your dad. We all love you just the way you are,' he added, pulling her to him.

'Thanks Jake,' she said, hugging him. 'I probably should phone her back,' Emily said quietly.

'Why not wait a while? Hopefully she'll go off and think carefully about what you said. Maybe she'll call you.'

'I doubt it,' Emily said thoughtfully, and fell silent.

'Hey, wanna see the progress on your bright, shiny shed?' he asked, getting up.

'Oh, you haven't finished?'

'Almost, but not quite. Just a half-day tomorrow. So I'm afraid more food is required,' he added with an apologetic shrug.

'That's no problem. Small price to pay for all everyone's doing.' She got up and allowed herself to be led outside.

As they were halfway across the expanse of rubble, first Steve, then Grant, and then Bob drove past. They slowed down and waved from their open windows. 'See you tomorrow.'

'Thanks very much. See you then,' Emily called back.

When they got to the work site, Des and David were packing tools into big aluminium boxes and winding up extension cords. Emily stared at the huge shed looming up in front of her. They were almost done. If only everyone had stayed until dark, they might have finished. But she couldn't be frustrated; a lot of people were doing her a huge favour. And it was probably safer to finish when they were fresh rather than rushing and working in poor light.

'It looks fantastic,' she said enthusiastically. 'You've made great headway this afternoon.

'Would have loved to have got it finished,' David said.

'Oh, well, there's no great rush. Are you coming back tomorrow, Dad?'

'Not sure. What are you cooking?' Des Oliphant replied with a lopsided grin.

'Oh, trust you,' she said with a laugh, and playfully made a swipe at his arm. 'Give me a chance to think about it. I've only just found out there's more to be done.'

'Well, whatever it is, I reckon it'll be worth the trip Des,' Jake said, putting an arm around Emily's shoulders.

'Add a bit of pressure, why don't you,' she said, turning her head and kissing him firmly on the cheek.

'Oh, look at the time,' Des said, checking his watch. 'Better get home before her ladyship sends out a search party.' He shook Jake and David's hands and gave Emily a tight hug. 'See you tomorrow around smoko time,' he added, laughing as he got into his ute. They waved him off in silence.

'Would you like a beer for the road?' Jake said to David.

'I'd offer dinner, but I'm sure Barbara is waiting for you.' Emily said.

'Thanks, but I'd better get cracking. I'll pass on the beer, thanks Jake. It might go down too well. Better stick to the water. See you tomorrow morning.'

'Okay, see ya. Drive safe,' Emily said.

He got into his ute and they waved him off before turning and walking slowly arm in arm back to the house.

Chapter Thirteen

The next morning, Emily and Jake enjoyed a light but lingering breakfast chatting about the cottage – they just couldn't stop calling it that. They had finished tidying the kitchen and Emily had returned to flicking through magazines for ideas when they heard the familiar friendly toot of David's ute. Jake kissed Emily goodbye, got up, and left the kitchen.

Emily watched him putting on his boots at the door, feeling dreamy and blissful. She finally had a great man in her life who respected her and treated her well. And they were about to embark on a great project together.

Out of the corner of her eye she noticed Grace get up from her spot under the cupboard to follow Jake. Emily called her back in a commanding tone. The downcast look the dog gave her as she trotted back in and lay back down made her feel mean, but she stuck to her guns. It just wasn't safe for her to be out where there might be tractors driving, things being dropped, and size-ten boots stomping around. And it wasn't fair on the workers to be keeping an eye out for her all the time. Grace could go with her when she took the food down, like she had the previous day.

'Yoo-hoo!'

She tilted her head at hearing a woman's voice. Mum? Emily frowned. She couldn't bear Enid bursting her bubble now when she was feeling so good. She stared at her magazine, annoyed at how just one thought could send her mood plummeting.

'Good morning,' Barbara called, as her head popped around the kitchen door.

'Oh. Wow. Hi,' Emily said, leaping up and almost knocking her chair over backwards in the process. 'I wasn't expecting you. What a lovely surprise,' she said as she embraced her friend.

'Thought you might like a hand with feeding the chaps,' Barbara said with a cheeky grin.

'Thought *you* said I was on my own.'

'Yeah, I might have said something like that. But the truth is, I'm avoiding doing the housework,' she added sheepishly. 'And I missed you.'

'Well, I'm happy to have the company.'

As Emily reached for the tea and coffee things, Barbara sat down on the chair Jake had vacated. 'What's all this,' she asked, peering at the paperwork strewn about. 'Looks a lot more than just an office reno,' she added, picking up the house plan.

'We've decided to rebuild the cottage – only bigger. How cool's that? Jake's thinking of setting up an agency for his business here and he thought the building would be a good display to show people.'

'Pretty hefty sample,' Barbara said.

'Well, I'm thinking I might run it as an art gallery – not that I know much about art. But I do know what I like and don't like, and that's half the battle, right?'

'I thought you wanted to run a B&B.'

'I've changed my mind. I decided I don't want to be waiting on people hand and foot.'

'Fair enough. Dealing with the public can be hard work. I didn't work for long as a hairdresser, but it was enough for me. But I reckon it'd be different running a gallery, though,' she hastily added.

'I'm going to call it The Button Jar.'

'Great name!'

'You don't think I'm taking on too much?'

'Girl's gotta have a hobby. And with all the antiques shops and cellar doors popping up, it's only a matter of time before art galleries and homewares shops are in demand too. You're smart to get in early,' Barbara said.

'Well, it might take up to a year to get it all set up.'

'Everyone has to start somewhere. I'm sure it'll be a roaring success. And it sounds like things are getting pretty serious with Jake.'

'Yes. You don't think it's too soon, do you?'

'Do you?'

'Yes and no. I *think* it's probably too soon, but it doesn't really *feel* like it is.'

'There's your answer. Go with your heart. It doesn't matter what I think, or anyone else.'

'I feel like I've known him forever, and that I can totally trust him. I'm so lucky.' She beamed at Barbara.

'He sure is a lovely man. And you deserve to be happy.'

Emily reluctantly dragged herself out of her love-struck daze. 'Can you look over the plans and see if there's anything you think we've missed?'

'As if you and Jake would have missed anything,' Barbara said, rolling her eyes. 'But I am a very inquisitive creature, so I'm dying to take a gander.'

They were silent for a few minutes while Emily got their teas and Barbara looked over the documents.

'So, what do you think?' Emily asked, putting their mugs on the table.

'Brilliant. Can't fault it. It gives great options for down the track – you could always rent it out if you decide you don't like running a business. Or live there yourself.'

'Well, I can't take any credit – it's all Jake, really.'

Barbara shrugged. 'Whatever you say. I love it.'

'I took a wee bit of convincing about polished concrete, but Jake assures me it'll look great.'

'You can always put carpets down if you don't like it. Ooh, just the thought of shopping for Persians makes my mouth water,' Barbara said, and actually wiped her hand across her lips.

'We'll see,' Emily said.

'Anyway, I bet it won't take you long to get used to. And it'll elevate it into chic rather than just country. Not that you need to. From the sounds of things, it's going to be one for the pages of *Belle* or *Home Beautiful*. So, why an art gallery and not a homewares shop?' Barbara asked.

'I want to give Jake and his sister, Simone, somewhere to exhibit. She's so talented. And I want to thank her for bringing Jake and me back together, and for all she did with the jam. You should see her work – gorgeous huge paintings of flowers.'

'Like the ones we have in our hall at home?'

'Not really – though yours are lovely too. Simone's are very modern looking; bright, and unframed. She uses quite thick paint so they seem to almost stand off of the canvas. I think it's what they call impressionist – I'm really going to have to bone up on art terms. Anyway, I just hope she doesn't think it's like charity or something,' Emily added, sipping on her tea.

'Have you told Jake? What did he say?'

'He's not keen to exhibit. But I've got plenty of time to work on him. Anyway, if one or both of them don't want to show, I'm sure there are plenty of good unknown artists out there. I don't think it'll be a problem.'

'Careful, or else Enid will suddenly be an artist wanting representation,' Barbara said with a laugh.

'Speaking of which,' Emily said, 'we had a bit of a moment.'

'Oh?'

'She and Dad dropped in out of the blue the other day. Jake and I had all this spread out on the table…'

'God, I can imagine she was none too impressed,' Barbara said, inclining her head slightly and raising her eyebrows.

'She said it was a silly idea, blah, blah, blah. Jake, bless him, leapt in to say it was something he was working on, but something in me snapped and I let her have it.'

'Really? What did you say?' Barbara asked cautiously.

'Oh, not a lot in the general scheme of things. I just pointed out that it's none of her business how I spend my money or what I do with my life. You're absolutely right; I'll never win with her.'

'And?'

'And she stormed off, leaving poor Dad here with no ride home,' Emily said with a tight laugh.

'Wow. Well, well done you. Naughty Emily.'

'I know you've been saying it for ages, but I think I finally see what you mean about her being insecure. It's just so sad.'

'Yep, sad but true.'

'Anyway, Dad was really supportive – he's even offered to sit and chip old mortar off the rocks!'

'Golly, that's dedication for you.'

'Yeah, I told him to be careful what he offers,' Emily said with another laugh. 'Speaking of offers,' she said, looking at her watch as they heard a number of vehicles drive in, 'didn't you offer to help me cook? We'd better get on with it.'

★

They were just delivering the morning tea when Des Oliphant drove in waving and grinning at them from his open window.

'I don't believe it,' Emily said, shaking her head and laughing. 'He turned up at the same time yesterday. Just in time for the scones.'

Emily and Barbara enjoyed a cuppa and slice of jubilee cake with the guys. They were expecting to finish just before twelve – in time for Grant and Steve to get to their afternoon games of sport. Emily offered to pack up sandwiches for them to take, but they refused. She suspected a crispy meat pie with sauce or a hotdog might be their Saturday ritual.

She invited Des to stay, but much to Emily's surprise, he announced he'd been called up last night to fill in on the local men's bowls team.

'But you've never even played bowls!' Emily cried, aghast.

'Well, apparently I'm better than them forfeiting. And, for all I know, once you hit sixty you might be automatically programmed to be able to play – I've just never tried,' he added with a chuckle. 'Who knows, I might uncover a hidden talent,' he said, miming an underarm throw.

Chapter Fourteen

The last few sheets of iron went up quickly, and then Emily, Barbara, Jake and David were tucking into sandwiches after saying goodbye to the guys.

'Why don't we go for a drive this afternoon?' Barbara said to no one in particular. 'Maybe look at a couple of antiques and second-hand shops for furniture for Em's study?'

'No, thanks,' David said.

'Ooh, yes please,' Emily said, and clapped her hands together a couple of times. 'Jake?'

'Er, sorry David,' he said, shooting David an apologetic glance, 'but count me in.'

'Jake Lonigan, you are a disappointment to the brotherhood.'

'You don't have to come,' Barbara told him. 'These guys could drive me home later,' she said, putting a hand on his.

'That's okay. I know when I'm beaten,' David said with a sigh. 'Anyway, it might be wise to have a less emotional participant. And I can keep hold of your spending, missy,' he said, tapping Barbara gently on the end of her nose.

'Goody, it'll be fun!' Barbara said, clapping her hands.

'I doubt it,' David muttered.

'Come on, show me this freshly painted room.' Barbara got up and collected her handbag from the floor beside Grace. 'I can't believe you didn't show me the other day.'

'Too busy with the shed and cooking.'

'Fancy a bit of antiquing, Gracie?' Barbara asked the dog.

The border collie cocked her head as if contemplating the question and then began flapping her tail against the floor.

'Great, even the dog's ganging up on me,' David said. 'Thanks a lot Gracie. I thought we were friends.'

'Ah, stop your whining,' Emily said with a laugh, and threaded an arm through one of his. They all trooped down to her office and surveyed the room.

'Wow, I love the colour!' Barbara said.

'It's very pink,' said David.

'Isn't it great?' Jake said. 'It's quite a masculine shade of pink.'

'You're kidding, right?' David looked incredulous. 'There ain't nothin' masculine about that. Oh, what would I know?' he conceded, throwing up his hands.

'You know lots, darling, just not about interior design,' Barbara said, wrapping an arm around her husband.

'I'm keeping the bed – I'll decide what cover later – but I'm thinking of adding a desk and chair and an armchair and floor lamp. So that's our mission for today,' Emily said, beaming at the others.

'What are you doing on the window?' Barbara asked.

'I would love curtains and a roman blind made in the same fabric as whatever armchair I find, but after our trip to Port Lincoln the other day, I now know that will cost an absolute fortune. I think I'll have to deal with window coverings later.'

'It doesn't all have to match, it just has to tie in and tell a story – isn't that what they say on all those TV shows?' Barbara said.

'Hmm, just thinking about what would go with what makes my head spin,' Emily said with a sigh.

'Best not to over-think it. Let's just go browsing and see what jumps out at you. Just pick pieces you love, rather than trying to follow rules,' Barbara added.

'Hmm, you're probably right.'

'Good advice,' Jake said. 'I think that's how my sister, Simone, went about her decorating. She started with the big pieces first and worked everything else in around them.'

'Emily told me how gorgeous her house is,' Barbara said. 'It's such a pity she's not here to advise us.'

'Right, so everyone take a mental picture of the room and keep that in mind while we're traipsing through the stores,' Emily said.

'All I'm seeing is pink. And I think I'm scarred for life,' David said, with a laugh.

'Is it *too* pink? Seriously?' Emily asked, looking from Barbara to Jake and back again.

'No way, I love it,' Barbara said.

'I'm only messing with you,' David said. 'I'm sure it's lovely – if you like that sort of thing,' he added with a shrug.

'*So* not helpful,' Emily said, laughing.

They walked outside to where David's dual cab ute was parked. 'Perhaps I should drive since I'm the only sane one,' he said. 'And it sounds like we might need a ute for transport.'

They chattered the whole way to their first port of call, around twenty minutes away. The sign swinging from a pole outside read ANTIQUES, but inside they only found flashy designer homewares – throw rugs, bedspreads, old-style French armchairs in beige fabric with grey cursive writing all over it.

'Not really what we're looking for, huh?' Barbara said to Emily as they all made their way across the car park.

'No. Bit of a nerve calling them antiques; isn't that false advertising?'

'Probably.'

'Hmm,' Jake agreed. 'It's everywhere in Melbourne, this French provincial look,' he said. 'I'm a bit sick of it.'

'Can you believe they wanted three hundred dollars for that birdcage with the faded paint out the front?' David said incredulously, shaking his head.

'Yep,' said the others at the same time, and then laughed at their synchronicity.

'What would you do with it? Surely not use it for storing fancy cups and saucers like they were – they hardly need securing,' David said.

'It's just decorative,' Jake explained.

David frowned.

Barbara laughed and put her hand on David's shoulder. 'My darling, ever the practical one,' she cooed.

'Right,' Jake said, pulling his phone out of his pocket to check the directions. 'I think we've got time to get to one more. The closest one is further south about another twenty minutes away.'

'I hope it'll be worth it,' David said as he slumped into the driver's seat. 'Should have brought something to read.'

'Now this looks more promising,' Jake declared.

In front of them was a shed with undeniably genuine old wares spilling out of the wide open doors. Leaning up against the corrugated-iron wall was a stack of wrought-iron bed frames. Rickety-looking wooden chairs in all shapes and sizes, most with seats missing, were scattered about haphazardly.

It was like going from one extreme to the other. This shop, if you could call it that, looked like it specialised in gathering its stock from the sides of roads on council clean-up day. If this was what people were using to decorate their homes with nowadays, Emily was way out of touch. It just looked like a lot of old junk.

David parked and they crunched their way across the gravel towards the entrance. *Perhaps all the nice stuff is tucked away in the back*, Emily told herself as she walked past the chairs and a collection of rusting watering cans.

'Hey, these would be great for the other project,' Jake said, pointing to some timber fire surrounds on the other side of the doors.

'What *other* project?' David asked.

'We're going to rebuild the cottage across from Em's,' Jake explained. 'Except, it won't really be a cottage; it'll be considerably bigger than it originally was. We just can't seem to stop calling it a cottage.'

'To live in?' David said.

'Maybe. But most likely to be an art gallery,' Emily said.

'I thought you wanted to run a B&B,' David said.

'Changed my mind – woman's prerogative.'

'Indeed. Well, I look forward to hearing all about it.'

Emily and Barbara left David and Jake to examine the fireplaces, and stepped through the doors. Inside, the building was fully lined and painted. Apart from the ceiling, you wouldn't have known it was a shed.

'Hi there,' called a woman from behind a glass counter in one corner of the space.

Emily glanced over and returned her greeting. Under the counter, the top shelf contained what looked like costume jewellery. On the bottom shelf, glassware was grouped in various shades. Now that she was looking more closely, Emily saw that everything in the shop was very carefully organised.

'There are a few rooms,' the woman explained. 'Feel free to go right through. Is there anything in particular you're looking for?'

'Just having a wander, really,' Barbara said. 'Although Emily here is looking for some office furniture.'

'Through to the back room and to your left,' the lady said, smiling at Emily and indicating with her hand.

'Okay, thanks,' Emily said. Whilst she was keen to see what office furniture was available, the main area was chock full of interesting stuff. In one corner was a range of vintage clothing, including a whole rack of fox furs in varying styles.

Another corner contained shelves full of books. Emily had only got back into reading since leaving John. How good would it be, not just to have somewhere special to read, but to dedicate a whole corner to floor-to-ceiling bookshelves?

As if bringing her fantasy to life, there was a comfy-looking armchair and an old floor lamp already set up. The items weren't quite to her taste – she had in mind a classic wingback-style chair rather than one from the nineteen sixties with curved wooden arms – but it gave her some great inspiration.

In the other corner of this main shed, there was a collection of old record players, gramophones and large and small valve radios in gorgeous restored timber cases. *How cool would one of those be?*

Emily walked to the back of the shed and through a small covered walkway into another space even larger than the previous one. She looked around, taking it all in. Again the room was divided into four sections.

To the left was an array of dining furniture, and rows of chairs hanging on the wall right to the ceiling. Tables were stacked three high and timber sideboards were lined up with space to walk between them.

'How great is this shop?' Jake said, appearing beside her. 'I love how organised everything is.'

'I was just having that very same thought,' Emily replied, smiling at him.

She looked to her right. The corner contained living-room furniture. Jacobean lounge suites with polished timber arms and cane sides were again carefully arranged next to more modern leather styles.

A couple of tub-style chairs caught Emily's eye, but they seemed all to go with three-seater couches. And there was no way she could fit that many pieces in the room.

She slowly scanned past them to a selection of side and coffee tables and a collection of single chairs. Suddenly she gasped and her mouth fell open as she spotted a wingback chair upholstered with a large floral print in monotone dark green – that could almost pass as black – on cream. She'd had in her mind a stripe or check design, but this was even better. She rushed over to it. *Please be perfect, please be perfect.*

And it is, she thought as she ran her eyes all over it. This was the chair for her – and her office.

'Wow, what a beauty,' Jake said. Emily was slightly startled. She'd become so focussed on the chair she'd almost forgotten she wasn't alone.

'Hmm,' she replied, as she stared at the chair and its price tag, hardly able to believe the bargain price of five hundred dollars. The new ones she and Barbara had seen the other day in Port Lincoln started at a thousand – and that was with the cheapest, plainest fabric. She didn't know much about fabric quality, but this sure looked expensive. And totally gorgeous!

'And a bargain,' Jake said, peering over her shoulder.

'It's great, isn't it?'

'I can attest to its comfort. It was one of mine.'

Emily turned at hearing the shopkeeper's voice.

'I've spent many an hour curled up reading in it,' the lady added. 'I had to downsize to go into business, so a few pieces had to go. The price you pay and all that,' she said cheerfully with a little flourish of her hand.

'Oh, right, fair enough,' Emily said, feeling a little awkward. What else was there to say?

'Did you see the back of the tag? There are matching curtains if you're interested. If not, I'll knock a hundred dollars off the price.'

'Oh, I wish I'd measured the window,' Emily said.

'If you've got an older house, they fit the standard single-sized double-hung window – if that's any help,' the woman offered.

'That's exactly what sort of window you have,' Jake said as Emily thought the same thing. *This is totally meant to be.* She was so excited, she felt like shouting from the rooftops.

'What have we found, kids?' David asked jovially, wandering up with Barbara.

'Oh, it's perfect!' Barbara cried.

'And there are matching curtains that should fit my window,' Emily said.

'Well, quick, snap it up before I do,' Barbara said.

'Don't you dare,' she said to Barbara. 'I'll take the chair and the curtains, thanks,' she said to the shopkeeper.

'Oh, I'm so pleased it's going to go to a nice home,' the woman said, smiling warmly.

Emily smiled back.

'Hey, this would be perfect for your cuppa and a book; just the right size and height I reckon,' Barbara said, holding up a small round occasional table in a medium-coloured polished timber. 'Go on, sit. Make sure it's comfy,' she urged, putting it down beside the chair.

Emily settled into the chair with a big grin. She reached over the side and pretended to pick up something from the table. Yes, definitely just the right height. It was big enough for a mug and book, and maybe even a small vase of flowers. 'It's perfect.'

'Lucky we brought the ute,' David said.

'I'll get the curtains out for you to see. They're in great nick, but I'll let you be the judge.'

'Jake, let's take the chair out the front,' David said.

'Thanks very much, you guys,' Emily said, and began making her way over to the back left of the shop, where she could see modern laminex office desks. Hopefully there were some pieces with character hidden behind.

'Well, this is clearly meant to be,' Barbara said, joining her. 'I bet you'll find the perfect desk here too.'

Emily stopped at a stacked pair of pedestal-style desks next to another stacked pair of simple desks with turned legs and a single drawer. She looked from one style to the other, unable to decide which she preferred.

'These are nice,' Barbara said.

'Which sort?'

'Both,' Barbara said with a laugh.

'That's the problem I'm having.'

'What problem are you having?' Jake asked, appearing beside them and draping an arm around Emily.

'I can't decide which style I prefer. I'd like a few drawers to put stuff in, but I also like the turned legs and slightly more dainty look of these,' she said, pointing.

'Take one of each,' he said.

She looked at him curiously. 'I don't have the space. Anyway, you can't have two desks in a room; that would look silly.'

'No, not both for your office. One for your office and the other for a reception desk for the gallery.'

'Isn't it a bit soon to be looking at gallery furniture?'

'I don't think so. That's the thing about buying second-hand. It's not like ordering new from a catalogue. You might not find the right thing when you want it.'

'He's got a point,' Barbara said, nodding thoughtfully.

Emily could see it too, but the conservative voice inside her was already saying it was pretty decadent to buy a chair *and* two desks. But the longer she stood there looking at the desks, the more she liked both styles equally. And, Jake was right, she might never see anything in this condition again.

She leaned closer to where white price tags dangled from handles, almost holding her breath.

'How much?' Barbara asked.

'Seven hundred and fifty each.'

'Bargain,' Jake and Barbara said at once.

Maybe, but that would mean she was spending two thousand, not including the small side table. She'd never spent so much in one hit in her life. Well, except when buying her car, but that didn't count.

'Hey, Dave, can you give me a hand to take this one down so Em can get a better look?' Jake said over his shoulder to David who had wandered up to join the small group.

'No worries.'

Soon the two piles were split and there were four desks sitting on the floor. Emily's mind began to boggle. Before she was struggling between the two styles, but now she liked all four desks.

'Oh, God,' she said, putting her hands to her head. 'They're all nice.'

'Well, if it helps, these two are nine fifty each,' David said with a shrug.

Hmm. Ordinarily Emily would have gone with the cheaper, but things were different now she had some money. She'd never been one to splurge, but perhaps she deserved a lift in standards. And, after all, an art gallery needed to make a good impression.

Jake was inspecting each piece with a critical eye and running his hands over them. Emily stood nibbling her lip whilst trying to decide.

'Aren't they great?' the shop woman said, appearing again.

'Yes, but I can't decide between them,' Emily said. 'I've got the decision down to one pedestal and one with turned legs, but that's as far as I've got,' she added with a laugh.

'Would a cuppa help with the thought process?' The woman asked kindly.

'Do you run a café here as well?' Barbara asked, looking around.

'No, but I've got a machine hiding out the back. I'm going to make myself a latte, but I can do a cappuccino, flat white, or short black. Or hot chocolate.'

'A latte would be great, thanks,' David said.

'A hot chocolate would be lovely,' Jake said.

'Ooh, yes, hot chocolate would be fabulous,' Barbara said.

'And for me, too. Thank you so much. Maybe a sugar hit will help me make this decision,' Emily said.

'You know, you can always sleep on it for a few days,' the woman offered. 'If someone else is desperate for one, I could call you.'

'Wow, that's very generous, but I think I really should make a decision today.'

'Well, at least wait until after you've had a cuppa. It always helps me,' the lady said, beaming, and left.

'Isn't she nice?' Emily whispered.

'Yes, lovely,' Barbara agreed.

'I wish more people in the city understood the value of good service,' Jake said from almost out of view beside a desk. 'Sorry, but I think you're definitely better off with the two more expensive desks. There is a bit of damage at the back of that one,' he said, pointing to the cheaper of the pedestal desks. 'Remember, in a gallery people will be walking up to what is the back of it if you're sitting behind it,' he added.

'Good point,' Emily said thoughtfully.

'And the legs of that one are a bit sturdier and the proportions seem better all round,' he said. 'Ultimately it's your choice, though.'

'Okay, done. I'll take both the more expensive ones,' Emily said, her mind suddenly clearing. *What's a few hundred dollars in the scheme of things?*

'And they are tax deductible,' Jake added.

'Your drinks are ready,' the lady called from the doorway a few moments later.

They all made their way back through into the other shed and over to the counter, where five steaming mugs sat next to a sugar bowl, some teaspoons on a plate, and a plate of chocolate Tim Tam biscuits. Below the counter, five chairs were arranged in a semicircle.

'Please, help yourselves,' the woman said, picking up a mug in one hand and Tim Tam in the other and then sitting down. 'I'll knock something off the price if you buy the chair and the two desks,' she added cheerfully as she dunked a corner of the biscuit into her coffee.

'I think I'll also take four of the timber mantelpieces,' Emily said. 'What do you say, Jake?'

'Sounds like a good idea to me.'

'I could do a good deal on restoration, too, if you'd like.'

'What do you think, Jake?'

'We've got plenty of time until we need them. Why don't we take them now and then bring them back for restoration later if we decide not to do it ourselves?' he asked.

'Fine with me. Whatever you decide. Are you renovating a house?'

'Building one, actually. I'm hoping to open an art gallery, but it's very early days. We're still in the planning phase,' Emily said. 'And I've never run a business before,' she admitted.

'Ah, nothing to it. I think a gallery is just what the district needs. You'll do great. And I'd love to come to the opening if you have one. I'm Maureen, by the way,' she added, extending her hand. Emily introduced herself and then the others.

Chapter Fifteen

It seemed as if they'd been sitting there for only minutes chatting with Maureen, but when Emily noticed long shadows crossing in front of the open shed door, she was surprised to find it was half past five.

'We'd better pack everything up and get going so you can close up,' she said, standing, putting her mug on the counter, and getting out her wallet.

'Oh, don't worry about keeping me,' Maureen said, getting up to attend to her. 'All part of the job. And I've enjoyed the company.'

'It's been lovely,' Emily said, handing over her card. 'I hope you don't mind if I borrow your idea about serving coffee to customers,' she said while waiting for the transaction to go through. She could imagine visitors browsing her gallery with cup in hand, or sitting and looking at art from strategically placed bench seats. Perhaps she could serve scones and jam and cream, too, so people could sample her jam.

'Not at all. And feel free to pick my brains about anything. We small business owners have to stick together,'

Maureen said, smiling as she handed back Emily's card. 'I'll just do up a receipt.'

'We'll start bringing everything out and loading the ute, right Dave?' Jake said.

'Absolutely,' David said.

'I'll get the little table,' Barbara said, setting off after the two men.

It was almost six by the time the four fireplace surrounds, one armchair, and two desks were loaded and securely tied down. Maureen had lent them a couple of old woollen blankets for extra padding, which they promised to return in a few days. The small round side table was stowed between Barbara and Emily in the back seat and they set off waving to Maureen, who was out the front of the shed bringing things in. They had offered to stay and help, but she'd insisted that she was fine and that as she had a good system down pat it was easier to do it on her own.

They drove away chatting excitedly about meeting someone new and how lovely Maureen had been. She and her husband, who was in mining and spent two weeks at home and two weeks away, were ring-ins – people from outside the district.

Barbara said with a laugh that it was lucky they had to return the blankets, because she'd been so caught up with Emily furnishing her office that she hadn't had a good look around for herself.

'That was probably the plan all along,' Jake said with a laugh.

'Yeah, you return the blankets, buy something else, take the blankets again, have to go back again et cetera,' David said, chuckling. 'Very clever.'

'Can you believe she gave me twenty-five percent off everything?' Emily said.

'Really? That's very generous,' Barbara said. David and Jake murmured their agreement.

Despite the saving, Emily still felt a little queasy at how much she'd spent. Oh well, too late now, as Gran would say.

'Golly shopping is exhausting,' Emily said, thinking aloud. But it was a satisfied exhaustion, she thought. Whoever said shopping was therapy was so right.

'Imagine doing it all day every day,' Barbara said.

'Don't you go getting any ideas, wife of mine,' David warned, raising his eyebrows and locking eyes with Barbara in the rear-vision mirror.

'I think you're pretty safe, darling,' she said, reaching forward and touching his shoulder.

They lapsed into silence, a sure sign they were all tired.

'Who's for tea at the Wattle Creek pub then,' David said a few minutes later. He was approaching the intersection where the dirt road to the right was a shortcut through to Emily's. If they stayed on the bitumen they'd end up in Wattle Creek.

There was a chorus of yeses and David sped the vehicle back up again.

'Oh, I wouldn't mind checking the mail,' Emily said. She hadn't checked it for a couple of days; she usually did it when she went for groceries, but they'd got them in Hope Springs the other day.

She thought again of how much she'd spent today. God, she was lucky to be in the financial position she was. Not so long ago she was freaking out about relatively small expenses such as groceries and eating out. She absolutely did not want to live like that again. And thanks to John and his parents, she probably wouldn't have to. But she would have to keep an eye on her budget.

Though, the diamonds... a little voice in her head reminded her. *No way*, she countered. She'd sooner move back in with her parents than reveal their existence.

Gran had kept them secret through all the financial ups and downs of her and Grandpa's lives, so Emily sure as hell wasn't going to fail her by parting with them. Not that she had any idea how one would go about putting rough diamonds up for sale, or even as collateral for that matter.

She could imagine doing so, only to have the Australian Federal Police or FBI turning up and arresting her for having blood diamonds. Was that only in Africa, or India as well? The little research she'd done online suggested that the diamond industry in Golconda was all but over.

In her overactive imagination she conjured up the relatives of the Indian prince. She imagined them turning up, declaring that the diamonds belonged to them and demanding their return. Then the media would get a sniff and life as she knew it would be over.

Emily almost laughed out loud as she pictured Enid putting up a fight with the Indian contingent and claiming that she was the rightful owner. No doubt they'd take off in fright.

Why had the Indian prince given Granny Rose the diamonds, anyway? There was no evidence of romantic feelings in his letter, but Emily couldn't help wondering what had captured his heart enough to send her such a gift – for her wedding to another man. God, she hated not knowing. But had to accept that she never would. The story had died with Gran.

Damn it! Of all the hours she'd spent with her over the years and all the anecdotes she'd listened to, why couldn't Gran have shared the most interesting one?

Emily had heard all about her school days, how she'd met Grandpa, how her wealthy parents hadn't approved and had all but cut her off after her marriage. She'd even talked about how they'd sent her off on a world trip with her uncle, who was some sort of diplomat. But she'd never once mentioned the prince. He *had* to have existed for the diamonds to exist – and they did exist because she had them in the button jar, and she had the letter. And there was no way her dear old gran, the most honest person she'd ever known, was an international diamond thief.

So why hadn't she ever told her?

Why didn't you tell her you were so unhappy with John? Emily asked herself. *But that was a totally different thing,* she countered, and folded her arms tight across her chest with a harrumph.

'Are you okay?' Barbara asked.

'Yeah, just thinking,' Emily replied.

'Your office is going to look fantastic,' Barbara said.

'I'm looking forward to getting it all set up. Not sure how much use it'll get, though,' she added with a laugh.

Moments later they were pulling up outside the Wattle Creek Hotel.

'I'll park out the front, so we can keep an eye on the load,' David said, putting on the handbrake and turning off the vehicle.

'Thanks, that'd be good,' Emily said. 'Now, don't let me forget to check the mail on our way past later.'

'Okay,' Jake, David and Barbara chorused.

They went inside and ordered their meals at the counter.

'So, tell me more about project cottage rebuild,' David said, when they were settled at a table.

Jake explained that as well as being a gallery space for Emily, the new, larger version of the cottage would be an advertisement for his business. 'I'm hoping it'll be a win–win situation.'

'So, if you're making it so much bigger, you're going to need more stone, right?'

'Probably double what we have.'

'Any idea where you're going to get it?'

'I haven't got that far yet. I'm hoping one of the owners of the land with piles dotted about will let me have it for a good price.'

'You shouldn't have to pay for it.'

'Maybe *you* wouldn't, but I'm an out-of-towner remember?'

'Ah, leave it to me. I know plenty of blokes who would love nothing more than to offload a pile of rock.'

'Thanks. That would be brilliant.'

'Hey, here's an idea. What if I help you clean your rocks and whatever else I can do while things are quiet for me? And then you do some hours on the tractor for me when the time comes?'

'Oh. Now there's a good idea. Are you sure?'

'Of course. I wouldn't suggest it if I wasn't.'

'You should be able to get away a bit when other trades are hard at work, right? Hopefully that will fit in with the break in the season.'

'It's a deal,' Jake said, holding out his hand for them to shake on the arrangement.

The dining room was empty and their meals came quickly. With no home games that afternoon, those who had travelled for sport were still on their way back. Thankfully they'd be out of the pub and on their way before the post-match crowds turned up.

They were a rowdy mob whether they won or lost; they got drunk and boisterous celebrating or commiserating. Emily quietly suspected that was why Saturday was schnitzel night at the pub – all those crumbs, chips and fat to soak up the alcohol. Not that she had any objection. She loved a beef schnitzel with mushroom sauce. And this evening's was no exception.

'God, that was good,' Jake said, rubbing his stomach appreciatively as they left the hotel. 'There's nothing like country pub fare,' he added.

Barbara, David, and Emily agreed.

'Right, to the post office we go,' David said, putting the ute in gear.

'Thanks,' Emily said.

★

David idled at the curb while Emily, with her two keys at the ready – one for John's box and one for the box she'd rented in her own name after leaving him – got out and bounded up the steps to the wall of numbered black doors. Barbara followed more slowly.

Emily emptied both boxes and flicked through the few business-sized envelopes as she made her way back to the ute. While they waited for Barbara, she chose the only two letters that didn't appear to be from a local business or bank, and that didn't appear to contain advertising material. The first was addressed to John.

She carefully slid her nail under the seal, opened it, and drew out its contents – a cheque. Her heart raced a little and she had to read the numbers twice: fifty-seven thousand dollars. It was the insurance payment for the totalled ute – and to go into the estate's coffers. She wondered briefly if anyone would object to her replacing the ute before probate was granted. The farm really did need one, didn't it? She stuffed it back in its envelope.

The second envelope was addressed to her. In the top left corner was a return address, but no company name or logo. She frowned a little as she prised it open and then carefully extracted the folded contents. Her eyes bugged as she realised it was John's life insurance payout. She stared at the numbers, trying to focus on more zeros than she'd ever seen in her life.

She suddenly felt ashamed of all the gleefulness she'd felt lately at the prospect of the money turning up, and of the plans she'd started making for it when it did. There was nothing to celebrate about this moment. She'd been expecting a cheque – not as large as five hundred thousand dollars – but she hadn't expected to feel like this when it arrived. There was no sense of relief at her financial security now being assured. This was blood money. Maybe she should have been excited, but she just felt sad. And a little sick.

'Are you okay?' David asked, turning in his seat to look at her.

Emily nodded. Her chest felt too heavy to speak, but after two carefully taken breaths, she managed to. 'They're cheques. John's life insurance money and the payout from the ute.'

'That's good,' Jake said. 'A bit more certainty.'

Barbara got back in the vehicle beside her. 'God, you look like you've seen a ghost,' she said, looking at Emily.

The second cheque was still in her hands in her lap. She held it out to Barbara.

'Oh.'

'I feel terrible,' Emily whispered, as tears threatened. Her heart thudded slowly and painfully.

'That's quite understandable. It's a strange situation,' Barbara said. 'But, remember,' she added with a whisper, putting her hand over Emily's, 'you deserve this. Be thankful, use it wisely, but do not feel guilty.'

Emily nodded.

'Okay, let's go. It's been a big day,' David said, clearly at a loss for anything else to say. He started the vehicle.

Emily wished she could have caught Jake's eye in the rear-vision mirror, wished they could have shared a reassuring look. She felt a million miles away sitting in the back, and desperately lonely, despite having her best friend right beside her squeezing her hand.

An hour later they stood in Emily's office surveying the newly added pieces of furniture and curtains. They had left the second desk and mantelpieces out in the enclosed verandah so as not to clutter the room.

'It's perfect!' Barbara declared, clapping her hands.

'Doesn't look nearly so pink now,' David said dryly.

'Well done,' Jake said, wrapping his arms around Emily.

'Thanks so much for all your help,' she said, looking around at everyone, forcing a smile. The room was just how she had imagined. But she couldn't muster much enthusiasm. The cheques had reminded her of the reason she was back here – John's death – and she wanted to be left alone for a while with her sadness.

'All you need now are some tall bookshelves wrapping around the corner to complete your reading nook,' Jake said.

'And a floor lamp to read by,' Barbara chimed in.

'Don't forget you'll also need a chair for your desk. Can't have you without the right ergonomics,' David added.

They all seemed to be making an effort to buoy her. She had to buck up. Barbara was right; no amount of moping would change the past. The thing was to look forward, and make a new future with Jake.

Chapter Sixteen

The day Emily had been concerned about finally arrived. The next morning Jake could barely muster the energy to turn over, let alone get out of bed.

'I don't know what's wrong with me. I thought I was doing well.'

She leaned over to reassure him. 'It's okay. You're meant to be resting. It's why you're here, remember?' She was happy to take care of him, but privately she was worried about how ill he looked; sweaty, shaky, his skin almost grey.

'I'm sure I'll be fine after some more rest, but you're right. I think I must have overdone things working on the shed. I feel terrible.'

'Do you feel like eating? I was planning bacon and eggs – I can bring it in. You need to keep your strength up.'

'That would be lovely,' he said, smiling wanly.

'Sounds like it's going to be a perfect day for staying in bed,' Emily added, as a shower of rain began pounding on the iron roof overhead.

★

Jake was asleep when she returned with a tray of toast, bacon and eggs, some cutlery, a mug of tea, a glass of water, and his vitamins. She placed it down and went to get the second tray whilst debating whether to let Jake sleep or wake him. Thankfully when she returned he was sitting up rubbing his eyes.

'How are you feeling?'

'A little better. Hungry, actually.'

'That's good.'

They sat up in bed side by side with their trays. Grace was nearby, looking like she was expecting to be tossed a morsel.

'You've already had some bacon, you greedy thing,' Emily warned her. They never fed her from the table, but they rarely ate in bed, so she couldn't be blamed for begging.

Outside, the weather turned into a raging storm. Emily opened the curtains so they could watch the dark sky being lit up by bolts of lightning that seemed just metres from the house.

Later that morning they were still in bed, Emily reading and Jake dozing, when there was a knock on the door.

'Hey, Em, Jake, are you there? It's David.'

Emily got up and opened the door with her robe on.

'Oh, sorry. I didn't realise you were…'

'It's okay,' she said. 'We've just been having a lie-in. Jake's not feeling so good.'

'I wondered if he'd been overdoing it.'

'So what brings you out on such a day?'

'I've come to bring the sheep in and give them a good look over. It's clear up our way. It looked a bit dark down here, but I had no idea it was this bad. Though, I think it's almost gone through.'

'Do you want a cuppa while it clears?'

'No, I won't bother you. I just wondered if Grace would like to come and play real farm dog. Or at least spend some time with her mum.'

'She'd love it. Did I tell you about the day Jake and I had a barbeque up on the rise? Grace went off and rounded up all the sheep while we weren't looking. She was ever so pleased with herself, weren't you, girl?' Emily looked down at the dog, who was waving her tail back and forth.

'Sounds like she already knows what she's doing – she's certainly got the genes. Sasha is getting close to retirement. Would you mind if I used Grace to help her a bit?'

'No problem. Actually, I have wondered whether she should be doing more of what she's bred for. She was so excited to be amongst sheep that day.'

'After finishing with your sheep, I could take her for a few days and do some work with mine, if you like? Really put her to the test. And then maybe she might be up for helping out with shearing. Sasha is getting a little old for paddock work, and she struggles to get up onto the sheep's backs these days, poor thing. If Grace comes home with me I can return her clean – she'll get pretty muddy out there today,' he warned. 'And I promise I'll take very good care of her.'

'Okay. All fine with me. I'm sure she'll love being a proper farm dog rather than a house layabout.'

'Brilliant. Say hi to Jake. I won't bother you on my way out.'

'I will. You have fun, Gracie. I'll miss you,' she said, ruffling the dog's ears. 'And be careful.'

'Don't worry, I know how much she means to you.'

'What was that all about?' Jake asked sleepily, hoisting himself up on his elbow.

'David's come down to look over the sheep and thought Grace might enjoy some time out with her mum,' she said, hanging up her robe and climbing back into bed. The sight of Jake's bare chest made her tummy flutter.

'I wouldn't have minded going out with him. I'd like to see what goes on with sheep.'

'I'm sure there will be plenty of opportunities. But not today. You're staying right here with me.'

'All right. You're the boss,' he said wearily, and snuggled back down.

Emily sighed at seeing his chest being covered up and picked up her book again. It was the first day they hadn't made love since he'd been there. But the day wasn't over yet... She forced her attention to rereading the line of her book for the third time.

She was just drifting off when she felt Jake moving beside her. Her heart leapt with anticipation as he sidled up to her and began nuzzling her neck.

'How interesting is that book?' he whispered after running his tongue around her lobe in the way they had discovered drove her crazy. An exhilarating shudder ran the full length of her body.

'Not *that* interesting,' she said with a seductive smile as she snapped the book shut and tossed it on the floor.

That afternoon Jake insisted he felt up to cooking an early dinner, since they hadn't bothered with lunch. They decided on lamb shanks for a quicker version of Sunday roast, and opened a bottle of red wine while it cooked.

'I feel so much better,' Jake announced over dinner.

'That's good. You look better. Are you still planning to go to Whyalla tomorrow?'

He'd mentioned an eleven-thirty a.m. meeting for the Civic Centre project. Emily had offered to share the driving – she didn't want him driving all that way and back alone, given he wasn't one hundred percent well. She also had her own reasons; the office still needed a chair and a lamp. It would be good to go and do some browsing.

'I'd better show up or else they'll think I've abandoned them.'

The problem was that Emily also wanted to bank the insurance cheques as soon as possible. She felt uneasy about having cheques for such large amounts hanging about in her handbag. Unfortunately, Whyalla didn't have a branch of her bank. She also needed to do some washing.

'I can't really go if I'm to get the cheques banked,' she said.

'Are you sure? I would actually feel better with a co-pilot, especially after today,' he said. 'And I really should be at that meeting. If you got to the bank right at nine-thirty when they open, you'd be back here by ten – leaving just enough time for me make it to my meeting.'

'That might be cutting it a bit fine,' Emily said. The drive to Whyalla would take ninety minutes, and she hated rushing of any sort, especially when Jake's professional standing relied on her getting back on time. 'And, anyway,

I need to do two loads of washing while the weather's fine. They're saying tomorrow is the only dry day for maybe the next week.'

'Hmm,' Jake said thoughtfully.

They were both silent for a few moments.

'Right,' Jake finally said. 'I think I have a solution. You give me the account details and I'll pop into town and bank the cheques. You can do the washing while I'm away, and then I'll pick you up. How would that work?'

'Perfect,' she said, beaming at him.

'It's probably high time I was seen in town. People will be starting to think I don't exist,' he added with a chuckle.

'We were in the pub the other night, remember? The whole town will know all about you by now. And what they won't know they'll make up. Are you sure you're ready to start mixing with the wolves?'

'What are you calling me, a chicken?'

'Not at all, but don't say you weren't warned,' Emily said, looking at him with a knowing expression.

'Don't worry. I've lived in a small town before, remember?'

They took the bottle of wine and went and sat on the concrete out under the verandah in the warm evening to watch the last of the lightning.

*

'So, how was the village?' Emily asked when they turned onto the bitumen main road the next day. She'd stayed silent until now, to let Jake concentrate on navigating the dirt road that was still wet and slippery from the rain.

'Good. Pity I was in such a hurry, though.'

'Really?'

'You're right about everyone knowing who I am – well, that I'm your *friend*. Lots of people wanted to stop and chat. I caught up with Nathan and he very briefly introduced me to Doris from Mitre 10. She seemed a good old stick, though I swear she was flirting with me. And she's probably old enough to be my mother!'

'I don't mind, as long as she gets us a good deal on our hardware.'

'Nathan apologised for not having had us over yet. He said that Sarah's doing training in Adelaide for the next couple of weeks and he's heading over to join her for the weekends. He asked me to tell you.'

'So you didn't get interrogated?'

'No. Everyone was very friendly. I can understand your concerns – you've lived here for ages and been on the wrong end of gossip. But everyone I came across was lovely. And I don't think you need to worry about them thinking you've moved on too quickly.'

'Oh? Why do you say that?'

'Two old ladies came up to me and one of them said they hoped I was sticking around because you deserved some happiness after, quote, "what that brute of a husband put you through," end of quote.'

'Oh. Wow. That's nice of them.'

'So maybe you've been judging the locals a little harshly?'

'Hmm. Maybe.' She still remembered how it had felt to have people whispering about her.

'It's understandable. You went through a lot. Perhaps you just heard what you were expecting to hear.'

'I didn't imagine some of the things that were said to me, Jake.'

'No, but perhaps you *interpreted* what was said differ-ently to what was intended. That's easily done when your nerves are frayed.'

'I didn't imagine Steve and Grant snubbing me in Mitre 10 – they apologised for it the other day,' she said a little huffily, feeling the need to defend herself.

'Well, you can let it go now. It's in the past. David said you've got a lot of friends around here, Em, so try to focus on that. It'll sure help when you're trying to get a business up and running.'

Emily felt a little stung, but she had too much respect for Jake to argue. He was certainly right about one thing. She'd seen businesses rise and fall depending on how people viewed the owners. Maybe she had been a bit over-sensitive. She'd been through a tough time. But that was behind her now. *Onwards and upwards.* She'd stop being so standoffish and get back to being how she'd been before leaving John.

She used to love escaping the farm and heading into town. Even with just a few things on her list her trips had the capacity to stretch into hours when people stopped her to chat.

It was as if most people on the street didn't have to do anything by a certain time. And, back then she hadn't either. The town seemed to run at its own pace – sort of like what some people on holidays called 'island time'. It was one of the things she'd always loved about Wattle Creek. That, and everyone waving and being friendly, even the policeman.

By retreating from society and then keeping to herself, she could see that in a way she'd as good as snubbed the whole town, just like Steve and Grant had done to her. Yes, she had been hurting, and embarrassed about people judging her – thanks to some sound conditioning by Enid – but she was free now. And happy. So blissfully happy with the man beside her. She looked across at him and smiled.

He smiled back. 'What's that look for?'

'Just because I love you. And because you're so wise.'

'Right,' he said a little quizzically. 'And I love you too.' He patted her leg. 'I feel a little bad that I was in such a rush. Those two old dears in the bank clearly wanted to chat, but I had to be a little rude to get back home on time.'

'What happened?'

'They were asking where I was from, how long I was staying and what I did in Melbourne. I'm trying to leave the building, shifting on my feet like I'm desperate for the loo or something, and they just kept firing questions at me.'

'So how did you escape?'

'I said I'd love to stay and chat but was in rather a hurry, and excused myself. I *might* have even agreed to go and have afternoon tea with them sometime. And to bring you.' He winced.

Oh. 'Who were they?'

'I have no idea,' Jake said with a laugh. 'One was on a walking frame and one had two walking sticks. They said they lived right across the road.'

'That would be the old Carrington sisters. John used to call them the smiling assassins. They're sweeties, but also the biggest gossips in town, even though they look like butter wouldn't melt in their mouths. But they'll be useful for getting the word out when the gallery is about to open. And they love nothing more than an outing. I can see we're going to have to have a big launch and invite the whole district.'

'Anyway, I hadn't been able to park right out front so I was a couple of cars down. So there I was, striding down the street with two old ladies chasing me. And, boy, you should have seen that frame and those walking sticks move!' Jake said with a laugh. 'I practically leapt into the car and locked the doors. I half expected the one with the walking sticks to jump into the passenger's side, or at least start banging on the window. It was a close call, I can tell you,' he added, looking at Emily with wide eyes and a cheeky glint.

'Thank God you made it out in one piece!'

They chuckled for a few moments.

'So, I didn't expect to have to queue up in the bank. Don't they have the quick cheque-deposit system in South Australia?' Jake suddenly said. 'I couldn't find it anywhere.'

Emily laughed. 'Well, they do. In theory. It's hidden behind the pot plant in the corner.'

'Oh?' Jake said.

'Now, how would the gossip train be helped if people didn't have to go up to the counter? All sorts of dots are connected through the most idle, seemingly benign, chatter. For instance,' Emily continued, 'it is now officially confirmed that the handsome guy seen in town on Saturday night with Emily, Barbara, and David is in fact living with Emily Oliphant, because: one, he was driving her car and two, he was doing her banking. And because you printed your name on the deposit slip, there's probably a whole gang of people around town typing your name into Google as we speak. Not to mention analysing your signature for indications of character flaws.'

'Haha, too funny,' Jake said.

'Believe me, the CIA is not a patch on Wattle Creek residents when they put their minds to it,' Emily said.

Chapter Seventeen

An hour and a quarter later the highway divided into two lanes each way to signal the outskirts of the city of Whyalla. They continued through to the city centre, Emily checking her watch repeatedly, despite there being ten minutes to spare. Jake found a park behind the Civic Centre and they both got out and stretched their legs. Jake got his briefcase out of the boot, handed Emily the keys, pecked her on the cheek, and then bolted off for his meeting.

'Good luck,' she called to his back before checking her watch again. Seeing that he would make it, she relaxed properly for the first time since he'd left for the bank that morning.

As Jake disappeared, she realised she was standing in front of his project. True to what she knew of his work, there was a great melding of old and new going on. The only hints of a new build were the cathedral-style windows high up in the new section, and the brighter, cleaner mortar amongst the stonework. Everything this end of Whyalla tended to have a bit of a red tinge thanks to dust from the nearby steelworks.

Standing before something that she knew to be Jake's work, Emily felt a surge of pride so strong she clasped her hands to her chest. She was a little overwhelmed at the thought that with all the awards and huge projects he'd excelled at, he'd chosen to stay in little old Wattle Creek and build something as modest as her cottage.

When someone walked across the car park, called, 'Hi,' and got into their car, Emily realised how silly she must look standing there gazing about. People were probably sitting inside their offices wondering what the hell she was doing.

She walked out onto the street and looked around. She didn't know this older part of the city at all. Her previous trips to Whyalla were always centred around the large shopping centre to the west. There the streets were mainly lined with plain brick semidetached houses dating back to the 1950s and 1960s. But here the buildings seemed to have more character. The two-storey hotel on the corner, especially, was quite lovely.

But she couldn't stand here all day admiring the view and looking lost; there was shopping to do. She'd printed a map she'd found online, but was now struggling to see which way she had to go to find the lighting shop. She turned it around in her hands, searching for a landmark, but the harder she looked and the more she concentrated, the more disoriented she got. Finally she decided there looked to be more going on to her left. She'd wander in that direction and see what she found. She could have driven over to the shopping mall on the other side of town, but she was afraid she might not find the Civic Centre again. Anyway, she told herself, it might be nice to explore a different part of the city.

Just a few hundred metres down the street, Emily came to a small cluster of shops. She almost let out a whoop of joy at the sight of a window jam packed with lights in all different sizes, styles and colours. There was also a variety of desk lamps and floor lamps on display. Everything seemed so modern, though, and she was after something more classic in design. She took a deep breath, mentally crossed her fingers, and pushed the heavy glass door open.

A woman of about Emily's age greeted her from behind a large counter. 'Is there something specific I can help you with, or are you just browsing?' she asked in a friendly tone.

'Bit of both, actually,' Emily said with a light laugh. 'I'm looking for a floor lamp, but a bit more old world in style than what you have in the window. I'm not sure exactly what I want, just that I don't want anything in chrome,' she added apologetically.

'Well, that's a good start. Come with me. I have a feeling you might find just what you're looking for out the back,' the lady said, getting up. As she stood, Emily noticed the name Karen on her name tag.

Emily followed her down a short hall that opened into a room that was possibly even larger than where they'd come from. Emily's mouth dropped open slightly as she took in the display of older style desk lamps and floor lamps. Above their heads, dozens of magnificent chandeliers, pendants, and glass light shades hung from the ceiling.

'Wow,' she said, looking around her.

'Thanks,' Karen said jovially, 'I'll take that as a compliment. I love the older styles.'

'I'm struggling to take it all in, to be honest,' Emily said, frowning.

'You said you wanted a floor lamp,' Karen said. 'Do you want to create mood lighting in a corner or have it over an armchair to read by?'

'Both,' Emily said. 'I'm putting a reading corner in my study.'

'Sounds lovely,' Karen said, as she made her way over to the far left corner where there were tall lamps lined up.

As Emily followed her, she began to see the method to the layout, which at first glance had just looked like everything in together. But now she could see banker-style desk lamps and an assortment of small, delicate lamps displayed on white melamine cubes of different heights in another corner.

She turned her attention first to the floor lamps. Some were just tall, straight sticks with shades and without, and some had hooks that the shades hung from. On a shelf, rows of glass shades were arranged by colour. There was also a selection of ruched and plain shades in all sorts of fabrics. They were all gorgeous; how was she going to choose?

'Would you like me to leave you alone to have a good look, or would you like some help?' Karen asked.

'Oh, I would definitely like some help please,' Emily said.

Karen beamed. 'Great,' she said, putting her hands together. 'What colours do you have in your furniture and paintwork? That's usually a good place to start. It's often easier to begin by eliminating anything you don't like at all, and any colours that won't work,' she explained.

'I've got some photos on my phone,' Emily said, fossicking in her handbag. She brought up the first of the photos she'd taken and leaned towards Karen to show her.

'Oh, it's gorgeous,' Karen said. 'That chair is divine. And is that carpet original? It looks like nineteen fifties or roundabouts.'

'I think so.'

'I love it.'

'Thanks.'

'Now, I'm sure I have the perfect lamp here. Just give me a sec to think it through,' Karen said, putting a finger to her lip and tapping thoughtfully. After a few moments she silently grasped the base of a tall lamp and set it in an empty space.

'I think you'd be better with this style. That one, as lovely as it is,' she said, pointing to another, 'won't be high enough. And the gooseneck style might take up too much space. I'm guessing you don't have a huge area to work with.'

'It is a decent-sized room,' Emily said, 'but as you can see, it's also got a bed and desk and chair in it. And, I'm hoping to put high bookshelves in when I find some I like.'

'The bed is just across from your reading corner, isn't it?'

'Yes.'

'Well, I think this would be perfect,' Karen declared with her hand around the slender brass stem. 'The base comes in a few different colours and finishes. This is solid brass, but it's lacquered over so you'll never need to polish it,' she added.

That had been a question on the tip of Emily's tongue. She ran her hand up the base, which had some engraved swirling detail.

'They're really well made. The base is nice and heavy so you won't have a problem with it toppling over, no matter what shade you put on,' Karen explained. 'It also comes in a simple fluted design, which I can show you in the catalogue. But I personally like this one for a more feminine room. The fluted one is a bit heavier set and tends to be more masculine looking.'

'Okay. I like it,' Emily said. 'What sort of shade would you suggest?'

'Can I take another look at your colours again?' Karen asked.

Emily found the photos again and handed the phone over. While Karen studied them, Emily took in the range on the shelves above them.

'I think you'd be best off with a glass shade; they give a gorgeous ambient glow as well as the targeted light for reading.'

'Okay,' Emily said, nodding.

'You'd think the obvious choice is pink, which it would be if you want the lamp to blend in. But if you want it to be a bit of a feature, I'd be inclined to go with green. It would tie in very nicely with the carpet and the chair. Of course, it's entirely up to you.'

'I'm not sure,' Emily said, frowning. 'I did have my mind set on pink. But that might just be because it seems the obvious choice,' she hastened to add. 'I'm sure you've got a much better eye than me.'

'Well, I have put together quite a few lamps over the years. Sometimes it's what you almost dismiss that turns out to be the perfect choice. Anyway, if you take something and then get it home and don't like it, you can always bring it back and change it,' Karen said with a warm smile.

'Oh, that's great, but I live near Wattle Creek.'

'That's no problem. I've got plenty of customers from over your way. I'm forever popping things on the bus or in the post,' Karen said with a dismissive wave of her hand. 'How about I set up one with the green and one with the pink shade – they take on a totally different look when they're on,' she offered, already starting to take the navy-blue shade off another lamp in the same style.

Emily looked back and forth between the two lamps and then closed her eyes to imagine each lamp in her setting. After a few moments she opened them and looked at Karen. 'You're right. Definitely the green one,' she said with a decisive nod.

'I think so. But seriously, you are allowed to change your mind,' Karen said.

'Um, how much is it?' Emily asked tentatively. She felt terrible asking, given how helpful Karen had been. If only she could just say, 'I'll take it!' without even asking. But that just wasn't in her nature.

'It's very reasonable,' Karen said. 'All up, two hundred and seventy-five dollars.'

'Oh, that *is* reasonable,' Emily said, her surprise evident. She'd seen some lamps in Port Lincoln at nearly double the price, and not nearly as nice.

Next they looked at practical desk lamps. They were all much the same design, but in a range of colours, none of which Emily was really taken with. 'There's one in antique brass that should be in a box that came in this morning, but I haven't had a chance to unpack it yet. Bear with me and I'll get it out. If you're in a hurry and have other shopping to do, I can call you when I'm done, if you like,' Karen offered.

'That's okay, I'm happy to wait. Don't rush, I'll just have a bit of a wander around,' she said, making her way to the far side of the room where a selection of crystal chandeliers hung from the ceiling. Hanging right above her was just what she had in mind for the gallery's entrance hall. She held her breath as she turned the price tag over. Two thousand dollars! Wow! Her eyes bugged slightly.

'It's genuine Italian crystal,' Karen called out from her spot nearby on the floor surrounded by boxes and bubble wrap.

'It's beautiful,' Emily said.

'I'll turn it on when I finish here. It's really quite spec-tacular. The genuine crystal makes a huge difference. I'll be there in a sec.'

'Please, don't hurry. I've got plenty of time,' Emily said, and then checked her watch to make sure. She was surprised to find she had already passed an hour in this shop.

'Right, here it is,' Karen declared. 'What do you think?' she asked, putting a brass version alongside the other coloured desk lamps.

Emily went over. She closed her eyes briefly and tried to picture it on her desk. It was traditional enough to blend in, and with the two joints on its arm, practical too. By attaching it to the lip of her desk, she wouldn't lose valuable working space. Once she put a stack of document trays, a computer monitor, a pen holder, a mug of tea, and perhaps even a laptop, she might be struggling for some-where to work.

'Perfect,' she said. 'I'll take it.' *And without even asking the price!*

'It's ninety dollars.'

'Fine.'

'Now let me show you how gorgeous that chandelier *really* is,' Karen said, going over to a bank of light switches on the far wall. 'There you go,' she said, as the chandelier suddenly lit up.

'Oh, wow,' Emily said breathily. She stood back for a better look, and put her hands to her face. It was truly breathtaking. In a hallway as a feature, without the distrac-tion of all the other lights in the shop, it certainly would make a statement. Just the sort of classy impression needed for the entrance of a successful art gallery, she thought.

'I've got one at home. I couldn't resist after putting it on display. I'm in an old house, but it would work equally well in an old or new space,' Karen said. 'Are you thinking for a hallway, or somewhere else?'

'It's a bit soon, but I'm planning to rebuild a stone building on my farm and turn it into an art gallery. My architect-builder thinks down lights in the ceiling would be best for my rooms. I've agreed, but only if I can have a nice big chandelier in the hall.'

'Sounds perfect. Down lights can take a bit of getting used to, especially if you generally like old-style things. But they are great for providing a well-lit space relatively energy efficiently, and with less shadowing. And with most of them you can change the direction of the light, which is perfect for a gallery space. When is it opening? I'd love to see it.'

'We're a way off yet – still in the planning stage,' Emily said apologetically.

'If you have a launch, please send me an invite. I love art exhibitions and, as I'm sure you're aware, the Peninsula doesn't have a lot on offer. Perhaps we can stock each other's brochures, since we won't be in competition? Here, take one of my cards. And do keep in touch. I'm Karen.'

'Okay, great. I'm Emily. I'm afraid I don't have a business card yet.'

She'd travel that *far for an art exhibition opening?! Wow, that's keen!* Her mind began trying to work out how far people would travel. Simone would be sure to come from Melbourne if she was exhibiting, but would any of Jake's friends travel that far? And what a great idea to swap brochures. That would really help each other broaden their customer reach. She'd mention it to Maureen at the antiques shop too.

'I'll do you a good deal on the chandelier since you're buying so much. And perhaps we can help with the down lights and anything else electrical when you start building? I'd appreciate the opportunity to quote. We've got a shed full of trade supplies out the back,' Karen said, distracting Emily from her thoughts.

Emily stared up at the chandelier. Part of her wanted to say, 'I'll take it,' but her cautious side held her back. She didn't want to get too far ahead of herself. She already had a desk and four mantelpieces for the gallery taking up space and not being used.

'As I said, we're a bit far off yet,' Emily said heavily. 'Perhaps in a few months, if it's still here.' She thought about what Jake had said about snapping up antiques on the spot.

'No worries. I always keep at least one of these in stock and I can order more. As gorgeous as they are, they're not one-offs. But they come from Italy so they do take a little while to arrive,' Karen warned.

'Oh, that's great,' Emily said, sighing with relief. 'I think I'm spending enough for one day,' she said, smiling warmly at Karen.

Suddenly the noise from the cars passing outside in the street become louder as the main door of the shop opened. Emily turned to see a tall, lean man in his late thirties or early forties with blondish-grey hair walk in, followed by...

'Jake! What are you doing here?' she cried.

'Here she is,' Jake said jovially, coming over and wrapping his arms around Emily. 'Em, this is Tom Green, my mate I've been telling you about. Our meeting finished early.'

Emily shook hands with Tom and said hello.

'I hear you're going into business together. You're in great hands.'

Emily nodded and smiled at Tom and then Jake. 'I think so.'

'Hey Karen,' Tom said, bending and giving Karen a peck on the cheek.

Don't tell me it's like Wattle Creek where everyone knows everyone? This is a proper city, for goodness sake!

'Karen's my sister,' Tom said, smiling at the look on Emily's face.

Of course she is. She almost laughed out loud. Just like Wattle Creek and Hope Springs; every second person is related. Too funny!

'How did you find me?' Emily said after introducing Jake and Karen.

'By accident, really. The car was still in its spot so I figured you couldn't be too far away. There aren't many shops. Tom here is relieving Karen for her lunch break, so I thought I'd tag along and see if I bumped into you before phoning. And here you are,' he added, kissing her and draping an arm around her shoulder. 'So, find anything nice?'

Emily grinned and pointed at the chandelier above them.

'Wow,' Jake said. 'Bit soon for that, isn't it?' he teased good-naturedly.

'That's what I was just saying to Karen,' Emily said. 'But I have found the perfect floor lamp, desk lamp, and light shade for my office,' she said triumphantly.

'Great, show me,' Jake said.

'That desk lamp,' Emily said, indicating her selection sitting on the counter, 'and everything else is out the back.'

Emily led them through to the next room.

'The green one,' she said proudly, pointing to the floor lamp, 'and that schoolhouse light shade for the main bulb,' she said, pointing to the shade on the small desk. 'All on Karen's recommendation. Lovely, huh?'

'Perfect,' Jake said. 'Looks like I've come at just the right time to be pack horse,' he added with a laugh.

'Yes. Now all I need is a chair. If only you sold office furniture.'

'I'm afraid not, but you'll find a great selection two shops further along,' Karen said.

Don't tell me, run by your cousin Alfred. I'm not going to ask.

'Tell Paul I sent you and he'll give you a good deal.'

No, you're not going to ask, Emily told herself sternly.

'He's our cousin,' Tom said.

She had to work very hard not to laugh.

'Do you own the whole city?' Jake asked with a chuckle.

'Alas, no, but our grandparents were in shoes and haberdashery many moons ago,' Tom explained. 'We seem to have inherited business brains from them.'

'Do you mind if I head off for my lunch break? I'm meeting up with a friend,' Karen said suddenly.

'Sure, no problem.'

'And can you fix Emily up and pack the lamps for her?' she added.

'Yep, that's fine. You go,' Tom said to Karen. As she left, he turned back to Emily and Jake. 'Why don't you guys go and look at chairs while I pack everything up for you?'

'Okay, thanks, we'll be back soon,' Emily said, and linked her arm through Jake's.

'So, how was your meeting?' she asked when they were outside on the footpath.

'Good. Everything's ticking along nicely. They've got a great project manager and team of builders, and won't need me as much as I thought they would. A bit ironic, given I'm only down at Wattle Creek now and not having to come all the way from Melbourne. Oh well, as long as they have someone else to blame things on if it all goes pear-shaped,' he said cheerfully, shrugging.

'Is that likely?'

'There's always the chance of a problem arising. But at the moment it's all coming along beautifully. Bit of a waste me being here, really. But at least their lunch was good. And you found your lights. That's good. Have you eaten?'

'No, I've been in choosing lights this whole time.'

'You must be starving. It's after one. Let's find you something to eat. We can do the chair after that.'

Emily smiled, enjoying Jake taking charge. It really was rather nice having someone to rely on.

Chapter Eighteen

Jake pointed the car towards the highway. After buying a pair of office chairs and collecting her purchases from the lighting shop, Emily had asked him if there was anything else he wanted to do. But he was as keen as her to head home.

'So, Tom seems nice,' she said, looking across at Jake, as the built-up area came to an end and the grey bitumen stretched ahead through red dirt dotted with low-growing grey-green saltbush and sparsely occurring taller native trees and shrubs. Emily had never liked this drive; she always found it desolate and quite depressing.

'Yeah. And I found out some very interesting information that will help us with our project,' he said conspiratorially.

'Oh, like what?'

'Like, that the Wattle Creek Council use either the building inspector from Port Lincoln or the one in Whyalla – taking turns.'

'And, don't tell me, Tom is the building inspector at Whyalla?'

'Yep,' Jake said, nodding.

'Wouldn't that be illegal, or at least a conflict of interest?' she said.

'Not really. He doesn't get the whole say, just makes recommendations for the council to rule on. And, anyway, it would be a fifty-fifty chance of him ending up looking at our application. But he did say that Wattle Creek are pretty easy to deal with. Basically, as long as the building meets the regulations, they're not all that fussed what you put up out on a farm. Though he did advise that applying for it as a house rather than a commercial space would mean less red tape. We'll be meeting all the regulations for disabled access anyway, but Tom said the process would be a lot slower if you go down that path. And he's absolutely right. I've done plenty of commercial spaces. The more regulations involved, the worse it gets.'

'Well, we are building a dwelling, first and foremost. It needs to be versatile if the gallery doesn't work out for any reason. So it's not as if we're being dishonest,' Emily said.

'Exactly.'

'What else did he have to say?'

'The next council meeting is Wednesday week. If we get the plans in by then we might get it through this month. Otherwise we'll have to wait until the next one. Not that it'll really matter; we've got plenty to keep us occupied sorting the stone and cleaning it.'

'Hmm,' Emily agreed. Thinking about what had to be done to turn the pile of rubble back into a building, and one double the size, was really quite daunting.

'Which reminds me. David rang just as I was coming out of the meeting. He's sourced the extra stone.'

'That's good,' she said.

'Except for the fact that it's only available because an unsentimental person has torn down another quaint old building,' Jake said with a grimace.

'Hmm.'

'Still, it's good that we'll be able to give it a new life. All in all, it's been a very productive day for both of us,' he said brightly.

'Yes,' Emily replied. She was exhausted, and the afternoon sun streaming in through the car windows didn't help. She closed her eyes and pictured the chandelier hanging in the hall. It would be perfect. Absolutely stunning.

★

Emily woke with a start as the gentle vibrations below her changed to a shudder and then gravel began spraying the underneath of the car.

'Hello sleepyhead,' Jake said, smiling at her and patting her leg.

She looked around. They were nearly home. 'Hi. So much for keeping you company while you're driving,' Emily said wryly. 'Sorry.'

'You were dead to the world. I can only ever doze in a car, I never go fully to sleep,' he said in awe.

'Must have been all that shopping. I'm totally worn out.'

'Yeah, all that brain power used for making decisions.'

Emily felt dishevelled. She'd been in a deep dream. *That* dream, the one she'd had a number of times before. She looked out the window and frowned as she tried to recall the details.

She'd been wearing tailored black pants and a formal wraparound silk shirt the exact colour of her unusual grey-and-navy-blue eyes. A photographer had been bouncing back and forth making exaggerated gestures with his hands while she posed against a mantelpiece with a large mirror framed in gold above it. Jake was beside her in a charcoal-grey suit. It was a very formal do, and an evening one, by the looks of their attire.

They were leaning in towards each other, his arm around her waist, her elbow casually placed on the mantel. Between them sat her gran's button jar.

They'd just finished the photo shoot when a car pulled up outside. The photographer scurried off to capture the event on film. And that's when she'd woken up.

As she stared out the car window, Emily felt calm and content that Jake had been so prominent in her dream. She took it as a good omen. When she'd had the dream before, it had never been clear who the man beside her was.

Previously, she'd always thought the house was the one she'd been renting from the Bakers. This time it had definitely been the cottage. Well, she supposed it must be, on account of the chandelier in the hall. What was the event? The grand opening? She hoped it was a sign this was all meant to be.

But, really, it could have been any building anywhere. Maybe it wasn't a gallery opening at all, but an engagement party, or a wedding. Emily frowned, trying to take her mind back to the image of them beside the fireplace. Did she have a ring on her left hand? Was that why she had her elbow on the mantelpiece? If so, why then include the button jar in the shot?

Oh for goodness sake, it was only a dream. They're not meant to make sense! Really, the dream was just a montage of all the topics currently on her mind: shopping for lights, indecision over the chandelier, Jake's presence in her life, the cottage project...

'Are you okay?' Jake sounded concerned. He gently squeezed her leg.

She reluctantly let the questions go and turned to look at him. 'Yeah. I was just thinking about a dream. I've had versions of it a few times now. It's some sort of formal function. The last couple of times I was sure we were at the other house, but this time it wasn't.'

'Well, that must be a good omen. And *we*? Even better if I'm with you,' he added, sounding genuinely pleased.

'Do you think dreams foretell good and bad?'

'God, they've been asking that question since the dawn of time. No idea. I, personally, take them with a pinch of salt,' Jake said.

Emily smiled at hearing yet another of Gran's sayings. She wondered with idle amusement if everything Gran had said over the years was just a series of well-worn quotes, clichés, and hackneyed old sayings. It was like she'd searched Google, except of course, Gran had never been near a computer.

The thought of her almost ninety-year-old granny trying to figure out how to turn on a computer, let alone punching requests into a search engine, struck Emily as hugely funny and she unsuccessfully tried to stifle a giggle.

'What's so funny?' Jake asked.

'Nothing really. I was just thinking about Gran and her use of sayings. I must be so tired I'm getting delirious. You were saying you take dreams with a pinch of salt,' she urged.

'I think they're just the brain's way of expressing what we're thinking about, really,' he said with a shrug.

'Yeah, you're probably right.'

'Hey, don't read too much into it, whatever you think you saw. The project is going ahead, it's going to work out well, you're going to set up a successful gallery, and *we're* going to live happily ever after. I'm not saying life won't have its challenges, but we make a great team, Em. We communicate well, and with good communication you can solve most things. Though, when kids come along, it'll change things somewhat.' He stopped his ramble abruptly.

Kids? Again?

Emily tried not to look shocked, which was exactly how she felt. They'd agreed to take their relationship nice and steady. What had changed? She *thought* she wanted kids one day, but certainly not right now. Pregnancy and childbirth sounded hideous! She'd never spent any time around pregnant women or small children – never even held a baby.

'Sorry, I don't know where that came from. I didn't mean to put pressure on you. We did agree to take it easy,' Jake said.

Emily looked across at him. 'But?' *There's clearly a but coming.*

'But I love you, Emily! I'd love nothing more than to spend the rest of my life with you, for better or worse.'

Emily wondered if the strange light feeling she was experiencing was the blood literally draining from her face.

He's not proposing, is he?

So what if he is? she thought, surprising herself with how she actually felt. The blood started to rise again and her face blushed pink. Her heart rate increased.

'Are you proposing to me, Jake?' she asked, and held her breath.

Jake hesitated for just a second. 'I guess I am. I didn't mean to. I mean, I didn't mean to do it like this.' He kept looking between her and the road ahead. 'But I mean it when I say I love you and want to spend the rest of my life with you. We can work out all the details later.'

Emily stared across at him. She reckoned he was more flushed than her.

Suddenly the car came to a stop right in the middle of the dirt road. Jake yanked on the handbrake and then turned and looked into her eyes.

'Hell, Em, marry me!' he cried.

'Really?'

'Yes, really! Please, as unromantic as my proposal is.'

Emily looked around, almost laughed. They were on an unsealed road surrounded by cleared farmland – practically nothing. As she tried to commit the scene to memory, she wondered what constituted 'romantic', anyway? It was so subjective.

What really mattered was that they got on well, were kind to each other, and agreed on the big, important things. But, most importantly, she couldn't imagine a life without him in it, couldn't imagine not having his towel hanging beside hers in the bathroom, his toothbrush snuggled up to hers, *her* snuggled up next to *him*. She loved him and he loved her, and of course she'd marry him.

Yes, of course I'll marry you!

'Please say yes,' Jake implored.

Emily nodded and swallowed. He was still waiting for an answer, and now her mouth was too dry.

'Yes,' she eventually croaked amidst another nod. 'Yes, I'll marry you. Yes, yes, YES!'

Jake undid his seatbelt and reached across, gathering her to him as much as the sides of the bucket seats and her seatbelt would allow.

'Thank you. We're going to have a great life together. And I will absolutely make up for this crappy proposal. I promise,' he muttered into her hair. Emily clung to him, trying to keep the tears at bay. Her heart surged and her soul glowed. It had come out of nowhere like a twister, but in a split-second her life had changed forever. For the better. Wow! What a day! Could she get any luckier?

They were both silent for a few moments. The word 'wow' kept repeating itself in Emily's head. She felt like she was floating.

'So, I suppose we'd better phone your parents and let them know,' Jake said thoughtfully.

'Oh, God,' Emily said, crashing back down to earth. 'No, you ring Simone first. I'm not ready to have my mother fluttering around choosing meringue dresses and three-tiered cakes just yet. Once you open that door, there'll be no closing it,' she added, rolling her eyes at him and sighing.

'We could always elope,' Jake suggested.

'Like to where?'

'How about India? We could go and see where your gran's diamonds came from.'

'Oh. Well, I suppose we could,' Emily said doubtfully. Though it would save her having to go through the palaver of another wedding...

But what if they got there and the royal family somehow found out that she had the diamonds? What if the prince had had no right to give them away in the first place? And what if the area was so poor they couldn't afford to feed or educate their children? She'd feel compelled to help by selling the diamonds and setting up a school, or something, and she really couldn't bear to part with Gran's treasure. Anyway, wasn't India full of open sewers, filthy streets, water you couldn't bathe in – let alone drink – without getting sick? Now her imagination was running away with her. If only she could just forget the diamonds. There was no way she was going to India.

As exotic as it sounded, Emily wasn't ready for her first overseas trip to be somewhere quite so... Well, quite so... *foreign*.

'I've always liked the idea of going to Tasmania,' she offered.

'Not very exotic. And India might give you some closure,' Jake said.

I've got all the closure I need, thanks, Emily thought, but stayed silent. Perhaps she was just being a scaredy cat. Perhaps it would be nice to see where Gran might have met the prince. And she would have Jake to look after her.

'Well, there's no rush. And there are plenty of wonderful places to go; we'll find somewhere nice,' Jake said.

Emily was incredibly relieved and grateful that he had picked up on her reluctance.

'Actually, what do you say we keep this to ourselves until we get a ring?' he continued, putting the car back into gear and moving off again.

'Oh, okay, probably a good idea.' The fewer difficult conversations with Enid the better.

They turned into the house yard and pulled up beside the gate to unload the car. The matter of their sudden engagement was set aside as they took the day's purchases in and set them up.

Chapter Nineteen

The following morning they were enjoying a cuddle when they heard the double-honk of a truck air horn.

'Jesus, he's early! What time is it?' Jake said, getting out of bed slowly.

'Seven-thirty. Who is it?'

'David's mate with more stone for us.'

Emily admired his back as he pulled his jeans on. As he fished around for a t-shirt, she got up and started getting dressed.

'Don't you rush, but I'd better just go and make sure he doesn't put it in the wrong spot.' Jake left the house at a jog.

As she made her way outside a few minutes later, Emily noted how much she missed having Grace trotting along beside her. The little dog was still staying with David and Barbara. She raised her hand in greeting to the truck driver who waved in return as he drove back out of the paddock and onto the road. She hadn't recognised him. *Whoever he is, he was quick.* She continued over to where Jake was standing beside a fresh pile of limestone.

'Looks like a perfect match.' He held a rock in each hand. 'See,' he said, smiling and holding them out for her to examine.

'I'll take your word for it. They just look like rocks to me,' she said with a laugh.

'Well, they are, but they're lovely rocks, except for the mortar still on them. But by the looks of what's already come off, it won't be too big a job to clean them.'

Emily looked around. She had been looking forward to sitting there knocking off the old concrete and mortar, like Jake had explained the other day. But now with a second pile that looked even bigger than the debris of the original building, the task looked huge.

'So, where do we start?' she asked.

'Well, you're not starting anything without gloves,' Jake said, in a kindly tone. 'Your lovely hands will be torn apart in seconds. We'll have breakfast, bring the tools over and then I'll show you what we have to do. And, remember, if you don't want to do it, you don't have to. It's hard work, Em,' he warned.

'I'm willing to give it a shot,' she said.

They walked back to the house.

'Actually, I do need to get a few things from the hardware store,' Jake remembered. 'Do you want to come and look at utes, since you have your insurance money in, or stay here?'

'Oh. Well I was going to wait until the cheque clears.'

'It can't hurt to look. With a brand-new one, you might have to wait a while for it to come in.'

'Hmm, good point. All right then. Let's go look at utes,' Emily said, with all the enthusiasm of someone heading off to visit the dentist.

'Come on, it's exciting!'

'We'll have to agree to disagree on that.' She laughed and tucked her arm through his.

It all happened in a bit of a blur, but three hours later, Emily was driving her car out of town followed by Jake behind the wheel of a shiny new bright-blue Ford twin cab four-wheel-drive ute.

She'd wanted to wait a few days until her funds cleared, but the dealership's chief salesman had insisted on doing all the paperwork then and there.

'I know where you live, remember?' he said with a wink as he handed her the keys. And it wasn't like she was leaving the district. If she wanted to purchase anything in town again – like, for instance, food – she'd pay.

Very few people could get away with running up debts around town. Farmers were a little different. They tended to run accounts because of the irregularity of their income. But Emily would die with shame if she couldn't pay a bill on time.

She'd encouraged Jake to drive the vehicle home, since he was the one who was really excited about it. He'd jumped at the chance. While she was proud of her driving ability and blemish-free record, she hadn't liked the prospect of taking the narrow driveway out of the showroom in front of the staff and other customers. The ute seemed huge and had a lot less visibility around it than her car. She'd get used to it on her own property away from prying eyes, thank you very much. Jake hadn't needed much encouragement to do the test drive on her behalf, either.

As she drove the familiar road, she studied the ute in her rear-vision mirror. It was a lovely sky blue. Oh, and it had four cup holders – two in the front and two in the back. She felt good about having the purchase ticked off the to-do list.

It had been a good morning all round. On their way into town they'd found a red parcel-to-collect ticket in the mailbox. At the post office, Bernice handed them a large tube over the counter. The plans! They'd been so excited that they'd foregone their trip to the hardware store in favour of rushing back home to examine them.

If all was well, they'd have to make a trip back in to submit the plans to council. Bit of a waste, but they decided that unrolling the plans in private was preferable to doing it in the pub or in the community library, or somewhere else in the public eye. They needed to look them over carefully, which meant being calm and focussed. Jake had done a great job with the plans for the other house, but errors could always happen.

It's really happening, Emily thought. *Fingers crossed the plans go through council first go.*

Surely it was meant to be. If it wasn't, she wouldn't have been able to afford it when the budget was done. It was time for her to take a risk. She had plenty of money in the bank. The worst that could happen was that her business didn't succeed, and in a few years she might have to start looking again for a part-time job.

It will all figure itself out, she told herself firmly. *If this isn't meant to be, it won't be – and no amount of worrying will change that.* It was a mantra she'd made up; she just had to walk the walk.

If she was meant to have a job in town then she would have found one back when she was so desperate, wouldn't she? Maybe everything was as connected as Barbara kept telling her it was: if John hadn't shot at Grace she wouldn't have left him, wouldn't have met Jake. If John hadn't died, she wouldn't have inherited everything, wouldn't be back in the house. And Jake wouldn't be back with her.

Sometimes thinking about it all made Emily's brain ache. It was all terribly confusing. Which, Barbara said, was why she shouldn't worry, but just accept that there was a whole lot going on out there beyond her control.

Emily really struggled with this concept of going with the flow. But she was trying. It helped having someone as calm and sensible as Jake to lean on.

They unrolled the plans and went over them carefully. Then they pored over page after page of fixtures, fittings, materials and hours with totals and subtotals beside them.

As always, when numbers were involved, Emily cursed not inheriting Gran's mathematical mind. The old lady could do almost any calculation as long as she had a piece of paper and a pen or pencil. Half the time Emily couldn't even do on a calculator what Gran could do in her head, and she'd tried, many times. Numbers tended to just swim in front of her eyes.

Thankfully the computer program had done all their calculations. Emily stared at the big number at the bottom: the total estimated cost of building and fitting out the cottage, excluding non-fixtures like window coverings and furniture. It seemed a staggering amount of money. But, as Jake reminded her, it wouldn't all be in one hit. There was a schedule of progress payments, which made it all less daunting, and meant she could put some money away and not have such a ridiculous amount in an access account earning nothing.

'Now,' Jake said, 'I didn't want to say this until I had checked with Simone – she's part owner of my business – but we'd like to go you halves. JKL and Associates would like to fund half the build.'

'That's far too generous!' Emily cried.

'Why not? It's as much about advertising our business as it is about you starting one, remember?'

Emily was about to say that it was *her* cottage on *her* property. But of course it would be *their* property when they were married. Though, the engagement hadn't been mentioned again. Perhaps he was having second thoughts… She shook the momentary doubt aside and returned to the conversation at hand.

'That would be great. But only if you're sure.' She knew how lame and ungrateful her response probably sounded, but was unable to do anything about it.

'Only if *you're* sure.' Jake took her hand. 'I don't want to push you into anything you don't want, Emily. I know I pushed you into the engagement yesterday.'

Right, okay, so we definitely are *engaged.*

'I don't want you thinking it's some plot to get hold of your land or something,' he added, sounding flustered.

Emily thought nothing of the sort. Well she hadn't until now that he mentioned it. It was all happening so fast. Was she ready for this level of commitment?

Of course you are.

'Thank you, Jake. I really appreciate the offer. It's very generous of you.'

'Well, it's not without its perks for me. So, what do you think?'

'I think let's go for it,' Emily said with a firm nod of her head. She and Jake formally shook on the deal before pulling each other into a tight hug.

Their embrace was becoming more when Jake abruptly pulled himself away. 'I'd better get these back to town.'

Emily was putting egg sandwiches together for a late lunch when she looked up at hearing the glass door slide open. *God, he's a gorgeous specimen of a man*, she thought, watching him saunter in. *And he's my man.* Her stomach flip-flopped.

'All in order at the council?' she asked.

'Yep, all good. Fingers crossed we get an answer next week,' he said, crossing over and sweeping her to him.

'Yes, fingers crossed.'

'Oh, and I got you something,' Jake said, putting a carry bag with hardware-store insignia on it on the end of the table. 'Doris thought these would be your size.' He was grinning cheekily as he first brought out a pair of leather rigger's gloves.

'Ooh, how romantic,' she said sardonically.

'And, wait for it… Your very own mason's hammer,' he said, bringing out a hammer with what looked like a chisel on one end.

'Goody,' Emily said, clapping her hands with excitement. 'I can't wait to get started.'

'You can't say I don't bring you presents,' Jake said, leaning over to kiss her on the lips.

'Come on, lunch is ready, let's eat,' Emily said.

'Yes, we're going to need our stamina.'

They ate while Jake explained, between mouthfuls, his plan for moving forward with the project. Emily listened and nodded her agreement occasionally. This was Jake's bread and butter; he knew exactly what he was doing, so she was happy to take instructions.

First they would take the front-end loader over and load into it whatever timber could be salvaged. This would be stacked into the newly moved hayshed. Some of the old timber might later make great seating and storage boxes outside in the proposed courtyard. In the meantime, though, it would be tidy and out of the weather.

David was coming to help with the heavy lifting, Jake added just as Emily was wondering if she'd be strong enough to help lift the big roof sections. Apparently he wanted the iron for something or other back at his farm.

'There's so much great material to be salvaged,' he enthused. 'It's just a matter of taking the time and making the effort to sort it out. It is the slow way to clear a site, but totally worth doing.'

It would probably be easier to take the iron, still mostly attached to the large timber beams and toss it all into a dump somewhere, but Emily was pleased at the consideration being given to recycling.

An hour later Emily drove the bright shiny ute over to the site. She was surprised to find it not nearly as cumbersome as she'd imagined. It actually had good visibility all the way around – better even than her car. Perhaps it was because she was that bit higher up.

'You know, I think I quite like you,' she told the vehicle approvingly. In the tray behind her, a mass of tools rattled about, and the trailer on the back banged loudly as she went over the bumps. Jake followed her in the small tractor with the front-end loader bucket on it.

She stood surveying the huge pile of debris with her hands on her hips. The throaty idle of the tractor ended as the machine was turned off.

'Right, so where do we start?' Jake said, appearing beside her. Emily looked up at him.

'I was just wondering that exact thing,' she said. It had sounded so much more straightforward back at the house.

Perhaps they should just load it all into tipper trucks and hide it back behind some scrub somewhere, like so many farmers seemed to do.

'I'm only teasing,' Jake said. 'It's not as bad as it looks. It's not unlike starting a jigsaw puzzle, really. Separating the timber and other stuff from the rock will be like taking out all the edge pieces.'

That made sense. 'Okay, so what shall I do?' Emily asked.

'Put your gloves on. I'm going to show you how to clean up the stone while we wait for David.'

'Okay.'

'Right. First, get it so it's comfortable in your hands.' Emily watched while Jake turned a stone around in his hands before picking up the special mason's hammer.

'Being old mortar, it's pretty loose and crumbly. All you should have to do is gently tap on it and it'll come off.' He tapped with the hammer, a lot more gently than Emily thought would be needed. Sure enough, the mortar just fell away.

'Just keep turning it and tapping away until the rock is clean. You'll get the odd stubborn bit. With these, you just use this chisel-shaped end, find the seam where it joins the rock, and tap. Again, you don't need brute strength. You don't want to crack the rock, just gently prise the mortar off. It'll make more sense when you start doing it. Here, you give it a go.'

Emily accepted the rock and hammer Jake handed her. She turned the rock over, chose a spot to start on, and tapped. A large chunk of mortar came off and shattered in the bucket below her. She grinned up at Jake.

'See, not so hard,' he said. 'You're a natural.'

'Thanks,' Emily said. It wasn't hard, but she did have to keep her wits about her or else she ran the risk of banging her fingers with the hammer.

Jake wanted the smaller rocks separated from the larger ones, and put examples at Emily's feet.

They were umming and aahing over what to do with the waste when Emily wondered aloud if it would work like gravel for filling potholes in the farm tracks. There was also an area at the back of the sheep yards that she knew got boggy in winter.

'Perfect!' Jake declared.

'Okay.' Emily was getting more confident. 'For now, why don't we fill the trailer and then dump it behind the sheep yards? Then we can use it to fill potholes later.'

So there she sat on an upturned bucket, picking up rocks, gently but firmly chipping the mortar off into another bucket, and then tossing the clean rocks into one of the two piles depending on their size.

The first time Emily stood up and tried to lift her waste bucket to empty it into the trailer, she thought her arms might drop off. She sheepishly called Jake over to lift it. She'd thought she could lift a three-quarters-full bucket, but had totally overestimated her strength and underestimated the weight of the mortar.

'Maybe in a few days when you've built up your muscles,' Jake said encouragingly, neither mocking her nor being exasperated by her needing his help. 'Until then, perhaps just fill it to half.' He smiled kindly.

Emily got into a rhythm and was able to block out all the goings-on around her. She liked the simple monotony of the task, the little bit of thought required, and the feeling that she was actually achieving something. They had a hell of a long way to go, but she could see she was making slight headway. *Slowly but surely.* That's what Gran would have said.

At one point she heard a vehicle coming in off the road towards them. She glanced up and saw David's ute, with Grace on the back. Her heart swelled. She'd really missed the little dog. When she looked back down to her piles of cleaned rock, she was pleasantly surprised and quietly chuffed with her efforts. But, by golly, would she need a long soak in a hot bath later – her back was already starting to ache.

That night after a warm bath and dinner, she lay on the bed for a massage. Jake said in a serious tone that it would help her muscles recover so she wouldn't be too sore to do it all over again tomorrow. She played along, soaking up his touch, and by the time he moved on to areas that had nothing to do with muscles she'd used in her manual labour, she was almost too relaxed to respond.

Almost, but not quite…

Chapter Twenty

Thankfully the predicted wet weather didn't occur and over the next few days they got into a great routine, leaving the house straight after breakfast with an esky of food, thermoses of tea and coffee, and a large bottle filled with ice and water. It was better to get a full day in, and there were times when Emily knew if she went back to the house and sat somewhere comfortable she might not be able to get up and return to the work site. It was hard but satisfying work. She still sometimes worried about Jake, but rather than nag him, she decided to keep an eye out and make sure he took enough rest breaks.

The same went for Des. Emily had accepted her father's offer of help, but emphasised that he wasn't expected to put in a full day's manual labour. He had been popping by now and then – the first two times right at smoko time. Though he tried to hide his disappointment at only finding sandwiches, she noted that his arrivals then tended to be after lunch.

On the morning of their first full day, a hire toilet had been delivered. Emily had no idea where it had come from, though there were probably all sorts of local businesses catering to the needs of the building industry. She'd just never needed to know about them before.

The more services and tradespeople Jake unearthed, the bigger the district seemed to get. It was like there was a whole subculture going on she didn't know about.

It took David and Jake three full days to separate the debris from the stone. Wood they stacked into the shed for safekeeping. Other debris, like the horsehair and plaster ceilings, they took to the council's refuse dump.

Luckily they hadn't had asbestos to deal with – the original cottage predated its use, and had never been renovated or extended. They had made an allowance in the budget to get professionals in should any be found, so they saved quite a bit of money there.

But Jake warned Emily not to get too excited as sometimes other areas blew out down the track – like the travel and accommodation expenses they'd had to since factor in. What mattered was how the figures looked at the end, he said, adding confidently that his projects usually came in on budget.

After the first week, Emily's muscles had settled down and she was starting to feel tight and well toned rather than sore. Gradually she increased the weight in her bucket, which saved her a little time by not having to get up and empty it so often.

On the ninth day, Jake, Emily, Des, and David were sitting on their row of upturned buckets, chipping away at mortar. They mostly worked in silence – with the tapping of hammers and the radio in the background, they had to raise their voices to have a decent conversation, so they tended not to.

Every so often they broke into song when a favourite tune came on, but mostly they were content to be lost in their tasks and own thoughts. Emily was really enjoying the routine and sense of accomplishment, especially working alongside the guys and being considered an equal.

With them spending most of their time on the building site, there was little news from town. Jake and David had brought back groceries after their visits to the dump, but Emily now needed to do a decent shop. As much as she was looking forward to a change of scenery for a few hours, she didn't like the idea of her share of work stopping. But there was no choice; they needed to eat.

The sound of a vehicle in the distance distracted Emily from her thoughts. When it became clear the vehicle was approaching, she looked up. Barbara's car was turning in.

They hadn't been in touch for more than a week, and Emily missed her friend. She felt a little guilty about not checking to see how Barbara's pregnancy was going, but she had been falling into bed each evening not long after eating. Her face lit up into a broad grin as she watched her friend get out of the car.

'Hi everyone,' Barbara called, as she walked towards them carrying a cardboard box. 'Having fun yet?' David quickly vacated his bucket seat, relieved his wife of the box, and urged her to sit down.

'It's so good to see you!' Emily cried. She was about to pull Barbara into a tight hug, but took a quick glance down her front, which was filthy with dirt, spiders' webs, and mortar dust. Instead she stepped back and raised a hand in a lame, helpless sort of greeting. Barbara smiled in return, but she really wasn't her usual bouyant self. Perhaps the pregnancy was making her feel tired.

As Barbara sat down beside her, Emily thought she detected the smallest of baby bumps.

'I come bearing gifts,' Barbara said wearily from her spot perched on the bucket. 'Thought you people might like some cake and scones since you're probably living on sandwiches. I got bored with resting and watching daytime television.'

'Ooh yeah,' David said, rubbing his hands together.

'You little ripper,' said Des.

They all ate greedily, devouring scones with cheese and tomato, and cheese and gherkin, and others with jam and cream, tossing Grace the occasional morsel. They left the cake until last.

'I've missed you,' Emily finally said.

'Me too,' Barbara replied. 'I'm so sorry I can't be here helping.'

'I wouldn't expect you to. I'm just sorry I can't be keeping you company.'

'I'm a big girl, Em. It's not your job to entertain me. Hopefully this time next year I'll be popping by your gallery for a cuppa with a baby in tow,' she said wistfully, staring down at her hand resting on her stomach.

'I look forward to it, and being the best sort-of-auntie in the world,' Emily declared.

'Careful what you offer or else I might be dumping it on you when the screaming gets too much.' Barbara laughed tightly.

Emily wondered how Barbara was brave enough to go down that path again after losing two babies. She couldn't imagine the pain she must have gone through. Whilst she didn't have any direct comparisons, she knew if anything happened to Grace she'd never recover from her heartbreak. Yet Barbara was still able to be light-hearted. Was she using mild gallows humour to ease her fears?

As a friend, she should perhaps be encouraging her to talk about it. But the miscarriages had happened before they'd met, and she didn't want to pry.

Then again, sweeping these things under the carpet and pretending they had never happened was something Enid would do. And such an old-fashioned response. That wasn't considered a healthy course of action these days, was it?

'Oh, no, I'm sure your baby will be perfectly well-behaved; no screaming, no projectile vomiting,' Emily said.

'Haha, one can only hope. So, you seem to be making some headway,' Barbara said.

'It's very slow, but we are getting there. I can't wait until the foundations are poured and the walls start going up. It'll be wonderful to look across from the bedroom and see progress rather than a pile of rocks.'

'David tells me Jake's got some guys coming from Melbourne to do the stonework.'

'Yes. They should be here in a few weeks. It's a bit of an expensive option, but there's no one around here who Jake knows well enough to trust with something like this. At least they'll be staying here with us, which will keep costs down and save them time running back and forth to town each day.'

'But, God, just think of the cooking involved,' Barbara said.

'Oh well, no pain no gain, they say. And I'll need something to do to keep me occupied after being over here day after day. It's been an experience, but somehow I don't think I'll miss chipping mortar off rocks for hours on end,' Emily said.

'No, I imagine not. Surely there's an easier way,' Barbara said, looking around and frowning.

'Not if you want to reuse old stone. It's actually not too bad, quite therapeutic in fact.'

'Well, I'll take your word for that,' Barbara said.

After the last of the cake was gone, they drained their cups, screwed them onto the tops of the thermoses, helped Barbara repack the box, and then waved her off.

They had been back at work for a few minutes when Jake's mobile rang and he stepped away to take it. Emily had got used to tuning out his conversations while she worked, and also tuning out her concerns that he was doing too much. He was looking great, and the night sweats seemed to have stopped. He'd assured her the jittery feeling had lessened too. His hands still sometimes shook a bit as he held his cutlery, but that could be put down to all the work they were doing. Her own shook sometimes as well. She looked up at hearing Jake exclaim.

'We've done it! We've got council approval. We can officially start,' he cried.

They leapt up and jumped about – Jake, Emily, and David – dancing around in a circle like children. Des looked on, smirking and shaking his head slowly in mirth. Grace just looked confused.

Chapter Twenty-one

From then on, the pace seemed to go up a gear. A few days after news of the council approval, David announced that the Bureau of Meteorology's long-range forecast was indicating that the winter crop-growing season would break in mid-April. That gave them about nine weeks to get as much done as possible before the rain came. Meanwhile, David would also need two weeks at the end of February to shear his sheep, and Emily's. All depending on the weather of course. Almost everything to do with farm life was reliant on the weather.

Emily hadn't really thought about the significance of Jake's birthday being near the end of April before – other than their apparently excellent astrological compatibility. Now she realised that, as he had promised to drive David's second tractor during seeding, there was no point trying to organise a trip away or probably even a barbeque – he'd be too busy.

Since she'd found out when his birthday was she'd been unsuccessfully racking her brain for a gift. What did you get a successful guy who could probably afford to buy anything he wanted? A few days on a tractor? Well, whether he wanted it or not, that's what he'd be getting. And probably a whole lot more than a few days. Poor fellow. She could imagine it turning into one of those 'careful what you wish for' situations.

The only thing Emily remained a little concerned about was that there had been no further discussion of their engagement. It was as if it had been forgotten, or had never happened in the first place. A couple of times it was on the tip of her tongue to mention it, but each time she chickened out. She really was trying so hard to not be like Enid; just let things happen and not nag or control.

She hadn't had much to do with her mother recently. They'd had a brief conversation where Emily had declined an invitation to dinner – she was simply too tired from chipping mortar all day. Predictably, Enid got all huffy – it was fine for her to be busy, but apparently not for Emily – and put Des on the phone. But instead of trying to persuade Emily to change her mind, he'd chattered excitedly about the project's progress.

One evening Emily emerged from the pantry with her arms full of dinner ingredients and found Jake on the phone. There was nothing unusual about that, but the frown on his face as he paced back and forth piqued her concern.

'Is everything okay?' she asked when he'd ended the call.

He ran a hand through his hair. 'One of the Melbourne jobs has had to be halted – the client's run out of cash.'

'Oh no, that's terrible. Does that mean you'll lose money?'

'Not a lot. At the most, thirty grand. I can wear it if I have to. Thankfully the progress payments are up to date.'

'God, not a lot? Thirty thousand dollars sounds like a lot to me!'

'I suppose, but not in the context of the whole job,' he said with a shrug. 'Anyway, it's not something I'm going to waste time worrying about, Em, so you shouldn't worry about it either,' he added, grasping her gently by the shoulders and looking into her eyes before kissing her on the forehead.

God, to not have a problem with losing thirty grand! He must be very successful indeed, Emily thought, feeling a whole new sense of respect for Jake. They'd never discussed Jake's financial situation in any great detail. If they were officially engaged, should they be discussing merging finances, getting a joint bank account?

'The good news,' he continued, 'is that my team will be here in a few days.'

Instantly Emily's brain started whirring with all that had to be done to make five men comfortable. Upon first mention of the team coming across from Melbourne, she had expressed concern about where they would fit them.

After a few phone calls, Jake had assured her they were happy to stay in swags in the shearing shed. It might be different if the weather was cold, but as it was, it would be okay. Emily couldn't believe they would be happy to spend months in swags on a hard floor. They must really like him, she decided. They'd agreed that if it got too cold, or too much for the men, they would scout around the district and find caravans for them. And with that agreement, Emily had put the accommodation side of things out of her mind.

They would come up to the house to eat and shower. It would be a strain, but it had to be done if the project was going to come along as quickly as possible and remain within budget. In a way Emily was looking forward to retreating to the kitchen and playing host. But another part of her would miss being in the thick of the action; making a visible contribution. Fuelling the workers was important, but it wasn't the same as actually being out there.

Emily also worried about backlash from businesses in Wattle Creek for bringing in labour from elsewhere. But there was nothing she could do about it. They would have hired local people if available, but as Jake had explained, stonemasonry wasn't the same as bricklaying. They'd be hiring a local concreter, electricians, roofers, and cabinet-makers when the time came. In the meantime, they'd have to cop whatever flak they got on the chin.

By Wednesday the twenty-second of February, David and Jake and Emily had most of the stone cleaned and divided into two different sizes. David announced that he wouldn't be available for the next two weeks – he was shearing Emily's sheep down here and then his own up at his place the week after. He again declined Jake and Emily's offer of stopping what they were doing to help – he had a good team set up. David's crew brought all their own food, so Emily wouldn't have to feed them. Soon she would have five men to feed full-time anyway.

Grace had proven herself and she was excited that David wanted to use her. He had put her through her paces, and she had turned out to be a natural in both the yards and the paddock. And she was still very young, so would only get better. Emily puffed up with motherly pride at the thought.

She thought back to her first ever conversation with Barbara when she'd gone to pick up the tiny puppy. Grace was the runt of the litter and hadn't been wanted by anyone else because she was so much smaller than the others. *Well, so much for that!*

She was also glad that Grace would be occupied. It was much better than being locked in the house yard, which she would need to be to keep her safe from all the extra foot and vehicle traffic. She felt dreadful locking up Grace, but they were expecting Jake's team from Melbourne at any moment.

Speaking of which, she thought, as a dual cab ute with five men aboard arrived on site.

As the men poured out of the vehicle, Jake greeted them like they were great mates. She heard them ribbing him gently about not taking long off work after all.

'Missed you guys too much,' Jake said in reply. 'This is David, a friend who's been helping out. And this is Emily,' he said, with his arm around her. 'She's co-boss, so just watch out,' he said with a laugh. 'Em, this is Toby, Ben, Stan, Bill, and Aaron.'

'Hi Emily, lovely to meet you,' they each said whilst offering their right hands.

'Likewise. Thanks so much for coming. I'll try not to be too bossy,' she said, smiling and shaking hands with each of them in turn whilst desperately trying to commit their names to memory. A couple of them – blond, blue-eyed Toby and pale, redheaded Aaron, in particular – had a bit of a larrikin look about them. Emily pegged them at around her age or maybe a bit younger. Stan and Ben were older – nearer early to mid-forties – and a little shyer. Bill, the oldest of the group, had more salt than pepper in his mid-brown hair, and had the weathered look of someone who had spent most of his life in the sun.

She warmed to them instantly. They all seemed like really nice guys. It would be fun having them around.

Despite the long drive from Melbourne with only a night in Adelaide, they got right to work. Jake unrolled the plans on the back canopy of the ute whilst gesturing in the direction and general layout of things. While David returned to work on the rocks, Emily left to go back to the house. She had to finish preparing for the big barbeque she'd organised to welcome them, and double-check that everything was organised regarding their accommodation.

Until David had finished with the shearing shed, the men would be sleeping in the house's two spare rooms. She'd gathered five swags: John's, her own – only ever used once – David's, Barbara's, and one they'd borrowed from Grant, but left it up to them to decide if they wanted to share the double beds or camp out on the floor. After deciding it would be a nightmare trying to keep track of towels if they were all the same colour – Emily, taught by Enid, only ever had sets of matching towels, hand towels, bath mats, and face washers – she had gone to town one afternoon and bought five new towels in different colours. Now she put up a clothes airer in the enclosed verandah for the stonemasons to keep them on.

Chapter Twenty-two

From the kitchen window, Emily watched the sheep race past the house on their way down to the yards. Her heart swelled and she felt a wave of emotion as Grace came into sight behind them, making her way back and forth, pushing them forward. She seemed to be doing a great job. Next came David's ute with Sasha aboard. Emily laughed, feeling like the proudest mum in the world. She reluctantly dragged herself away and got back to work on dinner. She yearned for a nanna nap, but she had too much to do to stop for even half an hour.

The welcome barbeque had been a triumph. The five guys, her parents, Barbara and David, Nathan and Sarah, Bob and his wife, Grant and Steve and their wives, and two babies, had all joined in to celebrate the official start of the building. Everyone seemed to have got along well and had fun. And they'd all raved about the food, especially the pavlova piled high with cream and fresh fruit she'd served for dessert.

She was glad that Nathan and Sarah had made it. They still hadn't got around to inviting her and Jake over – Emily quietly suspected they were too busy getting to know each other intimately – so it was good to have them over at last.

It had been getting harder to find excuses to dodge Enid's invitations, though, and she had figured the opportunity of notching up a dinner with her mother whilst being busy with other guests was too good to pass up. Besides, she'd really wanted her dad there for what was both a kick-off party for the cottage and thank you to the other guys for doing the shed. She'd also wanted Jake's mates to meet some locals. She didn't want them feeling they were stuck at the farm on their time off.

Thankfully it hadn't been too late a night, with everyone having left by ten and the guys settled in their rooms by ten-thirty. The stonemasons had even insisted on staying to help her clean up!

That night the kitchen was a hive of chatter as the Melbourne men talked excitedly of seeing sheep being shorn – most of them for the first time ever.

'It doesn't hurt them at all,' Toby said. 'I thought it would, but it doesn't.'

'They don't pluck them, mate, it's just clippers – like what you should use on your hair occasionally,' Stan said.

'I didn't mean the actual shearing. It always seemed a bit harsh them being dragged across the floor when you see it on the telly.'

'I wouldn't like to be stooped over like that all day – you can see why those blokes need so many breaks,' Bill said.

'That's because you're old,' Aaron said. Out of the corner of her eye, Emily saw him pick up a bread roll and aim, but then put it down again after a glare from Jake.

'I can't get over how precise it all is with the testing of the fleeces and categorising them.'

'And how careful they are with contamination. It's really very clean,' Toby said.

'Yeah, probably cleaner than your house, eh, Tobes?'

'Yeah, probably.'

'Your dog was amazing, Emily. Pretty gutsy for such a little thing – climbing on all those big woolly beasts. David told us she's never actually been trained. That's incredible,' Bill said.

Emily beamed back. 'I snuck a peek when they came past the house. I felt all silly, like a proud mother.'

'Where is she, anyway?' Stan asked, looking around.

'She's staying with David for a fortnight until he's finished his own shearing, playing at being a real farm dog.'

'Well, it looked like she was loving every minute of it.'

'I just hope she'll want to come home eventually.'

'Don't worry, if necessary we'll mount a covert operation to kidnap her for you,' Aaron said.

'You can't do anything quiet, Aaron, with feet that big,' Toby said, laughing. The others joined in.

'Thanks Aaron, I'll let you know,' Emily said, playing along. She really enjoyed their banter. 'I hope you won't find the shearing shed too smelly to sleep in. They're a bit on the nose straight after shearing,' Emily said.

'Nah, we'll be right,' Bill said. 'Won't we fellas?'

A chorus of 'yep' made its way around the table.

'If not, there are always the spare beds and floor space.'

'I think I might be scarred for life from the pink in that room as it is,' Toby said.

'Ignore him, Emily. It's a nice colour. And don't you worry about us,' Stan said.

'I was only kidding,' Toby said. 'I actually don't mind it.'

'It's okay, Toby, I know it's an acquired taste,' Emily reassured him, smiling at the thought of David's reaction. 'It is very pink.'

For the first week the Melbourne guys were there, Emily would stay for a cuppa and look over progress whenever she could spare the time after delivering the meals. There didn't seem to be much going on in the beginning – mainly tidying up the site and levelling the building area. She couldn't wait to see stone walls going up. Thankfully the weather was kind and all the rain they had occurred overnight. Nor was David's shearing affected – each evening he managed to get enough sheep safely under cover for the next day's work.

Every night Jake spent an hour or so updating her on progress while they lay in bed. They didn't have a lot of other time to themselves away from the men. And the only time they seemed to have the energy to make love was on Sunday mornings.

She was a little disconcerted that they had settled into such a companionable way of life so quickly, but she told herself it was temporary and that their situation was quite an unusual one.

It wasn't as if she didn't still find Jake hugely attractive. Every time she looked at him her heart skipped a beat and a tingle ran right through her down to her toes. Seeing the ease with which he directed the guys, and the way he managed the project whilst remaining calm and even-tempered, and not even all that stressed, was very impressive. And a big turn-on. The man was quite something.

She quite often found herself hovering with her box of
food listening to him, feeling awestruck by him, and very
grateful she had him in her life.

Emily hoped Jake was okay with the way things were,
but kept her thoughts to herself. She wasn't about to raise
their significantly reduced sex-life and introduce a problem
if there wasn't one.

She worked hard to keep the amazement that he had
chosen her at bay – it was negative and she was trying
so hard not to be. A lifetime of not measuring up in her
mother's eyes would most likely always remain with her.
But she was finally beginning to address the self-esteem
issues that had plagued her for so long.

Emily was an adult and responsible for her own happiness, as Barbara had pointed out more than once. She was
doing her best to retrain herself to be more positive, not
depend on her mother's approval, and not let her past and
her insecurities negatively affect her future. She *was* good
enough, damn it! There was no reason why she couldn't
achieve whatever she wanted to.

The Sunday after he finished shearing her sheep, David
brought down an old television, DVD player, and set-top
box for the boys.

'This might make it feel less like you're living back
home with Mum and Dad, fellas,' he announced.

It had been too crowded for all of them to sit and watch
television in the lounge. But they hadn't complained –
they'd instead taken to playing poker around the huge
kitchen table.

Aaron and Toby had so far not revealed themselves
to be major pranksters or larrikins – well, not in Emily's

vicinity – but both had quite the lucky streak when it came to Texas Hold 'em.

Stan had turned out to be a good cook, and whenever he had the time he was inside offering to help Emily. He confessed that cooking was what he did to relax, and she was only too happy to indulge him. He was coming up later to make bread on his day off.

Ben had also proven a great help and wouldn't leave the house until the kitchen was tidy. He also liked to help with cooking, and was good with instructions, but wasn't as confident as Stan. Emily was so used to having her kitchen to herself, it was taking a bit of getting used to. But she was really enjoying having them there, and playing mother to all five men.

Late in the afternoon, Emily joined in as everyone stood in the shearing shed with their fingers crossed, biting on bottom lips, hoping the TV would get good enough reception through the rabbit ears antenna.

After lots of tweaking, they managed to achieve a reasonably clear picture. Hopefully it would hold when the warm, still weather became more unsettled with the onset of autumn.

Chapter Twenty-three

After the second week, Barbara started dropping in after lunch for a quick cuppa after she'd been into town. Emily would stop for ten minutes before resuming her buzzing around, chattering away as she got on with things. That was one of the great things about their relationship: she could just be herself. It was a busy time, but Barbara was as happy as Emily to just have the company for an hour or so. And there was no expectation that she would stop what she was doing and then start up in a mad panic again to catch up later.

Barbara helped her fill sandwiches and cut and butter cake and do simple tasks, but was equally happy to sit back and stay out of the way. They'd both done enough catering to know that it was sometimes easier to just let someone do their thing and not waste their time explaining a process in order for the other person to assist.

On the other hand, Enid didn't get it at all. She had dropped by once in the first week and entered the kitchen like a tornado demanding to know what she could do. Emily had firmly told her mother that she was welcome to sit and have a cup of tea, but that she didn't have time to stop. And, no thank you, she had everything under control. Enid had sat at the table, tapping her fingers impatiently. Clearly she thought if she waited long enough, Emily would stop what she was doing and give her the attention she demanded. She eventually left with a harrumph and, 'Well, if you don't need me, I'll be off,' after draining her cup.

'See you, thanks for the visit,' Emily had called over her shoulder from the bench where she was making a meatloaf for lunch.

She was especially grateful for the extra pair of hands in the laundry when Barbara visited. Emily had taken on the guys' washing since they were working so hard and she didn't like them having to do it on their only day off. It was more work than she'd expected, but it wasn't hard, just a matter of fitting in the loading, unloading, hanging out and bringing in around her other tasks. The gift of efficiency was at least one good thing she had inherited from Enid. Though, working with your best friend was nothing like working with your overbearing, critical mother. On the days Barbara visited, her friend would get in a load of washing and fold it while she pegged out another lot on the line.

One afternoon they were sorting a load of freshly dried laundry.

'You need to get someone in to help,' Barbara said.

'I couldn't trust the cooking to anyone but you.'

'Sorry, but I can't do it.'

'Of course you can't – you've got to rest and take care of your baby. But there's no need to apologise.'

'I suppose it would be a ridiculous waste to have someone come and just do the washing,' Barbara said thoughtfully.

'Yeah. They'd spend all their time sitting around waiting for the machine to do its thing.'

'I actually did a ring-around the other day looking for a cleaner. Just out of curiosity.'

'Well I could certainly palm off the dusting, vacuuming, and cleaning of the bathroom and toilet right about now.'

'Sadly, I couldn't find anyone.'

'Bugger.'

'Hey, maybe we should start a cleaning company,' Barbara said after a few moments of silent folding.

'Er, we both hate cleaning, remember?' Emily replied with a laugh.

'Well, *we* wouldn't be doing it; we'd be the bosses just running the show.'

'Except, of course, for having no one to *do* the cleaning, which is our current problem. Remember?'

'Hmm.'

'Not to mention the fact that I have a paddock full of men building me an art gallery. And you're going to have your hands full with a new baby soon.'

'Yes. I'm still trying not to think about it.'

'Come on, Barb, you can't jinx it. You know that. Aren't you always telling me that these things are out of our hands? What will be, will be?'

'Apparently I'm much better at running someone else's life than my own,' she replied, smiling weakly.

'It will be fine, Barbara. You need to stop worrying and start living again. All this worry can't be good for the baby, can it?'

She stopped short of pointing out that Barbara was running the risk of creating a self-fulfilling prophecy, if her own views of the universe and its workings were to be believed. Again Emily wondered where all Barbara's positivity and faith had got to.

'Come on, time to feed the workers,' she said, trying to change the subject and lighten the mood. *I really don't have the knack Barbara does with pep-talks*, she thought, putting the milk in the top of the large box. The first day she'd tried to carry everything over in an effort to make up for missing her morning walks – she hadn't had a proper walk since they'd begun cleaning the stone – but by the time she'd got to the building site she'd been almost ready to drop the heavy box. Now she made the short trips back and forth in the car.

Sometimes one of the guys did the afternoon smoko run, but today Jake had specially asked Emily to come across. They worked it out via UHF radio. The day after the guys arrived, he had been into town and returned with a few handheld devices so they could all communicate free of charge rather than the expense of using mobile phones.

Curious about why Jake had specially asked her to come across this afternoon, Emily and Barbara arrived a few minutes before three.

She gave her father a hug hello. 'What's going on?' she asked.

'You'll see,' he replied, and winked.

Emily and Barbara exchanged shrugs as the other men scurried around nearby.

'Right, all ready to go?' Jake said, looking around the group.

There was a chorus of murmurs of 'Yep.'

'Stan, you do the honours,' Jake said. He grasped Emily gently by the shoulders and turned her towards what she knew would be the front of the cottage.

She felt the realisation dawn as she watched Stan trowel a bed of mortar onto the concrete foundation and then place a stone on top, carefully pushing it down and tapping it into place with the handle of the trowel. A cheer went up, followed by a round of applause. Emily's chin began to wobble.

'Oh, wow,' Barbara said, beside her. 'God, I think I'm going to cry.'

Emily felt Barbara's hand grasp hers and her father's hand squeeze her shoulder. She turned to them in turn, wanting to speak, or at least smile. Acknowledge them somehow. Here were the three people who had given her the most support during the hardest time of her life. Where would she be without them? All she could do was bite down on her lip and try to keep the tears at bay. This stone was the official line in the sand. Everything would be better now.

She turned her tear-filled eyes to Jake. 'Thank you. Thank you. You don't know how much this means…'

'Oh, come here,' he said, kissing her and pulling her into his chest.

Chapter Twenty-four

March passed. Once the walls started going up, the building progressed very quickly. Each day Emily looked out her bedroom window and saw the piles of cleaned stone getting smaller, and the walls growing higher. It was looking more and more like a bigger version of her old, beloved cottage.

They'd had a very dry period with mild weather and hadn't suffered any down time on the building project, but in early April, clouds began to gather. Ten weeks into the project and around seven weeks after the Melbourne stonemasons had turned up, Emily was well-entrenched in her new routine. Thursday morning dawned overcast, just like the weather bureau had been forecasting.

Around town the farmers had been getting antsy about the lack of rain. David hadn't really commented beyond sticking with the Bureau's original prediction of a break in the season around the twentieth of April. That date was still a week away.

He was philosophical like Barbara usually was. He would often shrug and say that no amount of worry and complaining would help.

While they were eating lunch the sky darkened and rain began to fall, beating down heavily on the iron roof.

'So, when do we start on the tractors?' Jake asked.

'At this rate we'll have enough to get started tomorrow, but I'd like to give it a couple of days to soak in and for the weeds to poke their heads up. That way when we go over it, we'll deal with them at the same time.'

'That makes sense,' Jake said. 'I'm looking forward to doing my bit.' Jake had told Emily a number of times how keen he was to see how another part of farming worked.

'You okay to leave the cottage project?'

'Yep, no worries. The guys know what they're doing. It won't be long until they're done and the local roofers can start. I'll only be a phone call away. It should be fine.'

Emily would miss the guys when they headed back to Melbourne. They were nice, cheerful, respectful fellows who really livened up the place. She would miss the banter around the huge kitchen table. The attention they'd given her, being the only woman amongst so many men, had been nice too, not that there had been any flirting or innuendo. Or even dirty jokes, for that matter. They'd kept things very clean in her presence – she hadn't even heard the 'f' word uttered.

Even though she was around the same age as the younger guys, it was as if they considered her more like their mother and like a younger sister to Bill and Stan, such was their treatment of her and their effusive praise of her cooking. It had been fun, but she certainly wouldn't miss all the extra work involved in having them staying. At least the roofers, and other trades that would be following them, would bring their own lunch and thermoses.

She would still take over cake and batches of scones – knowing that the way to a man's heart really was through his stomach. If the builders were happy, they'd turn up each day until their work was done and not disappear and leave the project behind schedule. It had worked so far, anyway.

Jake was in regular contact with Simone, and Emily often chatted to her of an evening after he had finished updating her regarding the project and discussing business matters. On a couple of occasions, Simone had said she was keen to come over and see it all firsthand. Emily had always suspected it was one of those throwaway lines, so she was surprised when Simone phoned a week before Easter and asked if she could impose on them for the long weekend. Despite it being so late in the year, Easter had snuck up on them all.

Only a week or so ago she'd realised she and Jake had completely forgotten Valentine's Day – months ago now. She couldn't recall now what had reminded her, but she was glad Jake had forgotten too. She'd always considered it a ridiculously commercial event. And she'd had enough trouble thinking up a birthday gift for him! At least with Easter the gifts were obvious.

Emily was thrilled that Jake would have his sister there for his birthday, not that they were planning a huge cele-bration. Jake, like Emily, wasn't one for giving birthdays much acknowledgement.

She told Simone an emphatic yes, but warned her that Jake might not be around much due to them hopefully getting stuck into sowing the crops. It was a pity Jake would be busy helping David on the farm, but it would have been the same if the holiday had occurred earlier; only then it would have been the building project keeping him occupied.

Emily was really looking forward to getting to know Jake's sister better in person. It would also be the perfect opportunity to discuss the subject of her exhibiting, which she hadn't actually mentioned to her as yet. She'd been telling herself she was putting it off in case she changed her mind about the building becoming a gallery, but really she was concerned that, like Jake had, Simone would decline the opportunity to have her art hung in public for sale. That she chattered on the phone excitedly about getting back into painting did bode well, but Emily didn't want to rush things and scare her off. The weekend would prove the perfect opportunity to have that particular conversation, and to pick Simone's brain for decorating ideas.

The stonemasonry team was working hard to get back to Melbourne in time for Easter. Bill and Stan were keen to get back to their families and do the Easter egg hunt they did every year. Aaron, Ben, and Toby wanted to watch Collingwood play live at the MCG on the Saturday.

'No wonder they all get on so well,' Jake had said one night after he'd found out they all supported the same team. Emily wasn't into AFL – or any sport, for that matter – but she knew of people so passionate they even came to blows with opposing supporters. She imagined it was rare to get so many Melbourne people in one room who supported the one team – Bill and Stan were also Collingwood supporters, but not quite as ardent as the younger fellows. Their project really did seem to be blessed. Emily hoped for their sake they would be finished by Easter.

Simone would be staying in Emily's office. Although it had been empty since the men had moved down to the shearing shed, she hadn't had a chance to look for book-shelves to complete her reading nook. In fact, she was a little ashamed to admit, she had barely stepped foot in it since adding the pieces of furniture.

She and Jake tended to sit at the kitchen table or in bed with his laptop working on the budgets and going over things. The non-cottage paperwork was still piled up and unfiled in the other room. When she thought about it, the amount of stuff she had to do was quite overwhelming. And when she started the business, there would probably never be an opportunity to sit and read for pleasure.

All she hoped was that Jake and David would be able to spare at least a few hours off the tractors for them to spend all together. A barbeque at one of the picturesque spots on her farm or David and Barbara's would be great to give Simone a real rural experience.

As Jake had done all those months ago when he'd visited Emily, Simone was going to fly to Whyalla, collect a hire car, and drive herself to Wattle Creek. She was planning to arrive mid-afternoon on Good Friday – the twenty-second.

Chapter Twenty-five

Two days before the Easter long weekend, the stonemasons finally completed their work on the building across the way. Emily was very chuffed when they called her over before putting the final stone in place. Then she, Jake, David and the guys all left their mark by carefully carving their initials in the mortar. It was a wonderful permanent reminder of their contribution.

Now when she threw open the bedroom curtains, she was greeted by nice straight stone walls standing tall. And she was truly a part of it. Soon the building would look less naked and exposed when the roofers did their work, and the joiners put in doors and windows. Everything seemed to be slotting into place perfectly.

They had a farewell dinner for the guys on Wednesday night. Jake had offered them a choice between a night out at the pub or a roast dinner at home, and to Emily's surprise they'd gone with lamb roast. She couldn't believe they'd want something so stock standard, especially when she'd already cooked them numerous roasts. But the weather was dreary outside and as Jake pointed out, these were city folk who hadn't had a lifetime of good country fare. And they had spent a few Saturday nights out in the pub with Grant and Steve and Nathan.

So they stayed in and Emily did a roast with all the trimmings. To compensate for what she considered a simple meal – hell, she'd made dozens, maybe hundreds, of roast dinners in her time – she made rich individual chocolate fondant puddings from a recipe she'd seen recently on a cooking show. Afterwards, the guys headed back to the shearing shed for the last time going on about how good the food was and how full they were. Emily was pleased, even more so when Jake showed his appreciation that night in bed.

On Thursday the guys left after breakfast. As she hugged them and waved them off, Emily felt a tug of sadness – she was going to miss them. She spent the day feeling a little melancholy as she pottered around the house cleaning up after them and preparing for Simone.

On the morning of Simone's visit, Emily and Jake got up early, both keen to get the day underway. Over breakfast, Jake was like a little kid who was antsy to go and play outside. 'Look at you,' she teased. 'You can hardly sit still.' He and David were starting their stints on the tractors.

'Gotta go,' he said, getting up with the last corner of his breakfast toast in his hand. He kissed her quickly.

'I suppose I'd better bring your lunch down later then, since you don't look keen to wait for me to make it.' Emily laughed.

'Oh. Sorry. Would you mind?'

'Not at all. You go plough those fields, oh handsome man of mine,' she said, slapping at his thigh as he passed by.

'Don't you start,' he replied, grinning back and pretending to bat her hand away.

'But seriously. Good luck. Call me if you need anything. I'll be right here,' she said.

'Speaking of barely able to sit still,' Jake said.

'I know. I can't wait to see Simone.'

'Me too. It's going to be great. Well, this crop isn't going to get planted on its own,' he said, and left the kitchen with a wave of his hand.

There was only around a week of solid work on her property, but timing was everything when it came to getting the seed in the ground. It was just a pity it was all happening when Simone was visiting.

Meanwhile, the construction work would continue across the road. Jake had been astounded when the roofers had offered to work right through Easter. Emily was surprised to learn that they didn't need supervising; they had the plans, had already met with Jake on site, and so would just set to.

After Jake left, Emily sat at the table with her coffee. Although she had often been alone in the house during the day while everyone else had been over at the building site, it suddenly seemed very quiet with no one around. Well, except for the chatter of all the neighbouring farmers on the UHF radio fixed to the wall above the bench. The whole district was abuzz with seeding. As much as she'd have liked to turn down the radio, she had to keep one ear open in case Jake called her. They could use mobile phones, but Jake wanted to use the radio for anything not too personal – that was what real farmers did!

Just after four o'clock, Emily heard a car pull up outside. She looked out to see Simone getting out of a little white sedan.

'Hi Simone,' she called, waving an arm as she raced down the path. 'Welcome to Wattle Creek.'

'Thanks. It's wonderful to see you again,' Simone said.

'I'm so glad you could come – especially for Easter.' They hugged like old friends.

'And you must be Grace,' Simone said to the dog beside them, bending down and patting her. 'What a gorgeous girl. Jake's told me so much about you, oh yes he has,' she said, ruffling the dog's ears.

'So you found us okay?' Emily asked after Simone was again standing upright.

'Piece of cake. Jake gives very precise directions.'

'Yes, that he does.'

'What a great spot,' Simone said, slowly turning around to take in a full three-hundred-and-sixty-degree view of her surroundings. 'I love the big gum trees.'

'They are lovely. And thanks. It's home.'

'It's a lot greener than I thought it would be. It looked quite dry flying into Whyalla.'

'Yes, we've had quite a bit of rain down here. You might have noticed tractors out in some of the paddocks along the way – they're busy sowing the winter crops.'

'And is that *the* project back there?' she said, turning and pointing over towards the creek.

'Yep. It's coming along really well. Much quicker than I thought it would. The guys worked like demons.'

'They're hard workers, and nice guys. Are they still here?'

'No. They finished Wednesday and left yesterday.'

'That's a shame. I mean, a shame I didn't get to see them. But I bet you're glad to see the end of all that cooking.'

'They said they'd come back for a holiday sometime and do a stone wall for us, if we want one,' Emily said.

'Pity you're not doing a B&B; they could be your first guests.'

'And do all their washing? I think I've learnt that lesson.' Emily smiled. 'Come on in. I'll give you the grand tour of the house. I'm leaving the cottage until tomorrow when hopefully we'll have a bit of roof on. I hope you don't mind.'

'Not at all. Anyway, I'm dying to see this office of yours. Jake's told me all about it — says it's absolutely gorgeous,' Simone said as they made their way up to the house.

'I'm not sure it should be called that — I haven't done anything remotely office-related in there. And I don't have anywhere near your flair for interior decorating.'

'I'm sure you're selling yourself short,' Simone said kindly.

Emily shrugged. 'Welcome,' she said, throwing open the glass sliding door and allowing Simone to pass.

'Oh, what a great space,' Simone said.

'It is, but it's just so big and open. I'd love to pick your brain about how I could improve it, not that I have the time at the moment. I started on the office to give myself something to do, but then the cottage happened. And as they say, the rest is history,' Emily added.

'Some strategically placed dividers – even strips of fabric hanging from the ceiling – would make a big difference,' Simone said, looking around. 'I'll draw you a diagram so you know what I mean.'

'Okay. Great. Thanks. The bathroom and toilet are at the end,' Emily said, pointing to her right. 'Bit of a hike from your room, I'm afraid,' she added apologetically.

'No problem. I don't exactly have en suite facilities myself, remember?' she replied, smiling broadly.

Emily smiled back, remembering the long, thin Melbourne terrace. She felt like hugging Simone again. She was so nice.

They made their way through the house, deliberately leaving her new office – Simone's room – until last.

'Oh wow, it's beautiful. Even more lovely than Jake described,' Simone said when they were finally standing in the doorway.

'You don't think the pink is too dark? Honestly?'

'No way. It's perfect. As you know, I'm quite partial to a bit of colour.'

Yes, about that, Emily thought. She was desperate to discuss the possibility of Simone exhibiting. At the rate they were going, the gallery might be up and running before spring. If Simone agreed, she'd need time to get some paintings done, and she'd have to fit them in around her job. She really hoped Simone was still painting 'like a demon' as she'd said all those months ago.

'I'm hoping to put tall bookshelves behind the chair in the corner. And I still haven't worked out what to do on the bed,' Emily said with a shrug. 'The cottage really has taken over.'

'These things always take time. Far too often I've rushed into buying something and it's ended up in a cupboard after a few months. I think you're better off living with a space for a while if you're not immediately sure.'

'Well, that's what I'm doing, but not really by choice. I've hardly spent any time in here at all.'

'Jake was telling me how busy you've been. I don't know how you do it. I struggle just to keep my house clean with working full-time, and I don't have a heap of blokes to cook and do washing for. I took on a cleaner a few weeks ago, and it's the best thing I've ever done. Wish I'd done it years ago.'

'I wish I could, but there aren't any around here,' Emily said.

'Maybe you need to set up a cleaning company.'

Emily laughed heartily. 'Sorry,' she said in response to Simone's puzzled look. 'It's just that my dear friend, Barbara, and I had the same discussion the other day.'

'So, is Jake out playing farmer?'

'Yep.'

'He was very excited about it.'

Emily checked her watch. 'Well, he's been out there for about eight hours. By now he's probably bored out of his brain with driving round and round only seeing dirt. I'm sure it's not nearly as glamorous or exciting as he was expecting, but he is helping David, so that's a good thing.' She explained that David and Jake had been swapping labour, both taking the opportunity to learn about the other's work.

'I hear David and Barbara are great. I can't wait to meet them.'

'Barbara's coming down for dinner tonight, but I'm afraid it might be just us girls. We're going to have a barbeque all together on Sunday, so you'll get to meet David then.'

Back in the kitchen, Emily brought out her scrapbook and they settled in to discuss the finer details of the cottage.

'It all looks fantastic,' Simone said. 'And Jake tells me you're thinking of using it as an art gallery. How exciting!'

'Yes.' Suddenly Emily felt a little nervous. 'Actually, I was hoping to talk to you about that. I'd like you to be my first artist to exhibit,' she blurted, her cheeks starting to redden.

'Don't be silly, I'm not a real artist,' Simone said dismissively. Then, noticing Emily's slightly mortified expression, 'Oh, you're being serious?'

'Of course I am. I loved the paintings in your house and I'm sure plenty of other people will too. They're gorgeous.'

For a moment Simone didn't reply. 'I'm very flattered,' she finally said. 'But they're just paint slapped on canvas.'

'Now you're selling *yourself* short.'

'That's what Jake said once,' Simone said thoughtfully.

'Well, he can talk. I wanted him to exhibit his photography, but he flatly refuses.'

'He's just very private. My reluctance is about lack of talent, not shyness,' Simone said with a laugh.

'Since there's clearly no problem with lack of talent, can I count you in then?' Emily said cheerfully, and crossed her fingers in her lap under the table.

'Er...'

'Oh, come on, Simone, please. I need an artist for the opening and I really want it to be you.'

'Flattery, flattery.'

'So, you'll do it?' Emily prodded.

'Before I decide, how long do I have and just how many paintings do you think you'll need?'

They discussed the details and Emily watched as Simone became more and more enthusiastic. She said she'd actually done quite a few canvases since being inspired to pick up her brushes again after Emily's visit. She'd even done some landscapes, abstracts, and experimented with architecture, like Jake had with his photography. She explained she'd once had aspirations to live as an artist, but didn't like the 'poor, struggling' part that seemed to go hand in hand with such an existence. Perhaps this was a sign, the break she needed.

'All right, I'll do it,' she said, and leapt up and hugged Emily, thanking her for the opportunity. 'But I'm not sure when I'll get the time to paint.'

They were still talking it over and chatting animatedly about styles, colours, and textures when Barbara arrived.

'Guess what?' Emily said after the introductions had been made, Barbara was settled in a chair, and there were fresh cups of tea in front of each of them.

'What?' Barbara asked.

'I've got my very first artist signed up – well, not literally signed.' She opened her arms to indicate Simone.

'Oh, that's fantastic,' Barbara said. 'May it open a whole world of opportunities for you, Simone, and mark the start of a successful venture for you, Emily.'

'I'll drink to that,' Simone said, and they all raised their mugs and tapped them together to complete the toast.

'Hey, I drove by to look at the cottage before coming in. I can't believe how much they've done on the roof already,' Barbara said. 'It looks like most of the beams are up.'

'They're going to be here all weekend. I couldn't believe it when I heard they wanted to work over Easter. Neither could Jake,' Emily said.

'Probably the fishing forecast wasn't good or there'll be too many tourists out on the water, or something. The owner of the business is a keen fisherman,' Barbara explained to Simone.

'Lucky for us,' Emily said.

'There were heaps of vehicles towing boats all the way from Whyalla,' Simone added, taking a sip of her tea.

'Well, I'm just happy the show goes on while David and Jake are off doing other things.'

'Indeed. How's Jake going out there all on his lonesome?' Barbara asked.

'Fine. I think. Haven't heard a peep since I took his lunch down earlier. He really is having a ball. I think being in charge of heavy machinery is good for his masculinity,' Emily said with a laugh. 'How's David going?'

'Trundling along. Not a peep there either.'

'So do you want to go for a few laps with Jake?' Emily suddenly asked Simone.

'Ooh, yes please, that'd be fun.'

'Come on then, we'll take him down some cake,' Emily said, grabbing the cling-wrapped bundle she'd placed on the bench that morning.

'Should I take a jacket or something?' Simone asked.

'It wouldn't hurt, but you should be in a nice warm cab.'

'I'll get it from my room, just in case,' she said, leaping up and disappearing from the kitchen.

'She's lovely,' Barbara whispered.

'Yes, isn't she?' Emily replied, also keeping her voice low. 'Though of course I knew she would be, being Jake's sister.'

'It's so good to be spending time getting to know each other properly. And I'm so relieved she's agreed to be my artist,' Emily said. 'That's a huge weight off my mind.'

'Well, everything sure is coming together. It's great to hear,' Barbara said.

'Speaking of coming together, how are you and the little one doing?'

'So far, so good. I'm doing my best not to worry, but it's hard. I'm meant to be in the safe period now, and I know I'm just being paranoid, but I'm still on tenterhooks. I'll probably be a nervous wreck by September.'

'You're going to be just fine,' Emily said, patting her friend's hand. She thought Barbara's overall appearance did have a slightly drawn look to it.

'I'm taking a camera too,' Simone said, reappearing. 'I just *have* to get some shots of Jake with his tractor!'

'Good idea,' Emily said, smiling and thinking how alike she and Jake were. Right from the start of the cottage project he had recorded every bit of progress with his camera. 'Come on then.'

'Do you mind if I stay here?' Barbara asked. 'Seen one tractor, seen them all.'

'No problem at all,' Emily said. 'I won't be long, and there are plenty of magazines in the usual place.' She called Gracie to her and pulled the glass door shut. It was a lovely, warm, still afternoon.

'Barbara's not her usual self,' Emily explained to Simone as they made their way down to the paddock where Jake was working. 'She's pregnant, but she's had two miscarriages before, so she's really worried about it happening again.' She hoped Barbara wouldn't mind her telling Simone, but thought it important she knew.

'Oh, the poor thing,' Simone said. 'No wonder she's being super-careful. I'm sure I'd be a nervous wreck. It's amazing; you hear of all these people – especially teenagers – getting pregnant at the drop of a hat and all the lectures at school about safe sex, but it seems it's actually quite difficult to get pregnant when you really *want* to. Not that I know anything about it.'

'No, me neither.' As they walked, the shadows were growing long, signalling that dusk was on its way.

They fell silent for a moment until Simone cried, 'There he is!' In the distance, a green John Deere tractor was making its way slowly along the far side of the paddock, the soil changing colour to a rich shade of brown behind it.

'So, what exactly is he doing?' Simone asked.

'Seeding. Sowing the seeds for a wheat crop.'

'Oh, don't they dig it up first? I'm just thinking of how normal gardening is done. You dig everything up and then plant the seeds.'

'They used to do that. Now they do what's called direct drilling – digging the soil and planting the seed in the one go. It keeps the nutrients in, or something. I'm not the one to ask. I was raised in a town, not on a farm, so I don't know a whole lot more than you. My husband wasn't one for sharing.'

'Oh, well, at least you have Jake now – he's one of the most generous and kind people I've ever met. Though, I might be a little biased,' Simone added, grinning.

'I love him,' Emily said blissfully as she brought the ute to a halt at the paddock gate.

'I know you do. And he loves you,' Simone said.

They got out and walked over to where a small truck was parked nearby. Emily explained that the large divided bin on the back contained the seed and fertiliser for refilling the hoppers on the machine behind.

'John used to have all sorts of trouble with the auger motor,' she said, remembering how he'd regularly cursed the machine. Hopefully it hadn't been giving Jake any trouble. *No news is good news*, she thought, quoting another of Gran's favourite sayings. 'We'll wait here for him to come around. It's not a good idea to drive over what's just been sown. He should only be a few minutes.'

They silently watched, mesmerised by the slow, steady progress of the tractor moving around the paddock in front of them.

It took around ten minutes for Jake to pull up nearby and the loud throaty engine to reduce to a gentle idling hum. He stepped down from the high cab and strode across the paddock towards them.

'Hey you,' he said, greeting his sister with a tight hug.

'Having fun playing farmer?' Simone said.

'I will have you know, I am *being* a farmer, not just playing at it,' he said, pouting.

'So, how's it going?'

'Good. No problems. Touch wood,' he added, putting his hand on his head. 'It's just time-consuming. But listening to talkback or music on the radio isn't a bad way to spend a day. So, who's coming for a lap or two? I can't fit both of you in, though,' he said.

'Simone's turn,' Emily said. 'Barbara's waiting for me back at the house.'

'Okay. Come on sis, we've got a crop to sow.'

'Are you going to finish this paddock before tea, do you think?' Emily asked.

'Should do, if it's not until around seven,' he said, looking at her questioningly.

'Do you want to be out here that long, Simone?'

'I don't know. Do I?' she asked Jake.

'She'll be fine. If I am, she will be,' he said.

'Well, if you do get sick of it, get him to call me up on the UHF and I'll come and get you,' Emily said. 'Oh, and here's some cake to tide you over,' she said, handing over four pieces of cake wrapped tightly in cling-film.

'You're wonderful, thank you,' Jake said, wrapping his arms around her.

'My pleasure,' Emily said, smiling up at him.

Simone and Jake walked across to the tractor and then got settled up in the cab. Emily watched as the tractor moved off with a puff of thick black smoke from its exhaust.

After waving them off, she got back into the ute with Grace, feeling happy and content. Everything sure was coming together and coming together well. Life was pretty damned perfect. It would be nice to sit with Barbara for a while. She'd missed that during the last few busy months.

Chapter Twenty-six

Even though it was Jake's birthday, Easter Saturday was a work day for the farmers. That morning they all got up early for a quick breakfast together before he set out on the tractor. Emily held her breath as he opened the present she'd agonised over.

'Oh wow, Em, this is great,' he said, getting up and kissing her.

After much deliberation, she'd ordered him a brown Bushman Driza-Bone oilskin jacket and fawn Stockman-style Akubra hat. She'd consulted Barbara and David to make sure she got traditional enough styles so that he would blend in with the locals.

'Hopefully I'll look less like the bloke visiting from the city now,' he said, putting on both items and doing a three-sixty in front of the girls.

'Maybe when you've worn them at bit and been in some dust,' Simone said.

'Well, there's no way I'm rubbing dust into my hat, if that's what you're suggesting,' Jake said indignantly, taking off the hat and stroking it protectively.

'Don't worry, I'm sure you'll look less clean and shiny in no time,' Emily said.

'This is from me,' said Simone, dragging a navy-and-white-striped parcel from the floor onto the table. 'Happy birthday, brother dear.' She leaned over and gave him a peck on the cheek.

'Thanks, sis.' He tore off the paper to reveal a nice thick woollen jumper in steel grey, a checked shirt, and two paperback novels. 'Brilliant. Well, I'd better go and get some real dirt on my new jacket and hat,' he said, getting up from the table with a huge grin. He kissed Emily on his way past.

'See ya later,' he said, doffing his hat at the door as he left the kitchen.

'Have fun,' Simone and Emily called.

Emily and Simone rugged up and headed off for a long walk soon after. They started with a tour of the new building, spending almost half an hour discussing upcoming fixtures and fittings.

It was an amazing feeling to stand underneath the timber roof trusses and imagine the finished building. Looking down at her feet, she couldn't wait to see how the concrete floor came up when polished. Even with all the dust on it, she could see small colourful stones glinting where the sun shone through the window openings.

They chewed over ideas for seating in the large rooms. Simone was right; large flat ottomans where people could sit and look at one wall and then swivel around to look at the next was a much better idea than couches with backs. It was the sort of thing all the government-owned galleries had. The tricky thing would be deciding the size, shape, and fabric. Leather would be hard-wearing, but would probably require quite a large outlay.

'I love leather, but you don't want to look too conservative and old-fashioned,' Simone said thoughtfully. 'Especially when it's going to be called The Button Jar. That makes me think fun, vibrant, colourful, eclectic.'

'That's what I'm going for,' Emily said, pleased the meaning behind it was so obvious.

'So you don't want it looking like a state or national gallery,' Simone continued.

'No, I don't really.'

'Don't worry, we'll come up with the perfect thing.'

When Simone suggested bright Indian fabrics, like those used for saris, Emily almost froze to the spot. There was India again. Had Jake employed Simone to convince her to change her mind about their honeymoon?

No, get a grip! They hadn't even seriously discussed going to India. It had been suggested as a place to visit, just like she'd suggested Tasmania. Simone didn't even know about their engagement yet. No, she was being silly and paranoid. Though she did let out a sigh of relief when Simone added that there were some places in Melbourne importing the gorgeous fabrics. And they are gorgeous, Emily thought. The only problem was how hard-wearing would they be.

She liked the idea of brightening the space they had deliberately left neutral. Though, would Simone's bright paintings be overshadowed by brocades in even richer colours? Gosh, there was still so much to think about. Of course, she mightn't always have bright artworks in here. But her priority was for everything to look perfect on opening night. If she went for fabric, she could always have a selection with zips so they could be changed. She could get out her sewing machine and make some herself once she had one to cut a pattern from.

As they left the unfinished building, the roofers were driving in off the road towards it. Emily and Simone waved in greeting, but kept walking in the opposite direction.

'Come on, I want to see sheep and kangaroos in their natural habitat!' Simone said, linking her arm through Emily's. 'If we have a good walk I won't feel guilty about all the chocolate eggs I'm going to eat tomorrow.'

'I can't guarantee you'll see kangaroos, but I'll do my best,' Emily said with a laugh. She took them towards a secluded area where she'd seen a mob of kangaroos hanging out a few weeks ago. The perfect, lush spot she'd first taken Jake to was a little far to walk. They'd try there tomorrow if they didn't see any roos here today.

They silently crept the last fifty metres and stopped amongst the trees, hidden. Just ahead of them, beyond the edge of the scrub, a dozen kangaroos of varying sizes were grazing.

Emily bent down to hold Grace's collar. 'Stay,' she said quietly in the dog's ear.

'Oh, they're beautiful,' Simone whispered, clearly in awe.

Her voice was low, but at that moment all the kangaroos lifted their heads in their direction. And, then, in one fluid movement like a grey blanket being caught up in a gust of wind, they turned and bounded off into the security of the trees on the far side.

'Sorry,' Simone said. 'I thought I was being quiet.'

'No matter how quiet we were they would still have noticed us. They probably smelt us well before they heard us. They have amazing senses. It's pretty late for their morning feeding, so they were probably ready to head off anyway. They usually come back around dusk.'

'Well, I'm so glad I've seen them. I think it's great you living in harmony with them and not getting out the gun,' Simone said, walking out into the open area the kangaroos had just vacated.

Emily laughed. 'Well, it's not quite harmonious, but the years of drought have kept their numbers down naturally. Hopefully we won't need to cull any for a while yet. I hate the thought of it, but in large numbers they make a horrible mess of crops.'

Leaving the area, they did a large loop that took them way up behind the new building. The whole time the faint background hum of Jake's tractor could be heard.

'So, Jake's looking well. Certainly much better than last time I saw him. Is he better, or is it just being out in the sun and fresh country air?'

'You'd have to ask him how he's feeling.'

'Yes, but you must have some idea. Has he shaken the adrenal fatigue, do you think?'

'It's hard to tell, really. It seems to be one of those illnesses that has a lot of symptoms you could put down to other things. Like, take his hands shaking. My hands were shaking when I spent all that time with a hammer cleaning up the rocks. I worry constantly that he's overdoing it, but I can't nag him. He's a grown man. And you know what men are like. Unless it's man flu and they're snivelling and moaning in pain, no one knows about it.'

'I know. I'm sorry; I shouldn't be putting you on the spot. I'll talk to him.'

'It's okay,' Emily said, in a gentler tone. 'And I don't mean to sound evasive. He hasn't had night sweats for ages and he hasn't really struggled to get up in the mornings since the project started, if that helps. But I don't know if that means he's over the illness or just that he loves being in charge.'

'Perhaps it's being away from city life, tough clients, and big projects that's done it.'

'I don't know, but he has certainly been in his element with this one. He hasn't seemed at all stressed or strung out. God, he's hot when he's in charge,' Emily mused, then realised she'd said the words out loud. 'Sorry, that was a little off of me.'

Simone laughed. 'He's my brother, so I can't say I find him "hot", but he is pretty impressive when he's in charge. And, I'm sure being in love has helped,' she added, linking her arm through Emily's again.

Emily smiled back in response.

They walked across a small ridge of hills and finally caught sight of Jake's tractor three paddocks over, turning the earth from the grey of old, dried summer grass and leftover cereal crop stalks to rich dark brown. Emily's bright blue ute shone in the sun at the gate beside the little old truck. *It's all just so right*, she thought, smiling contentedly to herself.

At eleven o'clock Sunday morning, after a bit of a lie-in and a breakfast of hot cross buns, Jake, Emily and Simone piled into the new ute and headed off for the barbeque. As they arrived at Barbara and David's favourite picnic spot – a secluded oasis tucked away at the back of their farm, hidden by scrub – Simone cried out in awe.

'It's gorgeous!' she said. 'Like a postcard.' She got her camera out and started snapping away.

Thanks to the recent rains, it was looking more lush and beautiful than the last time Emily had been there.

David and Barbara were unpacking their ute when they pulled up. David had laid down a tarp and secured it at the corners with tent pegs, and was now spreading picnic rugs over the top.

'Happy Easter!' they all cried, and went through the ritual of everyone hugging and kissing. Jake introduced David and Simone and then David took orders for drinks.

'I'm on the sparkling apple cider,' Barbara said, 'if anyone would like to join me. No additives. Just pure juice with bubbles from Tasmania.'

'Ooh, yes please,' Simone said.

'Yes, me too, thanks,' Emily said.

'Looks like I've got two designated drivers,' Jake said.

'And I've got Barb,' David said. 'We could get hammered, mate.'

'You're on your own there. I'm way too old for that sort of caper,' Jake said.

'Yeah, me too, really. So, just a light beer then?'

'Yes, thanks,' Jake replied.

When they each had a drink in hand, David welcomed Simone and toasted, 'To good friends.' They clinked glasses, murmured their agreement and took their first sips.

As soon as she tasted the sparkling non-alcoholic cider, Emily thought she might never go back to the alcoholic version. She liked the gentler, sweeter sensation of it on her tongue. 'This is lovely. I must get some,' she said, studying the bottle.

During a quick trip to town the day before – where Simone had been stunned to find the shops shut at noon – Emily had bought a loaf of squishy white bread and a few standard sausages from the local butcher. These items were their homage to basic, old-fashioned barbequing amongst an otherwise quite gourmet selection. Barbara had brought marinated skinless and boneless chicken thighs, rissoles, and grilled pumpkin, zucchini, capsicum and potato.

After the salads, plates, cutlery, serviettes, and condiments were set up on the table, the girls took their place on the rugs with their backs to the sun. Meanwhile, David and Jake got to work on the portable gas barbeque.

'Thank you so much,' Simone said. 'This is perfect. What a great way to spend a Sunday, let alone Easter Sunday!'

'Thank goodness the boys took some time off,' Barbara said.

'Yes, plenty seem to be still at it,' Emily said, cocking an ear. The hum of tractors could be heard droning away on nearby farms.

After lunch they sat around nursing their full stomachs.

'I'm eating for two,' Barbara announced, 'and I still think I've eaten too much.'

'As long as you've left room for Easter eggs,' Emily said. 'We've got stacks of them.' She got up and retrieved the chocolate eggs from the esky.

'Before you dish them out,' Jake said, getting up, 'I've got something to say.'

'Oh, okay,' Emily said, surprised, and sat back down with the bag beside her.

'As you all know,' Jake began, addressing the small group, 'it's been a few months since I came here to Wattle Creek, and in that time I've become very settled with Em. What most of you don't know is that around three months ago I proposed.'

Emily blushed. She looked at the ground with no idea why she was feeling embarrassed. Out of the corner of her eye she noticed David and Barbara's bug-eyed, open-mouthed expressions. But Simone didn't look at all surprised.

'I made a hash of it, really, blurting it out when the timing was all wrong,' Jake continued. 'But now – if you'll still have me, Em – I'd like to make it right.'

Suddenly he was on his knees in front of her. He took her hands in his and looked deep into her blue-grey eyes.

'Emily Katherine Oliphant, will you do me the honour of becoming my wife?'

Unable to speak, Emily nodded. Tears blurred her vision as Jake reached into his pocket. She blinked them away as he brought out a small, square velvet box and then opened it in front of her. She focussed on a large diamond sparkling in the sun. She put her hands to her throat. *Oh. My. God. It's huge!*

'Oh wow! It's gorgeous!' Barbara cried, speaking the exact words Emily hadn't yet got out.

'So? Do I get a yes – again?' Jake asked, grinning.

Emily nodded furiously. 'Yes, yes, YES!' she finally blurted, and threw her arms around him. They fell back, entwined. The ring box snapped shut, still firmly in Jake's grasp.

'Pity I can't drink champagne,' Barbara said wistfully as she watched them kiss.

'Oh, come on, get a room, you two,' David said after a few moments.

Jake and Emily sat up, grinning from ear to ear.

'But seriously, congratulations. You make a lovely couple,' he added. He leaned over and hugged Emily and then shook hands with Jake before pulling him into a manly hug and slapping him on the back.

'Yes, congratulations,' Barbara said, hugging first Emily and then Jake.

'And from me, of course,' Simone said. 'I helped choose the ring, so it goes without saying that I totally approve.' She smiled and leaned in to kiss them both. 'Now,' she said, clapping her hands together, 'it must be time to bring out the chocolate.' She reached across, took an egg and passed the bag to Barbara. 'More for us if they're too busy,' she added, nodding at Jake and Emily, who were once again entwined.

'Not so fast,' Jake said, sitting up. He intercepted the bag just before it was handed to David.

'Oi,' said David, pouting.

'We're newly engaged, we should get priority,' Jake said.

'Not until she has your ring on her finger you're not, mate, not officially,' David replied.

As Jake slipped the simple, elegant ring over her finger, Emily stared at the massive clear round solitaire diamond.

'I hope you like it,' he said quietly, 'but if you don't, it can easily be changed.'

'No, I love it. It's perfect.' It was the largest diamond she'd ever seen up close in a ring, but it was in a style that didn't sit too high and would be practical enough to wear every day. She made a silent vow to never take it off.

'I'm so glad you like it,' Simone said when they'd settled into the Easter eggs.

So, Simone had been involved. Well, of course she had to have been. Perhaps this was the whole reason for her visit. She was so pleased she was there.

Emily looked around at the group of people who meant the most to both her and Jake. The only ones missing were Des and Gran – she was a little sad about that. And her mother too, but knowing Enid, she'd probably have said something to ruin the moment.

Her eyes kept moving back to admire her ring.

'Here, give us a look now it's on,' David urged, and Emily held out her hand and wiggled it in front of them. The diamond glinted magnificently in the sun, sending tiny brightly coloured rainbows across the picnic rug.

'So, when are you going to get married?' Barbara asked when the commotion of oohs and aahs had finally died down.

Emily looked at Jake and shrugged.

'Better give Enid enough time to put together the full catastrophe,' Barbara said quietly. Emily was surprised by her friend's lack of animation. Where was the smirk? Probably no one else would have noticed, but she did. Barbara was usually the life of the party and had been known to be merciless with her sarcasm.

'Oh, God, don't remind me,' Emily said, pushing her concern aside, and making an exaggerated show of putting her head in her hands. Barbara did have a point, though. She'd have to try to stop her mother bolting off to book visits to bridal-wear shops, florists and bakeries in Adelaide. She and Barbara had discussed their weddings a few times and there was one thing she knew for sure – this time she did not want Enid involved at all.

'Speaking of which. I'd better call Mum and Dad,' Emily said, and got her mobile out, stood up, and moved away from the group.

'Hi Dad, Happy Easter,' she said. 'How's things?'

'And a happy Easter to you too. Anything out of the ordinary happening that I should know about?' Des Oliphant enquired. 'Like perhaps an exciting announcement?'

'You already know?' Emily looked back at Jake who grinned at her and raised his eyebrows knowingly.

'Jake might have mentioned something. I hope you said yes.'

'He actually asked your permission?' Emily asked, fixing her gaze on Jake who now shrugged, looking proud of himself.

'Very good manners, that young man. I believe he'll be very good *to* you and very good *for* you. I wouldn't have given my blessing if I didn't think so.'

'Thanks Dad.' Tears filled Emily's eyes again and a lump worked its way into her throat.

Just as Emily was about to ask to speak to her mother, there was a commotion in the background at her father's end. She heard the muffled words, 'What's going on? What blessing? Is that Emily? Here, give me the phone.'

'Emily, what's going on?' Enid Oliphant's shrill voice boomed into her ear.

'Happy Easter, Mum.'

'Yes, happy Easter,' she said brusquely. 'Now, what's going on? What's this about Des giving his blessing? For what? And why aren't I being consulted?'

'Jake has asked me to marry him. We're engaged,' Emily said quietly when Enid's rant finally ended.

'What? Oh. But you hardly know him. It's a bit soon, isn't it?'

'We don't think so. You could at least be pleased for me.'

'I am. Of course I am pleased for you. Congratulations, both of you. I'm sure you will be very happy together.'

'Thanks Mum.'

The next thing she heard was Enid berating her husband. 'You *knew* about this Des and didn't tell me? How long have you known?'

Emily rolled her eyes and sighed. As usual, her mother had managed to make it all about her.

'I'd like to speak to Jake, please,' Enid said suddenly.

Emily moved back towards the picnic rug. 'Mum wants to speak to you,' she said, and handed the phone over with pursed lips before sitting back down heavily.

'Hello Enid. Thank you, we're very happy. I hope you approve.'

Emily wished he'd put it on speaker so they could all hear.

'No, we haven't set a date yet. This is all very new; we haven't discussed any plans.' He looked at Emily and winced. 'We're not in any rush. When we've decided what we want to do, you'll be the first to know. But it will probably be something low-key.'

'No, you're right, I haven't been married before. But I'm not a big one for white weddings. As I said, we haven't discussed the actual ceremony as yet. Look, I'm sorry Enid, this phone is going flat. I'm going to have to go. It's probably going to cut out any second. I'll have Emily phone you back later.' And with that he ended the call and dropped the phone onto the rug like a hot potato.

'Phew,' he said, and let out his breath loudly.

'Well handled, mate,' David said. There were ripples of agreement from around the group. Simone frowned.

'Emily's mother can be somewhat…um…interfering,' Barbara explained. 'And not, generally, very supportive.'

'That's putting it politely,' David said.

'Ahh,' Simone said knowingly, and nodded.

'So, it sometimes calls for affirmative action to protect our dear Emily from her clutches,' Jake said.

Chapter Twenty-seven

In the ute on the way home, Emily still couldn't take her eyes off her ring.

What a surprise, she thought, twirling it around on her finger. Not one mention of their engagement in almost three months and then, bang!

'You like it, don't you?' Jake asked, putting his hand on her thigh. 'Because if you don't...'

Emily grasped his hand. 'It's perfect, and I love it,' she said, beaming across at him. She almost added, 'Perfect like you, like us,' but stopped herself. This scene – them sitting in the front of the ute, Simone in the back – was too much like a scene out of a low-budget movie as it was without adding soppy dialogue as well.

What a wonderful day, she thought, again looking back down at her ring. She wondered what it would take to convince Enid she was not having another big wedding. There was no way she wanted to go through that palaver again. Then again, maybe it would be easier just to give in? She could leave all the preparations to her mother and just turn up on the day.

No way, I'm better than that. Look how I've been standing up for myself lately.

It was hard work keeping the defences up, but the peace was worth it. And there was Jake to think about now too.

She knew she'd have to phone her mother back, but she decided to sleep on it. In the morning she would be stronger and more tolerant. Right now she wanted to let the joy of her engagement sink in. She settled back into the seat and let out a deep sigh.

'I hope that's a sigh of contentment, darling,' Jake said.

'Of course it is,' she said, turning towards him and smiling warmly.

'I've never properly asked you, Em,' Jake said, 'but what do you want? Would you like a big white wedding, a smaller, more casual affair, or to go away, just the two of us? What would you like to do?'

Emily felt a little uncomfortable having this conversation with Simone in the vehicle with them.

'I'm not sure, but I certainly don't want the full shebang. I'd feel like such a hypocrite doing that all over again, when I didn't get it right the first time.'

'I'm sure you made a beautiful bride,' Jake said kindly. 'It wasn't your fault you married the wrong bloke.'

Whose fault was it then? It wasn't like I was dragged down the aisle kicking and screaming.

'Your mum didn't sound all that happy about the engagement. Doesn't she like Jake?' Simone asked.

'No, she thinks he's lovely. Well, she did the first few times they met. I think she blames him for what she would see as my sudden wilfulness. You see, I've finally started standing up for myself after a lifetime of accepting her control, interference, and lack of support,' she explained to Simone. 'I'm thirty-two, and my mother still thinks she can run my life. I'm finally trying to throw the shackles off.'

'I think eloping to somewhere exotic would be perfect,' Simone said wistfully.

'Honestly, I've got too much else taking up space in my head to even think about it right now.'

'Yes, one thing at a time, I think,' Jake said. 'Like remembering to phone Enid back,' he added, shooting her a grimace. 'Sorry. Maybe I shouldn't have hung up on her.'

'Forget it. I'll deal with it tomorrow, when my head is clear and my defences can withstand her.'

They got back just as the last light was fading. Emily was pleased she'd thought ahead and left the outside light on. They were weary but content. She couldn't remember when she'd last spent a day without all her attention on the building project or under pressure in the kitchen.

After unpacking everything, Jake and Emily retreated to the lounge to watch some television – which they hadn't done for ages – while Simone packed so she would be ready to leave early in the morning.

Emily would be sad to see her go. She had been wonderful company while Jake had been off planting the crop. And Emily hated goodbyes of any sort.

Sometimes she wondered if this little twinge she felt whenever she and Jake said goodbye – even for the shortest time – was fear that what she had found was too good to be true and that it was all about to be taken away. She had to work hard to force the negative thoughts away. She was so lucky to be where she was now. And she'd been doing so well at being positive. If only she could just focus on the good all of the time and not let the insecurities seep back in.

Barbara had told her more than once that if you thought too much about what you feared happening, it could become a self-fulfilling prophecy.

In recent times, Emily had often wanted to say something similar to Barbara regarding her fear over losing the baby, but had never found the right way to say it. She didn't want to sound like she was throwing Barbara's philosophical beliefs in her face. But she couldn't help thinking that if Barbara just got on with life – instead of fretting about doing the tiniest thing in case it might harm the baby – she would be better off.

But really, what would I know?

What she *did* know was that she was neglecting their friendship because of the cottage project. She knew Barbara didn't resent her for it, but perhaps if they could hang out together more, her friend might be in a better place psychologically and emotionally.

It was even worse now that seeding had started and David was spending most of his time off in the paddock, leaving Barbara home alone with her fears. Even though Emily wasn't religious, she did still sort of pray. Well, raised her eyes skyward and silently begged the atmosphere around her to give Barbara a healthy baby and return her well-adjusted, laid-back friend to her.

She knew a baby would change everything, but she just hoped Barbara would return to trusting the universe to do its thing.

'All packed and ready to go,' Simone announced, entering the lounge and throwing herself onto the vacant couch.

'I'm going to miss you,' Emily said. 'It's gone far too quickly, but it's been so good to have you stay. And to get to know you a bit better.'

'Me too. But we've got lots of time to get to know each other now we're going to be related,' Simone said, beaming. 'I'm so happy for you guys. Anyway, I'd better get back home and get busy on the paintings,' she continued. 'I wonder if the boss would let me take a month off to play artist like he's playing farmer,' she said, raising her eyebrows in question at Jake.

'How many times do I have to tell you two? Tractor driving is *not* playing. And, anyway, I'm still running the project while I'm doing it. I'm *multi-tasking* like you women are always on about. It's actually not so hard,' he added with a challenging grin. 'But seriously, Sim, do you want some time off to paint?' he asked.

'I wouldn't mind, actually,' Simone said a little coyly.

'Well, you've got plenty of leave owing.'

'But you're not there.'

'But Angus is. And Toniette. It's JKL and *Associates*, remember? You keep telling me not to worry, that everything is going along fine without me. And that Andrew is proving a great asset. Winter is coming and the Hansen job has had the plug pulled, so it's quiet anyway. The other guys can run the place and focus on looking for new work while you take a month off.'

'Are you sure?'

'Of course. As if I'm going to shackle you to the place if you don't want to be there. I don't want my best employee and business partner getting so jack of it all she ups and leaves me permanently.'

'What if my paintings sell like Emily's jam and I become a famous artist overnight,' Simone said, waving her arms theatrically.

'Well, we'll discuss how we're going to move forward then.'

'You're pretty safe. It's not as if that's likely,' Simone said.

'How many times do I have to tell you to stop selling yourself short? Your paintings would look right at home in plenty of the galleries I've visited,' Jake said emphatically.

Emily chimed in. 'Jake's right, Simone. I loved the paintings in your house. And I bet plenty of other people will too once they get to see them.'

'Well, you're both very kind,' Simone said.

'So, take a month off and enjoy your painting,' Jake said. 'End of discussion. I'll phone Angus on Tuesday morning. Anyway, we don't want you working so hard you end up a basket case like I almost did,' Jake said.

'You seem good now, so if that's what getting out of the office does for the psyche, sign me up!' Simone said.

'That and good country cooking, fresh air, and the love and attention of a good woman,' Jake said, putting his arm around Emily and pulling her towards him. 'I will be forever grateful for you calling Emily that day, Sim,' he continued. 'So, consider this the first step in repaying you.'

'You don't owe me anything, Jake. You're my big brother and I love you.' She leant over and kissed him on the cheek.

Watching this exchange made Emily sad about being an only child. But at least gaining a sister-in-law was better than nothing.

The flickering television was ignored as the three of them sat up chatting about the next stage of the build and the fit-out before saying an early goodnight and heading off to their rooms just before nine.

'Are you okay?' Jake said when he and Emily were snuggling in bed. 'You seem a bit down.'

'Maybe just a bit tired. It's been a big day.'

'Yes, sorry about that. It's my fault, springing the ring and second proposal on you.'

'Don't be sorry, it was lovely.'

'Are you sure you're okay?'

'I am a bit worried about Barbara,' Emily said. 'I'm not sure what to do.'

'Yes, she was very quiet today.'

'Hmm.'

Just then the home phone rang beside Jake. Emily checked her watch: right on nine. She didn't like to answer the phone after nine o'clock. It was how she'd been raised.

'Do you want me to answer it?' Jake asked.

It might be important. 'Yes, thanks.'

'Hello, Jake speaking.' He listened, mouthed, 'It's your mother,' and then pressed the button to activate the speaker. 'Hello again Enid. What can I do for you?'

'Emily hasn't phoned me back. You said she would.'

'She'll call you tomorrow. We've just got home after a long day out and we're really quite tired.'

'Oh, where have you been?'

Jake shot stricken raised eyebrows at Emily. She felt the urge to say, 'None of your damned business.' But he was too well-mannered, so he did what she always did and conceded details.

'Er, we've been out for a picnic barbeque with Barbara and David Burton. My sister Simone is visiting from Melbourne for the weekend. She's leaving first thing in the morning, so we've got a very early start.'

Hint, hint.

But Enid never seemed to get hints, and tonight was no exception. 'Oh. Well, I'm very disappointed not to have had the opportunity to meet her. You could have all had lunch here with us. It would have been nice to spend at least *some* part of the holiday weekend with my daughter. I haven't seen her for ages,' said Enid indignantly. Jake pursed his lips and stared at Emily whilst slowly shaking his head.

And there it is, Emily thought. *The guilt trip. She's blaming Jake for me not visiting.*

'We've been very busy with the building project, and it hasn't been *that* long since we've seen you,' Jake said calmly.

'Oh, did you go ahead with that?'

'Well, yes, we did tell you that. Quite some time ago,' Jake said into the phone whilst frowning bewilderedly at Emily and shaking his head.

You were at the bloody launch party! And where do you think Dad's been spending all his time these last few months? Has Alzheimer's set in? Like Gran? Do I need to talk to Dad about getting her assessed? She bit her lip.

'Well, I still think it's a silly idea,' Enid said in her perfected holier-than-thou tone.

Jake was becoming exasperated. 'With all due respect, Enid, it really makes no difference whether you approve or not. Now, if there wasn't anything else…?'

'I'd like to speak to Emily. I need to discuss the wedding arrangements.'

'Enid, Emily and I are not even sure we want a wedding, as such. Look, could we do this another time? We have an early start in the morning, as I've already said.'

'You can't not have a wedding!' Enid said, clearly aghast. The words, 'What would people think,' remained unsaid, but Emily knew they were on the tip of her mother's tongue – they always were.

'We will celebrate our wedding as we wish. Enid, we only became engaged today and really haven't had a chance to discuss it as yet,' Jake said. Emily was impressed with his patience.

'Put Emily on, will you please?'

Jake raised his eyebrows in question.

Emily reached out for the phone. 'Mum, it's Emily. What's the problem?'

'You didn't call me back.'

Oh, God, here we go, right back at the start. She took a deep, calming breath, and silently counted to five.

'I haven't had a chance yet,' she said with a deep sigh. 'I was going to phone you in the morning. I've had a long day and I'm very tired.' She almost added, 'What with getting engaged and all,' but there was no point. Enid would still find a way to bring everything back to her.

'You can't be serious about not having a wedding.'

'Actually, we're very serious about it, Mum. And, honestly, we've got enough going on with the gallery right now…'

'Gallery? What gallery?'

'The *building*. It's going to be a gallery.'

'As in an *art* gallery?'

'Yes.'

'Whatever do you know about art?'

'I know what I like,' Emily said boldly.

'Oh for goodness sake, Emily.' This had always been Enid's fallback line when she disagreed with something but didn't quite know what to say next.

'Mum, I'm having the courage to take a risk and do something with my life. I have Jake's full support. And Dad's. It would be nice to have yours.' *For once.* 'Now, if you don't mind, we have an early start tomorrow and a very busy day ahead, and need an early night.'

'Oh. Right. Well. Of course I'm supportive, Emily,' Enid said indignantly.

'Goodnight Mum,' Emily said, and hung up without waiting for further comment from the other end of the line. She flopped back onto her pillow, feeling considerably more exhausted than before the call.

'She really is something else, isn't she?' Jake muttered. 'I don't think she'd approve of *anything* that wasn't her idea.'

'Probably not,' Emily said absently while raiding her memory. She came up empty.

Chapter Twenty-eight

The next morning they saw Simone off at seven o'clock. Then Jake left for another day on the tractor, along with Grace, who had taken to riding around with him.

It would be his final day sowing on their property. Tomorrow, all going well, David would be moving the tractor and equipment up to his much larger farm. It was a major production that involved utes with flashing orange lights driving ahead to warn oncoming traffic that large machinery was coming along the road. Barbara and Emily would be needed to provide taxi and escort services back and forth.

Once they moved farms, Emily would hardly see Jake for weeks. He'd come in late, sleep, and leave early the next morning. Everything depended on getting the crop sown as quickly as possible.

Sitting at the kitchen table with her hands wrapped around a steaming mug of coffee, Emily felt tired, to the point of queasiness. She looked down into the coffee she'd lost all interest in. Her mouth tasted weird – sort of metallic. She got up and went to the sink and emptied the mug.

She considered phoning Barbara to see if she wanted some company, but they'd spent most of yesterday together.

She then thought about going back to bed. She was actually starting to feel quite unwell. No, she'd go out and check on the orange tree growing in the back corner of the house yard. Maybe make a batch of marmalade. That might make her feel better. She'd been working so hard for so long taking care of everyone and being involved with the project, she needed to take a day out and do something for herself.

Emily retrieved her stack of buckets from the laundry, and then checked on her stash of jars. Thankfully John hadn't disposed of them. She hoped the oranges were ripe and hadn't gone rotten. She hadn't been around that side of the house in months – there was never any need to.

She was in luck. The lone tree surrounded by bare earth was full. It was the one fruit John had liked, and she'd planted it for him to celebrate their engagement. They had discussed planting a veggie patch here as well, but had never got around to it. She picked up the few oranges that had fallen to the ground. Her heart and mood brightened at the prospect of a fun day in the kitchen, just cooking for herself and feeling close to Gran. It would be nice to have enough to send a box to Simone's friend, Billy, who had the produce store, and to sell in the gallery when it opened.

*

It took them all day Tuesday to move the machinery to David and Barbara's farm, and the whole time Emily continued to feel a little off. A dull nagging nausea always seemed to lurk below the surface, flaring up every now and then. She was sure that if she threw up she'd feel much better. But, as close as she got, she never seemed to cross that particular line. Whatever it was hadn't turned into a cold or the flu. If she rested and kept eating well, hopefully she would keep whatever was ailing her at bay.

That evening, after poached eggs on toast for dinner, they went to bed early and sat up discussing progress on the cottage project. Emily would have preferred to just go to sleep, or at least snuggle silently. But Jake was keen to chatter about the building, which now had a completed roof and protection from the rain.

'The doors and windows will go in in the next few days and then the building will be lockable. A major milestone,' he declared.

'Yes, it looks almost finished from over here now the roof is on,' said Emily, struggling to focus on the discussion.

'Still quite a bit to do, but it'll be great to have it at lock-up, especially since I'll be away at David's for a while.'

'Yes, perfect timing.'

'It's going like clockwork, all round,' Jake said proudly. 'Thank goodness everyone has been available when we needed them.'

'Yes, we certainly do seem to have luck on our side.'

'And you deserve no less. Once it's weather-tight, the concrete can get polished and then we're ready for the cabinetry to go in and the tiling to be done. Then the major heavy work inside will be complete.'

'Great.'

'That, my dear, means we only have a few weeks to decide on the finishing touches. We'd better get back up to Whyalla and buy your chandelier.'

'Yes, we'd better.' Emily was looking forward to that milestone. They'd left the chandelier until last after deciding that the extra expense of having the electrician come back especially to put it in was a better bet than running the risk of it being hit by ladders being carted in and out.

She couldn't believe how fast it was all happening. She'd watched plenty of reality TV renovation shows when contestants only had a week to do a whole room, but she'd never totally believed they didn't turn the cameras off for a few days here and there. Now she was starting to see that it could in fact be done that quickly.

She was glad they had started discussing opening functions and guest lists so early after all. When Jake had first mentioned it, she had thought he was jumping the gun a bit, but now she could see he'd been spot on.

'We really need to nail down a logo, if we're having one. Or at least something to use as branding for the invitations and sign by the road.'

'Hmm,' Emily replied.

They had thrown around a few ideas and had decided to try using a photo of her actual button jar instead of having a logo designed. Jake had done some experimental shots and while Emily thought some were great, she wasn't entirely happy. Did it look too kitsch to include the object? Would people think she was selling buttons? Maybe it would be better to just have the name of the business in a decorative style.

Jake had some contacts in graphic design, so she put him in charge of coming up with some concrete ideas. There didn't seem to be any rush; he had said they would be able to turn such a small job around in a week or so.

'Right,' Jake said. 'Here's my guest list.'

Emily had already put together a list of her own, which consisted of a few close friends and people in the district she knew reasonably well. She was also going to put an open invitation advertisement in the *Wattle Creek Chronicle*, so as not to have anyone feel left out. They were keen to have the building full. People could spill out onto the verandahs if necessary.

'Right, so the first column is good friends and family, and close business associates: must invites. The second is people I know and like, but who I don't know quite so well or aren't in touch with as much. We can cull from the second list, if necessary. That's why I've included occupations – we can be a bit strategic.'

Looking at the list, Emily thought the problem would not be culling the invitees, but people not wanting to travel. Other than a few people in Whyalla, everyone on Jake's guest list lived in Melbourne or in another state.

But she certainly wasn't going to be negative. Jake was smart; if he'd put them on the list then he'd done so with some confidence they'd be interested in attending. Listed were journalists, other gallery owners, business people, some people in finance, some in insurance, and a couple who ran a travel agency.

'Isn't it a bit weird to invite other gallery owners? Aren't they the opposition?'

'While there's a certain amount of rivalry, I think they're generally reasonably supportive and careful not to step on each other's toes. I've had people recommend other galleries showing artists they think I might like when I've been in browsing. And by making contacts with different gallery owners, you'll be in a better place to source good artists for the future. It's just an idea. None of them might want to travel this far.'

It was at this moment Emily began to feel a little overwhelmed. She was just a youngish woman opening a building to sell some art and a mix of other things she hadn't fully decided on yet. Simone was to be her first exhibiting artist, but beyond her, she hadn't considered where to look for others, or if she even would.

That was the beauty of calling it The Button Jar; it wasn't locked into being an art gallery. But Jake was right; she had to start thinking ahead. It could take ages to secure an artist; for all she knew, good ones might be booked out years in advance.

It was all coming together rather too fast. Soon it would be really happening. And if she didn't want to make a hash of her first foray into business – and prove her mother right – then she'd better get her act together.

When Jake began talking about public relations consultants, he must have seen the sheer bewilderment on her face. 'So people know about it,' he explained. 'You could have the best idea and run the best business in the world, but there'd be no point if nobody knows about it.'

'But isn't that what journalists are for?' Emily said, frowning in confusion.

'Yes, but how do you think they find out about what to do a story on?'

Emily shrugged helplessly. She was way out of her depth.

'Darling, all those little snippets of advertorial in papers plugging products and services are all deliberate. It's the work of public relations people to get the media to talk about what they're being paid to promote.'

'I thought public relations people were the ones who stand up at press conferences on behalf of companies to make statements or say they have no comment, or whatever,' she said.

'That's still PR, but a slightly different sort than what we're looking for here.'

'Right. Well, I'll just leave all this to you then, okay?'

Jake reached for her hand. 'You can't leave *all* of it to me. You'll need to be able to talk about what you'll be stocking at The Button Jar, where the name came from, Simone's style, and all that sort of thing, during any interviews. You'll need to *sell* the place and the concept, entice people to drop by.'

'I'm going to be interviewed?'

'Hopefully. We'll need publicity if this is going to succeed. And no offence, Em, but I don't think just the *Wattle Creek Chronicle* will cut it.'

Emily liked his drive and determination, and belief in their success, but it was all getting rather serious. She had no intention of creating an empire. All she wanted was a little shop to keep her occupied and make enough money so she could remain viable without relying too much on the farm or her savings.

'Are you okay?' Jake suddenly asked, looking at her with concern in his eyes.

Emily rubbed her head. 'Just a little overwhelmed, and a bit queasy still.'

'As for being overwhelmed, you have me to hold your hand. I've been through this before. It's not exactly the same as launching an architectural-building firm in Melbourne, but I'm sure some of the principles are the same.'

'Thank goodness I've got you,' Emily said wearily, and leaned over and kissed him.

'Well, you do,' he said, dragging her into a tight hug. 'And if you're still not feeling well in the morning, you should see a doctor. We've got a big few months ahead; we need you in peak condition.'

They were still snuggling in each other's arms at midnight when the phone rang. Emily's heart instantly began to race, as it always did when anyone phoned late in the night or very early in the morning. In her experience, it usually only meant bad news.

'Who could it be at this hour?' Jake said, voicing her thoughts. He sat up and picked up the handset.

'Hello, Jake speaking,' he said, looking at Emily. 'No, that's okay, we weren't actually asleep.'

For Emily, only being able to hear half the conversation was frustrating, and the wait excruciating. Who was it on the other end of the phone?

'What's happened?' Jake asked, sitting up straighter. Emily watched the blood slowly drain from his face.

'Oh no. Is she okay? Are you okay? What about the baby?'

Now she sat up and brought her hands to her mouth. She stared at Jake, who had his eyes locked on her.

'Okay, I can do that. You just call if there's anything else we can do. Anything at all.' He reached for Emily's hand and squeezed. 'Well, you hang in there. You just have to trust the doctors to do their work. We'll handle things here; you're not to worry about a thing.' He listened again. 'No worries. All the best. And send our love to Barbara. Call again when you know more. Right. See you.'

Jake put the phone down, let out a deep sigh, and rubbed his hands across his face.

'What's happened?' Emily said. 'Is it the baby?'

'Barbara's experiencing some bleeding. They've flown her to Adelaide. They've just arrived. She's being assessed.'

'Oh, God, poor Barbara. And David. They must be terrified. What can we do?'

'I'm going to carry on as planned with the seeding. David's going to phone Bob Stanley in the morning and see if he can do a couple of night shifts. Poor fellow, you could hear how torn he was. He needs to get the crop in or else he'll lose a year's income, but he can't leave Barbara.'

'No, that he absolutely cannot do,' Emily said emphatically. 'And she said she was feeling so much better today too,' Emily added sadly. 'She was even affectionately talking to her bump.'

'Yeah. Hopefully it's just a false alarm and everything will be okay.'

'Hmm. Hey, what about Sasha?' Emily asked.

'He didn't mention her. I'll pop by on my way out to the paddock first thing and check she's got food and water. I'm sure David will know more in the morning. If they're going to be away for more than a few days we'll bring her over here. But let's hope it won't come to that. Fingers crossed it's just a false alarm.'

They lay there in each other's arms knowing they should get some sleep, and that it would be nearly impossible now.

Poor Barbara, Emily thought. *Why does such a kind, loving person — someone who would be the best mother in the world — have to go through this? It just isn't fair.*

'Come on,' Jake said. 'We should try to rest. They're going to be relying on us and we need to be on top of our game.'

'Hmm,' Emily agreed. But she was thinking, *you maybe; I'm just going to be uselessly sitting around. What can I do to help?*

She rolled over and Jake spooned in behind her. She concentrated on saying the mantra, 'Please let everything be okay for all of them,' over and over in the hope sleep would come.

Just when everything was going so well…

Chapter Twenty-nine

They woke with the grey of early morning peeping through the tiny gaps in the bedroom curtains. Jake gave Emily a quick peck on the lips and said good morning before getting slowly out of bed. The mood was sombre, as gloomy as the day outside. It was a far cry from three days ago when they'd been celebrating their engagement and Easter with Simone.

Emily watched Jake get dressed, unwilling to face a day that promised to be anything but good. She felt the nausea creeping back in, so reluctantly got out of bed and began dragging her own clothes on. She didn't have time to feel unwell; she had Barbara and David to focus on.

'You're very pale,' Jake said as they sat down for breakfast, which, yet again, held little interest for Emily. 'You really had better go and see a doctor.'

'Maybe you're right.' Emily didn't really think her general heaviness and lethargy warranted a trip to the doctor, given what Barbara was going through. It was probably just a virus. But it would be good to know what was going on. 'I'll go down to Hope Springs and see if I can catch up with Dad too. And I suppose I'd better check Mum's not off booking churches,' she said, smiling and rolling her eyes in an attempt to lighten the mood.

Jake smiled back, clearly appreciating her efforts. But it didn't help. Nothing would until they heard all was well with their friends. Though, if they lost the baby...

Emily tried not to think about that. She didn't know what she'd do if that happened. They just had to hope it didn't. *Trust in the universe.* Though look how it had turned on Barbara and David.

Emily packed sandwiches, some cake, and a thermos of coffee, and saw Jake off at the door with a lingering hug. Her heart was heavy as she watched him walk down the path and turn and wave at the gate. Grace, obviously sensing she was needed by her mistress' side, remained with Emily.

She sat back down at the kitchen table. Her fingers itched to phone David. But she resisted. They would call when they knew more or needed something from them. Meanwhile, she had to give them their space. The thought of a day with nothing to do looming ahead was a little terrifying. She had to phone and order the chandelier, but as excited as she'd been about it last night, it all seemed so insignificant now. She'd said as much to Jake over the muesli she pushed back and forth in her bowl.

'Life must go on, Em,' he'd replied. 'It's not about us. I don't think Barbara and David would want us putting our project on hold because of them.'

It was all right for him; he was actually doing something constructive – something to help. She just felt useless and frustrated.

She watched the clock's minute hand tick painfully slowly towards nine, and then phoned the medical centre.

She was in luck; there had been a cancellation, so she secured an appointment for later that morning. Then she phoned Karen, who told her the chandelier she'd seen a couple of months ago was still available. The day was looking up.

As Emily drove towards Hope Springs, half an hour away from her farm, she glanced at her ring twinkling above her finger on the steering wheel. Her parents would be seeing it for the first time today, if they were home. They should be excited, celebrating, cracking open champagne. But how could she even think of her happiness and future when Barbara and David's hung in limbo?

She went straight to the medical centre, parked, went in, presented her Medicare card, signed the form, and took a seat between a pimply faced teenager and an old man wheezing with emphysema. She picked a magazine from the stack and settled in, willing her nausea to subside. She'd had a wave of it so strong as she was leaving the house that she'd grabbed one of the empty fruit buckets and taken it in the car.

As she opened the magazine, her ring caught her eye again. She probably should organise a notice announcing their engagement in the *Chronicle* before too long. She made a mental note to mention it to Jake that night. Emily smiled to herself at recalling how Gran always referred to that section in the paper as hatch, match, and dispatch – births, marriages, and deaths.

She had just become engrossed in an article about Gwyneth Paltrow and Chris Martin – 'Conscious Uncoupling'; how bloody ridiculous! – when she heard her name called. Already? With a slight sigh, she dumped the magazine and made her way to where a tall, straight-backed male doctor with a receding grey hairline, kind eyes, and a gentle smile stood at the open door with a file in his hand.

'So, my dear, what can I do for you today?' he asked. She had no idea what his name was.

'Well, I'm just feeling a bit off; a bit queasy. I have been pretty busy lately, but for a few days now I've been feeling weary all the time. I seem to have gone off coffee too, but that's hardly likely to be a symptom of anything, now is it?' she finished off with a flutter of her hand.

'You do look a little pale,' the doctor said, after patiently waiting out her ramble. 'Any other symptoms? Vomiting, diarrhea?'

Emily shook her head. 'No. It doesn't come on suddenly with cramps or anything. Not like I've eaten something that's disagreed with me. I didn't overindulge in chocolate over Easter.' She let out a nervous little laugh. 'And I haven't actually thrown up – just felt like I might. Quite a bit.'

'Right. So, really, you just feel a bit off? Not quite right? And for a few days now?'

'Yes. But I actually feel perfectly fine right now,' Emily said with some surprise, as she suddenly realised she did in fact feel perfectly fine. 'Maybe I've just been doing too much.' She pulled the handbag on her lap tighter to her.

'Well, you're here now. It might just be a virus, in which case you'll just have to ride it out, I'm afraid. But you could be low in iron or deficient in something else. Best I check you over and take some blood. Just to be sure.'

He put his hands under her jaw and felt her glands.

Brrr, cold hands!

'Your glands aren't up, so I doubt it's glandular fever.'

He took a little light on a stick from his top drawer and looked in her ears. Then held her tongue down with a wooden spatula and looked into her mouth. Next he inserted a thermometer in her ear for a few moments, then drew it out and read it without so much as a murmur. He wrapped the wide strap of the blood pressure cuff around her arm, pumped the rubber ball until Emily thought her arm would be crushed, undid it and released her, and then got up and went out of sight where Emily heard him fossicking about.

A few moments later he came back. She tried not to look at the needle in the little bowl. She pulled up her sleeve, looked away as the needle went in, and concentrated on breathing calmly and evenly like the doctor instructed.

'There, all done,' he said, putting a little round sticking plaster over the hole in her vein. 'I'll order a full count. The results should be here in a week.'

He sat back in his chair and linked his hands in his lap. He seemed to be looking her over, not just looking *at* her. Emily squirmed a little under his scrutiny. *Is he still consulting, or am I meant to be leaving? He'll get up to show me out, right? So I sit tight until then?* She frowned to herself. A few more moments passed with Emily feeling more and more awkward.

His glance momentarily passed over the ring on her finger, then he smiled. 'There is another possibility. Could you be pregnant?'

The question hit Emily like a bolt of lightning. She felt what little blood was remaining in her face drain. She blinked at him in disbelief. She tried to speak; opened her mouth a few times, but when no words came out, closed it again.

Could I? The words echoed in her head. She tried to think, but the sharp tick of the wall clock and a new gurgling sound in her ears made it impossible.

'When was your last period?' the doctor continued.

Emily frowned and tried desperately to rack her brain. Ages actually. She was on the pill, but often started the next month without taking the little white sugar tablets that filled in the days of the period.

'Well, um.'

Slowly the fog in her mind started to clear. Now she thought about it, she had meant to get another prescription a while ago. Right around the time the whole cottage project had started to take shape. And then she'd been flat out busy. She must have clean forgotten. *Oh God.*

It became even clearer. She'd put her foil of pills, which she usually left out on the bathroom vanity top as a reminder, in the drawer when the guys had come to stay to do the stonework. *Shit, that was around two months ago.*

Emily felt her face go bright red.

'Er. I can't remember,' she said quietly. 'I suppose I could be pregnant.'

'Well, the blood test will tell us for sure,' the doctor said, smiling kindly. 'We'll know next week.'

God, that'll be an excruciating wait. But the thought of standing at the chemist's counter with a pregnancy test kit for the world to see was even more excruciating. How was she meant to go on business-as-usual for a whole week? Damn living out in the sticks. She wouldn't mind betting results came back the next day in the city.

'Meanwhile,' the doctor continued, opening another of his desk drawers, 'take one of these.' Emily looked at the box in his hand – labelled Home Pregnancy Test – and almost leapt up and hugged him. *Thank you, thank you, THANK YOU!* This way she'd find out in a few minutes and wouldn't have to suffer the embarrassment of purchasing one.

'Thanks very much,' she said.

'I'm sure it can be a bit daunting to buy one of these in a small country town. Not to mention carrying a little jar of pee across the waiting room for me to test,' the doctor said, smiling warmly at her. 'But this will do the same.'

Emily nodded.

'Come back in a week and we'll see where things stand then,' he said, getting up and clearly signalling the consult was over.

Emily stuffed the small oblong box into her handbag and left the room. She walked past the desk where a few people were being attended to. She knew she should wait and book in to get her results, but found herself walking out of the building in a daze. She'd have to phone them at another time, when she felt less like a rabbit caught in headlights. She had a strange out-of-kilter feeling – as if her whole world had tilted on its axis.

She sat in the car for a few minutes, wondering what to do next and trying to figure out if she was pleased or not pleased – or just terrified – at the prospect of being pregnant. All of the above, she decided. She thought about going back into the medical centre to use the loos to pee on the little strip. No, she'd wait until she got home. What difference would a few more hours make? Was it something she and Jake should do together? Like a ceremony? She'd seen that in movies but had always thought couples leaping about clutching a stick someone had just peed on quite disgusting. What would he want?

Despite the shock, Emily decided to carry on with her original plan to visit her parents before she left town. She wasn't sure she had the necessary tolerance to deal with her mother, but she wanted to see her dad. A warm hug was just what she needed. And she really should show them the ring before everyone else saw it. Enid would have a fit if someone told her they'd seen it first.

Chapter Thirty

Emily took a deep, fortifying breath and got out of the car, dragging her handbag from the passenger seat as she went. She rang the doorbell and waited, choosing to ignore the usual custom of just entering. She no longer wanted her mother doing it to her, and wanted to set a reasonable example at her parents' home.

The door opened and Des stood there in front of her. Suddenly she felt like she was twelve again; helpless and innocent after a day of being bullied at school and needing a hug and kind word from a loving parent. She almost burst into tears.

'Hi Dad,' she said, struggling to compose herself.

'Em, what a wonderful surprise,' Des Oliphant said, drawing her into a warm, welcoming embrace.

Emily breathed in his scents – Imperial Leather soap, Old Spice aftershave, and wool with just the slightest hint of eucalyptus clinging to it – before pulling away. If she stayed like that too long, she might crumble.

'Enid, Em's here,' Des called as he led his daughter into the open-plan kitchen–dining area.

'We weren't expecting you, were we?' Enid said, looking up from the sink. Her mother had pink rubber gloves on and was scrubbing the stainless steel with white cream cleanser.

'No, I was just in town and thought I'd pop by for a quick visit,' she said.

'Oh,' Enid said. Her hands stilled but remained in the sink. 'What are you doing in Hope Springs that you can't do in Wattle Creek?' she enquired, eyeing Emily.

'Just this and that.'

'Like what?' Enid persisted.

She racked her brain for a plausible excuse. Seeing the doctor wouldn't cut the mustard because she didn't look sick – no sniffling nose, croaky voice, or other symptom.

She looked down at her hands for inspiration and spied her diamond blinking up at her.

'Isn't it enough that she's dropped in, Enid?' Des said. 'Well, *I'm* pleased to see you, pet,' he added, looking pointedly at Enid and draping a protective arm around his daughter.

Enid let out a quiet harrumph and resumed her scrubbing in the sink.

'I thought you might like to see my engagement ring,' Emily said, putting her left hand out and wiggling her fingers.

'Ooh, yes please,' Des said, grasping her hand mid wiggle. 'Oh what a beauty! It's lovely. Look Enid.'

Enid made a show of leaning across, still with gloved hands in the sink, and trying not to be impressed. But Emily noticed her eyebrows lift and her eyes grow just that bit wider. 'Yes, lovely,' she said primly, and then turned on the tap.

'Right, well, who's for a cuppa?' Des asked.

'Do you have anything herbal, like peppermint, or something?' Emily asked.

'But you always have regular tea, coffee, or Milo,' Enid said, looking at her suspiciously.

Emily was half expecting her to add, 'What, too good for your usual now you're sporting a large diamond, eh?'

'Come on, Enid, give the girl a break. She wants something different. It's a free country. Now let me check. I do vaguely remember seeing some peppermint in there. It came as part of a Christmas hamper from the Greens last year,' Des said, and made his way across the kitchen.

Emily stood at the end of the bench while her mother continued to give the stainless steel sink all her attention. At her hip was her handbag, where the pregnancy test kit was practically burning a hole through the leather. As the silence went on, punctuated only by the sound of her father fossicking in the large pantry cupboard, Emily grew more and more restless.

'Ah, found it,' Des said, and reappeared clutching a small cellophane packet with tightly packed green envelopes inside it. 'Will this do the trick?'

'Perfect, thanks Dad,' she said, offering him a warm smile. Well, that was what she was going for. It might have come out more as a grimace.

'Excuse me, Enid,' Des said, as he held the kettle near the sink and swivelled the spout of the tap around to fill it. Enid reluctantly stepped aside and he turned on the water.

'Do you mind if I just use the loo?' Emily said.

'Of course not, pet. You don't need to ask. Go right ahead,' Des said. 'Are sure you're you okay? You look a little green around the gills.'

'I'm fine,' Emily said. She rushed past her mother, who was now using the dishcloth to wipe away imaginary drips from the bench top. She shut the toilet door behind her and sat down while letting out a huge breath.

Why does it have to be so hard?

Was Enid still angry with her about not wanting a wedding? Well, she'd have to damn well get over it, because Emily was not giving in. Not this time. Anyway, would Enid still want to parade her daughter around if she was sporting a prominent baby bump? The thought of her quickly backpedalling from organising the wedding almost made Emily giggle.

With shaking hands she drew the long box out of her handbag. She read the instructions, pulled out one of the two foil sealed packets and opened it. Holding the test stick, she reread the instructions and tried to commit to memory if one line or two pink lines meant she was pregnant. But her brain was failing her.

She undid her jeans, pulled everything down, and tried to position herself over the white stick just inside the toilet bowl. *Please don't get pee everywhere*, she begged, as she tried to let out just a small amount.

Ew, yuck. Gross! Rather than just a nice little targeted dribble on the stick, she'd managed to wee all over her hand. A few wayward drops fell on the seat as she brought it up to eye level. Apparently she had to wait five minutes for the reading. How was she going to get away with being in here for that long without another inquisition?

'Are you all right in there?'

Emily cringed at hearing her mother's voice. She rolled her eyes. *She's like a bloody heat-seeking missile!*

'Yes, fine, coming,' she called back, looking around desperately. She yanked a few tissues from the floral plastic-covered tissue box matching the soap dispenser and toilet brush holder and quickly wrapped the stick in them. *As if it could it get any grosser*, she thought, holding the wad with the tips of her fingers. With her nose turned up in distaste, she pushed it into her handbag along with the remaining stick in the box and did up the zip. She carefully wiped the seat, rearranged her clothing, flushed the loo, and washed her hands. Drying her hands on the coordinating hand towel, she composed herself in the mirror.

Emily opened the door to find her mother standing on the threshold, and got such a fright she leapt back slightly and almost dropped her handbag.

'God, Mum,' she said, bringing a hand to her chest. 'All yours,' she said brightly, and quickly made her way back to the kitchen where a steaming mug of peppermint tea awaited her on a coaster on the table.

'Everything all right, pet?' Des asked, looking up from his own mug.

'Yes, thanks, fine.'

'It really is the most beautiful engagement ring,' he said, nodding at Emily's hand. 'Congratulations again. He's very lucky to have you.'

'Thanks, Dad. I think I'm pretty lucky too. I can't believe he actually asked you.'

'Shows a lot of respect, in my book. I did feel bad about keeping it from your mother – and I'm not entirely off the hook yet – but I couldn't have her... Well, she can be so...' He gave up with a shake of his head and picked up his mug.

'I know,' Emily said, following suit.

As she sipped her tea, Emily couldn't decide if she was hoping the little white stick would turn out to be positive or negative. She wasn't afraid of what Jake would say if she was pregnant. He definitely wanted kids. And they were engaged, so it wasn't as if they weren't committed. But she did feel very jittery about the reality of being pregnant – all the awful medical things she'd heard about. And, oh God, if Barbara lost her baby after such a battle only to find Emily had accidentally got pregnant and all was well…

'You haven't been overdoing it, have you?' Des quizzed her again. 'You're looking awfully pale.'

'Just a little washed out. You're probably right – just been doing too much.'

'I'm not surprised. You had a lot of work taking care of all those men. And the project certainly has come along quickly.'

'It has. We're already starting to put the guest list together for the opening party. Oh, and Jake's sister Simone has agreed to be my first artist,' Emily said proudly.

'I didn't know Simone was an artist,' Enid said, returning to the room with her handbag. 'Not that I know *anything* about her,' she added.

Emily ignored the pointed comment. 'Well, she dabbles. Mainly in acrylic at the moment. She's got some gorgeous large, bold floral pieces in her home, but this will be her first ever exhibition.'

'Sounds very modern. I'm not sure I like the sound of them. And do you think that's wise, Emily, if she's completely unknown?' Enid said.

'She's very talented, just chose a different career path. All the famous artists had to start somewhere, Mum. And I like the idea of helping her.'

'How wonderful that you can give her the opportunity to shine in public. I look forward to seeing her work,' Des said enthusiastically.

'Thanks Dad.'

'Well, it sounds like an awfully big risk to me. I hope you know what you're doing,' Enid warned. Emily tried hard to not roll her eyes.

'Oh, I forgot the biscuits,' Des added, getting up.

'No, don't bother. I'd better get going anyway,' Emily said. She drained her mug and stood up. 'Jake started up at David's today.' Emily had no idea how this was meant to explain her need to get going. It had just slipped out. She couldn't exactly say that she needed to rush off to check if she was pregnant or not. 'Thanks for the cuppa,' she said, putting her mug in the sink.

'I have to head off to a Lions Ladies meeting,' Enid announced, and offered Des and then Emily air kisses from about six inches away.

Des walked Emily to the front door while Enid made her way to the door off the kitchen into the garage.

'Bye Dad,' she said into her father's neck as he hugged her goodbye. She waved to her mother backing out of the driveway as she got into her car and then waved again to Des, who was still standing on the front step as she pulled away from the kerb.

Emily considered stopping in the next street to check the little white stick, but the last thing she needed was Enid or one of their neighbours pulling up alongside her and asking what she was doing. She couldn't exactly claim she was looking at a map for directions.

As she drove back to the farm, she thought about going straight out to David and Barbara's to see Jake and have them see the result together. But she didn't want to distract him from his work for their dear friends in their time of need.

And, anyway, did the result stay on the little stick indefinitely or go away after a while? The last thing she needed was to have to squat in the middle of the paddock to use the second tester. No, she'd find out for sure and tell Jake later.

Back in her own kitchen, Emily dumped her bag on the table, unzipped it, pulled out the wad of tissues and unwrapped it. She stared at the two pink lines, trying to remember what that meant. She reached into her bag for the box, struggled, and then gave it a good tug. It flew from her hands and fell on the floor. She bent down to pick it up and then banged her head on the underside of the table as she stood back up. She almost laughed. The universe clearly didn't want her to know the result.

Finally she calmed down, sat back on the chair, and compared the picture on the box to the plastic tester. She looked from the box to the tester a few times to make sure, and then stared at the stick.

Two pink lines. She was pregnant.

Emily wasn't sure how she felt, other than numb. At least the nausea seemed to have gone away in all the excitement. *Uh-oh, spoke too soon.* She put a hand to her mouth and bolted to the toilet. This time she actually threw up.

She flushed the loo and washed her face in the bathroom next door. As she did, she stared at herself in the mirror. What was she expecting to see? That she looked completely different as a result of what she'd just learned? Probably. She laughed at her ridiculousness. Sure, one pee on a little white plastic strip had totally changed her life. But she didn't actually look any different than she had five minutes ago. She was almost disappointed. Where was the radiant glow? She went back to the kitchen and put the kettle on, as much for something to do as wanting to actually consume anything. As the machine hissed into life, she thought about the magnitude of what she had just learnt.

Was she ready to be a mother? At the barbeque back in February, she'd held Steve and Grant's babies and just felt paranoid about dropping them. She'd felt nothing remotely like maternal stirrings inside her. So, no, she probably wasn't ready. *But who is?* Did she want a child? *Maybe.* Though the timing wasn't exactly perfect. In a few months she was opening a gallery and would be run off her feet keeping track of a new business. *The timing is never perfect.*

'You'd better be a quiet one, or else Mummy won't cope,' she told her stomach. 'Lots of sleeping, little one.'

She thought of her own mother, wondered how Enid had felt when she had learnt about her pregnancy with Emily. But of course that was different. She had been married. *She'll have a fit at me getting pregnant out of wedlock.* Would Enid be the cold, children-should-be-seen-and-not-heard style of grandmother, or would she surprise them all and be the warm, doting mother figure Emily had never had? *Like Gran.*

'Oh, Gran, I wish you were here,' she said, looking up towards the ceiling.

What sort of mother will I be? What sort of parents will we *be?*

She suddenly had the overwhelming urge to tell Jake.

Chapter Thirty-one

Emily drove through Barbara and David's yard, past the house and the shearing shed and on down to where she saw her bright shiny blue ute parked near some equipment a couple of hundred metres ahead in a small paddock of old silvered stubble. The place was eerily quiet, like a ghost town. She reached over and patted Grace beside her for comfort.

For about the hundredth time that day she crossed her fingers and hoped all would be well. The wait for news from Adelaide was excruciating. She could only imagine how Barbara and David must be feeling while they waited on test results and doctors' opinions.

She made her way slowly, not much more than walking pace, letting the car roll down the slight decline, following the smooth, worn earth track cut deep from sheep and vehicle movement over the years. Jake's green tractor was creeping its way along the far side of the next paddock. It must be a big paddock; he was only on his first lap. She didn't want to sit for too long pondering and worrying about Barbara and David, and how Jake might react to her news. But she had no choice. She'd have to hope he'd see her car and pull up. She didn't want to phone and disturb him – especially when he was on his first lap and needed to get the far edge of the wide machine as close as possible to the fence without hitting it. She wouldn't have minded letting sleeping dogs lie – another favourite saying of Gran's – but that wasn't an option either.

The rational part of her knew he'd be fine – he'd said he wanted kids one day – but fear and insecurities still burbled away deep within her. People often said things they didn't mean, or changed their minds when put on the spot. Hell, no one could really say how they'd feel about something as life changing as this until it actually happened.

She was terrified. Not just of Jake's reaction, but the whole thing. The nine months – or however long there was left – of changes to her body, then the trauma at the end. And then the next thirty years raising a child and doing your best to ensure they turned out to be a well-adjusted, fully functioning contributor to society. And happy. She wouldn't care what direction the kid wanted to go in as long as he or she was happy. She would make sure they knew that that was what mattered.

God, what if there was something physically or mentally wrong with him or her? The fear flared up in her again and she struggled for breath. Would she have one of those tests to see if there was anything wrong before the birth? Would she ever have the nerve to terminate?

Oh, God, there's so much to think about.

She came to a halt beside the ute, a little way away from where she knew the tractor would need to get access to the truck to fill up. She put the handbrake on and turned off the key. Her heart was racing. At least she had Jake to share the load with. Hopefully he would be happy about it.

Of course he'd be happy about it. They were committed, *engaged*, for goodness sake. It wasn't as if they'd had a
one-night stand. And he definitely wanted kids. She knew
that. So what was her problem? Was this irrationality down
to hormones? Perhaps all the worrying about Barbara and
David was affecting her.

Emily leant back against the headrest, closed her eyes,
and focussed on breathing slowly and deeply, and enjoying
the warmth of the sun through the window. *It will all work
itself out for the best*, she told herself, and repeated the words
over and over in her head.

Finally the throaty tone of the tractor's huge diesel
engine became much closer and she opened her eyes. She
watched Jake making his way along the fence line to her
left. At last he was level with the gateway and lining up to
start his second lap. The roar turned into a burble as he put
the tractor into neutral and left it idling.

Emily watched as the door on the far side opened, Jake's
figure disappeared from the cab, and the door closed again.
She got out and began walking in his direction. And then
he appeared, in practically a run, new Akubra in hand and
the bottom of his oilskin jacket flowing out behind him.
She stopped in her tracks as she watched possibly the most
handsome man she'd ever set eyes on – her man, the father
of her child – coming towards her. Her heart flip-flopped
and her emotions surged. Grace bounded off to greet him,
the white tip of her tail bouncing up and down above her.

Jake patted Grace, and then moved on and swept Emily
off her feet and into his arms, taking her so by surprise that
she let out a little gasp.

'I'm so glad to see you,' he said, spinning her around.
'What a lovely surprise. I wasn't expecting a visit.' Then
he set her down and scrutinised her features. 'How are you

feeling?' he asked, touching her face gently with the tips of his fingers. 'Did you go and see a doctor?'

Emily nodded.

'Well? Is everything okay, or do I need to come home and look after you?'

Emily smiled softly and shook her head.

'No, what? No, you're not okay or, no, I don't need to come home and look after you? What's going on?' His face became creased with worry.

'I'm pregnant,' Emily said quietly.

'Oh! Wow!' His face lit up. 'That's great news. Well, it is to me. Are you okay with it? I know we hadn't exactly planned it?'

'Guess I have to be,' she said with a shrug. 'But we've got a lot going on,' she added with a bit of a grimace. 'The timing's not exactly great.' *And I'm fucking terrified.*

'Well, I've always thought people worry too much about the timing of these things. I don't think you'd ever find the perfect time.'

'So you're okay with this? Really?'

'Of course. I think it's wonderful news. Seriously,' he said, looking intently into her eyes. 'Oh, wow!' he said, picking her up again and holding her tight to him and kissing her. 'Sorry, I'm probably crushing the little one,' he said, and carefully set her back down.

'I'm not sure there's much there to crush yet,' Emily said.

'So how far along are you?'

'No idea. The doctor took some blood, and I've just done one of those pee-on-the-stick-test things. And that's all I know at this point.'

'Oh, so the whole district already knows,' he said, grinning cheekily.

'Thankfully I didn't have to go into the chemist to buy one! The doctor gave it to me. It seems they've figured out small country towns hold no privacy.'

'Fancy that,' Jake said lightly. 'So,' he continued, 'did the pill fail? I thought it was meant to be ninety-nine percent effective.'

'Probably is, if you remember to take it,' she said sheepishly.

'Oh. Right.'

Emily explained where she might have gone wrong.

'Oops,' Jake said, grinning.

She smiled back and let out a small sigh. All would be well. Jake was genuinely excited about it. His eyes were even sparkling.

'So, are *you* okay with it?' he asked. 'You don't exactly sound over the moon.'

'I'm probably in a bit of shock. And, to be honest, I'm scared.'

'Of what?'

'Everything. Getting fat, being sliced open or ripped apart, never enjoying sex again, being a crap mother, not actually liking it.' Emily became breathless. She was getting a little hysterical, but couldn't stop. 'I don't feel the least bit warm and fuzzy and maternal,' she wailed, tears spilling over. 'What if I'm a terrible mother?'

'Hey, don't cry,' he said, wrapping his arms around her. 'You'll be fine. We'll work through it together. Like you said, it's a shock. That, and what's going on with Barbara and David is pretty traumatic.'

'But what if I'm cold and horrible like my mum is with me?'

'You're nothing like Enid, Emily. And there's more than one type of mother. I've had women friends who've said they never felt maternal. Some said they felt a rush of love when they held the baby for the first time, and others confessed to never feeling that way about their children at all, despite knowing that they would throw themselves in front of a truck to save them if they needed to. You feel what you feel, you can't control that. Don't beat yourself up. I'm sure Enid loves you in her own way. She might not have been the warm, demonstrative, loving mother you wanted, but I'm sure she would've done anything to protect you,' he said, smiling sympathetically and stroking her hair. 'You just be you and you'll do great. Anyway, there's plenty of time for you to get used to the idea. It's all very new. But I'm glad you felt you could be honest with me about how you're feeling,' he added, looking deeply into her face. 'I love you, Emily. We can get through anything together if we keep talking. Just remember that.'

'I know. Thanks, Jake. I love you too,' she said, wiping her tears away. She felt much better. Gran was so right when she said that a problem shared was a problem halved. She wasn't alone; she had to remember that. 'So how are things going here?'

'Well, I had to fill everything up, so I've only just started. I got a call from Bob. He'll be here tonight. I think they're going to put together a roster around their own work – all chip in a few hours here and there.'

'It's a pity I can't drive a tractor,' Emily said, glancing across at David's larger John Deere parked nearby.

'I'm sure you *can*, you just haven't tried,' Jake said.

'Do you think you could teach me?' she asked. John had never given her the chance.

'I'd love to, but I don't know enough myself. David taught me what gear and revs to use with this tractor. But his is bigger, so I'm sure it'll be different. Anyway, hopefully they'll be back very soon with tales of a false alarm and he'll be able to finish his own cropping,' Jake added, clearly attempting to sound upbeat.

'So, you haven't heard anything?' Emily asked. She knew he would have said if he had, but she had to ask anyway.

'No.'

After a pause that neither of them knew how to fill, Jake changed the subject. 'I'd better get back to it,' he said with an apologetic grin.

'Yes, you go,' Emily said, pecking him on the lips and then making shooing motions with her hands.

'Thanks for coming up and telling me straight away,' Jake said. 'And don't worry so much, I think it's great news,' he added, giving her a quick hug. He blew her a kiss and strode off.

'Have fun,' she called as Grace trotted after him.

After a few more steps, he stopped and turned. 'Okay if she comes with me?' he asked, nodding at the dog.

'That's fine,' Emily called back, and waved. 'You have fun too, Gracie.'

She stood with her hands thrust deep in the pockets of her thick fleecy jacket, suddenly aware of the icy wind rushing around her. She normally enjoyed watching him drive off, in command of the big, powerful machine. It was so manly. But she was getting really quite cold; what was taking him so long?

Emily waited a few more moments and then got back into the car to wait. Maybe he was checking the air seeder or something. But he was taking ages.

And then Jake's long, lean frame appeared behind the machine and he was walking back towards her with Grace beside him. This time his stride was slow and heavy. What was wrong? What could have happened in the last minute and a half? Had he suddenly realised the impact of them bringing a child into the world? Was he having second thoughts? Then she saw the mobile phone in his hand.

Emily got out and went over to meet him. His face was ashen, his lips fixed in a grim line. Gone were the bright, cheery features, the happiness and excitement twinkling in his eyes.

'David just phoned,' he said, standing in front of her. 'Barbara lost the baby.'

'Oh no,' Emily said, bringing her hands to her face. She looked up at him, his features blurring as the tears filled her eyes. Jake drew her to him and they clung to each other. Emily began to sob, letting go of all the tension, nervousness, fear, and sadness. Amid her sobbing she felt Jake begin to shake as well. He too was crying. They stood there for a few minutes wetting each other's shoulders until the tears slowed to a trickle and the raw emotion had subsided.

They parted and looked into each other's tear-stained, shattered features.

'How are we going to tell them our news? They'll be devastated,' Emily said quietly, her chin quivering.

'I have no idea,' Jake said, shaking his head slowly.

'I'm sure they'll put on a brave face and say they're happy for us, but it will tear them apart too,' Emily said.

'I know,' Jake said, now running a hand through his hair. 'It's all too soon. Perhaps when the dust settles,' he said, a little helplessly.

'But what if they can never… We'll be a constant reminder.'

'Em, we'll just have to wait and see, cross these bridges when we come to them, as they say. Oh, God, what a mess,' he said, rubbing his hands roughly across his face.

'Did David say how long they'll be away?'

'No. I think they're still in shock. They're going to need some time. I think we'd better organise people to finish the seeding. At least that'll be one less thing on their minds.'

'Do you think I should call?' Emily asked.

'I honestly don't know.'

'God, I wish I was there with them.'

'They probably just need each other right now,' he said kindly.

'You're right. But I feel so helpless,' she said, lifting her hands up and dropping them again.

'I know you do.'

They turned at the sound of a vehicle and saw a white ute pulling up. Bob Stanley got out and walked towards them. From the grim look on his face, it seemed he had just had a phone call from David as well.

'Hey Jake, hey Em,' Bob said, and bent down to briefly pat Grace.

'Hey Bob,' Jake said, accepting the hand Bob offered.

'Hi Bob,' Emily said.

'Nice to see you, though I wish it were under better circumstances,' Bob added.

'So you've heard?' Jake said.

'Yes, David just called. Terrible,' Bob said, shaking his head. 'They're such good people, they don't deserve this.'

Emily thought she saw tears in his eyes, and looked away. She didn't want to embarrass him.

'Right, so I can't stay now, but I can do the night shift,' Bob said, suddenly all businesslike.

Better than getting all mopey, I suppose, Emily thought.

'I'll do a ring-around. We should be able to get enough blokes and machines to knock it off in a couple of days. I hear you've got the map of what's being planted where.'

'Yep, it's in the ute,' Jake said.

'Great. I reckon put it in the front of the truck so if you're not here anyone who comes in knows what the go is.'

'Righto, fair enough.'

'Well, I'd better get back. I've left my wife to do a few laps at our place. If she finishes the paddock while I'm not there I might have a gate to replace,' he said with a smile.

'Hey, before you go,' Jake said, 'could you tell me what gears and revs to use for the other tractor? I'm a bit new at all this and maybe Emily here could do some driving as well?'

'Have you driven a tractor before?' Bob asked her.

'Er, no.'

'Don't worry, there's nothing to it. Best you steer clear of first laps though.'

'I'm just about to start the second one here,' Jake said.

'Good, we'll put her into that one. Emily, I'll give you a quick lesson. Wait here while I just show Jake what's what with the bigger beast.' He and Jake left with Grace trotting alongside them.

Emily waited, gradually becoming more and more nervous. She was glad she always carried water in the car – she might be out here for a while. She had her bottle in her hand when Bob came back a few minutes later.

'Righto, come on. Time for tractor driving one-oh-one.'

'Thanks so much for this, Bob,' Emily said, as she hurried to keep up with his long stride. 'Sorry you have to do this and get held up,' she added a little breathlessly.

'No worries. It'll be good to get a second tractor going right away, anyway. Makes me feel better about not dropping everything over my way. I've only got a few hundred acres left. I figured it's best to just finish and then be free to help David,' he added.

Driving a tractor turned out to be quite similar to driving a manual car, though you didn't start in first and there were two gear levers to worry about rather than one. Once you got going and managed to get to the right revs – revolutions per minute, rather than kilometres per hour – it got even easier. Bob explained that it was important to keep the revs at a constant speed so the seeds went in the ground evenly.

The main concern for Emily was making sure the far tyne of the huge machine behind her lined up neatly with the edge of the previous lap. There were a few wobbles to start with while she figured out how sensitive the power steering was – very.

'Try and straighten it up next lap,' Bob said. 'Otherwise when the crop comes up the lines will be wonky for the whole district to see – and possibly the world, thanks to Google Earth.'

'How embarrassing!'

'Don't worry about it too much. David will be grateful enough for the help not to be concerned about a few gaps or extra thick patches here and there.'

In addition to keeping everything straight and at the right, even speed, she also had to continually keep turning her head to check on the gauges showing the levels of the seed and fertiliser in the machine trundling along behind. It was easy enough to drive, but there was so much else to keep an eye on. Thank goodness it wasn't one of the totally computerised systems. That would probably do her head in. She tried to ignore Jake making his way around ahead of them and concentrate on what she was doing.

Bob was a good teacher; calm and patient. He stayed for the whole of her first lap, which took over an hour. Finally they got back level with where everything was parked.

'Right. You'll be fine from here,' Bob said. 'You did well for a first-timer. John was a fool not to utilise your skills, stupid idiot,' he muttered, shaking his head. With that he leapt out, shut the door behind him, bounded down the steps, gave her a smile and a wave, and ran over to his ute.

Let's hope I can do all this on my own.

Emily successfully got the vehicle back in motion and gave herself a little mental fist-pump of achievement before focussing on the speed and direction. Bob had turned off the radio the moment they'd started their lesson. She would have liked to turn off the UHF and shut out the annoying chatter that seemed to have suddenly picked up, but it was her lifeline to Jake across the way. She just had to do her best to block it.

'You there, Em?' his voice rang out clear amongst the chatter. 'Got the hang of it okay?'

'Yep,' she said after retrieving the handset from its hook.

'You're doing well,' he said.

'Thanks. It's not nearly as hard as it looks, is it? It's actually quite good fun.'

'Tell me that when you've driven fifty laps!' He laughed. 'I'll leave you to concentrate.'

'Thanks.' She hung up the hard plastic handpiece and returned her attention to the dials inside the cab, lines of freshly sown earth on the ground, and gauges and levels on the huge machine behind her.

Three hours later, the only parts of the paddock not a rich chocolate brown colour were the small sections in the corners that got missed with each lap as the wide machines swept around. Emily had often heard mention of 'headlands' on the UHF in the house while married to John. Now she finally understood what they were referring to.

Bob had explained that because the big machines couldn't do really tight corners, a gap was left as you swept around the bend of the corner. These were the last parts of the paddock to be done. It was quite fascinating now she was actually a part of it. Once all the laps had been done and all that was left were the gaps radiating out to each of the corners, you drove out one corner, turned around – but being careful not to turn too sharply – and headed back the other way. Thanks to Bob's instructions, Emily knew exactly what Jake meant when he told her to just drive out the first one and leave the rest to him.

It was rough driving across the furrows, and she was a bit shaken up by the time she got back to the gate and stopped. But she felt an incredible sense of achievement. For three hours she'd had something to concentrate on other than Barbara and David, and her guilt around her own change of circumstances. For three hours she'd been doing something concrete and practical to help, rather than sitting around feeling helpless.

She sat with the tractor idling while she waited for Jake to complete the other headlands and pull up behind her. Bright orange late-afternoon sun streamed in the windows. Jake leapt up the steps beside her and opened the door and leaned in. He must have left Grace in the other tractor.

'How was it?' he asked after giving her a kiss.

'Good, but not exactly relaxing. There's so much you have to keep an eye on.'

'It gets easier. You did great,' he said.

'Well, we'll see how wobbly David's crop comes up,' she said with a grimace.

'I'll take it through the gate for you; it's a bit of a tight squeeze.'

Emily vacated the comfy seat and let Jake sit down. She remained standing beside him and watched, fascinated, as he manoeuvred the machine through the gateway that seemed barely wide enough. He parked the tractor in the paddock beside the truck and left it idling. Emily got out and waited beside her car and watched while Jake walked back and brought the second tractor through the gateway. Then he got out and lifted Grace down.

She called the dog to her so she'd be safely out of the way and then watched as Jake filled the hoppers. She was cold, but wanted to continue being a part of it all.

Jake had filled the first machine, moved it out of the way, brought the second in, and was almost finished filling the last pair of hoppers when he turned his head towards something in the distance. 'Looks like the cavalry has arrived,' he shouted above the *pop pop* of the little petrol motor running beside them and the drone of the idling tractor.

Emily looked over, had to shade her eyes from a sudden burst of sunshine, and saw a convoy of tractors, trucks, and utes coming up over the rise towards them. Her heart surged. She'd seen her district band together in times of need before, but it never ceased to choke her up. Even seeing vision on the TV of another community far away doing the same flooded her with emotion.

You didn't need to be a born-and-bred farmer to appreciate genuine mateship and camaraderie. She'd heard of farmers banding together to harvest crops for a mate who had been struck down by illness or for his wife and family upon his death, but Emily had never actually been a part of it before. If she wasn't so awestruck, and there weren't people about to see her, she'd have retreated to the car for a weep. Instead she swallowed hard and pulled herself together.

Soon there was a small group of men, and a lad of about fifteen, standing around introducing themselves and shaking hands with Jake. Emily smiled and nodded at Grant and Steve, and raised her hand in greeting. They were the only two in the group she recognised. Their presence made her feel a little less self-conscious about being the only woman. She watched as Jake unrolled David's map on the bonnet of the nearest ute and gestured at the paddock, telling them it was the one that they'd just sowed and then indicating where it was on the map.

Heads nodded, voices mumbled. Emily felt a part of it, but also separate. But she didn't mind. She was suddenly feeling very weary. The day was catching up with her. She turned at hearing a voice very near.

'Okay if I drive your tractor?' the young lad asked shyly.

She blinked, frowned slightly, and then nodded. Of course it *was* actually her tractor, just like the farm and all its equipment. The probate notification had arrived in the mail a few weeks ago.

'Thanks, that'd be great,' she said, offering the lad a warm smile. She didn't need to ask if he knew how – around here kids were driving from as young as eight years of age, often propped up on cushions they had to get down off in order to stomp on the brakes and clutch.

Thankfully with tractors, the throttle was hand operated and so once you got going you didn't need to be able to reach the floor until you wanted to stop. Emily had had to slide off the seat slightly to reach the pedals, but then they hadn't taken the time to adjust the seat for her shorter legs – it wasn't as necessary as when driving a car.

The lad moved away and Emily made her way around the group to Jake.

'I'm going to head off,' she said. 'I'll take Grace with me.'

'Righto. Thanks for your help; you saved us a heap of time,' Jake said, smiling warmly at her.

Emily smiled back, pleased with her accomplishment. 'Thanks.'

'Good idea to take Grace. It's getting too busy and dangerous – especially with the sun going down. Can you pick up Sasha on your way past the house? We should take her home with us.'

Emily gave him a quick hug and kiss, feeling a little ill-at-ease at being watched by so many who knew she'd so recently been John Stratten's wife.

'Come on Gracie, let's go see your mum,' she said as she turned the car around.

Chapter Thirty-two

Emily stopped the car outside the shearing shed where she knew Sasha liked to snooze the day away. Her heart ached when she thought about how quiet the place was. There wasn't even a squawking or chirping bird to be heard.

Grace raced ahead and disappeared through the gap where the door was always left ajar for Sasha. Emily looked through the small opening and blinked while her eyes adjusted to the darkness. She spied Grace's white tip.

'Come on Sasha, girl,' she called. 'You're going on a little holiday.'

Grace trotted past her and back into the daylight. And then Emily felt a gentle nudge to her leg. Sasha was looking up at her and waving her tail slowly back and forth. Seeing how forlorn the dog looked, Emily had to swallow hard to stop herself from giving in to tears.

Though, really, she told herself, Sasha didn't look any sadder than usual – she was a quiet, pensive-looking creature at the best of times. Did she have any idea of the drama going on within her family? She'd been fed, which was probably all that mattered to her. She wasn't a pampered house dog like Grace. Barbara and David came and went from the place quite a bit; nothing was really out of order for her yet.

Emily drove home with Sasha and Grace, thinking about where she'd put the older dog. Sasha wasn't used to living inside. She could put her in the outdoor laundry, but then she might whine at the door, wanting to be with her daughter. And if she left Grace out there the spoilt younger dog was sure to demand to be let in as soon as it got chilly.

In the end, she decided to set up another bed in the kitchen and just keep her fingers crossed that Sasha was smart enough to ask when she needed to go outside. David might be a little annoyed at her turning Sasha into a softy, but that was just too bad. She was playing Auntie Em, and could spoil her if she wanted to!

At home, Grace was ecstatic about having canine company. She trotted around after Emily while she gathered extra bedding and bowls, pausing to give Sasha a smooch every time she passed her.

The older dog stood in the one spot patiently looking on, seeming to take it all in. When everything was set up, she lay on her bed as instructed.

Emily sat at the table and looked at both dogs. Their demeanours were so different. Grace was curled up snoozing contentedly. But Sasha crouched with her head on her paws, her eyes following Emily's every move. Her heart lurched again as she looked at the sad expression.

She looked away and tried to blink back the forming tears. But they kept on coming. She folded her arms on the table, laid her head on them and let the tears flow. She felt so sad for Barbara and David, and so helpless, and so bloody guilty. How cruel of fate to do this just when everything was going so well. It wasn't fair.

Finally the tears stopped and she pulled a wad of tissues from her sleeve, mopped her face, and then blew her nose. The two dogs were sitting at attention, heads identically cocked in concern, looking at her.

Wanting to feel a little less disconnected, she picked up the phone, found David's number, and dialled. Her heart pounded slowly and heavily while she waited for it to start ringing. It was answered straight away.

'Hi Em,' David said.

'Oh David, I'm so sorry. I was out at the farm and Jake told me.'

'We're pretty shattered.' He sounded like every word was a huge effort to get out.

'I wish there was something I could say.'

'I know. There's nothing anyone can say. We just have to do our best to get through it. At least we have each other,' he said, sounding less than convinced.

'How is Barbara doing?'

'Trying to put on a brave face. You know how she is. I'm really worried about her, Em. She won't talk about it – to me or anyone.'

'Would she talk to me, do you think?' Emily asked.

'I tried to suggest it, but I think she's still too shocked.'

'Would it help if I came over?' Emily asked. At the same time she looked down at the dogs and wondered who would look after them if she went away. It was too much to put on Jake while he was busy with the cropping. And while her father would happily take over, her mother would have a fit if she even suggested having a dog in her house. Enid Oliphant did not do pets – inside or out.

'It's lovely of you to offer, but it's a hell of a long way to come.'

'I wouldn't mind,' she said.

'I know you wouldn't. We'll be home in a few days. Until then, I'm hoping she'll agree to see the counsellor here.'

And what about you? She hoped David wasn't ignoring his own needs whilst keeping it all together for both of them.

'I've already seen him,' David said. 'It helps to talk. I've just got to convince Barbara of that.'

'Well, if anyone can, you can,' Emily said lamely.

'So, how are things with you two?' David asked, taking her by surprise.

'Us? We're just worried about you guys,' she said.

'I hear you've had a go at driving your first tractor. Well done.'

Emily smiled despite herself. 'How could you possibly know that already?'

'Bob rang just before. He said you did really well.'

'You'll see just how well, or otherwise, when your crop comes up,' Emily said, allowing herself the tiniest chuckle.

'Indeed we will. I really appreciate everything you guys are doing. Words can't really express…'

Emily sensed him choking up and cut in. 'It's our pleasure, David. We'd do anything for you guys. I just wish we didn't have to, not like this,' she said, choking up again herself. She swallowed hard and cleared her throat. 'Hope you don't mind, but I've got Sasha here with me.'

'Turning my dog into a softy, I suppose?' She could tell he was smiling.

'Yep. Good luck turfing her back outside when you get home.'

David let out a small laugh. 'Oh well, worse things happen at sea,' he said.

A heavy silence enveloped them.

'I'd better let you get back to Barbara,' Emily finally said. 'Please give her my love and tell her I'm thinking of her – you both – every second. If there's anything at all you need, just let us know.'

'Thanks, Em. You're a gem. And thanks for the call.'

'You just take good care. Hopefully we'll see you soon.'

'Okay. Bye then.'

Emily hung up, relieved to have the call over with. If only she could have been there to wrap her arms around them instead. No words would have been needed.

'Right,' she said to the dogs, 'we've got some cooking to do,' and went to her freezer to look for inspiration.

'What's all this?' Jake asked later that night when he finally walked in looking dirty, worn and dishevelled. 'Shouldn't you be resting, in, er, your *condition*, oh mother-of-my-child-to-be,' he said, grinning and sweeping her to him.

'I'm fine. Need to keep busy. It's for Barbara and David. Spaghetti bolognaise, beef stroganoff, lamb casserole, and chicken cacciatore,' Emily said, pointing. 'I spoke to David. I'm not sure when they'll be home – maybe in a few days – but when they do, I don't want them to worry about cooking for a while.'

'Good idea,' he said, nuzzling her neck. 'Oh hello, you,' he said, spying Sasha on the floor looking up at him. 'I hope David's not going to object to you being spoilt.'

'He's fine with it. I told him. I couldn't leave her out in the cold in a strange place.'

'How was he?'

'Holding up remarkably well, I'd say, though it's hard to tell.'

'Hmm.'

'So, what do you fancy for tea?' Emily asked. 'Take your pick.'

'Oh, beef stroganoff, please. I haven't had it for years.'

'Good. Well, you go and have a shower and then you can tell me all about the last couple of hours.'

'Okay. You're the best, Em,' he said, kissing her on the top of the head. 'Have I told you that lately?'

'Yep, but feel free to repeat yourself,' she said, grinning at him.

*

The next morning, after a quick trip into Wattle Creek, Emily drove home with a boot full of groceries and enough ingredients to bake a small mountain of cake and biscuits for Barbara and David. Thankfully she had arrived early enough to miss the older shoppers – who tended not to leave the house before ten – and later than those who popped in to fill lunchboxes before school. She practically had the supermarket to herself.

She was relieved that no one stopped her to ask about Barbara and David. It was not her business to discuss. And with hormones messing with her emotions and causing her to cry at the drop of a hat, she didn't want to embarrass herself by crumbling in public. That wouldn't help anyone.

As she passed the bakery, she remembered their first lunch there, and began to miss Barbara all over again. They hadn't caught up for lunch for months. She'd been too busy with Jake and the cottage and everything. Now she wished she'd made more effort. Maybe Barbara would have been more at ease with the baby and everything and…

'Oh dear, little one,' she told her stomach, 'it's not your fault, but this is not going to be easy.' Emily sighed.

What should be an exciting time was anything but. She still wasn't feeling all gooey and maternal. She cared about the little being growing inside her, she really did, but she was also very concerned about how the news would affect Barbara and David. How could they possibly tell them? And when? What would poor Barbara think, watching Emily's belly grow bigger and bigger, knowing how close she'd come to having her own child only to have it snatched away?

'It's all a bit of a mess, isn't it,' she said, stroking her belly as she drove.

Emily was usually happy when she was on a baking mission, and could block out most other things. Today, though, the tasks that had become automatic over many years gave her too much space to think. Normally that was a good thing; she'd worked her way through many a problem whilst rolling out dough, mixing cake batter or dropping balls of soft biscuit mixture onto trays, pushing it flat with a fork or poking cherries or almonds into the tops with a finger. Today it just made her sad and worried.

Some of the items she cooked were Barbara's favourites and she was taken back to the day they had spent cooking up a storm for David's father's funeral and the CWA trading table. Today the happy memories were tinged with sadness, so Emily didn't linger like she normally would, stretching out the enjoyable experience as long as possible.

Whilst everything was cooling enough to package up, she checked her emails. There was a message from Simone. She opened it to see a beautiful image of arched shapes within a circle, the main colour being salmon pink. Was it architectural or a design from somewhere else? It looked familiar, but she couldn't quite place it. Being so different from the pieces Emily had previously seen, she was excited to know more.

From: Simone Lonigan
Subject: Busy artist at work
To: Emily Oliphant
Cc: Jake Lonigan

Hi Emily (and Jake),

Thanks so much again for your wonderful hospitality. I would have loved to have stayed longer. Oh, well, no rest for the wicked, as they say! I've been painting like a demon at any moment I can get. And totally loving it! Thanks so much again for the kickstart!

Here's a pic of a small piece I did last night. Working title is *Gothic Sunset* – hence the pink tones. It's the window at the top of the gorgeous Gothic ANZ Bank on Collins and Queen – yes, inspiration taken from Jake's lovely photo. It's been raining cats and dogs here since I got back, so I haven't been able to get out with my camera. But hopefully I will soon. I want to have a good variety for you to choose from for the exhibition.

Hope you guys are well. Please send my best to Barbara and David – I did so love meeting them.

Lots of love,
Simone xx

Emily felt a new wave of sadness. Jake would have to phone and tell her about Barbara. She forced her attention back to the more positive: Simone's lovely art and the pace she was working at.

If Simone could continue to work so quickly, an opening in the not-too-distant future wouldn't be a problem. It was looking likely that it would be in winter.

When she and Jake had discussed it the other night, she'd said she thought people ought to be given at least six weeks' notice – that was the etiquette with wedding invites, anyway. Jake thought they could get away with a month and they'd struck a compromise where he would email an advance notice of a general time period to those he wanted to come from Melbourne. He'd do that in the next few days when he finished tractor driving.

Emily wrote a quick reply.

From: Emily Oliphant
Subject: RE: Busy artist at work
To: Simone Lonigan
Cc: Jake Lonigan

Hi Simone,

It really was wonderful having you stay. We wish you could have stayed longer too. But, wow, you're really burning the midnight oil – I hope not literally! ☺ I love the image. It's gorgeous. I'm looking forward to seeing what else you come up with.

Jake's off on the tractor up at David's property and I've been cooking up a storm – just because. Better run and rescue a batch of biscuits before they burn!

Happy painting!

Lots of love,

Emily xx

She reread her message before sending and cringed at her few white lies. They were small enough not to matter, weren't they? She couldn't tell Simone via email what was really going on. She pressed 'send'.

As she turned off the computer, she wondered if the image would be suitable for the invitations. She was keen to get them finalised and off to a printer.

There were quite a few fiddly things left to get done. Jake was looking after most of them, but they were still on her mind.

She remained undecided about the sign having an actual button jar on it. Were they running the risk of looking too quaint and unsophisticated? The last thing she wanted was to be mistaken for a hospital auxiliary shop selling tea cosies, lamingtons, and crocheted knee rugs in local footy team colours. Not that there was anything wrong with that – it just wasn't what she had in mind for her business.

Jake kept assuring her the logo would be classy, but so far she was yet to see an actual design. Maybe just plain block lettering on a cream background might be better – ruby red to match the glossy front door and other timber highlights. Or perhaps on a gold background.

Chapter Thirty-three

Emily pondered the sign as she drove out to Barbara and David's. The more she thought about it, the more she felt that they were over-complicating things by including a logo. They should just stick with the plain and classic:

THE BUTTON JAR
Fine Art and...?

Fine art and what? Bric-a-brac? No, too casual. *Homewares?* A bit too limiting. *Knick-knacks? Curios?* No, to Emily these words suggested wares of an ordinary nature, and diminished the term fine art. And it was definitely *fine* art she would be selling, as opposed to decorative art; the stuff brought in by the container load from China.

Sure, she'd be selling the odd jar of jam, but the focus was to be art. If only she could think of the right word for an eclectic mix of good-quality *stuff*. Was there one? Until then, it would simply be:

THE BUTTON JAR
Fine Art Gallery

Or, even better: Gallery of Fine Art.

She pictured it in her mind. The more she thought about it, the more adamant she was. That was the tone she wanted to set.

She fought back the sadness as she entered David and Barbara's home. She unloaded her goods from the car into the fridge, freezer, and pantry. She tossed out the old milk and replaced it with a box of unopened long-life. There was nothing worse than arriving home after being away and not being able to have a cup of tea or coffee. She could only imagine how they would be feeling coming home after this particular trip.

It was clear they had left in a hurry. The place was tidy enough, but on the table were two mugs and a chopping board with a knife lying across it, and a few scraps of pear core and stalks. Barbara never left anything on the table; it was always cleared and wiped off immediately after every meal.

Emily did the few dishes and tidied up. She hesitated at their bedroom where a dirty clothes hamper was overflowing. Would it be overstepping the bounds to do her friends' laundry? She tried to reverse the situation in her mind. How would she feel in the same position? While it might be nice to have the simple act of washing to distract from other things, it also might be nice not to worry about running out of clean clothes.

She grabbed the hamper and took it to the laundry. Thankfully it turned out not to be as full as it first appeared.

While the load was whizzing around in the front loader, Emily pondered changing the sheets. She loved fresh sheets, and would change her own every day if it wasn't a hideous waste of water and electricity. But some people might actually like coming home to familiar smells – especially after an ordeal. In the end she decided to leave the neatly made bed as it was. There were plenty of clean sheets in the linen press if needed.

She waited and hung out the clothes on the outside line, thanking the sun for being out and shining brightly, and the brisk breeze for blowing. While she was waiting for them to dry, she decided to check on the progress of seeding.

From the verandah, all she could see were acres and acres of rich brown turned land. The work must be happening out over the next rise. She called the dogs, who were snuffling about nearby, and they piled into the car.

Sure enough, a few kilometres further into the farm, Emily came over the second rise from the house and discovered a mass of activity. She let the car roll to a halt and stared in awe. As far as she could see in every direction, tractors in all sizes and colours were trundling around paddocks. She counted them: four paddocks, five tractors in each. Twenty tractors. She tried to pick out which one Jake might be in, but couldn't. There were a few green John Deeres and they all looked pretty much the same.

She continued over to what looked like the nerve-centre. There was a cluster of utes parked a little way from a line of trucks with seed and fertiliser bins on the back and shiny metal field bins with augers sticking out of them. It was so well organised. Parked out of the way, she watched as a tractor came in and pulled alongside the front truck. A bloke ran over and pulled the cord to start the small motor to drive the truck's augers to fill the air seeder hoppers. It was fascinating to watch.

In just a few minutes that tractor was driving off and another, a red one this time, was pulling in. Emily got out her camera, told the dogs to stay, and exited the car. She walked around, being careful not to get in the way, and started snapping away. Then the bloke on the truck augers, the noisy little motor now silent again, called and waved her over. As she moved closer she recognised Bob. She shook his hand.

'Wow,' she said. 'What a production.'

'Yeah. Least we could do. Taking a few photos?'

'It's an amazing sight.'

'Climb up here and you'll get a great shot right across the paddocks,' he said, indicating the ladder on the back of the truck.

'Okay, thanks.'

'Here, I'll take that while you go up,' he said, holding out his hand for the camera.

Not keen on heights, Emily carefully negotiated the ladder. She leant down and thanked Bob as he passed up the camera.

'Wow, what a spectacular view.' She gulped back a wave of intense emotion. Seeing the activity from ground level had been amazing, but up here it was awe-inspiring. She could see the brightly coloured, evenly spaced tractors making their way around the paddocks – all at the same speed – the patchwork of landscape changing colour behind them. She snapped away. When she was confident she'd got enough good shots, she handed the camera back down to Bob, and carefully descended.

'How was it?' Bob asked.

'Brilliant. What an amazing turnout.'

'Yeah. You certainly tear through the acres with this many machines going. We'll be finished in a few hours.'

'Which one is Jake?' she asked.

'Over there to your left. He's in David's John Deere. Young Stevie Richards is in yours still.'

Emily felt a surge of pride on Jake's behalf. Helping out here would mean he was accepted into the fold more quickly than he might otherwise have been. Though he'd met lots of locals thanks to the cottage project.

The district could be a little standoffish when it came to outsiders. It was often said that you weren't local until you were third generation born and bred. That was if you were a farmer. Emily often thought townies needed five generations to earn their stripes, farmers being the dominant species. There seemed to be different rules for everything.

'Okay, that's me again,' Bob said, as another tractor came in to fill up. 'Catch ya later,' he said with a wave as he raced over and retook his position by the side of the truck.

Emily got back in the car, but she couldn't make herself drive away. Watching this, being part of it, was so special. She sat there watching tractors coming and going and making their way around paddocks, and lost all track of time. She was in a mesmerised daze when a tap on her window startled her. She smiled at seeing Jake and wound the window down.

'Hey there,' he said.

'Hey there yourself.'

'What a sight, eh? I can't believe how many are involved now.'

'Yeah, it's amazing. I can't tear myself away,' she said with a laugh. 'I've been at the house, doing their washing. I'm waiting for it to dry.'

'Perfect weather for it.'

'Yes, thank goodness. Have you heard from David today?'

'Not me personally, but Bob spoke to him late last night. They're planning to be back the day after tomorrow. Hence the additional workforce.'

'Do you think we might be able to go up to Whyalla tomorrow?' She wanted to pick up the chandelier and sort out an outfit for the opening before Barbara and David got back so she would be close at hand if needed. 'I suppose I can go on my own if I have to,' Emily ventured.

'Funny you should ask. I've finished here now. And I actually just got a call from Tom Green. He wants to do a final sign-off on the Civic Centre. I was waiting to ask you if tomorrow would suit.'

'Great,' Emily said, feeling relieved. She didn't want to be distracted when she saw Barbara and David. Thank goodness she wasn't needed on site at the cottage. Jake was constantly in contact with the trades, and regularly assured her he had it all in hand. The windows and doors were going in today – or was it yesterday? After the plumbing and electrics had been done, the gyprockers would get to work, and then the tilers. She was happy to leave it in his capable hands and see it when it had come together.

'I'm going to head off,' she said. 'The washing should be dry now. Oh, did you see the email from Simone, the one with the image of her painting?'

'Yes. It looks great. Though a little small on the phone's screen.'

'Do you think it would work for the invitations? I'd really like to get them started.'

'I don't see why not,' he said.

'And I've also been thinking about the sign and the general branding,' she added.

'Me too. I'm thinking perhaps leave the button jar image off. If that's okay with you. Perhaps just have classic, stylish lettering. But we can discuss it later.'

'Great minds think alike. I totally agree. I think using the jar might make us seem a bit quaint. I want to be taken seriously.'

'And you will be,' he said, leaning in and giving her a kiss. 'We'll look at fonts later. I've got a few ideas.'

'Great. Thanks. See you later.'

Emily drove off feeling buoyed. Things were good as long as she didn't let her mind dwell on Barbara and David's grief. For a few moments she'd even managed to forget her own pregnancy. Thinking about it now made her quiver with nervousness.

One thing at a time, she told herself. *Washing in and folded, ironing done, and then home.*

As soon as Jake got back that afternoon, he retreated to his office. When he emerged a few hours later for dinner, he had lots to share. He'd been speaking with Simone and had got her to agree to a deadline for the paintings.

'Allowing a week for unforeseen circumstances, we can have the opening on June twenty-fifth,' Jake said. 'Lucky we decided to put gas log fires in; we might need them.'

'Is it fair to put that sort of pressure on her?' Emily asked. 'I didn't think creative people worked like that.'

'No idea, but she agreed. I'm sure if she had a problem she would have said so.'

'I suppose.'

Jake went on to say his graphic designer contact had agreed with keeping their branding simple and had suggested a font.

'God, that was quick,' Emily said. 'Perhaps we'll have six weeks for the invitations after all.'

'I phoned him with the brief as soon as you left. It was a piece of cake.'

Jake laid a sheet of paper printed in the perfect cranberry colour on the table. It was plain and classic.

'It looks good,' she said. But her voice must have betrayed her mood, because Jake looked up sharply.

'I'm not taking over too much am I?'

Emily couldn't lie. But she couldn't tell him the truth. She nibbled the inside of her cheek, unable to quite look at him.

'I am; I've overstepped the mark, haven't I?'

Emily cursed the heat starting to flow into her cheeks. What came to mind was to say, 'Well, it's my gallery, and my business. What right do you have to discuss deadlines with my artist, even if she is your sister?' But the words in her head sounded like the complaints of a petulant teenager, so she kept them to herself.

'We're a team, Jake. I love that you have all these great contacts and experience, but I'd just prefer you talked to me before getting designs drawn up and bullying Simone into a deadline, that's all,' she said.

'I didn't *bully* Simone. She offered,' he said.

'But why were you discussing it in the first place?'

'To try and get some idea of a date for the opening.' His words started off defensively, but petered out when he seemed to see Emily's point. 'Which really wasn't my place, was it?' he added sheepishly. 'I'm sorry, Em, I just want to help. It's not that I don't think you can do all this – I know you can – but I just think it's wise to use all the resources available. And I happen to be a very good resource. And now you're pregnant...'

'Don't worry about it. I appreciate your help, I really do. But I want to be involved too. When it's a success, I want to be able to say, "Look what I did," not "Look what Jake did for me." And if it all goes pear-shaped…'

'It won't. It's going to be a huge success; *you're* going to be a huge success. I'll back off,' he said, raising his hands, 'and wait for you to come to me.'

'I don't want all or nothing, Jake,' she said, thinking momentarily of Enid. 'I want us to be a team, to be sitting together writing lists and making decisions. Like we did before you went off tractor driving,' she added, suddenly realising that was when things had changed.

'Fair enough. I suppose I did go a bit rogue on you. It's just that the only time I could contact people was during office hours and I was so knackered at night.'

'I can always make calls and send emails,' Emily said.

'I know. Sorry. I'll do better from now on,' he said, offering her an innocent, puppy-dog look.

'You're forgiven. I'm probably just being needy and insecure.' Emily kissed him and then finished dishing up their roast chicken and vegetables.

Over dinner they discussed their trip up to Whyalla the following day and consulted the list Emily had prepared. It wasn't long, but everything on it was time-consuming. In addition to going to the party hire place and Karen's light shop, she wanted to get prices for business cards and stationery for when the design was finalised. Jake said he could get all that done in Melbourne, and probably cheaper, but Emily wanted to do as much locally as she could.

But the main thing bothering her was what to wear for the opening. She'd never really been much into fashion – preferring to be comfortable in jeans and a t-shirt, or an ironed shirt if she needed to be a little more dressed up.

She felt daunted by the prospect of doing it alone, and with Barbara and Jake both unavailable – he'd be in a meeting for most of the afternoon to celebrate the conclusion of the project – she was jittery about the experience.

She knew of women who would dedicate months and multiple big city shopping trips to the quest for the perfect outfit. Emily needed it dealt with in two hours – and in Whyalla.

Chapter Thirty-four

Emily's eyes bugged when they walked into the huge warehouse filled with glassware, crockery, cutlery, balloons, streamers, and serviettes. On the wall, on an angled shelf, was a display of place settings in every colour imaginable. The choice was mind-boggling. As much as she wanted her opening to be classy, she was not remotely interested in ironing hundreds of linen napkins. If paper serviettes were good enough for the Governor's visit the year before, they were good enough for her.

'We don't need plates either,' Jake said as they stood chatting out of earshot of the two staff members behind the counter. 'Let's just go with small paper serviettes. That's what they do at all the business functions I go to in Melbourne.'

'I really don't want plastic glasses,' Emily said. 'I know that means someone will have to wash them all, but I hate the idea of them ending up in landfill.'

'Fair enough. It's a big dishwasher, so quite a few will fit in at a time. And they'll only need a quick cycle. Anyway, won't they wash them for you? In Melbourne the hire places deliver them clean and pick them up dirty.'

'We can ask. But I'm sure they'll be arriving on the bus or we'll be collecting them. And, at the risk of sounding like my mother, I'd rather wash them myself and know they're clean for my guests.'

'Okay, so that's settled. Proper glasses it is,' Jake said.

'Crikey, have you seen the prices?' Emily said, looking at the price list on the counter.

'Don't you go getting all freaked out on me now, Em, it'll be fine. As I'm sure your gran would say, "If it's worth doing, it's worth doing well." You want to arrive with a bang, give people something to talk about.'

They still had to get prices for the catering. Oh, well, Emily kept telling herself. It was business, not just a lavish party for themselves.

They took a heap of photos with Jake's mobile phone, and decided they'd need more precise numbers before going any further. They didn't know how many would turn up from the ad they were putting in the paper. The staff assured them they didn't have any functions around their date so there should be no problem with availability.

'Wow, I had no idea how much stuff there was to choose from, and how expensive it is,' Emily said as they returned to the car.

'At least we don't need chairs or chair covers,' Jake said.

'Yes, lucky that.'

'Thank God we're not having a big white wedding!' they both said at once and then laughed.

They got into the car and headed the rest of the way into the city centre.

Emily's head was still spinning with confusion, indecision, and numbers when Jake parked the car in the Civic Centre car park and then kissed her goodbye before making his way across to the main building.

Right, we're going to find something to wear, Emily told herself forcefully, picturing the blue-grey wraparound silky shirt-like top from her recurring dream. She knew being set on something so particular was dangerous, but hoped that having the same dream so many times was a good sign.

She paused out the front of the first of the two boutiques on the now familiar shopping strip. The display was a sea of colour and seemed quite casual. She hoped they had a more formal section inside.

Fingers crossed, she thought, taking a deep breath and pushing open the door.

'Hello,' the young lass behind the counter called brightly.

'Hi,' Emily called back. She was friendly, but couldn't quite muster the same level of enthusiasm.

'Is there something I can help you with?'

'I hope so. I'm looking for quite a specific outfit for a semi-formal evening function.' She went on to describe it.

'Oh. That *is* specific. I can't remember seeing anything quite like that. And the colours we have right now are still a little summery – lighter. When is it for?'

'Winter. End of June.'

'You might be better off waiting a couple of weeks until the winter stock is fully in. But let's have a look. Our more formal wear is over here,' she said, leading Emily to the other side of the store.

She flicked through the first rack, shaking her head. 'No, nothing of that colour. Here's a wraparound dress in green,' she said hopefully, holding it up.

'Thanks, but not really me,' Emily said. It was nice, but she had her heart set on the outfit of her dreams – literally. They went through two whole racks. Despite telling herself to open her mind to other possibilities, Emily didn't see anything worth getting undressed for.

If Barbara was there she would have been more likely to try on and see. But her heart wasn't really in it. The girl was still smiling and showing as much patience as when she had walked in, goodness only knew how long ago, but it wasn't to be.

'I'm really sorry,' she finally said, 'but that's all I have. There's another boutique down the street. Perhaps try there.'

Emily admired her tolerance. In her place she probably would have thrown up her hands by now. *God, who would work in retail and have to deal with the public day in day out?*

Er, you, Emily, her inner voice said. She almost laughed out loud. *Christ, what am I getting myself into?*

At least with a gallery it was more a case of what you see is what you get. She couldn't imagine a gallery client saying, 'Oh I like that, but do you have one with more blue in it, or a bit more red here or there?'

'Thanks so much for your help, anyway. You've been great,' Emily said, but was somehow hesitant to leave. She so desperately wanted to get her outfit sorted with minimal palaver.

'I'm just so sorry I couldn't help,' the girl said. 'I hope you find something. But, if all else fails, you can't go wrong with a little black dress. This one would really suit you,' she said, plucking one out of the rack and looking expectantly at her.

Emily looked at it and ummed and aahed. *It is nice*, she thought, *and the shape might look okay on me*. It was in a stretchy fabric, so it wouldn't matter if she changed a bit in the next two months. The three-quarter-length sleeves would hide her not-so-lean arms. She should probably put the blue-grey out of her mind – nothing like that colour seemed to be in at the moment.

'Good idea,' she said. 'I'll try it on.' She offered the girl a grateful smile and headed into the change room just behind her.

The patient lass was not so patient when waiting for someone to get out of one outfit and into another. Twice she enquired if everything was okay in there and twice Emily called back breathlessly that it was. *Damn dressing to be warm*, she thought, as she struggled with her three layers. She hadn't considered how long dressing and undressing would take.

Finally she dragged the stretchy black dress over her head and pulled it down and into place. She looked in the mirror and thought it fitted her curvy shape rather well. But she still couldn't get enthusiastic. Every second woman would be in a little black dress. She was the host, for goodness sake. She'd wanted to look much more striking than ordinary.

Oh well, better than nothing, Emily thought as she stepped out of the change room and did a twirl in front of the girl. It would work as a fallback if she didn't find anything else. At least being disappointed was better than being stressed over having nothing to wear.

'Oh, it's perfect on you. I knew it,' the girl cried. 'Do you want to try on any others now you're undressed?' she called, as Emily wrestled the clingy garment back over her head.

'Um, thanks, but I don't think so,' she called back when she had finally extricated herself. She emerged re-dressed in her jeans and multiple layers, and boots, and put the dress on the counter.

'Would you be able to hold this for an hour or so? I really want to check the other shop before deciding.'

'We do have a full refund policy, even if you simply change your mind. You could take it now and then return it if you find something you like better. It's entirely up to you though.'

'Oh, that's very good of you. That would be great. Thanks so much.'

Emily left the shop with her purchase. She was tired, but relieved she had found something she liked. Her legs were heavy as she moved down the street to the second boutique. She paused in front of the window display, which suggested the shop was targeting an older clientele. And, again, none of the colours looked anything like what she was looking for. But she was there now, so she pushed the heavy glass door open and walked in.

'Good morning,' called a short, rotund, slightly past middle-age woman with perfectly coiffed grey-rinsed hair.

'Hello,' Emily replied as the door closed behind her with a thud. The atmosphere in here was totally different to the previous shop – not nearly as warm and friendly. Emily almost turned and walked out, but not wanting to appear rude, started on a circuit of the store. Again the colour she wanted was nowhere in sight.

'Is there a special occasion you're shopping for?' the lady asked.

'Yes, a cocktail party for a new gallery that's opening.'

'Now where's that then?'

'Sorry? Oh, down near Wattle Creek,' Emily said, taken by surprise at the woman's inquisitiveness.

'Oh, I haven't caught up with that yet. I do hope I get an invitation, I know a few people down that way.'

Emily remembered the conversations she'd had with Jake about spreading the word as far and as wide as possible.

'The opening is the twenty-fifth of June,' she said. 'It's called The Button Jar. I'll send you an invite if you like.'

'That would be wonderful. My name's Mavis,' the woman said, holding out her hand, which Emily accepted. 'Thank you. I'll look forward to it. Now, let's find you a wonderful outfit. You have a gorgeous figure,' she said, eyeing Emily up and down.

Being looked at like that – the way Enid did all the time – made Emily bristle. But she swallowed it down, reminding herself that Mavis was only trying to help her find an outfit that would look good on her.

'Would you, by any chance, have anything in blue-grey?' she asked.

'This is probably the closest thing I have,' Mavis said, selecting and then holding up a lace dress in almost the exact colour of the top in Emily's dream. Her heart surged for a moment. At least the colour existed. But the dress wasn't right.

'The colour works well on you, but the dress is really a bit too mother-of-the-bride, I'm afraid. Unfortunately I don't have anything else in that colour. How about this burgundy one?' Mavis offered, putting the dress back and holding up another.

'No, I don't think so, thanks all the same. It's a bit too similar to what we've chosen as our main business colour.' Was that the right way of putting it? Jake kept calling it their corporate colour, but Emily thought that sold the business as being bigger than it actually was.

'Right. Well, you don't want to feel like you're in uniform, do you?'

'No, exactly.' She was warming to Mavis. The lady was a little brusque, but seemed to know about dressing people for specific occasions. And, like the younger woman in the previous shop, was very patient.

'You know, you can never go wrong with black. Always classy, and always appropriate,' Mavis offered, holding up a sleeveless dress.

'I actually just bought a black dress up the street,' Emily offered with a grimace, indicating the bag in her hand. 'As a fallback.'

'Can I see?'

'Um.' *How awkward is this?* She couldn't exactly refuse to show her. 'Okay.' She drew the dress out and held it up.

'Perfect choice. I bet the nipped-in waist looks great on you. And the longer sleeve will keep you warm if it's a cold night.'

Emily sighed with relief. 'Thanks so much for saying so. I really wanted something in blue-grey because, I know it's silly, but I saw it in a dream.'

'That's not silly at all. Dreams are interesting things. I'm just sorry I don't have your *dream* outfit for you. New stock comes in regularly, so pop in if you're up again before the event.'

'I will. Thanks so much for your help anyway. I'd better get going,' she said, stuffing the dress back into the brightly coloured carry bag.

'Here's my card. And I'm serious, I'd love to come along to your opening if you've got space on the guest list.'

'Okay. Great. I hope to see you there.'

'Hey there,' Jake said, startling Emily, who had managed to become engrossed in the novel she'd picked up in the newsagent. 'How was the shopping?'

'Okay.'

'Are you okay? What are you doing here in the car?' After leaving the dress shop, Emily had eaten a quiche and salad for lunch, and had returned to the car park to wait for Jake.

'I'm fine, just feeling a bit weary and not really in the mood to shop. It's not the same without company,' Emily said.

'Do you want me to come with you?'

'Thanks, but I sort of meant Barbara,' she replied apologetically. 'I ended up with a black dress. It's nothing very special, but it'll do the trick,' she said with a shrug.

'I'm sure you'll look gorgeous,' he said, leaning in and kissing her. Are you sure you're all right?'

'Fine, maybe a bit moody. I'm missing Barbara and worrying about them too.'

'Fair enough. Let's just pick up the chandelier and be off then.'

'I'd rather not go in and see Karen, if that's okay? I'm just not feeling sociable today. I'll see them at the opening if they come.'

'It's okay, Em. I understand. I'll go in myself.'

Emily's strange mood couldn't be totally explained away by being concerned about Barbara and David. If she was honest, she was bitterly disappointed about not finding the outfit she'd seen in her dreams. She'd seen it as an omen. If she had walked in and found it hanging there right in front of her then everything would have been okay; the business, the opening, Barbara and David and their friendship. But it hadn't been there. And maybe everything wouldn't be all right.

Jake parked a few doors away from the lighting shop so Emily could remain unseen in the car. Within minutes he was back and had stowed the boxed chandelier on the back seat and wrapped a seatbelt around it to keep it secure.

In bed that night, Jake swept Emily into a tight, comforting hug. He rubbed her belly gently and told her how much he was looking forward to seeing the first ultrasound pictures, whenever that was. He was clearly excited about it all.

She was still terrified and trying to stay in denial. It was okay for men. They didn't have the yucky side of it all. The only yuck they had to deal with was cleaning up after the baby. If only Barbara was here to discuss it with, or she got along well enough with Enid. But she didn't, and she was dreading telling her mother of this new development. Hopefully Enid would prove to be one of those women who was thrilled at the idea of becoming a grandmother. She wasn't ready to face the alternative.

Emily fell asleep in Jake's arms with the thought that she'd better go back to the doctor. It was important to know how far along she was and there was no doubt a heap of other stuff she should find out, like what the next steps were and what to expect going forward. She hoped soon she would start feeling better about it all. It wasn't that she felt *bad* about being pregnant, but she was afraid.

She was always apologising to her belly – silently and out loud – and berating herself for her ridiculousness. What was wrong with her? Pregnancy and birth was a natural, normal phenomenon. Millions of women went through it every year, and the majority of them were ecstatic about it.

So why not me?

Chapter Thirty-five

The following day, Emily pottered around the house trying to pretend she wasn't just waiting for a call from Barbara.

Jake spent most of the morning in the office sending images back and forth to the graphic designer and being careful to keep her in the loop.

By that afternoon the invitations, branding for the stationery and outdoor signage were set, and with the press of a button, Jake put the order in. In the end they had decided to get it all done through the place in Melbourne that he knew and trusted.

Emily hadn't been over to the cottage since she'd taken Simone through. She'd liked Jake's suggestions of tiles and fixtures and fittings, which he'd used before, and had been happy to be spared from having to choose. They had similar taste; both liked to keep things simple, neutral and elegant and leave any 'jazzing up' to soft furnishings and other temporary items. It was all running much smoother, and quicker, than she'd ever have imagined. And while she was keen to see how things were progressing, she also wanted to wait and get the full experience of seeing the chandelier in situ after opening the gorgeous glossy front door, just as visitors to the gallery would.

The painters were just finishing up outside and would come back and do the inside later. They had already done the highlights on the external woodwork in the rich garnet shade that Emily and Jake had chosen as their brand colour.

White crushed limestone and quartz rubble had been laid out the front so there was no chance of the car park area becoming boggy when it got really wet.

They'd tossed around ideas for low-maintenance land-scaping, but had decided to leave it for the time being. Later they might add a pair of pots with camellias on either side of the front door.

At present it looked more like a commercial building than a domestic home. And it tied in well with their branding vision: simple, classic, high quality.

Around three o'clock, Jake came in and said he'd just had a call. David and Barbara had arrived home safely. 'They were absolutely blown away to find that their seeding had been done.'

'Oh good. I'm sure it's a huge weight off their minds. And now David can focus on taking care of Barbara.'

'Yeah. He got a bit emotional on the phone, poor bloke. He said Barbara asked him to pass on her thanks for all the food and for doing their washing.'

Emily felt a little hurt that Barbara hadn't called herself. But then she caught herself. This wasn't about her; Barbara needed to do what was right for her, and if that meant not phoning Emily yet, well, that was fine.

She forced herself to admit that maybe, just maybe, she'd done an Enid; that some of the things she'd done were in part in order to be thanked and therefore get some attention in a situation where she was feeling helpless and left out.

Oh, God.

'I'm sure she'll contact you when she feels up to it,' Jake continued, obviously catching the disappointment in her eyes.

It was more than that – she wanted to share her dear friend's pain, ease it, and take some of the burden. Not that there was really any way she could; she couldn't begin to know what they were going through. But she wanted the opportunity to learn, to help in a more emotional sense.

'She really does appreciate all you've done, Em,' Jake persisted. 'As does David.'

'Did he say how she is?' she asked.

'No. But I think she was nearby when he made the call. I get the feeling he doesn't want her out of his sight.'

I could look after her, sit with her. She wouldn't have to say a word, Emily thought.

'Probably a good idea,' she said instead of voicing her thoughts. 'How's everything over at the cottage?' she asked, changing the subject.

'Great. All on track. Soon we'll be able to start making it look lived in – well, you know what I mean,' he said, laughing.

Emily nodded. She was still so impressed with how quickly it had all come together. She should be beside herself with excitement, but all she could think about was Barbara. *What right do I have to be pleased and proud as punch with our dream when they've lost theirs?* She put a protective hand over her tummy.

'How's it all going down there?' Jake asked, nodding at her stomach.

'So far, so good. The morning sickness seems to have gone for now – touch wood,' she said, putting both hands on the table. 'Must have been the little one just trying to get my attention,' she added with a laugh.

'Well, it worked. Should we be getting books and swotting up on what to expect?' Jake asked.

'Honestly, I think I'd rather not know too much,' Emily said.

'Okay. But don't think I won't be Googling like crazy on your behalf! When do you think we should tell your parents?'

'I think it's normal to wait until the three-month mark. I don't even know yet when I'm due. We need to know that first. Then we can give them a date. It also means we can wait until after the gallery opening.'

'Good point.'

'Maybe we should let Enid get over the engagement before dropping another bombshell.' What she really meant was that she was keen to put off the announcement for as long as possible. Maybe before too long she'd figure out how to tell her – and be strong enough to deal with the backlash if it came.

'I don't mind waiting. But they'll have to know before anyone else – it's only right.'

*

Jake and Emily were still in bed at eight-thirty on Monday morning when the phone rang. With seeding finished, so little left to do on the cottage, and the business side of things pretty much taken care of, they had decided to have a lie-in. They'd be run off their feet again soon enough.

They had just made love and were catching their breath and luxuriating in the feeling of closeness. Jake extricated himself from Emily's embrace and leant over to pick up the phone handset.

'Hello,' he said. He looked at Emily. 'Oh hi, Barb. How are you doing? Yes, she's here, I'll put her on.' He handed the phone to Emily, who was now sitting up.

Her heart started to race. *God, what do you say to a friend who has just lost her baby?*

'Hi Barbara. Welcome home.' She was disappointed with how inane she sounded – how *normal* – but it was the best she could do.

'Thanks so much for all you did,' Barbara said.

'It was nothing. I wanted to do something for you, and…' She stopped herself, started again. 'You're my best friend, Barbara. If there's anything I can do, anything at all, you only have to ask.'

'Actually, there is one thing,' Barbara said quietly.

'Yes?'

'Can you come out this morning for a cuppa? I need some human company. And some help to eat all the cake and biscuits.'

The last comment was probably meant to be an attempt at humour, but Barbara's voice remained tight and flat. She sounded so low. Emily's heart ached for her. She so badly wanted to make it better, but knew she couldn't. Barbara and David would never be the same again, but hopefully they would regain their humour and easygoing personalities. It would take time.

'When?'

'Any time. I couldn't sleep last night. I've been up since five.'

'Oh, you poor thing. I'll get changed and then come on out.'

'Thanks Em.'

'You're welcome. See you soon.'

Barbara hung up without another word. Emily stared at the handset, a mix of different emotions surging through her.

'That's good,' Jake said.

'Yeah.' Emily had been waiting for this, wanting it so desperately for two days, but even so, she felt nervous and apprehensive. 'What if I say the wrong thing? I could upset her even more. I told her everything would be fine, remember, and look how that turned out.'

'So did I, to David. Friends reassure, it's part of the job description. We couldn't have known, they know that. You'll be fine,' Jake said. He rolled over and drew her back down onto the bed towards him. 'You don't need to worry. You're best friends. The right words will come to you, and if they don't, it won't matter. Just be yourself,' he said, giving her a gentle kiss on the nose.

Emily was quivering inside when she parked just below Barbara's verandah. The door opened before she had a chance to knock. Sasha and Grace pushed past Barbara and into the house. Emily thought to call them back, but was too taken aback by her friend's appearance.

Barbara looked like she'd lost five kilos in the past week. Was that even possible? Her track pants and windcheater hung loose on her long, lean frame. Her attire was as much a shock as her limp hair, pale complexion and sunken, red-rimmed eyes with dark shadows beneath.

'Oh Barb,' she said. As she enveloped her friend, she was further startled by the boniness of Barbara's shoulders. 'I'm so sorry.'

'I know. Thanks for coming,' Barbara said, and they dissolved into tears. They held each other tightly, both sobbing and ignoring the cold breeze rushing around them from the open front door. Barbara's shoulders shook violently. When Emily thought her friend couldn't possibly have any more tears left to shed, a new gentler burst started.

Finally the shuddering subsided. Emily pushed the door shut with one hand whilst keeping her other arm around her friend.

'Come in and sit,' she said, ushering Barbara into the lounge room a few steps away. Sasha and Grace were already sprawled out across one of the two long lounges. Emily looked apologetically at Barbara, whose face showed the faint signs of a smile.

'Come on you two, off,' Emily commanded.

The dogs obeyed, looking chastised, and promptly curled up on the carpeted floor.

'Sorry,' she said. 'I couldn't bring myself to leave Sasha outside at our place. David said it would be okay. Actually, he said, "Worse things happen at sea".'

'That's his way of saying it's okay,' Barbara said, smiling weakly. Every time Emily looked at her friend, she was stunned all over again at her appearance. And every time, her heart lurched and took on a whole new level of ache.

'You sit,' Emily commanded. 'I'll get us a cuppa. Tea or coffee?'

'Coffee, thanks.' Barbara didn't look like she had the strength to walk two more steps, let alone go to the kitchen and back.

Emily reluctantly left, hoping the dogs would stay with Barbara. As quickly as she could, she prepared a tray of biscuits, cake and mugs of coffee for Barbara and tea for herself, and made her way back down the central hall to the lounge. She hesitated at the door, unsure of what she might find. But what she saw wasn't what she expected. There sat Barbara with Grace curled up on the floor below and Sasha in her lap, her arms wrapped around the larger, older dog and her face buried in her fur.

'Here we are,' Emily said, putting the tray down on the coffee table. 'Yours is the blue mug.'

Barbara looked up, two fresh streaks of tears evident on her cheeks. She tried to wipe them away with her sleeve before reaching for a biscuit and a steaming mug.

'Thanks for this,' Barbara said.

'There's no need to thank me,' Emily said.

Sasha had moved off Barbara when she had leant forward to reach the coffee table. Now she curled up next to her. Emily sat on the other couch and Grace stayed on the floor. The air was thick with unasked questions and raw emotion being held at bay. There was so much Emily wanted to know, but she wanted to give Barbara the space to make the first move – all the moves, really.

It took almost an hour, two cups of coffee, one piece of buttered date loaf, and two melting moment biscuits, but she waited her out. *At least she's eating something.*

'Oh Em, I feel so sad,' Barbara finally said, her lip beginning to quiver again. In the time it took Emily to put down her almost empty cup, get onto the couch and draw her friend to her, the tears had already begun cascading down Barbara's face and were dripping off her chin and staining her windcheater. She began to cry again in sympathy.

'I cry all the time,' Barbara said into Emily's hair.

'Of course you do,' Emily said quietly as she stroked her friend's hair and back. 'It's okay. You need to grieve.'

'But when will the tears stop?'

'When they stop.'

'My whole soul aches.'

'Of course it does. I just wish there was something I could do to make the pain go away,' Emily said.

'I feel like my heart is being broken – literally. It hurts so much,' she said, erupting into a new, stronger bout of sobbing.

'It is, Barbara; your heart *is* being broken. It's going to take time. Oh Barb, I'm so sorry you have to go through this.' Emily's gentle crying became sobbing, the intensity of which almost matched Barbara's. The two friends clung together, tears pouring from their eyes, their bodies shuddering, their hearts aching painfully.

'I don't want another baby,' Barbara said suddenly when the tears had slowed.

Emily thought about her own baby sitting between them and felt a stab of guilt so great she actually gasped. 'It's too soon to think about anything like that.'

'I just can't go through this again. It would kill me.'

Emily nodded. She could believe it. At that moment she believed a person really could die from a broken heart. 'Did you see a counsellor?'

'Yes,' Barbara said, nodding. 'Really, they can't know exactly what you're feeling or going through. They can say what their books tell them to, but they can't really know, can they?'

'Probably not,' Emily said. 'I don't know.' She suspected that many grief counsellors went into the profession to help others after surviving their own ordeals, but she wasn't going to go down that path. This was all about Barbara. Whatever she needed, whatever she wanted to hear. It was all so raw; she wasn't anywhere near thinking rationally yet.

They sat in silence for a few minutes until Barbara broke it again. 'We called him Albert, after David's father – his middle name.'

Emily was so taken by surprise that for a moment she had trouble figuring out what Barbara was talking about. *Oh, the baby. It was a boy.*

'That's a nice name,' she said lamely.

'Albert Joseph.'

Emily nodded and watched Barbara fiddling with a wet ball of tissues in her lap. She should go to the kitchen and get the box, could have kicked herself for not bringing it in earlier, but didn't want to leave in case Barbara wanted to say more. It was agony to hear these details; how much harder must it be for Barbara to utter them? The tears welled up again, and she worked to force them back down.

She thought about how often people used the throw-away line, 'Build a bridge and get over it'. In her own limited experience with grief – and she included her failed marriage on her list – she had come to see that you never really got *over* it. You got *through* it. Somehow you got to a point where the grief was there, but it didn't affect you quite so much; didn't consume your every waking moment. You were changed as a result of this experience that stayed with you like a barnacle attached to your heart and soul.

'He looked so perfect,' Barbara continued. 'Tiny, way too tiny, but ten little fingers and toes, a little pursed mouth like David's.'

Emily watched as tears filled Barbara's eyes again and her chin began to quiver, and put her arms around her friend. The ache in her heart was so painful she found it difficult to breathe. She began to stroke Barbara's back.

'Let it all out,' she cooed gently as the sobbing became uncontrollable and Barbara's whole body began to shake again. She was fully aware of how clichéd her words were, but she didn't know what else to say.

Slowly the wretched sobbing and shuddering subsided. Barbara eventually sat back and blew her nose to signal that particular episode was over. Emily was prepared to sit here like this all day, and the next, and the next, if it would help.

She suddenly wondered where David was, hoped that he wasn't hiding out alone in some metaphorical cave somewhere trying to do the macho thing. She thought he was a bit more in touch with his feelings than that, but there was no way of knowing exactly how this would affect him.

'How's David doing?' Emily asked.

'He's so wonderful,' Barbara said, and promptly burst into tears again. This time she shrugged and waved off Emily's attempts to comfort her. And the bout was short-lived.

Progress, Emily thought, though she knew not to get her hopes up. Relapses were inevitable. This would be a long, slow process that could take weeks, months, or even years.

'I couldn't ask for a better husband.'

But how's he doing? Emily wanted to ask again as the silence rolled on.

'I think he's doing better than me,' Barbara finally said. 'Probably only because someone has to keep things together enough to make decisions. He'll probably crumble when, *if*, I ever get my act together,' she said with a wan smile.

Emily just looked on. She didn't know what to say.

'Hey, thanks so much for doing all the cooking and the washing, and everything,' Barbara said, abruptly changing the subject. 'It made such a difference to not come home to how we left the place. I know it's weird, but it sort of meant that something had changed. If the dishes had still been there on the table, the milk spoiled, the rubbish stinking, I think it would have done me in.'

Emily nodded. 'Sorry I didn't wash the sheets,' she said with a shrug. 'I thought you might like your bed being that bit more familiar after the hospital. I hope that was the right thing to do,' she added helplessly.

Barbara nodded, her eyes glistening. 'You were right. Oh Em, you're such a good friend. I don't know what I would do without you,' she said, and reached out for Emily as a new flood of tears erupted. Again they held each other tightly.

'And you're the best friend I could ever hope for,' Emily said through her own sobs as she rubbed her friend's back.

Slowly the episode ended and they parted again to wipe away their tears and blow their noses.

'Look what we've been through this past year,' Barbara said. 'What a fine pair we are,' she added with a faint smile.

What I've been through by no way compares to what you have, Emily thought. 'Thank God we've got each other.' They clasped hands and held on tightly as they looked at each other through sodden lashes.

Emily knew she would be forever grateful for having met Barbara when she did. Thinking about it again now made her want to shed tears for herself. But thankfully none came. Could you actually run out of tears?

'I'm exhausted,' Barbara suddenly said. 'Would you mind if I went and had a lie-down?'

'Of course not. Do you want me to wait for David? Will he be back soon?'

'He should be. I'll be fine though. Thanks so much for coming.'

Emily watched as Barbara got up shakily. She rose in case she needed help. The women hugged briefly and Emily was shocked all over again at how frail Barbara was.

'Do you need a hand?' she said, when it looked like Barbara might overbalance on her way to the door.

'Thanks, but I'll be fine,' Barbara said, her hand on the door frame. She left the room with Sasha, leaving Emily feeling helpless all over again. Somehow Grace knew to stay beside her mistress. She was grateful for the dog's loyalty.

She took the tray back to the kitchen, thought about leaving the mugs in the sink so the noise of washing them wouldn't bother Barbara, but decided not to leave work for David. And, anyway, she needed to do something while she waited for him. No matter what Barbara said, there was no way she was leaving her alone.

As she ran some water into the sink, she doubted Barbara would actually go to sleep. But a rest would at least help.

Crying really is exhausting. She could actually use a catnap herself. Grace nudged her leg and she bent down to ruffle her ears.

'I've been ignoring you, haven't I? Sorry girl, Auntie Barbara needed all my attention,' she explained in a whisper. 'And I'm afraid she's going to need a lot more of it yet.'

Emily made sandwiches for Barbara and David's lunch and was just drying the cutting board and knife when David came in. She put her finger to her lips.

'She's having a lie-down,' she whispered as they hugged tightly.

'Thanks so much for everything,' David said. He was clearly exhausted, but didn't seem as bad as Barbara.

When would he crumble? *No idea, but Jake and I will be there if and when he does.* 'My pleasure,' she said, smiling wanly at him.

'Having the crop in is certainly a weight off my mind,' he said.

Emily nodded, unsure of what to say. 'I'll head off now you're here,' she said. 'I just didn't want to leave Barbara on her own.'

'Thanks. It's been good to get out of the house for a bit. Can you just wait a minute while I check on her?' he said.

'Of course. No problem.' He made his way slowly from the room, standing a lot less tall and straight than usual. 'Carrying the weight of the world on his shoulders,' Gran would have said.

David re-entered a few moments later. 'She's asleep with Sasha curled up beside her,' he said, with a hint of a smile.

'Sorry about that,' Emily said, cringing.

'Don't be. I don't mind. Honestly. If having Sasha there will help Barbara get some sleep and feel a little better, then it's a small price to pay,' he said.

'There are some egg sandwiches in the fridge if you haven't had lunch. I made them while I was waiting.'

'Thanks, Em, you're the best,' David said and wrapped his arms around her. They held on tight for a few moments before both drew apart slowly at the same time.

'You take care,' Emily said, gathering up her handbag from the floor.

'I'll see you out.'

'There's no need, David, really,' she said, and made her way out and down the hall, being careful to tread quietly.

Emily hoped the heavy ache within her would ease with the closing of the front door. But it didn't. It stayed like a hand clenched around her heart, as did the lump in the back of her throat.

Chapter Thirty-six

Emily stopped at the mailboxes at the crossroad just outside David and Barbara's driveway, and looked left and right, checking for traffic. Without consciously making the decision, she found herself turning left towards John's parents' house instead of right towards the bitumen to go home. She drove in a daze, just like she had the last time she'd come out to see them – the day before his funeral. And here she was again, arriving at their beautiful home unannounced, dishevelled, and empty-handed. She didn't even really know why she was there, except that she felt compelled to be.

Emily briefly checked herself in the mirror before getting out of the car. She looked a wreck, just like last time. At least she was dressed a little better. And not wearing make-up meant no streaks of mascara or panda eyes.

'Gracie, you just wait here. There's a good girl.'

The front door opened before she had a chance to knock. There before her stood the impeccably presented Thora Stratten in navy slacks and a navy-and-white lightweight knitted jumper. A strand of pearls hung just below her throat.

'Emily, what a lovely surprise,' Thora said, enveloping her in a warm hug. Emily didn't want to let go, wanted to stand there drawing in Thora's strength. 'It's so nice to see you. Come in,' Thora said, releasing her.

Emily entered the house, having still not said a word.

'Gerald, dear, Emily's come to visit.' Thora ushered her into the lounge room. She heard Gerald's footsteps in the hallway, and when he entered the room, she was surprised at how much older he looked since the last time she'd seen him. He was stooped and his shoulders a little rounded. She felt bad for not keeping in touch better.

'Dear girl, wonderful to see you,' he said, clutching her to him and holding her tight for a moment before letting her go. 'Can I get you a tea or coffee?'

'Tea would be lovely, thank you.'

'Thora, darling?'

'Coffee, thank you, Gerald. And butter some of the jubilee cake and bring it in, there's a dear.'

'Right. Very good. You sit and catch up on your girly talk and I'll be back soon.'

Emily sat back into the leather sofa, feeling totally at ease. On the few times she's sat here during her time with John, she'd been so uptight, almost afraid of them. She really wished she hadn't let John's relationship with his parents influence her view of them for so long. They weren't at all what he'd made them out to be. But, she mustn't dwell. Things were different now, better.

'Have you been to see Barbara Burton?'

Emily nodded.

'How is she? How are they doing? I was so sad to hear their news. Poor things.'

'I think she's doing as well as can be expected.' She cursed her words. She sounded so cold and robotic – just like Enid. 'It's early days,' she added with a shrug. *There I go again.*

'Thankfully they have your friendship.'

'I feel a bit helpless, to be honest.'

'I'm sure just knowing you're able to be called upon is a huge comfort.'

'Thora, I'm really sorry I haven't been in touch properly since…'

'Oh, Emily, I didn't say that to make you feel guilty. You have nothing to feel guilty about. We're fine. I've thrown myself into CWA, The Rose Club, and a few other bits and pieces. Gerald is still pottering about the farm and talking about selling up. You've been busy too. We drove past the other week and saw the big building project. Didn't we, Gerald?' she said, as he entered the room carrying a tray.

'Sorry?'

'I was just saying we saw Emily's house being built.'

'Oh, yes, marvellous.'

'You should have stopped in.'

'We didn't want to disturb you.'

'I would have loved to see you. Promise me you will stop in, next time? It's an open invitation.' Emily took a sip of tea. 'Speaking of invitations. It's going to be an art gallery – the building, that is. I'd like you both to come to the opening. It's June twenty-fifth, from seven o'clock. You'll get an invitation when they're sent out.'

'Oh, how lovely. I'm so pleased you're building a future down there. It would've been quite difficult returning to somewhere you weren't entirely happy.'

'There's something you should know, so you don't hear from someone else. It's all happened rather fast,' Emily said, colouring. She picked up her mug to hide it, and took another sip.

'You've met a new man,' Gerald said.

'Er, yes,' she said, only just managing not to spit out her tea in surprise.

'And he's quite lovely, and very dishy, by all accounts,' Thora said, raising her eyebrows and grinning a little cheekily.

'I should have... I'm so sorry you...' Emily said, blushing furiously. She still found it mind-boggling that they had apparently not known that she and John had split up, despite their separation being the talk of the town for a couple of weeks.

'Nonsense. You owe us nothing, Emily. We're very pleased to see you getting on with your life and being happy, especially after what John put you through. Aren't we, Gerald?'

'We most certainly are,' Gerald said.

'I really appreciate you being so understanding. It must be hard for you, too, to hear.'

'Don't worry about us. We're all grown-ups. Have some cake.'

'Thank you,' Emily said, taking a slice from the offered plate.

'So, tell us about this young fellow,' Gerald said.

'Jake is his name. He's an architect and builder from Melbourne. He specialises in sympathetic renovations – merging the old with the new. It was his idea to rebuild the cottage. He's hoping there might be demand for his work locally. The building is going to be a gallery, and it's also going to double as a display home, advertisement.'

'Sounds like a very good idea. I'm sure people will welcome him with open arms.'

'Ah, and I see you're engaged,' Thora said, reaching for Emily's hand. 'How exciting! May I see the ring?'

Emily was a little startled. She had no idea she'd been fiddling with her ring, but now she realised she had. *Why didn't I take that off and put it in my pocket?*

'Yes, of course. It's all happened rather fast,' she said, embarrassed, holding her hand out for inspection.

'Ooh, it's just gorgeous. Love doesn't run to schedules, dear, so don't you worry about how it will look. What's important is that you're happy. And you are, you're practically glowing. Being engaged really suits you.'

Emily looked down and fiddled with the handle of her mug, shifted in her seat. 'Um...'

'Except, it's not just being engaged, is it?'

She let out a little sigh and shook her head slowly.

'You are, aren't you? Pregnant, that is?' Thora's eyes were wide.

'Yes. But please don't tell anyone – it's too soon.'

'I knew it!' Thora said, clapping her hands. 'I wondered that the moment you walked in the door. I have a nose for these things, you see. Oh, that's wonderful news. And my lips are sealed.'

'Hearty congratulations – on both counts,' Gerald said.

Emily nodded. 'Thank you.'

'It *is* wonderful news, isn't it?' Thora said, peering at her.

'Yes.' She hesitated.

'But? Is something wrong with you, the baby?'

'No. We're both fine, as far as I know. But, to be totally honest, I'm terrified.'

'Of what?'

'Excuse me, but I think that's my cue to leave,' Gerald said, standing up.

'Oh, please don't feel...' Emily started.

'I'll see you again soon. Visit any time.'

Emily got up to hug him and watched as he kissed his wife on the forehead and left the room.

'Don't mind him. He's just old-fashioned – baby discussions are the domain of women. Now, you were about to tell me what you're frightened about.'

'Everything, really,' she said, shrugging helplessly, tears filling her eyes.

'You can't let yourself worry about what happened to Barbara and David Burton happening to you.'

'I know. I'm trying not to think about it.'

'That's not all that's bothering you, is it?'

'No. I'm not *unhappy* about being pregnant, but I just don't feel...'

'Gushy, maternal?'

She nodded.

'I have no doubt you'll be a wonderful mother. Motherhood comes in all shapes and sizes, Emily. I felt gushy from the moment I found out, but I know plenty of women who didn't feel much other than sick, worried, and frightened until they saw the baby, and some who didn't ever feel the warm rush of gooey love. Oh, they loved their children, all right, don't get me wrong, but they just didn't goo and gah. Nothing wrong with that. Perhaps you're worrying too much about what you're *not* feeling. Maybe you've been keeping yourself too busy. But you can't run away from your feelings forever, Emily. Trust me, I know. How far along are you?'

'I'm not sure yet. Probably only a few weeks or a month. It wasn't actually planned.'

'Probably best that it wasn't, dear. I'd say someone or something has taken that decision out of your hands, wouldn't you?'

Emily wanted to laugh and cry at the same time. Thora sounded so like Gran.

'Jake is happy about it all, isn't he?'

'Oh yes. He'd probably be stocking up on onesies already if I let him.'

'And he's kind and supportive of you?'

'He's wonderful. I really am so lucky to have found him.' Emily stopped herself abruptly.

'Well, then, you have nothing to worry about. Together you'll get the job done just fine. And how is Enid coping with all this?' Thora asked in a concerned tone.

Emily really nearly did laugh this time. *Oh, you know her so well.*

'She doesn't know yet. We're trying to stretch out the shocks. We've only just got engaged. I haven't even got around to putting an ad in the paper yet.'

'And perhaps putting it off?'

'Yes. Guilty as charged.'

'I know your mum can be a little standoffish and, well, holier-than-thou, but I haven't yet met a woman who isn't thrilled with the idea of being a grandmother. Although, I have to concede, there is a first time for everything.'

They exchanged a wan, conspiratorial smile before sipping their drinks.

'But on a serious note, Emily, if you ever need a de facto set of grandparents or extra babysitters, I hope you'll think of us. As you know, John was our only child, so we…'

Noticing tears in Thora's eyes, Emily reached out and put her hand over the older lady's. 'Thora, I'd be honoured if you and Gerald would be another set of grandparents to my baby. Jake's parents died when he was young.'

'It would mean the world to us,' she said, clutching Emily's hand with both of hers. 'We meant it when we said you would always be part of our family.'

'And hearing you say that means the world to me, Thora,' Emily said with eyes awash.

'Oh, look at me, getting all weepy,' Thora said, extracting a handkerchief from her pocket and blowing her nose.

They chatted for a few more minutes before Emily made to leave. At the door Thora held both Emily's hands and looked deep into her eyes. 'Remember, I'm here if you ever need me, Emily.'

'Thank you, Thora. And if there's anything I can do for you and Gerald, you only have to ask. And please don't drive past again without dropping in,' she added, smiling warmly.

Emily drove away with a wave. She felt so much better after her visit. She was heavy with feelings of love and gratitude for Thora and Gerald, but lighter about the baby.

Chapter Thirty-seven

In the week following, Emily rang Barbara every morning to see how she was, but she was wary of overcrowding her. It wasn't that she avoided her friend; she just left it to Barbara to ask her to spend time together. She didn't want the sudden attention to make her feel like a charity case. Given how little time they'd been spending together before all this happened, it might look very contrived. Besides, she had so much to do regarding the gallery opening and didn't want Barbara sitting around feeling neglected.

She thought life had to start getting back to as normal as possible as soon as possible, not that she was in any way qualified to make such an assessment. It was probably tough love, but she thought Barbara needed to learn to live with the grief, and not bury it by filling her waking hours hanging out with her.

If questioned deeply, however, Emily would have had to concede that her actions weren't solely motivated by Barbara's best interests. As long as she didn't spend too much time with her friend, she wouldn't accidentally reveal her pregnancy, which she was slowly starting to feel better about. Admitting her mixed feelings might be worse than actually revealing the pregnancy.

She wanted to hold on to that news, and her relationship with Barbara and David, for as long as possible. She just didn't want to cause them any more pain. A big part of her knew it was absolutely ridiculous – of course they would be happy for her and Jake – but she just couldn't shake the fear that it could damage their friendship.

If the situation was reversed, she hoped she'd be pleased for her friends. Hurt and sad for herself and Jake, but happy for them. But there was no telling how they would react in their grief-stricken state. So, she hoped that if she kept it to herself long enough then they might be in a better place psychologically and therefore more inclined to accept it. That was her theory anyway.

Every now and then she wondered if it might be better to just sit Barbara and David down and tell them. But she wanted to get through the opening of the gallery first and didn't want to do it without her dear friends. After all, they had been instrumental in helping her get back on her feet all those months ago.

Though, really, would they be up to a big night out so soon? Getting dressed up, putting on a happy face, dealing with the expressions of sympathy?

Emily had finally got around to booking her appointment to see the doctor, only to find she couldn't get in for another week. Flu seemed to have well and truly gripped Hope Springs, the receptionist told her. When she heard that, Emily wondered if it might be best to hold off for a while. She didn't want to expose her unborn baby to a room full of sick people.

Wasn't the first ultrasound not until after three months, anyway? Surely she couldn't be any more than a month along. She'd been on the pill for years, and had always heard that women were unlikely to get pregnant straight away after missing a few doses.

No, she'd better get it over with while she had the time. The doctor had wanted her to return in a week for the results. Oh well, she'd only be a few days late. Not the worst thing in the world, considering everything else that was going on.

Soon she'd be enveloping invitations, recording RSVPs, keeping track of acceptances and declines, and sorting out the catering. She tried not to think about how it would be running the gallery with a baby in tow. 'Cross that bridge when you come to it, dear,' Gran had often said. No doubt Thora would say the same. Emily felt a little guilty about confiding in John's mother and not her own, but it wasn't as if she'd planned it.

'So, you're off to see the doctor this morning, right?' Jake said over breakfast one day.

'Yes. Nine o'clock. I'd better get going.'

'Want me to come along?'

'Thanks, but there's no need. I think I know what's going to happen: He'll tell me that I'm definitely pregnant, probably hand me a leaflet on what to expect, and give me a referral for an ultrasound.'

'Well, if you're sure…?'

'Totally.' She'd told him of her visit with Thora and that she was determined to think better of things.

A few moments later the phone rang. The handset was nearer Jake, so he picked it up. Emily instinctively checked her watch – a little after eight. She had to leave at eight-thirty, eight thirty-five at the absolute latest, to get there on time.

'Jake speaking. Oh, hi Barbara. Yes, she's right here, I'll just put her on.' He handed her the phone.

'Hi Barbara, how's things?' Emily asked.

'Hi Em, doing a bit better this morning, thanks.'

'That's good to hear.'

'Yeah, but another day here and I won't be.'

'Oh?' She raised her eyebrows at Jake.

'I need to get out of the house. Do you have any plans today?'

'Today? Um, I don't have anything major on,' she said, wincing.

'Can I come down and hang out?'

'What time were you thinking?' She crossed her fingers. *Hopefully I'll be back from the doctor in time.*

'Would nine o'clock work?'

Emily shot a stricken look at Jake. 'Oh, er, sure. Nine o'clock would be fine.'

Jake frowned back and she shrugged helplessly.

'Great, thanks so much,' said Barbara.

'No worries. I'll see you soon,' Emily said, and hung up.

'What are you doing?' Jake demanded.

'I couldn't really say no to Barbara,' Emily said. 'Not when she's made the first move to start coming out of her shell.'

'But what about your doctor's appointment? Couldn't you have told her to come over later? It's not like this is just a regular check-up.'

'I suppose. But it's done now. I can't exactly call her back now, can I? She'll want to know why.'

'Hmm, I see your point,' Jake said. 'Hey,' he said, after a few moments, 'Why don't I just go on your behalf? I could get the blood test results and ask any questions you wanted to know.'

'There's no way they'd give out my information, because of confidentiality,' she said.

'Maybe they would if I had written consent from you,' he suggested. 'It's worth a try.'

'Would you mind?'

'Of course not. It's my child as well. This is the least I can do.'

'Well, I guess it's worth a shot. It's that or miss the appointment. They don't open until nine, so I can't cancel it now anyway. If they won't accept you as my proxy, then they can put the results in the post.'

'You write the note and I'll get changed,' he said, getting up.

'You're the best. Thanks, Jake.'

Half an hour after Jake left, Emily heard the arrival of a car. Now there was less traffic coming and going for the building across the way, her ears were again tuned in to the sound of vehicles turning in off the dirt road out front.

She went out to greet Barbara and was surprised to see David getting out of the driver's side. She was even more surprised when he opened the back door of the dual cab ute and Sasha emerged.

'I don't want Barb driving at the moment,' David said as he embraced Emily. 'She's a bit distracted.'

'He means I'm a basket case who can't be trusted behind the wheel,' Barbara said, coming up beside them.

'Oh. Right,' Emily said, feeling a little uncomfortable.

'Probably best, I am a bit distracted,' Barbara added. 'Yesterday I drove down to the end of the driveway to check the mail and ended up in Wattle Creek. See, totally off the planet!'

Emily relaxed slightly.

'Hope you don't mind Sasha coming along, but we've become a bit attached.'

'Not at all. Grace will be pleased to have the company.'

'Is Jake in?' David asked.

'Er, no, you just missed him. He had to pop over to Hope Springs,' Emily said.

'Oh, maybe I'll head down there and see if I can catch up. I'll come and collect you in a few hours. You'll probably be ready for a lie-down by then.'

'Thanks darling,' Barbara said, and hugged her husband.

'Have fun,' David called with a wave as he got back into the vehicle.

'Here, this is a treat for later. Just bung it into the fridge,' Barbara said, handing Emily a brown paper bag.

'Okay, thanks,' Emily said.

'Isn't this nice? Just like old times,' Barbara said, as she linked arms with Emily and they walked up the path to the house.

To Emily, it was nothing like old times. Part of her wished she'd put Barbara off in favour of the doctor. Once upon a time they could just be together without either of them making any effort, but it certainly didn't feel like that today. When she'd visited the other day there was no pretence that things were normal. Now it all just felt awkward.

Inside, the dogs had a quick reunion and then settled onto their mats while Emily put the kettle on. Emily only remembered then that she hadn't removed Sasha's bedding – they'd been so busy with the cottage. While she explained the progress over the past two weeks, Barbara was alternately excited and subdued.

The two friends sipped tea amid long silences that regularly strayed into awkward.

'So, come on, I'm dying to see the place,' Barbara said suddenly after they'd finished their tea. She got up.

'Okay, just let me have a wee first.' Emily was finding her bladder capacity shrinking by the day. Recently she'd been trotting off to the toilet almost half-hourly. She assumed it must be psychosomatic; surely the baby was tiny. But telling herself that didn't make any difference.

'As you can see, it's a lot bigger than a cottage, but we've never managed to stop calling it one,' Emily said as they made their way towards the building site.

'Oh, well, sounds better than *the building* or *the house*,' Barbara said. 'And there was a real little cottage there once. Until a certain someone knocked it down.'

'Yeah, don't remind me. I try not to think ill of the dead,' Emily said.

'That's noble of you.'

'Thanks, but really, at the end of the day, it was only bricks and mortar.'

The words, 'not a living, breathing person' hung unspoken in the chilly air around them.

They traipsed on, both with hands thrust deep into pockets. The dogs bounded on ahead, Sasha struggling to keep up with Grace.

'I'm giving you the full experience,' Emily said. 'Hence going the long way around.' They could have climbed over the fence and cut across the paddock, but instead they were going up to the official driveway. 'Sorry for the extra walk.'

'Don't be. I've been sitting around like a blob for too long; some exercise will do me good,' Barbara said. 'And I'm not sure I could climb a fence at the moment.'

They paused at the edge of the road to take in the scene. The sun glinted off the galvanised iron roof and verandahs, and the pale stonework and creamy mortar was lit up in streaks where clear laserlight sheets had been used above the windows to help light the rooms inside. Even though she'd seen it plenty of times, Emily still felt a little awestruck. The sun was at a perfect angle, and was shining brightly.

'It looks brilliant,' Barbara said.

'Thanks. It's come up well.'

'It still looks very much like the old one, only better – more complete with its verandah.'

'I hope so. It's a lot different inside,' Emily said.

'So it should be – the previous incarnation was practically derelict! And it'll be nice to see it without all the pigeon poo!' Barbara declared. Emily was pleased to get a glimpse of her dear friend's sense of humour. She smiled to herself as she thought: *she'll come back, she'll be okay*. She could see that now.

'Oh, no, we kept that for posterity. You know how sentimental I am.'

'Still attached to a sample of old floorboards, I hope.'

'Yes, we've sent it off to be gold plated. It's going to hang above the fireplace behind my desk,' Emily said, grinning and playing along. 'But seriously, we were thinking of landscaping out the front,' she explained, as they walked off the road and started across the large white rubble and gravel parking area. 'But we couldn't decide what to do.'

'I like it like this; it looks like a real business. You don't want it looking too domestic. And you need plenty of parking for all those visitors you're going to get.'

'I hope so,' Emily said, smiling at her friend.

'It's going to be a huge success.'

Emily could see how hard Barbara was working to put on a happy face – she just hoped the façade wouldn't crumble from all the effort.

'Love the colour of the door and the timber highlights,' Barbara said. 'Not too brown, not too brick-red or plum-red; it's just right.'

'It's garnet,' Emily replied, glad that she had noticed. 'We've chosen it as our brand colour. I should have shown you when we were at the house. Remind me when we get back.' She inserted the key in the lock and threw open the door.

'Welcome to The Button Jar Gallery of Fine Art.' She took a moment to enjoy the way the name rolled off her tongue.

'Wow,' Barbara said, taking in the view for the first time. 'Is that polished concrete?'

'Yes, with chips of quartz and coloured stone in it. I was a bit sceptical to start with, but I love it now,' Emily said.

'It's brilliant, and will be a doddle to keep clean.'

'I'll get a hall runner at some stage.' She flicked a switch and the chandelier lit up above them.

'That is totally gorgeous,' Barbara said.

It was the first time Emily had seen it in all its glory. As rainbows from the Italian cut crystal lit up the ceiling and walls, she thought it worth every cent. It was stunning.

'I want to get ottomans for people to sit on, but I haven't decided exactly what shape and fabric yet,' Emily explained as they made their way through. 'We're leaving it empty for the opening though.' All the rooms were bare except for the one at the back left that held Emily's desk and chair. She was surprised to see the desk in place. Had, in fact, completely forgotten about it. Jake couldn't have moved it on his own; he must have got the electrician to help the other day when he was here.

Each room had high picture rails for hanging the art on. It was one nice clean line rather than having hooks sticking out of the walls.

Next Emily opened the doors to the bathrooms and they peered in. Nice and clean in neutral tones, but nothing over the top. Unlike the kitchen.

This was the first time she'd seen it fully completed. It was perfect, just what Jake had described.

'What a gorgeous kitchen,' Barbara said, running her hands over the stone bench top.

'I can't take any credit, really; it's all Jake,' Emily said, walking over and running her hand across the chunky raised gas cooktop. She'd seen it in the pictures, but Emily would never have believed a kitchen appliance could actually look so handsome, so *sexy*. But it did; the cast iron trivets, the gas ring below, all framed in sleek, shiny stainless steel. It was a work of art compared to the boring black coils and solid electric elements she'd used all her life. She was a little overawed.

Finally she unlocked the row of five glass café doors. They walked outside. A paved patio area held a stainless steel outdoor kitchen and a large timber table with bench seats.

'Gosh, you've thought of everything,' Barbara said, looking around.

'Jake has,' Emily corrected.

'I'm surprised you guys aren't going to move over here. I would.'

'Who knows what will happen?' she replied with a shrug, 'but for now it's definitely going to be a gallery.'

'And a very successful one at that,' Barbara added firmly. 'When is the grand opening?'

'The evening of June twenty-fifth. It's a Saturday. It's going to be cocktails standing up, so make sure you wear comfy shoes,' Emily warned. 'We're hoping for hordes of people.'

'I'm sure you'll be swamped.'

Emily smiled. 'We're still waiting for the invitations to arrive from the printers. Otherwise the two of us would've been stuffing envelopes and sticking stamps all day.'

'I wouldn't have minded,' Barbara said. 'It's good not to just be sitting around with my sadness shadowing me,' she added quietly. 'I'm so glad I'm here.'

Emily turned to her. There were tears welling in Barbara's eyes. 'I'm glad too. I've missed you.' They embraced and then Emily held her friend by the arms. 'I know you might not want to talk about Albert,' she said.

Barbara's lip trembled.

'But if you do – *whenever* you do – I'm always here. I want you to know that it's okay to talk. If you want. And if you don't, that's fine too.'

Barbara nodded, her eyes brimming with tears. 'Thanks,' she said with a gulp.

Emily smiled sadly at her friend before releasing her. It was chilly out of the sun and surrounded by stone, so they made their way back inside and she locked the doors behind them.

'I'm just going to test out the loo,' she said, and headed to the toilet with her head down.

'Are you okay?' Barbara asked when Emily emerged a few minutes later.

'Yeah, fine,' she said, avoiding eye contact.

'Twice to the loo in one hour?' Barbara continued.

'Must be the cold weather,' she replied, still unable to look Barbara in the eye. It had been the first thing that had come to mind.

They walked slowly back to the main house, long silences again the norm.

'I fancy some cheese,' Barbara declared when they were back inside.

'I'm afraid I've only got ordinary cheddar,' Emily said apologetically.

'No you don't,' Barbara said with a mischievous glint. She went to Emily's fridge and brought the paper bag to the table.

Emily retrieved a wooden chopping board from the open cupboard above the bench and put it on the table. She held her breath whilst hoping Barbara's selection didn't include anything soft. After her chat with Thora, she'd started swotting up online about pregnancy. She'd read that expectant women shouldn't eat soft, blue-veined or semi-soft cheeses like fetta and ricotta. Apparently they were more prone to growing bacteria, like listeria, that was harmful to unborn babies.

'We picked these up in Whyalla on the way home,' Barbara said, rubbing her hands together in anticipation. 'I've been craving soft cheese. I guess that's what happens when you deny yourself something. Avoiding cheese certainly didn't help me, though, did it?' she added bitterly, as she extracted a box of water crackers from her handbag and put it on the table.

Emily was without words. All she could do was offer her friend a sympathetic look. She focussed on unwrapping the package of cheeses and then stood staring at the four packets, only one of which wasn't soft. *Uh-oh.*

'Are you okay?' Barbara asked.

'Um, yep, fine, just got distracted for a moment,' Emily said, tearing her gaze away and moving to the utensil drawer to look for the cheese knife.

Think, Emily, think, she told herself as she pretended to fossick through the assorted implements for the cheese knife – which was clearly visible at the front of the drawer, right by her hand.

She couldn't claim to be on a diet; Barbara knew she didn't believe in them. She couldn't claim to have gone off cheese, because that would raise too many questions.

Oh God. Would it be easier just to eat the damned cheese? How great is the risk anyway? If only she'd got Jake to ask the doctor. But of course when he left she'd had no idea she'd be facing this dilemma an hour or so later. *Shit, shit, shit!* She felt like banging her head against the cupboard in frustration.

'Just a normal knife will do,' Barbara said.

'Got it,' Emily said, making a show of holding up the cheese knife as she shut the drawer. She reluctantly sat back down in front of the platter of unwrapped cheeses. Her mouth was watering. She handed the knife to Barbara.

'Which one can I cut for you?' Barbara asked, knife poised.

'Just a piece of the cheddar, thanks.'

'What, no blue vein or double brie?'

'No thanks,' Emily said, shaking her head. 'We had a big breakfast.'

'What's going on?' Barbara asked, eyeing her warily.

'Nothing,' Emily said, accepting the wedge of cheddar on a water cracker, but avoiding her friend's gaze.

'Don't you dare tell me you're on a diet,' Barbara said.

Emily shrugged.

'There's something you're not telling me. What is it?'

A sudden wave of nausea came over Emily and she bolted from the room like a rabbit in front of a pack of greyhounds. She made it to the toilet just in time.

Barbara was staring at her when she re-entered the kitchen a minute later. Emily failed to hide a sheepish look.

'What's wrong with you?' Barbara asked again.

She sat back down. 'Milk must have been off,' she lied, still feeling her friend's gaze.

'But I had milk with my tea and I'm fine.'

Emily looked up tentatively after Barbara had been silent for ages. Her friend's eyes were wide and still upon her.

'You're pregnant, aren't you?'

All Emily's resolve left her. She nodded slowly, and then put her head in her hands on the table.

'Oh my God! You're pregnant. I can't believe it,' Barbara said. And then, 'But what's wrong? Aren't you happy? You're in a committed relationship, why wouldn't you be happy?' she asked, clearly perplexed.

Emily looked up with eyebrows raised in a knowing expression.

'Oh. Oh! You're worried about upsetting me?' Barbara said. She put a hand over her mouth.

'Oh Barbara, I didn't know how to tell you,' she said, and burst into tears.

'God, what sort of friend would I be if I couldn't be happy for you?'

'But it's so soon.'

'I'm sure you didn't plan it that way,' Barbara said, smiling kindly at her friend.

'So you're okay with this?' She wiped her nose.

'Of course I am. Honestly, Em, I'm happy for you. Yes, I'm sad and bitterly disappointed for my own situation, but that doesn't mean I don't want good things for you. I love you. You're my dearest friend in the whole world.'

'Oh Barbara,' Emily said, 'I've been tying myself in knots about how and when to tell you.'

They got up together and hugged across the corner of the table.

'I thought you'd be upset.'

'I *am* upset, but not at you, silly,' Barbara said. 'So, when are you due?' she asked when they were once again seated.

'I'm not sure,' Emily said, wincing.

'Oh, so not planned then?'

'No. I'm so sorry.'

'Don't be, Em, please. Please don't pity me; I couldn't bear that. I'll just have to be the best auntie in the history of the universe.'

Emily nodded.

'Well, this changes everything, doesn't it?' Emily was trying to figure out Barbara's tone when her friend reached for the cheese knife. 'Looks like I get to pig out on the creamy cheese all by myself,' she said, offering Emily a wan smile.

They spent another hour together. Whilst Emily was relieved that everything was out in the open, she still had the gnawing feeling that Barbara's ready acceptance of her pregnancy was the calm before the storm. She really hoped she was wrong.

When David arrived back to pick Barbara up, they hugged goodbye.

After Barbara and David had left, Emily paced around the kitchen for a few minutes. Where the hell was Jake? Why hadn't he come back around the same time as David? She couldn't settle. She wanted to walk off her angst, but was afraid he might return while she was gone.

Finally she heard the ute and raced out to meet him. She flung her arms around him as soon as he was out of the vehicle, almost unbalancing him.

'Easy tiger,' he said. 'What's up?'

Tears filled Emily's eyes. 'Oh Jake. I'm so glad you're home.'

'What's wrong? It's not the baby is it?'

Emily shook her head. 'I'm fine. But Barbara knows. About the pregnancy.'

'Yeah, so does David,' he said sheepishly.

'You told him?' She didn't know whether to be annoyed or relieved.

'He caught me coming out of the doctor's. It just sort of came out.'

'So how did he react?'

'He was fine. What about Barbara?'

'She was fine too.'

'So what are you so upset about? It's good that it's out in the open, and even better that they're okay with it.'

'But what if they're pretending?'

'Of course they're pretending, Em. They're putting on a brave front, but inside their hearts will be breaking all over again. They'll be wondering why we got pregnant at the drop of a hat when they struggled, and why their baby was taken from them. Every time we talk about our child it's going to remind them of what they have lost. But they will put all that aside to be happy for us, because they are kind, considerate and unselfish people, and because that's what good friends do.'

'I just feel so terrible,' Emily said.

'I know. But they wouldn't want to take away from our happiness.'

'It's just not fair,' Emily wailed.

'No it's not. Life often isn't,' Jake said sagely. 'But we have each other. And they have each other. We'll all get through this. In a way I'm glad it came out now; hopefully it means that the dust will settle sooner rather than later,' he said. 'You know what them knowing means, though, don't you?'

'What?' Emily asked, genuinely baffled.

'We have to tell your parents as soon as possible. It's really not fair other people knowing when they don't.'

'Oh, God. Tomorrow?'

'Tomorrow. But no later.'

Emily remained silent, mulling it over for a few moments.

'So how did Barbara find out anyway?' Jake asked suddenly.

'Cheese. Bloody cheese!' Emily said, throwing her hands up in the air and letting them drop.

Jake frowned quizzically at her.

'She brought us a treat since she can now eat soft cheese again,' Emily said, rolling her eyes and shaking her head in exasperation.

'Oh, and now you can't,' Jake said, thinking aloud.

'Exactly.'

'But I can!' he said, giving her a squeeze and leading her up the path and into the house.

Chapter Thirty-eight

All the way to Hope Springs, Emily talked with Jake about the project and launch of the business. But it did little to keep the tension at bay. How would Enid feel about the prospect of being a grandparent?

'Don't worry about it. She'll be thrilled to be a granny,' Jake had said when Emily had voiced her concern the night before.

Since then, she had kept her fears to herself. She did tend to catastrophise, but was doing her best to be more positive. Her life was pretty damned perfect after all – a loving fiancé, an exciting new business venture, good friends. She was even starting to feel differently about her baby. After all, she had felt maternal about Grace from the instant she met her. How exciting would it be to meet someone who had been growing inside her belly for nine months?

At that moment, her relationship with her mother was the only thorn in her side. She really hoped Jake was right; that bonding over the baby might be a turning point in their relationship. She knew how important grandparents were, and she wanted her child to have the sort of relationship she'd had with hers.

'She's been through it all before, Emily. She might have a lot of good advice. And Des,' he'd said.

'Hmm,' Emily had said.

Des greeted them at the door and led them through to the kitchen. There was not a dish in sight, but Enid was at the sink with cloth in hand wiping furiously. How much time could one woman possibly spend wiping the sink and bench tops?

'Emily, Jake, lovely to see you both,' she said, going through the air-kissing ritual.

'Who's for tea or coffee?' Des asked. 'I've still got some bags of peppermint tea if you'd like, Em.'

'That would be lovely. Thanks Dad.'

'Tea for me – white with one, thanks Des,' Jake said.

'Bring the biscuits too, Des.'

'What's this?' Emily said, pulling out a chair at the table. In front of her was a neatly stacked pile of magazines, the top one being *Australian Bride*.

'I thought when you saw the gorgeous cakes, dresses, and flowers on offer you might change your mind about not doing things properly.'

'Mum, I've already had my white wedding. And it was lovely. Besides, didn't you say it was ridiculous of Debbie Argus to wear ivory for her second marriage?'

'Yes, but she was a much older bride.'

Emily concentrated very hard on not rolling her eyes as she took her place. You really couldn't win with Enid.

'Well, at least have a flick through.'

Deciding to pick her battle elsewhere, Emily began thumbing through the magazine. There were some gorgeous dresses, floral arrangements, and amazing cakes. But she still didn't feel inspired to go down that path again.

'Here we are,' Des said, delivering mugs to the table, and then a biscuit tin.

'On a plate, Desmond, not the shabby tin,' Enid said with a sigh. 'Oh, never mind, it's here now. Jake, I hope you will forgive our poor manners. Now, tell me, what are you wanting by way of food for the gallery opening?'

'Thanks Mum, but we're having it catered.'

'Oh, who by?'

'Most likely the CWA. They're raising money for the Royal Flying Doctor Service. I'm sure they'll appreciate the opportunity.'

'Good idea. But you should get more than one quote. I could help if you like.'

Emily wanted to defend her decision, but again chose to keep the peace. Enid had a valid point. She hadn't run it by Barbara yet – the idea had only just struck her – but she wondered if her friend might enjoy having something to organise or cook for to keep her mind off other things. She was helping Simone by launching her career. Perhaps she could in some small way help Barbara too. If not, there were plenty of others in the Wattle Creek CWA she could call on – like Thora.

'So, everything is on track?' Des asked.

'Yes,' Jake said, 'it's been fantastic. There's really just the launch party to organise now. The invitations will be going out this week.'

'It all sounds very exciting,' Des said.

Emily wondered if Enid had her nose out of joint for not being part of the non-existent organising committee.

'I popped in and saw Thora and Gerald Stratten,' she said, abruptly changing the subject.

'Oh?' Enid said.

'How are they doing?' Des asked. 'I keep meaning to give Gerald a call.'

'They seemed to be okay.'

'All very sad,' Enid said. 'I must invite her for afternoon tea.'

'Yes,' Emily agreed. 'Good idea.'

'Mum, Dad, Jake and I have something to tell you,' she started, breaking the stretching silence. She gripped Jake's hand under the table. *Here goes.* 'I'm pregnant!'

Enid breathed in sharply. The air seemed to be sucked out of the room. Emily blushed. Jake squeezed her hand. Somewhere in the house a clock struck the hour. There seemed to be a collective holding of breath. *Dong, dong, dong, dong...* She counted the chimes all the way to ten, trying to keep her nerves at bay, unable to quite believe everyone was still silent. It was excruciating. *God, say something, someone. Please! Dad?*

'That's wonderful, dear, congratulations. Both of you,' Des said. He got up and pulled Emily into an embrace, then turned and shook Jake's hand. Then he hugged and slapped him on the back. 'What lovely news!'

Across the table, Enid remained seated. The blood had left her face. 'Des, they're not married.'

'Well, I don't know about you, Enid, but I for one am very excited at the prospect of becoming a grandfather.'

'Thanks Dad. It's come as a bit of a surprise.'

'But...you're not married,' Enid said, apparently dumbfounded.

'That's right, Mum. We're not married. You can get pregnant without a marriage certificate, you know.' Jake squeezed her hand again – no doubt as a warning.

'But, what will people think?' Enid was now blushing.

'Who cares what they think? I've met a wonderful man who makes me happy. We're engaged. We're committed. And we're going to have a baby together. Can't you just be happy for us?'

'Of course I'm happy for you.'

'Well, it doesn't sound like it.'

'It's just. I don't know. It's just a bit of a shock. I just never thought…'

'God, Mum. Why don't you ever give me a break? As usual, you're making it all about you. "What will people think?" Well, what about what *I* think?' Emily felt her heart start to race. She snatched her hand out of Jake's. Her voice went up an octave and a few decibels. 'What about, "Darling, as long as you're happy?" A good mother should want her child to be happy, but I don't think you care about my feelings at all. I don't think you ever have.' She was starting to feel out of control, like a freight train heading downhill without brakes. Out of the corner of her eye she noticed her father and Jake shifting in their chairs, but she blundered on. 'Parents are supposed to love their children, no matter what. But oh no, not you. All you do is criticise me and put me down.'

'Oh, Emily, don't be silly. You're being hysterical. And of course I…'

'You what? You've encouraged me? You've supported me? When? How? You orchestrated a reunion dinner to try and get me to go back to John, for Christ's sake! I was miserable with John. He was cruel, and you knew it.'

'Emily, language!' Enid said. 'Marriage vows are important. You can't just give up when things get a little difficult.'

'A little difficult! He shot at my dog, Mum. For fun.'

'I'm sure he…'

'What? Had his reasons? What possible reason?' She took a breath, shaking with emotion. 'You're right, it doesn't matter now. It's too late for you to show your support on that. Thankfully I had Dad. But you… You've never encouraged me to be anything more than a wife and mother. Well, look, here I am, pregnant and engaged. Fulfilling my duty – my great career path. And I still can't bloody win! I never will with you. I've wasted all these years and so much energy tying myself up in knots seeking your approval. The truth is, you'll never approve of anything I do. You're cold, critical, and unsupportive. You're a bully. And I've had enough of it. If you don't want a grandchild, then John's parents will be happy to step into the breach.'

'And I suppose they've been told. Before your own parents?'

She felt a stab of guilt. 'Yes, as a matter of fact they have. I didn't mean for it to happen, but it did. And, despite losing their son, they were gracious enough to be happy for me and Jake. But that's not the point. The point is that you always make everything about you.'

'What ever do you mean, Emily? How do you think it feels to have…?'

'Oh, for fuck's sake. Are you serious? It's not about who knows first! It's not a competition. Jake and I are having a baby – your first grandchild. And are you excited, pleased for us? Oh no, all you're thinking about is what people will think about me being unmarried, and that someone might have heard before you. It's the twenty-first century, not the nineteen sixties. I'm sorry Thora and Gerald found out first, but it was an accident. And I'm sorry I continue to be such an embarrassment to you. But, you know what, I no longer care. I'm glad you're not interested in your grand-child, because I don't want my child growing up feeling like I did.' She leapt up. 'Come on Jake, we're leaving,' she said, and stormed towards the front door.

They drove in silence, as Emily played back the outburst in her head. It hadn't felt good to let her mother have it like that, but at least she'd got it off her chest. It had been a long time coming. After ten minutes, she finally asked, 'Aren't you going to say something?'

'I'm not sure what to say.'

'How about, "Well done for standing up for yourself."'

Jake considered that for a moment. 'You didn't stand up for yourself. You attacked your mother in front of all of us. It was cruel. It was embarrassing. And your poor father...'

Stunned, Emily looked at him and then turned towards the window. Tears welled.

When they got home, Jake made no move to get out of the car. 'I'm going into town to check the mail.'

Emily stayed put.

'Emily, please. We'll discuss it later, but right now I'm too disappointed to even look at you.'

'Why?'

'She's your mother, Emily. You might not like some of the things she says and does, but she's the only one you've got.'

'Don't you dare play the "at least you've got a mother" card.'

'It's the truth. I'd give anything to have my mum to call or visit.'

'Well, you're welcome to Enid! I don't want any child of mine going through what I have, feeling like I have.'

'And I don't want my child not having a close relationship with their grandparents. So, we have a problem.'

'We certainly do,' Emily said. 'And if you think I'm just going to fall on my sword and apologise after finally standing up for myself, you've got another think coming.' She ripped the door open, got out, and slammed it shut behind her.

Chapter Thirty-nine

Inside the house, Emily busied herself with baking a cake, hoping the noise of the beaters would distract her from her anger. She desperately wanted to phone Barbara and offload, but she was terrified that her friend might side with Jake. *Is it possible that I went too far?*

No. She assured herself she was in the right. But she still didn't pick up the phone. Barbara had enough on her plate without being subjected to more of Emily's issues with her mother.

'Oh, Gracie, mummy's made a mess of things,' she said to the dog, who was lying on the floor nearby. 'What should I do?'

She was just putting the cake in the oven and wondering how to distract herself next when there was a knock at the door.

'Coming,' she called.

It was Des. Emily was shocked to see how haggard and stooped he looked. His face was a dreadful grey colour. Guilt stabbed under her ribs like a twisted knife.

'Dad! Come in,' she said, hugging him tightly. 'I've just put a cake in the oven if you'd like to wait.' She was so relieved to see him – to feel she had an ally – she almost burst into tears. 'I'm so sorry about before. I feel terrible that you had to hear that.'

Des broke the embrace and looked at her solemnly. 'Darling, I've got your mother in the car.'

'Oh.'

'I've been sent as the advance party to check you were home, since we can't see the car.'

'Jake's gone off. He's upset with me.'

'Oh dear.'

'Dad, if Mum's expecting an apology, she's going to be sorely disappointed. Whilst I regret losing my cool in front of you and Jake, and embarrassing you, I stand behind what I said.'

'You don't owe her an apology, Em.'

'Thanks Dad. I'd better put the kettle on.' When she turned back from filling the kettle, Enid was standing in the doorway. 'Hello, Mum,' she said.

'Emily,' Enid said stiffly and walked into the kitchen, bypassing the air-kissing ritual.

Emily almost shuddered in response to Enid's glacial stare. She could have sworn the temperature in the kitchen dropped ten degrees.

'Tea, coffee, something else?'

'Not for me, thank you,' Enid said.

'Coffee, thanks sweetheart,' Des said.

Emily's heart thudded hard as she prepared the mugs and delivered them to the table, the silence only broken by the loud plastic tick of the wall clock. Mother and daughter faced each other on opposite sides of the table, with Des between them at the end.

'Don't you have something to say to me, Emily?' Enid finally said.

Emily tightened her grip on the handle of her mug, but said nothing.

'I think an apology is in order. And what *exactly* have I done that makes me such a bad mother?'

Des flashed Enid a look. 'Enid, we talked about this.'

'No, Des, I want to know.'

'I didn't say you were a bad mother, Mum,' mumbled Emily.

'Well, it was certainly implied. You attacked me, in front of Jake and your father. I'd like to know why you hate me so much.'

'I don't hate you, Mum. I love you, but very often I don't like the way you treat me.'

'And what is it that I have done?'

'I told you. You're not encouraging, you're not support-ive. You're critical, you're always putting me down...'

'Examples, Emily. I need specific examples.'

'God, Mum, it's hard to give specific examples.'

'Well, try, Emily.'

'The house I moved into. You weren't supportive about that,' she said, a little desperately.

'The place was a dump, only fit for vermin! Surely I'm entitled to my own opinion?'

'Of course you are. But it was my choice to move there. Can't you see how criticising my choices isn't very supportive?'

'Am I such a bad mother for wanting better for my daughter? Now you're just sounding like a petulant child, Emily. I came here to find out why you think I've wronged you so badly that you would threaten to not let me see my grandchild.'

'Mum, it's more about the way you behave towards me,' Emily said, tears of frustration filling her eyes.

'How am I supposed to be a better mother if you can't tell me what I do that upsets you so much?'

Emily wanted to beat her head against the table. This was just going around in circles. Enid would never see it. There wasn't an actual example she could cite without her turning it around to suit herself. You can't explain feelings.

'You said I don't encourage you enough. I'm sure if I did you would be complaining I push you too hard. I can't win either way. It's the curse of motherhood. You'll see what it's like yourself soon enough, Emily. You're a well-adjusted, intelligent young woman, so I clearly didn't do too bad a job.'

'Then why are you so hard on me?'

'I wasn't aware that I was. Perhaps I'm not as warm and demonstrative as you would like, but that does not make me a bad mother.'

Gah! 'Do you know how awful it feels to always have your mother looking you up and down critically, to never feel good enough in her eyes, to never measure up?'

Enid's mouth dropped open and she stared at Emily.

'I do not.'

'You do, actually. All the time. And it makes me feel terrible.'

'Well, I certainly don't mean to. I think you're beautiful. Of course I do, you're my daughter. If anything, I'm a little envious of your lovely curves. I would have liked a bit more up top. And your complexion is so much better than mine. I wish I could get away without wearing make-up.'

So, maybe Barbara was right when she said Enid was threatened by her.

'And of course I'm proud of your achievements. Look at the way you got through John's funeral and moving back here. And you're about to start a business.'

'But, you said it was a silly idea.'

'Well, maybe I was a little hasty. I thought you were taking on too much too soon with the farm, and Jake, and everything. And perhaps I was seeing it through my eyes. You're much younger and more energetic than me. If I'm being completely honest – and it seems I am,' she said with a sad smile, 'I'm probably a little overawed by your strength. Look at how well you've dealt with all the terrible things life has thrown you lately.'

A fine way to show it.

But Emily kept her thoughts to herself. This was hard for her mother. She knew that. Enid really couldn't see how she'd hurt her, but maybe it was time for a truce. She'd just have to accept Enid for the way she was.

'Thanks Mum,' she said with a faint smile.

'Now, you two, hug,' Des said. 'Properly.'

Emily and Enid both glared at him. Enid really didn't do hugging.

'I insist. We're not leaving until you do.'

Emily got up, walked around the table and opened her arms out wide. Enid stood up and embraced her, tentatively at first. And then she clutched on hard. Emily wrapped her arms around her mother. When was the last time they had hugged properly like this? Had they ever? Suddenly she felt Enid's shoulders begin to shake. *Oh my God, she's crying.*

'I'm so sorry I've been a cold, critical mother. I know I have. I didn't want to admit it, but I have been a bully, Emily. I've been trying to hide my own fears and insecurities by being cruel to you. Please forgive me. And please don't take my grandchild away,' she sniffed.

'It's okay, Mum,' Emily said, hugging her even tighter. She found herself rubbing her mother's back, soothing her. 'I'm sorry too. I shouldn't have spoken to you like that – in front of Dad and Jake.' She felt bad about humiliating them, and was glad to have apologised for it. It was just a pity Jake hadn't been there to hear it. If only he hadn't gone off in a huff. So much for good communication...

Finally Enid broke away. Emily was shocked to see just how broken she seemed. Her mother – the woman with the hard, brittle exterior that never wavered – looked absolutely shattered. She'd aged twenty years in the last two minutes, but somehow she'd never looked more beautiful. The lines down her face and the coldness in her eyes had softened. She grasped Emily's hands in both of hers.

'I want you to know that I love you and I am proud of you – I always have been. You'll be a wonderful businesswoman and mother, and if you'll let me, I'd like to be there for you and Jake and the baby.'

Emily could only nod and try to swallow back the tears.

Des smiled at them. Emily almost erupted again at seeing tears in his eyes and streaks down his cheeks. He held out the tissue box that usually lived at the far end of the table.

Enid silently plucked a tissue from the box, and then Emily did.

'Thanks Dad.'

They sat back down. Emily felt exhausted, but leapt up when the timer on the oven sounded. 'Who's for a slice of warm apple teacake?'

Chapter Forty

Jake still hadn't arrived home when her parents left. It was now mid-afternoon, and Emily was concerned. She wished he'd been there to see how well everything had turned out. She wasn't sure how she was going to convince him of what had gone on. She had invited them to stay for lunch, but Enid had said she had cold meat in the fridge that had to be used that day. In the end they had hugged goodbye – it seemed her mother now did hugging.

She had just finished forming a batch of raw rissoles on a tray and slid it into the fridge for cooking later when she heard a car drive in. She started running through what she was going to say in her head. But she was in for a surprise.

'Hi, honey, I'm home,' came the voice from the back door.

Emily turned to see Jake enter the kitchen with a bunch of multi-coloured roses, their stems held together with aluminium foil. She raised her eyebrows.

He handed the roses over with a sheepish look.

She was about to speak when he put a forefinger over her lips. 'Me first. I'm sorry,' he said. 'I was wrong. You have every right to speak your mind and defend yourself against your mother.'

'Thank you,' Emily said, almost lost for words. 'But you were right. Not about what I said – I still stand by every word – but about the way I did it. I shouldn't have put you in that position. I'm sorry.'

They drew each other into an embrace, and Emily found herself sobbing again. 'Oh God, Jake. I thought I was going to lose you. Let's never fight like that again.'

He kissed her deeply, and then looked into her eyes. 'I love you, Emily Oliphant.'

When he let her go, Emily sniffed the flowers, drawing in the gorgeous, heady mix of musky, spicy, and sweet rose scents.

'Where did these come from? Don't tell me you've been off sweet-talking the old ladies in town.'

'No. I went to see Barbara and David.' He sat down at the table. 'Something smells good.'

'Raw onion and garlic? I've made rissoles for dinner. There's some apple teacake, if you fancy.'

'That would be great. I haven't had lunch.'

'Here you are, help yourself. I've already had some,' Emily said, putting the open Tupperware container, a knife, and a plate in front of him.

'So I see,' he said. 'Just having cake won't be good for the baby.'

'Don't worry, Mum and Dad helped with the cake.'

'Oh?' he asked, raising his eyebrows.

'Not so fast, mister, I want to know why you've had a sudden change of opinion.'

'Well, I hope you don't mind me talking to Barbara and David, but I didn't know where else to go.'

'How are they?'

'They're doing well. They reiterated that they're happy for us, and said they'll be the best aunt and uncle our little one could imagine.'

'That's great. We're so lucky to have them as friends.'

'That, we are.'

'And what did they have to say about the, er, Emily–Enid situation?'

'Barbara told me some of the awful things she's heard Enid say to you. Honestly, I had no idea just how damaging she's been. I'm so sorry you've had to put up with that. And I'm really sorry for not supporting you. I see now how hard it's been for you to stand up for yourself. I feel awful that I let you down. Will you forgive me?'

'Of course I forgive you, Jake. I love you,' she said, suddenly choking up. 'We're going to be great parents together,' she said, getting up and wrapping her arms around him from behind as he sat at the table, and kissing his neck.

'So, what did I miss?'

★

The following morning, after another lie-in for Emily, Jake came home from the post office with the box of invitations. He handed the package to Emily, who tore off the sticky tape with the glee of a child unwrapping a Christmas present. They grinned at each other as she carefully slid one out. She almost gasped at seeing her vision depicted there on the card in front of her.

Everything about it was stunning. She loved how the thickness of the card felt in her hand. It was so professional looking, and smelling. She took a deep whiff. Jake raised his eyebrows at her.

'What are you doing?'

'They smell so, so *professional*. Yummy.'

Jake laughed. 'Darling, they *are* professional. Here, let me see.'

'They're absolutely perfect,' she said with a sigh, and handed it over. 'I can't believe how well Simone's art came out.'

Emily and then Jake turned it over and around and around, carefully looking for any errors, and finally agreed they were free of typos.

It was a cold, wet day, perfect for staying inside and enveloping and addressing the two hundred and fifty invitations. They had just laid everything out on the table to operate a production line when they heard the whoosh of car tyres on wet earth outside. Jake got up to investigate. Emily could hear David and Barbara's voices.

'This looks like fun,' Barbara said, as she came into the kitchen, followed by Sasha and Grace. Jake and David had paused in the closed verandah. 'Are those the invitations? How exciting.'

'You're just in time to help,' Emily said, hugging her friend.

'Is everything okay with Jake again?' Barbara whispered into her hair.

'Thanks to you,' Emily whispered back, giving Barbara an extra tight squeeze.

'I hope we didn't overstep the mark discussing it with him, but he...'

'No, never. Not at all. I understand.'

'And what about Enid?'

'You know, I think we might have turned a corner. She actually apologised to me.'

'Really?'

'Yep, really. It was good to get things out in the open. We'll see how long it lasts, but at least she seems to know the score now.'

'That's amazing.'

'I know. So how are you guys doing? I think about you every moment of every day.'

'Thanks. We're taking it one step at a time. We'll get there.'

'Sit,' she said, pulling out a chair for Barbara. 'I was only kidding about putting you to work. I'll just move these out of the way.' She started bundling everything up again.

'We're happy to help.'

'What am I being roped in for?' David asked, coming in and hugging Emily.

'We'll help them stuff the envelopes, label, and stamp the invitations to the gallery opening, won't we?'

'Of course,' David said, sitting down.

'That's lovely of you. But not before you've had a cuppa.'

'Don't mind our dog making herself at home,' Barbara said with a laugh, nodding at where Sasha and Grace had curled up together against the wall.

'They only have themselves to blame for turning her into a house pet,' David said.

'She's beautiful. We loved having her here, as did Grace,' Emily said.

'She's been such a comfort, you've no idea.'

Emily smiled and nodded knowingly. She almost shivered at the memory of that first night in the Bakers' old, empty house after she'd left John. She'd been terrified. If it hadn't been for Grace, she might have seriously contemplated giving in and going back to him.

'They look great,' David said, picking up an invitation from the top of the pile.

'Thanks, we're really happy with them,' Jake said.

'How many are you sending?'

'Two hundred and fifty. Basically everyone we could think of.'

'Wow,' David said.

'The rule of thumb is you end up with around one third attending. And since we're so far out in the sticks and lots of them are in Melbourne...'

'Though we are putting an ad in the paper so no one feels left out,' Emily cut in.

'Sounds good,' David said.

'Who's doing the catering?' Barbara asked.

'I've been meaning to speak to you about that. I thought you might like the fundraising opportunity for the CWA. There's no pressure though. If you're not feeling up to cooking, that's fine. Or you could run it and delegate. Or not be involved at all – it's entirely up to you. I just wondered if you might want something to...'

'I'd love to do it,' Barbara said.

'Don't decide straight away. Take some time to think it through. There's always the bakery if it gets all too hard and the CWA can't or don't want to do it.'

'Darling, we've spoken about this,' David said quietly, putting his hand over his wife's. 'You can't be putting a Band-Aid over everything by making yourself so busy you can't think about it. You heard the counsellor; you have to be kind to yourself. Now might not be the right time,' he added softly.

'At least let me think about it. It's over a month away, and I'm getting better every day. Soon I'll probably be climbing the walls for something to do. And I do so love cooking.'

'And you're so very good at it. But please don't feel pressured,' Emily said.

'I won't.'

'Promise?'

'I promise. I'll let you know in the next few days.'

As they settled down with their hot drinks, Emily watched Barbara. She could practically see her brain churning with ideas for canapés. And she was suddenly looking more determined. It was good to see some animation back in her friend who had given her so much.

'So,' Barbara said an hour or so later, when they were busy enveloping and stamping, 'you haven't told us when the little one is due. Jake got the results of your blood tests the other day, didn't he?'

Emily nodded.

'And...?'

Emily wasn't avoiding telling them, she was trying not to crack up laughing.

'Lucky you're sitting down,' she said.

'Why, when is it?'

'Er, Christmas Day.'

Barbara laughed out loud. 'That's hilarious.'

'Quite the gift for someone who doesn't *do* Christmas,' David said, laughing.

'Nor do the Lonigans, really. It's terribly ironic,' Jake said.

'Haha, even better. Oh, this is too funny! I tell you what, I'll let you off tinsel duty if you're in labour.'

'Oh, you're so generous. But the poor kid, having that date.'

'Well, missy, you shouldn't have been so anti-Christmas. It's a sign.'

'Everything's a bloody sign, according to you. The problem is figuring out what the sign is a sign *of*.'

'Sometimes these things are simply sent to entertain the rest of us. This is just priceless,' Barbara said, chuckling and shaking her head as she placed a stamp on an envelope and gave it a thump with her fist.

Now this *is more like old times*, Emily thought.

A few days later, Barbara rang to say she would be honoured to do the food for the launch on behalf of the CWA. She had already spoken to Thora Stratten, who was also thrilled to be involved. And Emily wouldn't have to hire glasses because between the bowls club and CWA they'd be able to secure plenty.

'I know this sounds way out of the box,' Emily ventured, 'but what about including Enid? I know she'd love to be involved.'

'Great idea. Thora will keep her in line, if necessary. Let me call her. I'll get back to you in a week or so with a menu.'

'Thanks so much, Barbara. It means a lot to have you doing this.'

'You're paying, don't forget.'

'Of course I won't forget. But I'm just so glad to have my best friend taking care of something so important.'

'Hold your applause until the actual night, Em. It could all go pear-shaped yet.'

'Yeah, right. As if. Don't forget there's a huge oven and plenty of bench and fridge space at the gallery if you'd rather do the cooking there.'

'Thanks, I'll bear that in mind. Well, I'd better go and get my committee together. I feel a bout of bossiness coming on.'

'Don't let me hold you up.' Emily laughed and hung up. It was so good to hear her friend so upbeat again.

'This is all coming together so well, little one,' she told her belly. She still wasn't all gooey and doe-eyed about her pregnancy, but she was intensely grateful to the little guy or girl growing inside of her for providing the impetus to sort things out with Enid. And she regularly rubbed her belly and said thank you.

She was looking forward to seeing the little bean on an ultrasound one day soon. They had decided to wait until after the opening so they weren't distracted. Meanwhile, they were still trying to decide if they wanted to know the sex of their baby or be surprised – they seemed to change their minds daily. Emily could imagine plenty of women in the district not bothering with some of the tests and scans, given all the travelling one had to do to either Port Lincoln or Whyalla. From the little she'd learnt so far, it was already clear that pregnancy treatment and birth services in the country were very different to those in the city.

Jake had initially been horrified that there were no obstetric or ultrasound services in Wattle Creek or the neighbouring towns. It had been Emily's turn to reassure him that everything would be fine. There was the St John Ambulance and the Royal Flying Doctor Service if anything did go wrong.

She had been feeling much calmer since she and Enid had sorted things out, and was determined to let nature take its course and be guided by the doctor in Hope Springs.

She'd quizzed Enid and discovered she'd had a smooth labour that hadn't been overly long. Though, to Emily, eight hours sounded an awfully long time to be in enormous pain. But Enid had assured her it was a different, fulfilling sort of pain.

Well, she'd have to take her word for it for now – they had the impending birth of their business to deal with first.

Chapter Forty-one

Time seemed to speed up, and the next few weeks passed in a blur of preparations, invitations, RSVPs, and last-minute arrangements. Suddenly it was the eve of the opening and Emily was cleaning the house in preparation for Simone's arrival.

She, Barbara and Thora had spent a day the week before choosing a suitable selection of hot and cold and sweet and savoury finger food, and everything was underway. All the women were getting along well. Even Enid was playing nicely.

When Emily had visited her parents to deliver personal copies of the invitation, Enid had asked whether it was okay if she put the word around Hope Springs and encouraged people to come along. Emily had laughed. 'Of course, Mum, the more the merrier – there's an advert in the paper, remember?' But she'd been really touched by how respectful Enid was being towards her these days. It certainly made for a much more harmonious relationship.

She had been surprised to receive an RSVP from her cousin Liz to say she was coming and bringing along her parents. She was even more surprised to receive an engagement gift in the mail – a gorgeous pewter photo frame. She was now really looking forward to seeing her again. They'd had a lovely chat when Emily had rung to thank her, and both had admitted to overstepping the mark during their last phone call. Afterwards, Emily had wondered if her relationship with her mother had also negatively influenced her feelings towards her cousin. For a while she had been quite angry towards all of her family – other than her dad. But Liz had been really supportive that day at Gran's funeral, and very generous to offer her somewhere to stay if she ever left John.

Aunt Peggy, Uncle Jim, and Liz were staying with Enid and Des. They were arriving today as well, and would no doubt be put to work on the food. Enid had assured Emily she wasn't expected to come down and help entertain them when she was so busy. That was a turn-up for the books, and a great relief.

While vacuuming her bedroom, Emily paused beside the button jar on the tallboy and looked out the window towards the cottage.

'So much has changed, Gran. You just wouldn't believe it.' She turned and smiled at the two signs that David and Jake had put up just inside the paddock – one for the gallery and one to advertise Jake's business. They really had made a wonderful partnership.

'And a wonderful family, Gracie,' she said aloud, bending down to rub the ears of the dog whose tail had just slapped her leg. 'Soon an even bigger family, too,' she added, rubbing her belly. Thanks to Jake's constant reassuring, she was feeling much better about the baby, the cottage, everything. She was so lucky to have found him.

'Too late to back out now,' he had said yesterday after unveiling the signs. He'd been grinning broadly, and had wrapped his arms around her.

'It's hard to believe it's really happening.' She was still astounded at how much they'd got done in such a short space of time. And how much had happened in less than a year.

If only Gran was here to see all this. When she thought about how much she missed the old lady, she physically ached. At least now the tears had stopped.

'Gran wouldn't want us moping,' she told herself, Grace, and baby bean as she stamped on the vacuum cleaner and it roared to life. After she finished the house, she would do the cottage. It probably should have been left until the morning, but she was keeping a lid on her emotions by keeping herself busy. She'd probably do it again then too.

She was also nervous and excited about finally seeing all of Simone's paintings in the flesh. Jake's sister had been hard at work since Easter, and had been sending regular updates with photos attached. Each was stunning, and Emily loved that she was tackling different subjects. She was confident there would be something to appeal to everyone who attended the exhibition.

She checked her watch. Jake had gone to town to check the mail and stock up on groceries. He seemed to have happily taken over this particular job, and she had no objections. Thanks to the build and the time he'd spent helping David, he had become friendly with loads of people and enjoyed stopping in the street to chat when he had the time. But hopefully he wouldn't be long today. Simone was due in less than an hour.

She packed up the vacuum cleaner and stowed it in the cupboard in Jake's office. At Jake's suggestion they'd got a second machine for the cottage. Better to have the place self-contained right from the start rather than be dragging things back and forth, he'd said.

They had decided Emily would just open on the weekends and see how that went for a start. They hadn't put opening hours on the sign, but a smaller panel swung beneath the main sign to state whether the gallery was open or closed. Jake's graphic designer had organised the website and Jake had done a Facebook page, so people could check without driving past.

They had also included details about being open by appointment and her phone number. Neither of them thought it would be a problem – it wasn't like they were ever too far away – and it seemed the usual thing to do. Emily had to take Jake's word for that; she knew diddly-squat about running a gallery, as she seemed to be reminded on a daily basis. But she was learning.

When they had gone over the final figures, Emily was delighted to see the project had come in twenty thousand dollars under budget. She couldn't understand why Jake wasn't more exuberant until he pointed out that the spare twenty grand was for landscaping – which they hadn't done yet. So, it had actually come in right on budget. Emily thought that was pretty good considering all the stories she'd heard of people's budgets blowing out.

She wiped the bathroom vanity one last time and re-straightened the already straight towels. She was starting to get a little jittery. Back in the kitchen, she'd just boiled the kettle in a last-ditch effort to keep herself occupied when she heard the *toot toot* of an unfamiliar car horn.

Here she is. Perfect timing, she thought as she heard another vehicle turning in behind it.

Outside, she found Simone stepping out of a white two-door ute with a fibreglass canopy. JKR & Associates was emblazoned on the side. They hugged like best friends.

'I can't believe how fresh you look after driving all the way from Adelaide,' Emily said.

'I'm so glad I did a stopover. It is a long way from Melbourne by road. But worth it to know the paintings would arrive safe and sound.'

Jake appeared beside them and hugged his sister. 'Good trip?' he asked.

'Not bad. I actually don't mind the ute,' Simone said.

'Wow, how many have you brought?' Emily asked, peering through the tinted windows of the canopy, where all she could see was bubble wrap. The whole back area looked chocker-block full of paintings. They'd offered to have them freighted over, but Simone had been adamant about bringing them herself.

'Heaps! I've been a busy beaver.'

'You must be exhausted,' Emily said.

'I'm not feeling too bad, actually, though I can't say I won't crash later,' Simone said with a smile. 'But not until I've seen this gorgeous building of yours.'

'I'll need your help to decide where to hang what.'

'I hope you came prepared to work, sis,' Jake said.

'Phew! And I thought I'd already done the hard work. Can I have a cup of tea first?'

'You sure can,' Emily said, leading her up the path.

'I'll get your bags,' Jake said, and retrieved a large duffle-style overnight bag and long, black garment bag from the passenger side. Emily thought she noticed him share a conspiratorial look with Simone.

'God, this weighs a tonne,' he joked, pretending to struggle under the weight of the luggage. 'We really don't need any more rocks or bricks,' he added with a laugh.

'Oh ha ha,' Simone said, slapping at her brother's arm.

Back inside, Emily boiled the kettle again and got out some homemade melting moment biscuits while Jake showed Simone to her room. She smiled at hearing Simone cry out in delight. They had finally put bookcases in and finished her reading nook. When she and Barbara had gone down to pick up the mantelpieces – they'd had them restored after all – Maureen had asked if Emily had found bookshelves, because a lovely pair had just come in. And they were; just perfect.

Just when she was starting to wonder what was taking them so long, they reappeared. Again, she had the feeling they were sharing a secret. They were chattering in the hall, but suddenly seemed to change the subject when they entered the kitchen.

'The shelves look great. They really complete the room.'

'Thanks. If only I had more time to spend in there! Now, you've had lunch, haven't you?' Emily asked, pouring the tea. 'I'm happy to make you a sandwich if you haven't.'

'I'm fine, thanks,' Simone said. 'I stopped at Hungry Jack's in Port Augusta. Naughty, I know, but just what I crave on a road trip.'

Emily nodded. She didn't think she'd ever driven to or from Adelaide without stopping for a burger in Port Augusta.

They chattered about the arrangements for the opening; what had been done, what was yet to be done. An hour or so later they took Simone's vehicle over, stopping at the signs by the road so she could take photos.

Emily struggled to stand still with the excitement fluttering inside her so furiously. When they finally got to the cottage, she had to take great care not to give in to the emotions threatening to swamp her. After they gave Simone a tour of the new building and all the oohs and aahs had died down they unloaded the paintings into the front room to the right and began unwrapping them, ready to hang.

'It's so exciting!' Emily exclaimed, clapping her hands together.

As well as her signature floral pieces, there were landscapes, cityscapes and examples of still life. With all the paintings now unwrapped, Emily could see Simone had a distinctive style: bold colour, use of thick paint, not quite precise brushstrokes, clear depiction of the subject without being exact like a photo. It was all there. Emily found it hard to believe that before all this, Simone had only dabbled, and only to decorate her own house and Jake's apartment. She was definitely talented. Her work wouldn't look out of place in a major gallery or museum.

Finally they had all the pieces lined up on the floor against the walls. The three of them stood back and took in the view. They had ended up with enough works to adorn the walls of the four main rooms and even out the back in the large open kitchen, dining, and lounge space. They were deliberately keeping the wide hall clear so guests could move about freely without risk of bumping into the art.

'They're even more gorgeous than the ones in your house,' Emily said, wiping away a tear of joy. 'I didn't think that was possible.'

Simone beamed back.

'Yes, well done sis, they're great,' Jake said, putting his arm around his sister's shoulders. 'Although by the looks of this, I'm about to lose my business partner,' he added a little morosely.

'Flattery, flattery,' Simone said, rolling her eyes at him. 'But seriously, thanks guys, it means a lot that you like them.'

'Like them? I love them!' Emily said.

Simone and Emily spent the next few hours directing Jake as to where to hang what. Left to her own devices, Emily would have deliberated for far too long over each one, but the decisions were made quickly with the three of them sharing the task. Jake had brought a spirit level, which meant they didn't have to stand there for ages making minute adjustments. And the picture rail running right around the rooms made the hanging process easy. Simone had fitted hanging wire to all the backs, and had even made laminated labels. As each painting was hung, Emily added the neat label to the wall beside its bottom right corner.

Finally they were finished. Emily walked from room to room, satisfied with how everything looked. But the dominant feeling was relief at having the paintings in situ and all up safe and sound.

The other night she'd dreamt that she'd been standing in the gallery on opening night surrounded by blank walls because the paintings hadn't arrived in time. In another dream she'd dropped one artwork after the other whilst trying to hang them, only to end up with a heap of torn and ruined pieces. She'd woken in a sweat and spent the whole of the next day with concern shadowing her.

She'd kept it from Jake; had blamed her mood on baby hormones and then later, in private, had apologised to her stomach. Luckily from then on her dreams had been dominated by happier thoughts.

They got back to the house on dusk. They each had a quick shower and then Emily put a shepherd's pie in the oven for dinner. Simone returned from her room clutching a bottle of champagne.

'I think we deserve to celebrate after all our efforts!' she declared. 'But I'm afraid we'll have to stick it in the freezer for a bit. I forgot to get it out earlier – too excited about getting over to the cottage.'

Emily looked at Jake and asked the question with raised eyebrows. He nodded back.

'What's up with you two shooting each other funny looks?' Simone said, coming back from the pantry fridge.

'Um,' Jake started.

'What?' Simone said.

'About the champagne…'

'What, don't tell me you guys have suddenly become teetotallers?'

'Er…' Jake said. 'Well, just for the next six months,' he said, grasping Emily's hand on the table and looking adoringly at her.

'Oh. My. God,' Simone said. 'You're pregnant!'

Both Emily and Jake nodded and burst into wide grins.

'Oh, wow, that's fantastic news!' Simone said, going up to each of them and wrapping her arms around their shoulders and kissing them on the cheek in turn.

'So, when are you due?'

'Christmas Day,' Emily said.

'Double celebrations then. Goody. But, ooh, you dark horses. I can't believe you haven't told me.'

'Sorry, it's just that we've been so busy and…' Emily said a little helplessly.

'I'm only joking. It's your business who you tell and when.'

'Thanks for understanding, Sim,' Jake said. 'We wanted to tell you in person.'

'And I jumped the gun, didn't I? Oh, I'm so excited for you both. So, do you know if it's a boy or a girl?'

'No, it's too early and we're not sure we want to. We haven't decided, yet, have we?' Jake said, looking at Emily.

'Sometimes I want to know. Sometimes I want to be surprised.' Emily laughed. 'Baby brain, I guess.'

'Oh, well, you'll figure it out. And I think it's very good that you're abstaining from alcohol as well, Jake,' Simone added sagely.

'I haven't been, until now. Well, not consciously. But we don't really drink much, anyway, do we? I don't think I've even had a drink since we found out,' he said.

'No, probably not,' Emily said. 'But you two don't have to miss out because of me.'

'No, I reckon one in, all in,' Simone said, smiling warmly at Emily. 'Like we did for Barbara that day. We can save the bottle for the birth. But I'd better get it out of the freezer so we don't end up with an explosion in the middle of the night,' she said, moving to get back up.

Jake put a hand on his sister's. 'I'll do it. I've stocked up on the non-alcoholic sparkling apple cider Barbara had. I'm sure it'll do the trick.'

Moments later he put a large green bottle and three champagne flutes on the table. When they each had a glass of liquid that looked just like sparkling wine only darker in colour, they raised them.

'To good friends, family, and life being pretty damned wonderful,' Jake said, smiling at Emily and Simone.

'Hear, hear,' Emily agreed.

'And to the baby,' Simone said.

They clinked glasses and savoured the first sip.

'Ah, yes, nectar of the gods,' Simone said with a sigh.

'Hmm, lovely. I could get used to this,' Emily said.

'Don't worry, I've got plenty for you,' Jake said. 'I picked up a case at the supermarket today.'

Emily smiled warmly from Simone to Jake. She sat back in her chair, thinking how lucky she was to have them in her life.

But just as she had that very thought, she noticed them sharing another look. This time she knew it wasn't her imagination.

'Yeah, go on. It's as good a time as any,' Jake said. Simone nodded and got up and left the room.

Emily frowned. 'What's going on?'

'You'll see,' Jake said with a cheeky grin.

A few moments later, Simone appeared with the black garment bag Emily had seen earlier.

'Ooh goody,' Emily said. 'I've been looking forward to seeing what you're wearing tomorrow night.'

Simone silently unzipped the bag and brought out part of its contents on a coathanger that she held up proudly.

Emily felt the blood drain from her face. Her mouth dropped open. 'Oh,' she said.

There in Simone's hand was the silk wraparound top from her dream. Her heart sank with so much disappointment it actually hurt. It was the perfect blue-grey colour; the colour of hers and her gran's eyes. The only difference was that this one had longer sleeves. She felt a stab of jealousy. Tomorrow night she would be wearing a black dress – a nice black dress, but plain black, nonetheless – and Simone would be upstaging her looking absolutely stunning.

Emily was glad she was sitting down. Time seemed to have stopped, along with her heart. She had to say something, at least appear gracious. But before she could form the words in her head, let alone utter them, Simone spoke.

'Come on, I'm dying to see it on you,' she said, shaking the coathanger slightly.

'What? Sorry?' Emily frowned, perplexed. 'Why would I be trying on your outfit?'

'It's for you, silly,' Jake said.

'What? Oh. Really? *Really!?*'

'Yes,' Simone and Jake said at once.

'Oh my God. Wow! I can't believe it,' Emily said. Had she ever told Jake the colour of the outfit in her dream?

'It's the perfect colour,' he said.

'Yep, perfect match,' Simone said, now holding the garment up to Emily's face. 'And the black pants will be just right.'

'Well, come on – go and try it on,' Jake said.

Emily accepted the hook and left the room.

As soon as she had the top on, Emily knew she'd never felt so glamorous before. It was just like what she'd seen in her first dream but with three-quarter-length sleeves instead of short; a slightly stiff wraparound shirt with a wide silk bow at the side, all in a brilliant deep blue with a hint of charcoal to it. With the long sleeves and ability to hide a camisole underneath, she'd be warm enough on the night. And the black pants with their slight sheen suited the top, and Emily, perfectly.

'You look absolutely stunning,' Simone said from the doorway. 'Here, let me tidy up the bow.'

Emily felt like a princess when she stepped back into the kitchen.

'Oh, wow,' Jake said. 'You look amazing.'

'Doesn't she just?' Simone said from behind her.

'Thank you so much. Both of you,' she said, looking from Jake to Simone.

'Don't thank me,' Jake said. 'Sim was the one combing the whole of Melbourne.'

'You poor thing, you also had the engagement ring to sort out.' Emily's guilt must have showed.

'It wasn't that bad, but it is hard when you're looking for something so specific.'

'Tell me about it,' Emily said with a groan. 'Why do you think I settled for plain black?'

'For the record, it was all Jake's idea to try and find something to match your eyes. They're so beautiful and unusual,' Simone said.

'I'm just totally blown away,' she said, looking from one to the other. She would have hugged them, but didn't want to crease the silk. 'So, what are you wearing, Simone? Can we see?'

'Well, all right, but it's nothing too exciting.' She reached into the garment bag again and brought out a green fine-knit top with a light long-sleeved black cardigan over it. Black pants, very similar to those Emily now wore, hung underneath.

'That looks totally gorgeous too,' Emily said, meaning every word.

'Yes, very nice sis,' Jake said with approval.

'I like it. But it took a bit of finding too.'

'Thank goodness for being a bloke and not having any choices – charcoal suit for me.'

'And a matching tie to Emily's,' Simone said, dragging a tie from the hanger and passing it to Jake.

'Oh, that's fantastic,' he said.

'How did you do that?' Emily asked.

'I had your top and the tie made at a great little tailor in Chinatown. Thought you two should match.'

'Trust you to think of everything, sis,' Jake said, beaming at his sister.

Chapter Forty-two

That night, Emily didn't think she'd sleep at all for the nerves and excitement rushing about inside of her. But she must have, because the next thing she knew, she was being gently prodded. She reluctantly opened her eyes.

'Time to get up, sleepyhead,' Jake said, kissing her before getting out of bed and gathering and pulling on clothes.

Emily rolled onto her back, wanting to savour one last moment before getting up to face what would be an extremely long and exhausting day.

'Come on, no time for lolling about,' Jake persisted, leaning across the bed and giving her a nudge.

She was still unable to make herself move.

'Are you okay?' Jake asked, sounding concerned. He came around to her side and crouched down.

'Just having trouble getting going. I'll be right,' she said, and dragged her legs out from under the covers and onto the floor.

'What you need is bacon and eggs,' he said cheerfully.

Emily cringed. The thought of it made her suddenly queasy. *Please don't make me sick today, little one*, she silently pleaded as she got out of bed. Jake headed out to the kitchen. She heard him greet Simone and begin clattering around, getting out pots, pans, and utensils.

Emily was slow to get dressed. By the time she entered the kitchen it was filled with the scents and sounds of cooking. She felt a strange sense of both longing and repulsion at the thought of greasy bacon and eggs. She looked on for a few moments, trying to work out which of the feelings was more dominant. Still undecided, she went over to where Jake stood at the pan and took a deep whiff of the rising steam.

'Yum,' she said hopefully.

'I wasn't sure if it might make you feel ill,' Jake said. 'I only realised when I was past the point of no return,' he added sheepishly.

'It's okay. I'm not sure myself. I guess we'll see,' Emily said with a sigh.

'Well, you need a good breakfast. We'll be on our feet for most of the day and then tonight. You and the little one are going to need all the strength you can get,' Simone said firmly. 'Try a couple of these.' She handed Emily a box of tablets.

Emily frowned and started reading.

'Ginger tablets for travel sickness,' Simone explained. 'I always have some on hand. I take them for flying and for travelling as a passenger in a car for long distances. They work a treat and it says they're also recommended for morning sickness.'

'Thanks, I'll give them a try,' Emily said, opening the box. She took two tablets per the instructions. She suspected that, like most homeopathic or herbal preparations, they might just act as a placebo. But she didn't care; she just wanted to feel well.

Twenty minutes later she sat down and devoured a huge plate of bacon, eggs, toast, mushrooms, and grilled tomatoes – all without a hint of nausea. 'I *am* eating for two,' she said when she caught Jake and Simone's stunned looks. 'Are you sure those ginger tablets don't increase the appetite as well?'

After breakfast they headed over to the cottage, armed with individual lists of tasks.

Jake was responsible for outside; sweeping the large verandah and patio, positioning some candles and making sure everything was presentable. He was also in charge of making sandwiches for lunch and bringing them over mid-afternoon.

Meanwhile, Emily and Simone were tasked with the final touches inside. First they wandered through the rooms, making sure they were still happy with the arrangement of the paintings. Then they wiped and cleaned every surface again. Next they set up and tested the EFTPOS machine, and stacked small pyramids of jars of marmalade on a corner of the large desk, the kitchen windowsill, and each of the mantelpieces.

They finished in the main gallery space by getting out the box of red dots that would be used to indicate when a painting had been sold.

Emily hoped there would be a sea of little red dots by the end of the night, as much for Simone as herself. She so badly wanted her future sister-in-law's foray into life as an artist to be a successful experience.

They had agreed on Emily taking twenty-five percent of proceeds as commission. The prices Simone had put on the pieces were based on the size of the painting, and

Emily thought them very reasonable – not so cheap as to sell Simone's talent short, but not too expensive for a country gallery either. Now they just had to cross their fingers and hope that lots of people would fall in love with the paintings enough to take them home.

The last thing they had to do before heading back to the house to get ready was to put all the glassware through the dishwasher for a quick rinse.

Just as they had unpacked the last load and lined all the glasses up on one side of the large bench, Barbara, Thora, Enid, Liz and Emily's aunt Peggy arrived. After hugs, greetings, and introductions to Simone, they left them to their work. Within moments they had aprons on and the kitchen was abuzz. Emily paused for a few seconds in the doorway. She was wondering where all the hours had gone.

'Come on, that's our cue,' Simone said, tugging at her arm. 'Time to get ready.' They had fifty minutes to get themselves showered and dressed.

Jake had already showered when they got back, next was Emily, and then finally Simone. That way Jake and Emily would be ready in plenty of time to have photos taken before guests arrived.

Ordinarily Emily took just thirty minutes to get showered and ready. Tonight, with her nerves bubbling up again, she was glad they'd allowed her the extra time. Though, she was determined to be ready ten minutes ahead of schedule. Enid had always taught her to be organised.

Thanks to the wraparound top, Emily was able to do her hair and make-up before getting dressed. Now, as she struggled with the row of small fabric-covered buttons down the side, she regretted Jake having already finished getting ready and gone from the bedroom. She was about to call for help when Simone came to the door, giving a gentle tap and asking if she wanted a hand with the tie.

'Yes, please,' she replied. 'And the buttons. My fingers just won't work,' she added, throwing her hands up in frustration.

Within seconds Simone had the buttons done up and was tying a perfect bow with the stiff fabric at Emily's side. 'There we are,' she said, standing back and surveying her work. 'Perfect. You look gorgeous.'

'Thanks. As do you. God, I'm nervous,' she added.

'There's no need to be. You'll be surrounded by friends and people who just want you to succeed and be happy.'

Emily smiled. Simone was right. Everyone there tonight would be excited for them, including her mother. She knew there was a chance that Enid would slip into old behaviour patterns at some point, but being a part of this event, it wouldn't be tonight. For the first time in years she was looking forward to her mother being there. How things change.

What a wonderful first half of the year it had been, she thought, sighing deeply. She put both her hands to her belly and looked down at her engagement ring.

'Anyway, you've done all the hard work,' Simone continued. 'It's now time to sit back and celebrate. I'm the one who should be nervous. What if my paintings don't sell?'

'Of course they'll sell; they're beautiful.'

'So if I agree not to worry about the outcome, will you?' Simone said. 'Tonight is all about celebrating.'

'It's a deal.'

Suddenly they were leaving the house. On her way out Emily told Grace to stay, before apologising profusely for leaving her behind. She would have loved to include her – they had been through so much together – but she didn't want the distraction of worrying about her. The next moment they were bundling into the blue ute and driving over to the building. As they approached, she was struck by what a gorgeous scene it made. The verandahs were lit up with candles. Small floodlights illuminated the stone walls, and beyond the cottage, huge ghostly gum tree silhouettes made an impressive backdrop. They were lucky with the weather; it was set to be an unseasonably warm winter's evening.

As they walked the short distance from where they parked, Emily took in the view of the chandelier through the open front door. It was stunning. She was so proud of what they'd done in such a short time. She paused for a moment to swallow back the sudden surge of emotion that had risen in her throat. The sight before her would have been right at home in any glossy home design or interior magazine. She absolutely loved the deep red colour gloss on the door and timber highlights.

'Hey Em, Jake, Simone,' someone called. The three of them turned around as one. A flash went off. And another. And another.

'Great shots!' the photographer called, beaming. Andre was a friend of Jake's from Melbourne. In return for airfares and room at the Wattle Creek Hotel, he had agreed to shoot the launch for free. He had been out a little earlier to capture daylight shots, and had returned for the main event.

Jake had told Emily he regularly sold images to media outlets in Melbourne, so they were optimistic about getting a photo in at least one of the major interstate papers and a magazine or two. When he'd said this, Emily had wondered why a Melbourne paper would be interested in an unheard-of art gallery out in the South Australian sticks. Only later had she remembered they were also promoting Jake's business and stone workmanship. *Not everything is about you, Emily,* she'd chided herself.

'Right, now, Jake, can I have you and Emily at the front door and then one of each of you on your own,' Andre directed. 'Brilliant, don't move. Just like that.'

Simone made her way inside to check on the kitchen, and for the next few minutes Emily and Jake were posed and told to smile or to lean this way or that way as the camera click, click, clicked away.

As they finally moved inside, Emily experienced a sense of déjà vu; it was as though all the dreams she'd had of a formal evening were coming together at once.

When Andre had them pose against the mantelpiece and suggested including the button jar for a bit of fun and a different, quirky look, Emily felt her legs go weak. Luckily she had Jake supporting her.

Finally he stopped clicking. 'That's me done,' he said. 'Thanks guys, you've been great. I've got some really good shots. I'll go get some images of Simone with her art, and then all the guests as they're arriving.'

'Thanks so much Andre,' Jake said.

Emily checked her watch. There were still fifteen minutes left until everyone was officially meant to be turning up. They were right on schedule.

'I'll go and get you a drink. You need to keep hydrated,' Jake said, leaving her standing and gazing around her in wonder.

The paintings looked even more beautiful in the different light of evening. She turned to see her dad entering the room and striding towards her, followed by her uncle Jim.

'Oh hi Dad.' They hugged tightly. 'Uncle Jim,' she said, hugging him. 'Thanks so much for coming. Good trip over?'

Jim kissed her on the cheek. 'This is incredible, Emily, a real credit to you and Jake. I'm looking forward to meeting him.'

'Yes, it all looks fantastic,' Des Oliphant said. 'I'm so proud of you, sweet pea.'

A lump lodged in Emily's throat. 'Thanks Dad. I'm a wee bit stressed,' she admitted.

'Nothing to be stressed about. You're amongst friends and family,' Uncle Jim said. 'How many have you got coming?'

'Upwards of two hundred and fifty.'

'Wow! No wonder Enid roped Peggy in.'

'So, how does one go about purchasing a piece of this lovely art?' Des asked.

'You don't have to do that,' Emily started.

'Do what? I've seen a painting and I'd like to buy it,' he said, sounding a little miffed.

'Okay. You tell me which one, pay for it, and we put a little red dot next to it to show it's been sold,' Emily said. She was suddenly bubbling with excitement.

'I'll go take a wander around before it gets too crowded,' Jim said. 'Great to see you looking so well, Emily, you're practically glowing. I'll see you later.'

'Thanks Uncle Jim.'

Emily and her father shared a look behind Jim's back.

'It's okay, we haven't said a word,' Des whispered.

'Thanks.' Emily found herself rubbing her belly gently. 'Come on and show me which painting you like.' *My first sale!*

'In here,' Des said, leading the way out and across the hall into the opposite room. 'That one straight ahead,' he said, pointing at a painting of a vase of deep blue-purple irises.

'A lovely choice,' Emily said, beaming. She put a red dot on the small label beside it, took the card Des offered, and walked back through the building to her desk. As she processed the payment, she wondered what her mother would think.

'Thanks Dad,' she said, getting up from her chair and handing him his receipt and card.

'No, thank *you*,' Des said enthusiastically as he tucked them into his wallet. 'And I didn't tell you how beautiful you look tonight. You're perfectly radiant,' he said, beaming at his daughter.

'Thanks Dad,' Emily said, smiling back. A moment later they were joined by Simone.

'Ah, here you are,' Simone said. 'Glass of bubbles.' She winked as she handed Emily a flute of bubbly liquid, which she knew to be the non-alcoholic apple juice. Emily introduced Simone to her father.

'A pleasure to finally meet you,' Des said.

'You need a glass each too, so we can toast our first sale,' Emily said proudly. She nodded at the tray of drinks in the hand of the waiter who had just materialised beside them. The CWA had organised all the wait staff – their children and nieces and nephews, by the looks of their young age.

'Oh, really? Wow,' Simone said. 'But there's no one here yet.'

'Dad's just bought *Blue Irises*.'

'Oh, that's great, thank you,' Simone said, suddenly a little bashful.

Fiona McCallum

'The pleasure is all mine. I love your work, but I'm certainly not the connoisseur of art that my daughter here is,' Des said, wrapping an arm around Emily and kissing her on the cheek before reaching for a glass.

When they each had a drink in hand – beer for Des and champagne for Simone – Emily raised her glass and said, 'To a talented artist, happy customers, and a successful exhibition.'

'Hear, hear,' Simone and Des said. They clinked glasses and then sipped their drinks.

'Well, I'd better mingle and leave you to all your other guests,' Des said after a few moments.

Emily turned around and was surprised to see people beginning to mill around her. She was swept into hug after hug and effusive greetings with people she knew. Most were locals, but then she spied Karen and Tom from Whyalla hovering in the hall just outside the room. She raced over to make sure they felt welcome.

'Wonderful to see you both. Thanks for coming so far. Did you find us okay?'

'Yep, no worries at all,' they said together. 'Having a map included on the invitation was a brilliant idea.'

'The chandelier looks incredible. It's the perfect choice,' Karen said, pointing.

'Grab a glass and some food and have a look around,' Emily said. 'I'd better keep on mingling.' She felt a little breathless, and a bit guilty at not being able to spend time talking. But she wanted to greet as many people as possible and make sure everyone felt welcome. There was Nathan and Sarah. She rushed over to greet them and noticed Grant and Stacy Anderson were behind them. And Doris from Mitre 10. Bob Stanley and his wife waved from the corner. Golly, she was going to be busy. Hopefully everyone would understand.

The room filled up and Emily gradually made her way out to find Jake and see if any of his Melbourne friends that she didn't know had arrived. She was further surprised to find each of the rooms and the hall quite tightly packed. On her way she said hi to Steve and Stan, who had to step aside to let her pass. It was becoming difficult to move through. Thankfully the waiters seemed to be doing well enough because everyone appeared to have a glass in one hand and a serviette in the other. The whole place was abuzz with lively, cheerful chatter.

The kitchen was a hive of activity. People bustled about constructing and plating canapés, putting food in and out of ovens, and emptying and replenishing trays of food and drink. Wait staff came and went. 'All good?' she whispered to Barbara.

'Yep. Have you seen David yet?'

'No, but I'll keep my eye out.'

'Thanks.'

'Mum? Thora? How are you going?'

'Too busy to stop,' Enid said, looking harried and waving her away.

'Everything is going well, dear,' Thora said, the picture of cool and calm.

Emily smiled and kept moving.

There was still no sign of Jake. She made her way back towards the front door, still unable to quite believe how many people had come.

Halfway down the hall, she spotted him standing alone on the verandah. As she stepped outside, the fresh winter evening enveloped her.

'Darling,' she said, sidling up to Jake and threading an arm through his. 'Can you believe how many people have turned up?'

'It's great, isn't it? Is it getting too stuffy in there yet? Do I need to turn the fires off?' he asked.

'I think we'd better, if you don't mind.'

'Not at all. Are you happy to stand here and meet and greet for a while?'

'Okay. But hang on. Wait a sec – here's David. Barbara was looking for him,' Emily said. 'What's he carrying?'

'You'll see,' Jake said.

Emily looked at Jake, but when he only returned a grin and a shrug, she turned back to watch David climb the steps and make his way towards them. 'What's this?' she asked. In his hands was a huge iced cake.

'Dessert,' Jake said.

'No celebration is complete without the cutting of the cake,' David said formally.

'Oh, you guys are just the best,' she said.

'Well, I'm just the courier,' David said.

'It's gorgeous,' Emily said, looking at it closely. There on the top was a very good impression of the gallery's sign, complete with the panel beneath; OPEN. A lump rose in her throat, and tears threatened. Emily forced them back.

Jake took David through to the kitchen while Emily waited to see if any more guests were going to arrive. After a few minutes she went back inside to get the box of red dots ready in case anyone wanted to make a purchase. When she entered the room with her desk, she was stunned to find a line of people with wallets out. Simone was sitting behind the desk, processing their payments.

How long have I been gone? Emily wondered. *Surely only a few minutes.* She checked her watch. Less than fifteen minutes had passed since she'd been standing here with her father. She made her way along the line, greeting each person she knew. There was Maureen with Karen and Mavis from Whyalla, and behind them Ben and Stan, who told her the other three stonemasons were next door.

Most of the people in line she would never have picked as art lovers, and quite a few hadn't been on the invite list. The advert in the *Chronicle* had clearly done the trick, as had the Carrington sisters, who had practically rubbed their hands together as they'd promised to spread the word.

Jake had made a special point of hand delivering their invitations, knowing the elderly pair would just love telling everyone about their special treatment. They had enjoyed several cups of tea and scones with the 'delicious' Jake, before Emily finally had to drag him from their clutches, and only after he'd promised to visit again before too long.

Thank God Tara Wickham hadn't shown up! Emily hadn't heard a thing about her since she'd turfed her out of the Baker brothers' house. She really hoped the woman was long gone, but she certainly wasn't going to waste another moment on the ghastly woman, especially on her night of nights.

Finally Emily made it to the desk. 'Hey, it's really not fair to have the artist doing all the work,' she said.

'It's quite okay. This way the buyers actually get to meet me,' Simone replied, before returning her attention to the customer in front of her. 'There you are, thank you so much for buying *Daisies*. I hope it brings you a lot of joy,' she added, smiling, as she handed over a receipt and credit card payment slip.

'But what about the red dots; who's in charge of putting them on?' Emily asked, trying to quell her rising anxiety.

'Don't worry. I put your dad in charge. He's got the red dots and a wad of post-its and a pencil. He writes the details down so we can keep a record here and put them on the receipt. Hello there, which one are you purchasing?' Simone said brightly to the next person in line, and held out her hand to accept a bright orange post-it note and card.

'*Passionfruit*. On credit, please,' said Sarah. 'Don't tell Nathan, it's for his birthday in July. Hopefully he's still out the back,' she said, looking around.

'I don't see him,' Emily said, beaming at her.

'See,' Simone said to Emily, 'a well-oiled machine. It's all under control. Seriously, Em, you go and schmooze. At this rate we'll be sold out in another half hour and I'll be free to mingle too,' Simone said cheerfully.

Surely not, Emily thought. *All sold in an hour?! Wow, wouldn't that be something?*

Chapter Forty-three

But Simone was right. Forty-five minutes later, when Jake called for quiet, every one of the forty paintings had a small red dot on the label beside it.

It took quite a while to get everyone to move through to the back patio area. They'd initially planned to have the speeches in the front room, surrounded by art, but there were far too many people.

Jake stood with Emily and Simone on either side. The cake was in front on a card table draped in white. Behind them, on Emily's strong encouragement, were Des, Enid, Thora, Barbara, David and the wait staff fanning out on each side.

'Right,' Jake started, microphone in hand. 'Can everyone hear me okay?'

Shouts of 'Yes' rang out around the space.

'Great. Don't worry, we're going to keep the formalities brief. A good speech is a short speech…'

Plenty of people chuckled.

'Firstly, I want to thank you all for coming, especially those who have travelled a long way to be here. To my

Melbourne friends, it means a lot to share this night with you. And to my new mates from Wattle Creek, thanks to you all for providing such a warm welcome to this city slicker.'

Now there were a few cheers.

'But the person I most want to thank is my partner and fiancée, Emily,' he said, looking deeply into her eyes and squeezing her to him, 'for bringing me to Wattle Creek in the first place.'

Raucous yahooing rang out, and a wolf-whistle from up the back.

'For those who might be wondering, I'm not actually a farmer.'

A few laughs. One bloke shouted, 'You had us fooled, mate. The way you handled a tractor.'

Jake smiled. 'I'm actually a builder and architect. And I've set up shop here. I'm hoping one day to take on an apprentice or two. So, while this building is Emily's Button Jar Gallery of Fine Art, it's also a showcase for my work. Everything you see here was built by my team – of which Simone, the artist, is a very important part. We were really pleased to find so many talented local tradespeople to put to work as well. If you'd like to know more or discuss a project with me, you'll find my business cards on the mantelpieces in each room. Give me a shout any time. Well, that's enough advertising. Tonight is really about Emily, and I'll now hand over to her.'

Emily waited for the cheering and applause to die down. She felt strangely calm, not at all nervous, which was amazing considering that just the thought of public speaking usually made her sweat.

'I, too, will try to keep it brief. But there are a lot of people I want to thank. Firstly, everyone who has helped on the building project and tonight's event – Mum and Dad, Thora, Barbara and David and all the wait staff. Tonight would not have happened without you – or we'd at least have gone hungry...'

Boos rang out, and then whistles and cheers.

'On a serious note, though, these wonderful people have donated all their time and done the catering and service to raise money for the Royal Flying Doctor Service. They are, quite literally, our lifeline at times. There are donation tins if you'd like to donate some cold, hard cash, and a percentage of every sale tonight is going to them. One of the wonderful things about small rural communities is our ability to be selfless and put aside our own problems to help others, so please dig deep.'

There was a brief round of applause.

'Our artist, whose work I'm so proud to be representing tonight, is one of the most generous people I've ever met. Without even knowing me, Simone took it upon herself to sell my jam at a Melbourne market when I was going through a really tough time. It's a bit of a long story. But she will never know just how much her kindness helped me. She gave me hope that things would turn out okay. Sometimes a little kindness can make all the difference to someone going through a rough patch. Oh, God, I think I'm going to cry.' Emily gasped, and tried to laugh off her sudden feeling of being swamped with emotion. She smiled at Simone before continuing.

'And, if it weren't for Simone, and a single phone call she made early this year, Jake and I probably wouldn't be together today – and we certainly wouldn't be celebrating this new venture tonight. From the first time I saw her paintings in Melbourne, I knew she had an amazing gift. She's going to be big. In five years time, Simone Lonigan is going to be a household name in the art world. And we'll all look back on tonight and remember how it started.'

Emily took a few breaths before continuing.

'You might be wondering why I've called the gallery The Button Jar, and for those who've seen the jar on the mantel in the other room, why it's there. Well, my granny Rose Mayfair was very dear to me. And one of my earliest memories is of sitting beside her as a small child, listening to her wise words while she sewed and mended. The day before she died last year, she gave me her precious button jar. I will always treasure it and the wisdom she passed on, and would like to dedicate tonight's event to her memory.'

She bit her lip and looked at Jake. He nodded encouragingly.

'Um, okay, moving on. To Mum and Dad, thank you. You've made me the person I am today. I know we've had our ups and downs, but I'm so glad you're here to share this with me. So, well, thank you,' she added a little helplessly, desperately trying to swallow down the lump making its way up her throat.

'Sorry, bear with me. Almost done.' She turned and looked at Barbara, and bit down hard on her lip before carrying on.

'Speaking of ups and downs. Barbara, you're my best friend. We haven't known each other long, but you've come to mean the world to me. My gran had a saying: "True friends are like diamonds, precious and rare. False friends are like autumn leaves, found everywhere." I don't think I fully understood what she meant until I met you. You have seen me at my worst and helped pick me up when I was at my lowest. I will be forever grateful to you for believing in me, encouraging me, and supporting me.

You were my rock when I didn't even know which way was up. Thank you.'

Emily swallowed again and turned to Jake.

'And, finally, my fiancé Jake, who I definitely couldn't have done this without. Thank you. Nothing I say can adequately express how much it means to me to have you in my life. I love you.'

She managed to stop herself just before putting her hand on her belly and saying, 'And our baby.'

'And now it's time to cut this gorgeous cake.'

Emily, Simone and Jake each put a hand on the knife and pushed it gently into the cake. Andre the photographer snapped away.

'I hereby declare The Button Jar Gallery of Fine Art officially open,' Jake said.

'Three cheers for Jake, Emily and Simone,' David shouted. 'Hip hip, hooray. Hip hip, hooray. Hip hip, HOORAY!'

The applause was deafening. Emily, Jake and Simone beamed at each other. It couldn't have gone any better.

'That was a lovely speech, Emily. Just lovely,' Enid said, appearing beside her and slipping her arm around her waist.

'Thanks Mum, that means a lot,' she said, smiling back at Enid, who she noticed had tears in her eyes too.

'I'll go and help with the cake and let you get back to your guests.'

'Do you want a hand?'

'No, you mingle.'

Gradually the crowd disbursed to fill all the rooms once again and the cake was handed around while people chatted.

The rest of the night passed in a blur. At some point the high-tech sound system Jake had had installed throughout the building was cranked up and people had danced.

It wasn't until two in the morning that Jake, Emily and Simone waved the final couple off and the last car horn honked goodbye. Enid and Des, Aunt Peggy and Uncle Jim, Liz, Thora and Gerald, and Barbara and David had left hours ago.

'What a night,' Simone said. 'And I thought gallery openings were sedate affairs.'

'A sell-out in an hour – that's brilliant, sis! Well done. Both of you,' Jake said, draping his arms around their shoulders and pecking them on the cheek.

'And you,' Simone said.

'I hope you get lots of business for JKL,' Emily said.

'Well, we'll have to wait and see, but plenty of people seemed interested.'

'A huge success all round then,' Simone said.

Before they left, Emily ducked back inside and grabbed the button jar from the mantelpiece. Maybe it was silly, but she wanted Gran close by, not left alone in the gallery overnight. Jake hadn't really wanted the jar there at all on public view – given its precious contents – but she'd insisted. They pulled the front door shut and then made their way back to the house with Emily behind the wheel of the ute.

Back inside, she thought she'd be too highly strung to sleep. But as she entered the kitchen, the feeling that she was home, and that it was all over, hit her with such force that she could barely muster the energy to clean her teeth or wash the make-up from her face.

'What time do we have to be up?' she asked as she lay in Jake's arms.

He was putting on a barbeque brunch at the cottage for all the people who had travelled over from Melbourne. When they'd organised it, they'd had no idea they would still be up at two o'clock. Hopefully their guests would be a bit slow in rising as well.

'You, my dear, can sleep in and wander over whenever you feel like it. I'll take care of everything,' he said, stroking her hair.

'You're a darling,' she muttered sleepily, already starting to doze off.

'Nothing you don't deserve. Good night, sweetheart,' he said. Then he kissed her, released her, and rolled over.

Chapter Forty-four

In the morning Emily stirred when Jake got up, but did not fully wake. She was vaguely aware of his mass leaving the bed, the rustle of clothes and quiet opening and shutting of cupboard doors and drawers. She knew she should be getting up as well to play host, but couldn't fully rouse herself.

Just a few more minutes.

She rolled over and pulled the quilt up a little higher against her chin.

Later she heard muffled voices in the kitchen, again thought she should be up helping, but again told herself just a few more minutes of dozing. Jake would come and get her if she overslept.

She woke with a start, sat up and rubbed her eyes. She felt more awake than before, but was still a little groggy – a sure sign she'd fallen back into a deep sleep. She tried to analyse the light filtering through the heavy curtains and peeping through the gaps. It couldn't be that much later, she thought;

it was still grey outside. She cocked her head to listen for sounds in the house and kitchen. Nothing.

She picked up her watch from the bedside cupboard and peered at it, willing her eyes to focus. She stared at the small dial, frowning, and blinked a few times. Could it really be eleven o'clock? No, surely not. Maybe her watch had stopped. She held it to her ear and heard the ticking. Shit, it *was* eleven o'clock! She'd slept in way past when she'd meant to get up.

When she moved to get out of bed she was surprised at how heavy she felt. If she didn't know better, she'd have said she was hung-over. She sighed, steeled her will, and pushed herself further. How embarrassing to be turning up now when everyone would have finished breakfast. Part of her hoped the guests had all left, keen to hit the road and get their long journey started. But she also wanted to see Ben, Aaron, Stan, Toby, and Bill. She'd barely spoken to any of them last night.

She dragged underwear, jeans, t-shirt and pink rugby top from her tallboy and gave the button jar a quick hug before getting dressed.

As she walked across to the cottage, rugged up in a thick coat, she revelled in the fresh, cool air in her face and cursed the overcast weather. No wonder she'd slept in; the sky was well and truly blanketed.

There were half a dozen vehicles parked out on the gravel in front. What would everyone think of her being so unsociable?

Oh well, too late now, she thought, as she stepped up onto the verandah and then into the hall. She glanced around as she made her way through to the kitchen. There was no sign of their late-running function the night before.

She felt even more guilty at having not played a part in the clean-up.

She stood in the kitchen at the threshold to the patio wondering how to make her entrance.

'Here she is,' Jake said, getting up and coming over.

'Hi,' Simone and the men sitting around the large timber outdoor table called. Emily blushed as a round of applause started by Toby at the far end of the table gathered momentum.

'Thanks for that, Toby. Trust you,' she said with a wave of her hand, as the noise died down. 'Hi everyone. Sorry I slept in.' As she looked at the empty plates with their scraps of bacon rind, her mouth began to water. She realised she was ravenous. All she'd eaten in the last twelve hours was some finger food and two small pieces of Barbara's delicious cake. 'I hope you left some food for me, you blokes.'

'Only because Jake's cooking isn't a patch on yours,' Aaron said.

'That's enough out of you,' Jake said, throwing a tea towel at him. 'Here, there's plenty of room,' Jake said, guiding her towards the nearest of the two tables. Everyone shuffled along to make extra space. Jake went over to the barbeque and opened the hood.

'That looks so good,' she said, accepting a plate of scrambled eggs, bacon, mushrooms and grilled tomatoes with toast perched on the edge. 'I'm so sorry I'm so late,' she whispered, leaning into his shoulder.

'No need to be sorry. It was a huge night. You needed your sleep. I would've woken you up if I thought you should be here. The guys don't mind; they're friends.'

Emily felt self-conscious eating alone in front of the dozen people, but they quickly returned to their conversations.

She had just pushed her empty plate aside when suddenly everyone started saying they had to get on the road. Next thing she knew, they were shaking Jake's hand and pulling him into a series of manly hugs. Emily got up and apologised for not getting much of a chance to talk to them. They brushed off her apology with promises to come back and visit again soon. Emily, Jake, and Simone walked them out and waved them off.

When they went back inside, Jake said he'd tidy up from breakfast while Emily and Simone organised and packed up the paintings Simone was taking with her to deliver.

Prior to the opening they had deliberated over what to do if people travelling from Adelaide and Melbourne wanted to buy art. Simone had suggested she take them back with her and deliver them along the way. They'd agreed that it would be better to have a few blank spaces on the walls than hold the paintings until the end of the exhibition and then risk damage by freighting them.

Before long the two young women were kneeling on the floor surrounded by bubble wrap, scissors, and the tape dispenser. Emily felt sad that Simone would be leaving them soon as well. A lot had changed for her in recent times, but she still hated goodbyes.

After farewelling Simone, Jake, Emily and Grace spent the afternoon relaxing inside.

Now and then Jake wrapped his arms around Emily and nuzzled her neck. No words were necessary; they were both grieving the loss of the sudden influx of visitors and company, and the end of a project that had consumed them for almost six months. They had to mourn the end of one phase of life before they could celebrate the new one they were embarking on.

Weeks ago Jake had told Emily it would feel like this for a few days. At the time she had thought he was being melodramatic. She'd experienced grief over Gran's death, the original cottage, her marriage, and then having to abruptly leave the other house. But she figured that was all pretty normal; genuine loss needed to be grieved over before the healing could start. But grief when a project had been successfully completed? That just sounded weird.

Now, however, she understood what he had meant. A few times during the afternoon she stole glances at Jake and offered silent thanks for having found such a beautiful soul who was so switched on when it came to human nature and emotion. In a weird way, he reminded her of Gran. They would have got on so well together.

Sometimes Emily wondered if Gran had somehow been responsible for sending him, but she quickly dismissed it as way too big a life question to get bogged down in. It would never be answered. It was easier to believe that it was all the work of the universe. That it was just meant to be.

*

Two evenings later they were sitting at the table enjoying a glass of sparkling apple juice after dinner when Jake's mobile began a series of tones that indicated the arrival of emails.

'I'm popular all of a sudden,' Jake said, as he leant over to retrieve the device. His frowned concentration changed to amusement as he scrolled through the messages, reading them quickly. After a few moments he handed the phone to Emily with raised eyebrows and a slight smirk.

The first message was from his friend Andre, and contained a few photos in the main body of the email. They were pretty small on the phone's screen but, from what she could see, looked to be very good.

Jake watched on, sipping at his wine.

At the end of the line of images was a note: 'Some great shots. Hope you don't mind me passing a couple on to Justin.' Emily looked away as she racked her memory for which one of Jake's Melbourne friends Justin was. Was he the public relations guy, the journalist, or the guy who owned the café? None the wiser, she held the phone out.

'The photos look good, but it's a bit hard to tell at this size,' she said.

'Keep going.' He had a smug, knowing expression on his face.

Emily did as he said. Her eyes bugged as the masthead of the online version of *The Age* newspaper came up, followed by a photo of her and Jake at the front door of the gallery and then a shot of one of Simone's canvases. To the right was the bold headline: 'How did Melbourne let this artist go unnoticed?'

The article gave a glowing report of the gallery's opening and praised Simone's work, reporting that the exhibition had sold out in an hour. Emily grinned wide-eyed at Jake, unsure what to say. Wow. They were being talked about in a major Melbourne newspaper!

She was still holding the phone when it began to vibrate and then ring. She got such a shock she almost dropped it. She noticed Simone's name on the screen as she handed it over.

'Hey Sim,' Jake said. 'How's things? You're on speaker – Em's here.'

'Hi Em.'

'Hi Simone.'

'God, you guys, you're never going to believe this!' Simone's excited voice boomed out of the speaker.

'What?' Jake and Emily said.

'I can hardly believe it myself!'

'What!?' Jake and Emily cried.

'Elwood Gallery of Fine Art have just called. They want me to do an exhibition!'

'That's fantastic news,' Jake said. 'When?'

'November. Eek!'

'Oh, Simone, that's brilliant. Well done.'

'Yes, it's wonderful,' Emily said.

'God, I'm so excited! Emily, this is all because of you; I'll never ever be able to thank you enough…' she rambled.

'You don't need to thank me,' Emily said. 'You're the one with the talent.'

'But no one would know if it wasn't for you.'

'I'm just glad I could help. We'll call it quits as long as you invite us to your opening,' Emily said. She felt so warm inside. She reckoned she knew how Simone felt; not unlike she did after Simone had sold her jam at the Melbourne market all those months ago. When she'd given her the hope she'd needed to carry on.

'So, November, hey?' Jake said. 'Please don't tell me you're leaving me.'

'Er, about that…' she said, suddenly sounding serious.

Jake gave a half-hearted groan.

'I'm only kidding. I'll figure it out. I can probably get enough done on the weekends and just take a day here and there.'

'I was kidding too. The business coped fine this time around, and it will again. If you want to paint, you paint. Honestly. We're so excited for you. How did they find out about you, anyway?' Jake asked.

'Justin got an article into *The Age* online today. It all happened rather fast. He rang earlier and asked if I was happy for him to give my number to the people at Elwood. Of course I had to think about that – not! I'll send you the link.'

'No need, he already sent it through.'

'It's a great write-up all round,' Simone said. 'And Andre's photos look awesome.'

'He's sent us a heap more – I'll forward them on,' Jake said.

'Thanks. Look, I'd better get going. I'm meeting Billy in half an hour. We're heading out to celebrate.'

'That's great. Have fun and say hi from us,' Jake said.

'Bye Simone. And, again, well done,' Emily said.

'See ya,' Simone chirped.

'Wow,' Jake said, after he'd turned off the phone. 'I certainly didn't see that coming. You know, Elwood is one of the top galleries in Melbourne. I reckon I'm about to have a famous sister and you're about to have a famous sister-in-law,' he said, leaning over and kissing her. 'And all because of you.'

'Well, I'm just so happy I could do something for her after her generosity in selling my jam. You guys will never really know how much that meant to me – you gave me hope when I was at my lowest.' Emily suddenly found herself tearing up.

'Hey, don't think about any of that now,' Jake said, delicately wiping away the one stray tear before pulling her to him. 'It's only good things for us from here on.'

'Thanks Jake. You always know the right thing to say,' she said, smiling at him.

'I know,' he said brightly. 'Now, come on, let me take you to bed and show you some of my other talents.'

Emily slapped at him playfully, but accepted his hand and allowed herself to be led from the kitchen.

Epilogue

Around four months later...

'Well, this is it, guys,' Emily said as she, Jake, Barbara and David pulled up outside Des and Enid Oliphant's home in Hope Springs. 'Time to see how the fur kids coped at Grandma and Grandpa's.'

'More to the point, how Grandma coped with having fur kids running around,' Jake said.

'It really was very good of Enid to take them for a week, considering how she feels about pets,' Barbara said. 'I just hope Sasha hasn't disgraced herself.'

'Mum's been amazing since our blow-up – trying so hard, bless her,' Emily said.

'Come on, we can't keep sitting here,' said Jake, and they tumbled out of the ute.

The front door opened before Emily could raise her hand to knock. A waft of savoury cooking smells greeted them. 'Yum,' they muttered in unison.

'Hello there, welcome back!' Des cried. 'Come in, come in.'

As the others went in, Emily held back so she could catch her father alone. 'How was it?'

'Good,' he said. 'Actually, great.'

'Really?'

'Well, just the one little teething problem, but that was quickly sorted.'

'What? What happened?'

'You'll see. Come on through.'

Emily arrived in the kitchen to see Enid coming down the hall from the bedrooms. Sasha and Grace were beside her with just their heads and tails visible. They might have looked like miniature horses in white dust rugs if their legs and feet weren't also covered. She brought her hands to her face to stifle a giggle. Barbara was also holding her mouth. The laughter was clearly visible in her friend's eyes.

'Oh, my God, they're wearing onesies,' David said, bringing his hands up and letting out a gulp.

'I hope you don't mind,' Enid said, clearly misreading their expressions.

'Come here, Gracie. Poor little thing, did Granny make you wear funny clothes?' Emily said.

'I think they look very cute,' Jake said, obviously the best poker player of the group.

'Thank you Jake.'

Emily just shook her head. 'Where on earth did you get onesies for dogs?'

'I made them. I can sew, you know, Emily.'

'Right. But, *why*?'

'They insisted on lying on the couch and the bed and I didn't want fur and dirty marks left everywhere.'

'They're dogs, Mum. They don't insist. You tell them to lie on their beds on the floor, and they do it. Or you put them outside.'

'Oh, Emily, if they can't get a little spoiled at Granny and Grandpa's, then where can they? Now, if you'll stop picking on me for a moment and greet me properly...' Enid held her arms out wide.

'Sorry. Thanks so much for having them. It was very good of you,' she said, hugging her mother.

'Yes, thank you so much, Enid,' Barbara said, accepting Enid's embrace.

'You're very welcome. How was the trip? Would you like an early dinner – I have a pot of braised lamb shanks on. I just have to mash the potatoes and steam the beans. Or do you have to rush off?'

The group looked around at each other and all shrugged.

'It's okay, I won't mind.'

'Dinner would be wonderful, Mum, though I'd like to be home before it gets dark. But, first, I really need to use the loo.'

'Again?!' Jake, David and Barbara cried in mock consternation, complete with exaggerated eye rolling. It had become the catchcry of their trip to Melbourne and back for Simone's exhibition.

Despite having four drivers to share the burden, they had had to stay the night in Adelaide in each direction because travelling took so long with Emily having to stop to pee so often. It had become a running joke that they were going to compile a map of all the public conveniences along the way. Emily didn't think it was a laughing matter. It was painful to hold on. And, anyway, it was quite unsafe to laugh with seven and a bit months of baby pressing on all the wrong spots.

'Of course you do. Go ahead, you poor thing. How is baby George doing?'

'Great, other than making me pee a lot,' Emily said, bolting.

Minutes later they were tucking in, having all helped finish making the meal and convinced Enid that it was fine to dish up at the table.

'You've no idea how good this is, Mum,' Emily said after her first bite. She groaned with pleasure.

'I hope you haven't been feeding my grandson greasy takeaway all week.'

'No, but we haven't had a home-cooked meal since we left.'

'Didn't Liz cook for you?'

Emily and Barbara shared a look. 'Mum, Liz doesn't cook. And to be fair, there really wasn't time.'

'It's the modern way, isn't it, especially in Melbourne, I hear. Peggy is quite beside herself with worry about it now...'

'Now, what, Mum?'

'Oh, I really shouldn't say.' Enid blushed slightly.

'Too late now, Mum. Spill.'

'Oh, all right,' Enid said, feigning duress. 'Liz is pregnant.'

Emily glanced around. Jake, Barbara and David had found their poker faces – or, more accurately, their acting faces. 'I didn't know she had a boyfriend,' she said innocently, playing along. Liz had told them the whole story, but she was letting Enid have her moment in the sun.

'She doesn't. That's just the thing. She's chosen to be a single mother, of all things. She used a...a sperm bank.

Have you ever heard of anything so…so clinical? It's all too much for me,' Enid declared with a sigh.

'Oh, well, each to their own, I guess,' Emily said.

'Yes. More beans, anyone?' Enid said, lifting the two large serving spoons from the bowl in front of her.

'So, how did the exhibition go?' Des asked.

'Another triumph. Simone's really going places,' Jake said. 'I'm so proud of her. And of Emily for giving her the chance to shine in the first place,' he said, pulling her to him and kissing her. 'I wouldn't be surprised if her next stop is New York or London.'

'Oh, that's wonderful.'

'Now, on a serious note, you two,' Enid said, putting down her cutlery. 'We really do need some ideas for an engagement present. It's been months. Thank goodness you're not having a wedding.'

'Actually, Mum, we've changed our minds on that.'

'Oh?'

'We've been discussing it in the car and think that maybe a nice simple ceremony and party, just like the launch, might be lovely. It was so much fun, and it really is the perfect venue. We could have the wedding and photos under the big trees. Though not until next year, after George is born.'

'That would be wonderful. You know, people still stop me in the street to tell me what a lovely night it was. We can contribute to that as our gift.'

'That's so lovely, but you guys have already paid for one wedding. Just having you there helping and looking after George will be wonderful.'

'Well, we can discuss the details later. Barbara, you did run a tight catering ship. Perhaps we…'

'Mum, I'm not having my only bridesmaid being tied up on the day with catering. Or the mother of the bride, for that matter.'

'Oh, yes, of course. Silly me,' Enid said, giggling.

Back home later that evening, they waved off Barbara, David, and Sasha – happily unclothed again.

As their friends pulled away, Jake and Emily watched their tail-lights fade into the distance while Grace sat patiently beside them. Staring up at the bright twinkling stars in the clear November sky above, they sighed loudly. The days were getting longer again, the nights warmer.

Emily thought back over the year that had been – her gran's passing, John's death, her eviction and the move back to the farm, Jake's recovery, and the rebuilding of the cottage. And now the baby, their greatest adventure yet. She squeezed Jake's hand.

'God, it's good to be home.'

Dear Reader,

I hope you enjoyed Emily's journey in *The Button Jar* series. At this stage, this is the end of the series, though I'm not ruling out more books being added in the future, which is why I've called it a series rather than a trilogy. But don't worry, I have a lot of stories yet to tell and lots of wonderful characters for you to fall in love with.

Next is *Leap of Faith*. After losing her nerve and giving up on her lifelong horse-riding dreams, Jessica must face her biggest fear in order to save their cattle and livelihood. Can she do it? Does she have a choice? I think it's a beautiful story – I hope you will too.

Meanwhile, you can keep up with all the latest news on my website, www.fionamccallum.com and follow me on Facebook at www.facebook.com/fionamccallum.author.

Thanks so much for your support in reading my books. With very best wishes,

Fiona

talk about it

Let's talk about books.

Join the conversation:

 on facebook.com/harlequinaustralia

 on Twitter @harlequinaus

www.harlequinbooks.com.au

If you love reading and want to know about our
authors and titles, then let's talk about it.